I0649285

All the Rivers Run South

All the Rivers Run South

Ouyang Yu

PUNCHER & WATTMANN

© Ouyang Yu 2023

This book is copyright. Apart from any fair dealing for the purposes of study and research, criticism, review or as otherwise permitted under the Copyright Act, no part may be reproduced by any process without written permission. Inquiries should be made to the publisher.

First published in 2023
Published by Puncher and Wattmann
PO Box 279
Waratah NSW 2298

http://www.puncherandwattmann.com

A catalogue entry for this book is available from the National Library of Australia.

ISBN 9781923099005

Cover image by Ouyang Yu

Cover design by David Musgrave

Printed by Lightning Source International

This is a work of fiction. Unless otherwise indicated, all the names, characters, businesses, places, events and incidents in this book are the products of the author's imagination and should not be identified with any persons living or dead.

This project has been assisted by the Australian Government through Creative Australia, its principal arts investment and advisory body.

For David

Blessed are the meek for they shall inherit the earth.
[Matthew 5:5]

*Writing isn't just telling stories. It's exactly the opposite.
It's telling everything at once. It's the telling of a story,
and the absence of the story. It's telling a story through its
absence.*

—Marguerite Duras, *Practicalities*

*I was once part of the flow, never thinking of myself
as a presence. Then I looked in the mirror and decided
to be free. All that my freedom has brought me is the
knowledge that I have a face and a body, that I must feed
this body and clothe this body for a number of years. Then
it will be over.*

—V. S. Naipaul, *In a Free State*

*天地之大也，人犹有所憾。故君子语大，天下
莫能载焉，语小，天下莫能破焉。*

—孔伋[1]

---

1 This is a remark by Kong Ji, Confucius' grandson, which goes, in this author's translation, 'Even if the sky and the earth are vast, people still do not think they are vast enough, which is why the gentleman says that, in terms of vastness, the sky and the earth are not vast enough to cover everything under heaven and, in terms of smallness, there may be things so small that nothing under heaven can break through them.'

Part I

Chapter 1

Under the moonlight, the deserted cemetery lay quiet and sombre, its headstones glistening with rain that was there a while earlier. I walked as I listened to my own footsteps on the footpath. The air was fresh after the rain. It was another one of those insomniac nights that I had when I couldn't help going out and doing my rounds in the neighbourhood as these sleepless walks would calm my nerves and restore my spirit.

That night, after I managed to sleep for less than two hours, I put on my coat, my trousers and closed the door behind me. Night, for someone like me, was always friendly; it embraced me with an armful of street lamps and acquiesced in my resistance when it saw me turn down a path less lit in the direction of the cemetery. It did not know what I wanted to do. But I knew. Or perhaps I didn't. All I knew was that I'd probably have to go there again, if only because of what I had seen the other day.

I first headed straight for the bridge across the creek. Leaning against the railing, I looked down, into the water. But I could see nothing much beyond the lights twinkling on the waves that were washing over the rocks. The noise of the water was soothing enough to induce a drowsy effect on me as it numbed my senses and dispel all thoughts from my mind like a swept room. But this went only for a moment before I realised that I had to keep going to my next port of call, or port of recall, so to speak. As my mind wandered, my feet dragged themselves across the tram tracks to the other side of the road, lined with tall, bark-peeling eucalyptuses, standing alone and separately.

When I reached the cemetery, its iron gate was closed. I stood there, looking through the bars at a narrow winding path amidst the gravestones, some taller than others, some broader, or more magnificent, but all written and wordless, dark or darkened, in a world of goneness. There was no one I could identify with here, not a single soul whose past life was related to me. And, yet, I felt close to them, a world of humanity lost, unfindable except in cherished memories of only the most intimate, so close in fact that I seemed able, in a way, to intuit their stories. Thinking the thought, I found myself moving away from the gate and walking outside by the wall till I came to a stop at a spot familiar enough to me. It was here a few weeks ago that I had come upon a sign bearing words indicating that this was a vacant lot for burial. In the darkness, I couldn't tell what the lot number was. But there was an eerie silence that reigned supreme here, unbroken for the duration of my stay, till I was about to step away when something stirred and said, in a voice that began indistinctly but that soon settled in a neutral tone. I stopped and listened.

'I am Ah Sin. I came to this country in the fifth year of Emperor Xianfeng. I came by ship. Ours would have been the first of its kind, captained by Mr Miller, a man of forbidding features with a cloud of a bushy beard surrounding his mouth, like Zhang Fei, in Romance of the Three Kingdoms. We, all of us, were different from him in that we had a long queue behind our backs, and our faces were clean-shaven except for a few thin whiskers legally allowed. We looked at each other and we looked at him. Then we laughed among ourselves. Not directly laughing into his face, of course. That would make him furious. But just laughing as we threw furtive glances his way. This happened in Hong Kong before the ship set sail for Australia, at the bottom of the Earth, as our shipping agent told us. At first, it was a mess. We lived in a crowded condition worse than in our villages. But our hope made us strong because we were going to a country described as an infinitely better and more beautiful one than our own. Freer, too. While waiting, I picked up a book to read. But I soon found all eyes were focussed on me. I was made uncomfortable by the way they looked at me, with a mixture of curiosity and contempt, it seemed. As I didn't know them well enough to accost anyone, I decided to plunge into the book instead of being browbeaten when a voice rose by my side and said, "What are you reading?" as a hand shot out and grabbed hold of the book, snatching it off me.

'I looked up, surprised. "Who are you?" said I, staring into a pockmarked face, slit-eyed and thin-whiskered.

'"Oh, I'm Ah Mao," the man said, without looking at me, his finger pin-pointing at a character. "What's that?"

'I took a look and saw that it's 鼉, so I said, "It's tuo, a muddy dragon." As I said so, I held out my hand in a gesture that indicated that he ought to give the book back to me. Without a word, Ah Mao relaxed his hold on the book and gave it back.'

Chapter 2

'Thank you for sending me this new chapter of your writing, Baohui,' Stacey began her email. 'Which I've quickly read, with great interest, and it seems to augur well as the beginning of your new novel. With your synopsis in mind, I think I am more concerned with the structure of the novel and the development of characters. You may have, I might suggest, to narrow down the scope by limiting it to a shorter historical period for easier handling.'

She stopped and glanced at herself in her iPhone, with the selfie mode switched on. Don't I look great today? She thought. But she turned instantly critical, examining the corner of her eyes, one at a time, to see if the number of the crow's feet had grown. 'Crow's feet?' A voice arose amidst her growing concern about another tiny foot that hadn't seemed there a day or two ago. Frantically, she started looking for her micro roller but in vain. The voice persisted, bringing her mind back to the seminar the other day in which Baohui raised concerns, imagistic, linguistic and cultural, in a talk focussed on a number of expressions, differently used, that meant the same thing. Two examples, both Chinese, that he used were impressive, one of 'fish-belly white' to denote colours of the sky at daybreak and the other, of 'fish-tail lines' to mean the crow's feet. The significance, though, according to him, was that neither language seemed to have the ability to absorb this vivid description into its own repertoire. In concluding his talk that lasted for about 10 minutes, he said that one falls in love in English whereas, in Mandarin, one loves up someone as if the object, the target, of one's love were superior and in fact it is, like climbing up a tree. Everyone burst out laughing, leaving Baohui bewildered, till Stacey came near and whispered something that got Baohui himself laughing as well when the meaning of the phrase, 'up a tree', sank in.

'I'll find a way to get rid of these fish-tail lines,' Stacey thought as she finished the email and clicked on 'Send', with these words below,

'Don't work yourself too hard. Be relaxed. Temper inventiveness with a practical sense of things. Be bilingual if that is how you feel the story could be enhanced. I'll see you again over coffee in a few days. Ciao.

'P.S. I really enjoyed your talk about the "fish-tail lines" and love "up a tree" the other day.'

'PPS. I suggest we meet up every two weeks with a new chapter from you and you will hear back from me regarding the previous chapter.'

Chapter 3

I realised that there was no Ah Sin. No voice speaking from the grave unless it was the result of a hallucination. But the sheer weight of history, or his personal history, a concomitant of a freak-out experience, was heavy upon me, pervasive enough to put me in a mode of historical thinking or living in parallel to the life of an imaginary individual. Despite the denigration of his people with that designation, Ah Sin managed to survive the vicissitudes of life in my mind, particularly when he began telling the story from the book he had got back from Ah Mao.

Amidst a crowd of rising clamorous voices, asking him to tell them the story, Ah Sin said, 'But this is a simple enough story that tells of how fortune is made in a strange way, captured in two poetic lines that go, "If you are fated to be poor, the gold you find turns into copper/But if you are fated to be rich, the paper you pick up turns to silk."

'There is this man in the Song dynasty, whose name is Jin (Gold). He spends all his life making money. Every once in a while, when the silver coins he earns reaches about 100 taels, he has them melted in a silver ingot and ties it in the middle with a red wool yarn. As time goes by, he has managed to amass eight such ingots. At his 70th birthday, he has his four sons over and promises that each of them will get two of the ingots in due course, to everyone's delight. That night, he is a little tipsy and, on his way to bed, he sees eight men appear in his house. One of them who looks like a headman says to him that they have known all along that he has been amassing a fortune. But it's not fair for him to hold onto them because they in fact belong to someone by the surname Wang living nearby. As soon as he finishes these words they walk off with the ingots. Jin wakes up from his dream in a cold sweat and is shocked to find none of the ingots there as he gropes around for them underneath his bed. He goes in search of Mr Wang and soon finds him, burning incense in front of his joss with his family. On learning of Mr Jin's intentions, Mr Wang, a pauper all his life, reveals that eight men did in fact give him eight ingots, which is why they are paying respects to their joss, to thank Him and to ask Him for protection. Before a bitterly disappointed Mr Jin leaves, Mr Wang gives him three taels of silver, which Mr Jin hides in his sleeve but can't find when arriving home. He's embittered in thinking that even his joss denies him this last possession when he realises that he puts it wrongly in another lining. In the end, he's happy that he has three taels of silver after all.'

'"Oh, I see. I've heard this story before," one man with a front tooth missing said. "Each of the eight men has a red thread tied around their waists and they tell Mr Wang that because Mr Jin's luck has run out it is time these ingots stayed with Mr Wang as organized by heaven."

'"Yes, yes, I know, I know. They then creep under Wang's bed and turn into the ingots themselves!" a young man said who happened to have a thread tied around his waist.

'"Ha, ha, ha," the tooth-missing man couldn't help laughing as he pointed at the white thread around the man's waist and said. "But it was of a wrong colour."

'"Oh, yes," Ah Fong, the oldest of them, said. "The colour has got to be right. A white thread denotes cleanness but also death; in our place, people wear white in a funeral. A black thread is certain death. A red one means good fortune. But a yellow one is of an emperor's colour." '

While all this was happening, there was someone who wasn't listening; instead, he lay in a ball, completely withdrawn into himself. This is Ah Toy, a boy of seventeen, who seemed to show no interest whatever in the happenings around him from the first day when he went on board the ship. He slept, slept, and slept, only doing the very basic things, like eating, drinking, and going to the toilet. Otherwise, he spoke not a word but just lay there in the corner.

*

An aside: I wonder if I need to switch modes here, from the first-person narrative to something I have not tried before, e.g. a second-person narrative mode. I'm encouraged by Yu in his approach shown in that novel of his, published in Chinese, as yet unavailable in English, in which a number of characters are narrated in a constantly switched mode. What is more, I wonder if I could even include this 'aside' in here as if it were said to an audience without the awareness of the other characters in my book. In any case, I think I shall give it a go. If my supervisor doesn't like it, I have time enough to delete it. Let me sample it for you here:

I know you come from Qishi (Strange Stone) Village. You are an orphan. Your father died in a storm when he was out at sea. Your mother died in mysterious circumstances. You were brought up by a rich uncle but was unfavourably treated by him. When the news came that gold was discovered in Australia, everyone wanted to go. But your uncle saw it as a good opportunity to get rid of you, so he signed a contract with an agent for you to go on the condition that you pay them double when you find enough gold and come home. You didn't want to because you were married. You in fact only slept a week with your wife before you were kidnapped after you were drugged. When you woke up, you were already on board. This was too sad for you amongst a crowd of total strangers, on board a ship bound for you knew not where. You liked nothing about you; you liked nothing about these people; you liked nothing about the ship. You slept because you were resentful of what had happened to you without knowing why. You blamed your surroundings and your circumstances for your misfortune. You didn't know why. You didn't want to know why. You did, though, throw a couple of glances, not at anyone, but at Ah Fong whom you found trustworthy because of the number of wrinkles on his forehead.

It was not till a few days after the ship had set sail that you decided to stay awake and speak only when spoken to. But no one spoke to you. They were either incessantly engaged in their fantan game or chatting about things you had no interest in. No one paid attention to the mouse of a man who had stayed quiet for days and seemed full of enmity. It so happened that Jack, a sailor, came under the deck for inspection.

*

A self-analysis. I think I must stop here to problematize the conflict that is about to arise from the contact between Jack and Ah Toy. From today's perspective, and based on a vast warehouse of historical material available online and offline, it would seem most natural that these two would come to blows as a course of conflict would seem to have been pre-set even for imagination. I suppressed the impulse the second it came to the surface. What is first contact? Is that a product of the mind or of the times? How many first contacts have already taken place before the real first contact occurs? Must all such contacts necessarily lead to conflicts? Must cultures necessarily come to blows with each other when they come into contact? Didn't Captain Miller have to make money? Didn't he have to have these Chinese customers on board even if he presumably hated their guts? Didn't he have to take them to Australia instead of throwing them overboard halfway because he, after all, was first of all a human being, second of all a professional and last of all a white man, hitherto the most criticized human dreg? And didn't he successfully arrive at the designated destination with all his human cargo intact? And in so doing didn't he deserve praises? I want to present the story as it is. As it 'is'? What story can be as it 'is'? As soon as it happens, it is no longer 'is'. It needs to be told or re-told, from what one sees in what one imagines. There is not a shred of truth in that, only what seems true or what is made to seem true. This is scary, not for me, but for a writer. I aim at completing a PhD thesis and successfully gaining a degree with it. But a writer has to do his or her utmost in making a product of a book good enough to make sales so he or she and his or her publishing company can live on a lucrative basis, divided along the line of 10% for the author and the rest for everyone else. But does he or she have to be conflict-prone even if he or she writes about a story that happened 150-odd years ago? Which leads to the next issue that constantly harrows me: Is everything that happened in the past necessarily wrong? Put another way: does the past have to be wrong because it is past, the past, a huge mistake uncorrectible except in academic papers with academic theories aimed at correcting the past errors or mistakes, theories awaiting correction themselves in a few years or decades? What about the present that is fast becoming a past and a distant past in the future? Would what is now correct be incorrect in a few decades?

Chapter 4

The day we arrived it was so hot I couldn't breathe. Blue was everything.
The sea water was blue. The sky was blue. The eyes of the sailors
around us were blue. Only the sun was yellow, a burning yellow. And
the line of the coast that emerged was brown, so brown my heart gave
a leap. The sea around my village was never this blue. The water was
grey, sometimes dark when the sky was overcast. And it smelt strongly
of fish. Here on board this ship, I felt I had come to a world of blue,
bathing me in its blueness till I wondered if my skin had turned blue.
It was. My cloth garment was wet and loose. The wind blew it flying,
filling it out like a sail. But for the man standing in my way and holding
me tight, I would have seen myself flying out to sea, right across the
railing. The man ripped my garment apart from the middle as I heard
the buttons drop in quick succession. In an instant, the lifting power
had subsided and I stood on my feet, like a half-naked fish.

'Want to swim, did you?' the man said.

'Sorry?' said I.

The man repeated his question. I was none the wiser. But I recognized him as one of the sailors, a thick-browed young man of 21, about
my age.

'This,' he pointed at my blue garment, shaking his head as he said.
'No good.'

That I understood and echoed, 'No good?' A remark, unuttered, flew
out of my chest, that made a staccato sound of 'ah, ah, ah, ah, ah', in a
painfully pleasant way.

'Ah, ah, ah,' he emulated the sound I had made, rolling his eyes, and
throwing up his hands, possibly in frustration but seemingly in an attempt to cheer me up.

'Name? Your name?' said he, almost yelling, against a blast of wind that instantly swallowed the words up.

'San, san, san,' said I, pointing at the tip of my nose.

'Sin?' the man shook his head incredulously, muttering to himself, 'what a name is that?'

'San, new, it mean new, not old, new, like first, like never before, like this, this, this,' I chucked words, like stones, in the baffled man's face, in a mixture of things I had heard or picked up or even dreamt of somewhere, somewhere else, anywhere else.

'Ah New, Ah New, that's you!' said the man whose brows swept from side to side, like a broad brush my calligrapher teacher once taught me to use in my village school.

'Yes, yes, yes, no, no, no,' I jabbered, gesticulated, blabbered, nonsensed, till the man held me with his hands and raised me above his head, saying, with a threatening voice, in a playful tone, 'I'll throw you overboard if you keep talking crap like that.'

I closed my eyes, becoming suddenly relaxed, deeming it a moment of heroic truth, in which a Taiping soldier was presented for execution, with a broad sword over his neck, to be beheaded shortly after. In that instant, I acquired a penetrating power to see my whole person suffused in blue, turning transparent, as a white seabird came flying, right through it, its shadow overlapping with that of my heart, and gone in a split second.

The man didn't throw me overboard. Instead, he put me down, and laughed out loud, saying to the other onlookers, a mixed crowd of sailors and passengers, 'This guy is so light it feels like a leaf.'

*

After weeks of overcrowding, food deprivation and much abuse in a language hardly anyone knew, we were finally arriving, not immediately close enough to shore so as to disembark over a gangplank, but not far enough to lose sight of a town as small as a seashell. How to get to shore? As the captain was in discussion with his men, I could see the locals come towards us in their boats. Sea birds rose and swooped down on any scraps of food chucked from the ship. There was noise of oars hitting water. A sense of excitement seized us. 'Au zau, Au zau,'[1] everyone yelled, from the bottom of their hearts as tears came to their eyes. Bitter memories of how money was scraped together, how promises were made to pay it all off as soon as gold was found, and how family members reluctantly tore themselves away from the departing loved ones came rushing back, only to make the moment the more relishable, appreciable. When it was decided that the lighter vessels, full of wool, on board the ship, would not be used for transport and everyone had to rely on the boats rowed in by the locals, we could do nothing but follow the instructions.

To our surprise, no one was allowed in the boats that were rowed alongside the ship. It was money that they wanted. These men of red hair, brown hair, grey hair, golden hair, no blue hair, wanted only one thing: money! And that was the first English word I had learnt: Money, and it sounded so much like another word, 'many'. I was later to learn that it also sounded like 'harmony'. In fact, the two words could be rolled into one: harmoney. No money, no harmony. That story later.

An intense session of haggling ensued. As I had no money to pay – 12 pounds, previously paid, was all I had as my fare from China, I watched them clinching the deal one after another, the lowest being 8 shillings, and the highest, one pound, as the crew threw their baggage into the boats. It went off to a good start as passengers laughed their way to shore, riding in their boats as if full of gold, until something dropped, making a loud splash in the water, taking the remaining ones by surprise. It was the baggage of someone that one crew member had thrown, landing outside the boat. The man, the owner of the baggage, was Ah Mao. He literally jumped on the deck, not into the sea, but at the man who had accidentally done the wrong thing, his hands tightening around the man's neck, forcing him down against the railing, till he raised his hand, gesturing that he would retrieve it for him, which he subsequently did by jumping into the water himself and diving for the sunken baggage. When he re-emerged, baggage in hand, the passengers cheered in a roar of history. After he climbed on board, Ah Mao was so moved that he went up to him, both his hands extended,

1 'Australia' in Cantonese.

meaning to shake hands with him, when the man, whose name was John, picked him up bodily and chucked him overboard, to everyone's dismay. But John laughed out loud, looking pleased with himself.

The last remaining two were Ah Toy and I myself. Ah Toy had no baggage, no money, and I had baggage but no money. He did not want to join the others as he seemed to develop an attachment to me, staying by my side and listening to my stories over the last few weeks. When I ascertained with him that he was a good swimmer, my mind was put at ease. Someone came along and said,

'How would you guys like to leave?'

I had a look and saw that it was the same man who had held me up skywards earlier this morning, so I told him in Cantonese that we'd just swim ashore. Seeing that he didn't understand, I held out my hands and drew them back in a semi-circle, indicating an act of swimming, when a gnarl blasted behind him, saying, 'David, stop talking nonsense to these bloody chinks! Just throw them overboard, along with their shitty baggage.'

David held up his hand towards the gnarling voice and said, 'Hang on, no such thing, as these are good-fellow human beings.' As he said so, he threw me a rope, tied one end to the railing and got me to hold onto the other. I refused because I wanted Ah Toy to go first so I could look after him should anything untoward happen.

As David let Ah Toy down by the rope, holding it with both his hands and letting it out inch by inch, I took a piece of string and tied my bundle, not exactly baggage, to my waist, getting ready for the water.

Shortly after, both of us were down in the sea, swimming towards shore as all the boats had deserted us, two moneyless beings, my illusion of people welcoming us and cheering for us gone for good, followed by this piece of reasoning that, perhaps, this was what was going to be for the rest of our journey to this country. No money, no receiving boats. No money, no welcoming smiles. No money, nothing. Still, we've got our arms and legs intact on us and they can take us ashore.

The water, though, was really welcoming. It felt so cool, even cold, pleasingly so. Ah Toy, without a word, gave me help as he swam, half holding my bundle to ease its load, further away from the ship till it dwindled into a fading memory.

*

A beach strewn with names, unknown names, unpronounceable to the degree of gobbledygook, unknowable except by their own owners, unlearnable even, that were stretched in a long queue, under the scorching sun, in front of a table, a white table, behind which sat a man, a white man, with a pen and a notepad on it. He was Mr Melville, currently in charge of the local Customs House, a one-man affair that had come into contact with something the place had never encountered in tens of thousands of years. The names, for example, were 刘百贵、杨春、赵先河、李积、伍亚仲、雷捷广、司徒恒大、甄广文、陈瓒伦、余勳集, taken from a Chinese novel on the event, titled, *Taojin di*, published in China in 2014, p. 16. One could transliterate them as Liu Baigui, Yang Chun, Zhao Xianhe, Li Ji, Wu Yazhong, Lei Jieguang, Situ Hengda, Zhen Wenguang, Chen Zanlun and Yu Xunji. In those days, when Wade-Giles was used, however, they would have become Leo Pai-Kui, Yang Chun, Chao Hsian-Ho, Li Chi, Wu Ya-Chung, Lei Chieh-Kuang, Situ Heng-Ta, Chen Wen-Kuang, Chen Tsan-lun and Yu Hsun-Chi. That way, you get a sense of how the names would sound to Mr Melville when he first heard them. Even then it was difficult because they were uttered in Cantonese, a dialect totally different from Mandarin in pronunciation although written exactly in the same way, different again from what's copied from the novel, like this, in the traditional Chinese script: 劉百貴、楊春、趙先河、李積、伍亞仲、雷捷廣、司徒恆大、甄廣文、陳瓚倫、余勳集. More difficult.

I am struck dumb as I realize I am not writing a novel. That is, I am not Ah Sin. But Baohui. I need to be Ah Sin enough to be Ah Sin, in a less Baohui way.

The bearers of these names stretched themselves from end to end, across the beach, with Ah Toy and Ah Sin standing at the tail of the queue. They moved inch by inch towards the table as they chit-chatted.

'How are you going to survive without any baggage?' said Ah Sin, turning around with his back towards the sun to sun-dry his wet pigtail.

'Don't you worry,' said Ah Toy. 'I can always manage.'

'You can wear mine if you feel cold,' Ah Sin offered.

'No, I'll be fine. It's quite hot.'

'But anything may happen, you know. They say it's the strangest place in the world where it may snow in summer and people shit from their mouths.'

'Oh, yes, I already did on board the ship,' said Ah Toy, remembering how he had vomited for days on end.

'So you'd have to be prepared; anything might happen,' said Ah Sin, recalling how baggage and even people were thrown into the water.

'I'm not afraid of anything,' said Ah Toy, recalling how he was kidnapped and put on board with nothing on his back, just whatever he was wearing at the time.

'Hey, hey, stop talking, will you?' A middle-aged man wearing eyeglasses hurled these words in the direction of the last two men and he could see that at least the loudness of the words seemed to produce an effect as the two started running, one oddly without any baggage and the other, carrying a light bundle with him.

He watched till the barefooted lank young man came to a stop before his table when he said, 'What's your name?'

'Ah Toy, Ah Toy,' said the young man, as if he was calling the man Ah Toy.

'I'm not a toy,' said the man. 'What are you talking about?' But Ah Sin could see, over Ah Toy's shoulder, that the man had already inscribed two words on his notepad: Ah Toy.

He waved for Ah Toy to step aside as he directed his last question, also his first, repeated ad infinitum, 'What's your name?'

'My name Gam Dai Sin,' Ah Sin said.

'What, Gum Die Sin? You don't have an "Ah" that goes with whatever?' the man looked up at him in surprise.

Ah Sin was lost and looked to Ah Toy for help. The latter said in Cantonese, 'Just tell him Ah Sin. Just do it.'

It suddenly dawned on Ah Sin that he ought to have done this a long time ago because it seemed like a passport everyone recognized and accepted. If he had told them what his real name in Cantonese-Chinese was, they would have got totally lost. As soon as he hit this thought he blurted out, 'My name Ah Sin, Ah, Ah, Ah, Sin, Sin, Sin, Ah Sin, Ah Sin, Ah Sin, very, very Ah Sin.'

The man with spectacles shook his head and studiously put down the two words, 'Ah Sin', as he muttered to himself, 'What an evil name!' and waved them off, as if to chase off two blowflies.

Chapter 5

We agreed to meet at Café 22 and we did, on a day of 39 degrees. As usual, I ordered a latte and she, a chai latte. 'That,' I said, pointing at the creamy froth on top and shaking my head. 'is no good.'

'Oh, no,' she said. 'Don't be so critical. I like it. It's symbolic.'

'Symbolic? In what way?' Our eyes met and locked. In that instant, my heart missed a beat and I quickly looked away as a thought emerged from the depths of my unconsciousness: I liked the way she looked at me through those eyelashes.

'You know you made a mistake when you wrote about Ah Sin in third person?' she avoided my question and my eyes when she got outside, lighting up a cigarette for herself by the street-side in the shade of a scarred gum tree.

'Yes, I do.'

'You know you can always correct it later in a second or third draft,' she blew the smoke off but I was quick enough to catch an elusive glance of hers through the dispersing smoke.

'I don't know about that,' said I.

'Why?'

'Not on this occasion at least,' said I, looking up at a daylight half-moon drifting, it seemed, among the gum leaves. 'because I want to keep track of mistakes made, I want to keep the trails or traces they leave behind. If I don't, or if I correct or keep correcting them, my readers, or my imaginary readers, won't be able to see them and they will be left with a correct and corrected version upon which no improvement is possible, reaching a state of perfection that is equal to death.'

'Are you suggesting you expect your readers to mentally improve upon your textual errors by correcting them?'

'That and also the fact — '

'Did you know what Hemingway said about first drafts? He said and I quote, "The first draft of anything is shit."'

'I don't agree. A baby is a first draft when he or she is born. Is that a shit?'

'More a shift, actually.'

Seeing that she wasn't offended, I went on, headlong, 'Yes, a shift, for better or worse. But you appreciate that and you record moments of its passage through life despite illness or mistakes.

She was silent, and smoking, her eyes on my forehead.

'Years ago I met an Asian composer who rejected the notion of revision by saying that as far as he knew from his experience the last draft, even if it was the 100th, was never as good as the first.'

'But you know what? This is not a real novel; this is a PhD thesis. Your target market is not the readers; it's me your supervisor and a couple of examiners, you know that?'

'I know, I know,' I said, my tone toned down a bit as a remark made by the composer swept through my mind and I heard him saying: Don't tell me about the beauty of revision. You can't revise a cloud, can you? Least of all, you can't revise lovemaking, can you? That is to say, you can't say to your partner: No, no, not like this, like that, no, like that, this is more correct, more right, if you do it like this, not like that. You just do it and take it right to the end, the way Auden did with his 'The Platonic Blow'.

But I kept mum and said not a word.

She finished another cigarette and chucked the butt into the bin next to her as she rose and said, 'Chai and latte, you and me, that's what.'

I rose, too, and went to the counter to pay. But the Italian girl behind it said, her chin pointed towards the back of Stacey, 'But she's already paid for you.'

*

An email sent, as follows:

Dear Stacey,

Thank you so much for your lovely coffee and the time you spent with me, discussing my work in progress.

I happen to be reading a book, entitled, *A Four Books Reader*, in Chinese, and found a remark by Confucius that is quite illuminating to me. He's basically saying that he won't look at a major annual sacrificial service, known as *di*, held by Duke Wen of Lu, in memory of his father Duke Xi of Lu and Duke Min of Lu, his father's older brother. But in arranging the wooden idols, he placed his father's idol in front of his older brother's instead of doing it the other way round. This, in Confucius' opinion, is a breach of etiquette, which is why he doesn't want to look at it, the least he can do in an act of defiance and criticism as a serving minister in the regime.

My immediate reaction to this is that rather than a breach of the etiquette it is probably a lapse of memory on the part of the duke or an error in judgement made by him for lack of knowledge without realising what he had done, much to Confucius' chagrin as the latter was obsessed with properness and propriety. But the crux of the matter is that history is not lived according to books or etiquette. It is strewn with mistakes, deliberate or accidental, which is probably why one can't set out to correct historical mistakes, particularly something that happened some 2500 years ago. One can try to understand them or seek to shed new light on them from different angles.

Further on that point, history and fiction do not often match, sometimes deliberately so because the nose has shifted its place of breathing or has stopped breathing altogether 100 years after its birth. Where do you pin that breath down? Which word do you pin it down to, on which paper written where? In the imagination of a particular person, anything can happen anywhere anytime to anyone without even having to resort to a subjunctive mood. Even a historian is allowed to resort to imagination when she does not have the language. A lot of words written, having to be written anyway. The future watching helplessly, ready to pounce on them and to correct. All we do, all I do, is compare notes, compare knows and compare nos.

This is just part of my musing on the matter, not an excuse for not wanting to remove my remission. Already, I realise that I may have to shed thousands, if not hundreds of thousands, of words in latter stages of revision. Did I tell you that in writing about Ah Sin, I have already given up on the idea of making him a 180-year-old man telling his story from the grave or a bad guy as Bret Hart, Mark Twain, Hume Nisbet and Mrs Campbell Praed did in their respective days? There's no other bad guy in this novel than myself. You'll find out if you keep reading.

By the way, as part of the work you said you would pay me to do on the number of hours worked, I have begun researching into gay and lesbian literature in ancient China and have dug up a number of works that I have never heard of, such as *Longyang yishi*. 'Yishi', no equivalent in English, refers to history that escapes or hides itself from the orthodox history, or a hermit history. Longyang is the name of a well-known gay man in history who lived in or around B.C. 243 and his name survived him as a referent for the gay people ever after. Hence the title, *A Hermit History of Longyang*, available online for free access except that it is in Chinese. I think it's high time you started learning the Chinese language. But I had a quick look at the novel. It has 20 chapters and each chapter is about the affairs between one particular man and other men and sometimes women, too. I won't go into detail because I am not sure how much you want to know and whether your interest lies more in gay or lesbian or both. I'll provide you with a bibliography of the literature in time.

We must catch up again but do let me pay for the next round of coffees.

Best,

Baohui

In the spirit of reconciliation I acknowledge the Traditional Custodians of country throughout Australia and their connections to land, sea and community. We pay our respect to their elders past and present and extend that respect to all Aboriginal and Torres Strait Islander peoples today. I also pay respect to multicultural Australia for giving me the opportunity to study and live in the country.

*

My notes, partly in poems:

<u>10/1</u>
Wrote a poem to entertain myself in an attempt to diffuse the burden of fiction or history or both, not to show Stacey, for the moment:

Numbers

In January 1853, 2 ships arrived
By the following year, 3000 had arrived

On 17 January 1857, *Land of Cakes* arrived
And 264 landed

On 27 April 1857, 3 ships arrived
1300 disembarked

In the preceding 6 days
1513 had arrived

On 30 June 1857, *Koenig Willem II* arrived
16 crew lives were lost

During 1857, 32 ships had arrived
And 14615 unloaded, with only 1 woman among them

In total, 62990 arrived in the goldfields
48000 returned to China, the rest remaining without a trace[1]

<u>19/1</u>
I found I wrote more and more poems in Chinese, probably in a way that matches the poems written by the early diggers or digger-settlers except that theirs were never published as far as the historical evidence available demonstrates or that theirs were never even meant for publication, written as they were in multiple individual and separate heads, deleted, or forgotten, the minute they were born, as poetry, like air, breathed in and out, dies as instantly as it is birthed. Do I make sense to myself? Anyway, here's the Chinese poem, for myself, too [Deleted based on Stacey's recommendation against the inclusion of anything linguistically Chinese in a textually English context and my self-caution against it based on a precaution inferred from Wen Ho Li whose material written in Chinese found by FBI at his home to be subversive and self-incriminating because his 'writing in Chinese was treated as evidence of some kind of crime'—See his *My Country Versus Me*, p. 117 although I'll keep what follows below]:

[A Chinese poem deleted in its entirety for reasons cited above—BH]

I'm not sure if there is a need to Google-translate or self-translate this poem. But I'm sure where there is an interest there is a way.

<u>20/1</u>
Already, I thought of ending every letter for Ah Sin with 'Yours Ah Sincerely' even though I have never read a single one left by him; I've only imagined them.

One note on the pronunciation of Guichen Bay. I can never look at

1 Based on the statistics in this article here: https://m.bendigobank.com.au/public/__data/assets/pdf_file/0012/95979/Heritage1209_Chinese-Gold-chinese-Trek-to-Gold.pdf (accessed 10/1/19)

'Guichen Bay' without saying to myself how Chinese it is as I blurt out: "桂臣湾", Gui for 桂, and Chen for 臣, which literally means a laurelled minister, even though the Australian-English pronunciation renders it like 'Guy Ken', and the French, 'Gee Shang', which, in another twist, sounds like the Chinese expression, *jixiang* (auspiciousness or propitiousness).[1]

---

1 See the pronunciations of the words: http://www.pronouncekiwi.com/ Guichen%20Bay

Chapter 6

A few words by Stacey Ahsin on supervisor intervention:

First of all, please accept my deepest condolences on the passing of Zhang Baohui who, sadly, had taken eir own life shortly after they submitted this draft, supposedly eir final draft, coded as 'v11.0'. Second of all, I shall have to exercise supervisor-initiated intervention wherever I see fit, just so that the book manuscript could eventually be published. Third of all, my understanding from the readers who have read this manuscript is that while some feel 'very moved', others simply hate BH, my student who is also a fictional character in the book, because of eir various criticisms. I hereby propose to myself and my potential—I mean eir potential—publisher that I shall practise supervisor-imposed censorship so that neither the publisher nor the readers are hurt by eir possibly improper comments. Let me add that they was actually a very likeable person when they was alive, someone who never minces eir words, with the result that the trait finds its way into eir writing but bearing in mind that I shall keep it at a maximum minimum. And, last, but not least, of all, I shall not provide any extensive explanations for my censorship, for a good cause, except a brief note or two, and that as far as I am concerned any extensive inclusion of Chinese passages in an English book oriented towards the English-speaking readers is bound to meet with failure however innovative the idea is, particularly in a country whose book-based bilinguality is yet to arrive in decades if not in centuries. I shall work in close consultation with any potential future publisher as to what more contents deemed unacceptable to be pruned or removed.

我们在巴特勒湖边安营扎寨，这座湖不大，对岸的树历历在目，能分得清树枝，湖水清澈透底，湖水在右边的远处缩成一个颈口，那是入海口。我尝了尝湖水，却不咸，脸上便露出一个开心的微笑，脑子里闪过一段诗句：明月松间照，清泉石上流，可是这儿没有松树，只有清水。我也不是王维，只是一个来淘金的，还不知淘不淘得到，但无论如何，淘不到金，是绝不回头的。为了这趟转道香港的船费，很多人已经到了砸锅卖铁，倾家荡产的地步，赚不到钱，回去就没有意义。我掏出烟枪和烟具。"十载寒窗无人问，一举成名天下知"，我的粉色鸦片烟的烟荷包上竖着绣着这两行字，我点燃烟灯，又把烟膏放上竹管，点着后徐徐吸食起来，把个小阿辛看得如痴如醉，小脑袋跟着我的每个动作转动。我说："来来，阿辛，你来抽一口。"说着，就把烟管给他递过去。

谁知他横了我一眼，说："No way！It's evil."我听懂了，他是说：这不行。这是很邪恶的。

我心想：看来这小家伙很不简单嘛，就没理他，管自抽了起来，顿觉筋骨酥松，疲劳尽消，进入了杜牧"烟斜雾横"的状态，想起家里的两个女人，此时不知在做啥，心里不觉有些儿难受。

此时晚霞消退，炊烟四起，湖上升起袅袅雾气，一轮不同于中国的残月，低垂在地平线上，淡淡的颜色，仿佛轻云的一抹，就那么一点月的意态。[Struck out but not deleted—SA]

We set camp by the side of Lake Butler, a small lake. The trees on the other side of the lake were clear enough to distinguish between the branches. The water of the lake was see-through right to the bottom. In the distance, the lake narrowed to a bottleneck, where the water emptied itself into the sea. I had a taste of the water, not salty, as a delighted smile came to my face and a poetic line flashed across my mind: 'A bright moon was shining on the pine forest / as a clean spring was flowing over the stones'. But there were no pine trees, only clear water. Nor was I Wang Wei, only a gold miner, not even knowing whether I could find gold. Still, if I did not find gold, I would not return home. The passage here via Hong Kong had made many a miner go bankrupt.

It wouldn't make sense if one didn't make money. I got out my smoking set, my pink opium pouch embroidered vertically with these two lines that go, 'No one pays you any attention while you study for ten years by the cold window / But once you become famous you are known across the under-heaven.' I lit the opium lamp, put the tobacco paste on the bamboo pipe and started taking slow drags. Little Ah Xin was fascinated watching me, his head rotated following every movement of mine. I said, 'Come on, Ah Xin, give it a go', as I passed the pipe to him.

But he rolled his eyes, saying, 'No way! It's evil.' I got it. He was saying: That won't do. It's evil.

I thought: The boy is awesome, and went on smoking, ignoring him. Soon, I felt completely relaxed, all my fatigue gone, and entered into the state of 'smoke mixed with a mist' as described by Du Mu. Then I thought of my two women at home and felt miserable because I had no idea what they were doing at the moment.

The evening glow was receding as smoke was coming out from the kitchen chimneys everywhere. Wisps of mist rose from the lake. A waning crescent, different from the Chinese one, lay prostrate on the horizon, of a colour so light that, like the smear of a light cloud, it had the slightest resemblance of a moon.

*

Silver banksia. Dryland tea-trees. Coast daisy bush. Red holly grevillea. Round leaf wattle. Dark-red wallaby saltbush. Creeping boobialla. Cushion bush. Native fuchsias. Native pigface. Coast spear-grass. Coast tussock grass.

Drooping she-oaks. Narrow-leaf bower wattles. Creek lilly pillies. Willow myrtles. Rusty gums. Yellow bloodwood. Red flowering gums.

Dead trees. Burnt. Dead. White bone-like trunks. Dead branches and trunks washed clean that were bleached and pale. Dead trees covered in creeping green leaves. Dead trees of many years' standing. Dead trees that thrust right into the skies. Dead trees that stood in a row, high and tall and towering.

And this is where Ah Sin and Ah Toy, along with the rest of the group, were travelling through, hacking their way to their destination of gold, said to lie some 350 miles away. If they could walk 20 miles a day every day, they might be able to reach their destination in about 15 days.

'Why are there so many flies?' said Ah Toy, waving a fly off his eyelash.

'Stop talking!' said Ah Sin as he spat out a fly that had flown into his mouth the second he opened it.

A chuckle from behind drew their attention. As both of them turned their heads around, they saw a face dark with flies but its mouth covered with a thin strip of white cloth. It was Ah Mao whose forbearance astonished them.

When they lit a fire to cook their dinner by the side of the lake, Ah Mao was able to tell them what had happened. He had swallowed quite a few stray flies before he realised he had to take immediate action by covering his mouth with a spare shoelace.

'I wonder if these devils will stay inside my stomach and breed more,' said Ah Mao.

'Then turn you into a huge fly?' said Ah Toy.

'What are you talking about?' said Ah Mao, his pockmarked face flushing red.

'I remember an ancient poem about the flies,' said Ah Sin.

'What did it say?' said Ah Toy, ignoring Ah Mao's remark.

'If you say that again, I'll break your neck,' said Ah Mao, staring at Ah Toy in a way that could have swallowed him up like a fly.

'I'll tell you what it is,' said Ah Sin as he silenced Ah Toy with a meaningful look and started chanting the poem off the top of his head,

Walking with a Burning Incense Stick

A fly flew into a smelly pot
obsessed with its sweetness, it went straight to the centre
forgetting to lift itself off
its feet stuck
its wings stuck

its shape lost
I sighed, my heart moved
there's bitterness in sweetness
the same way disasters were bred in happiness
once you had a taste of it
you should have removed yourself from it all
but you were just not nimble enough
such a big fly!

'Who wrote that?' Ah Fong, who had remained silent so far, spoke for the first time.

'No idea,' said Ah Sin, looking at his grave face of wrinkles. 'I think it's by an anonymous poet, a poet without a name.'

'One ought to remember all the best poems by the best poets throughout history,' said Ah Fong.

'I'm going to catch fish,' said Ah Toy as he took off his shoes and ran to the edge of the water.

'You are probably right,' said Ah Sin, not to anyone, his eyes fixed on the fire which was growing more brisk underneath the wok, filled with water found in a creek nearby. 'But I'm not a poet. I just like it.'

'Many people died, like flies,' said Ah Fong.

Ah Sin looked up in surprise. His lips moved but words refused to come out.

'Well, you know,' Ah Fong began his story in a slow, drawn-out voice, in a matter-of-fact tone. 'Hundreds if not thousands died.'

'How did you know?'

'I saw with my own eyes; I was there; I crept from out of the corpses in the fields.'

'What fields? Where?'

'Don't remember. Have forgotten. But do remember how Wei Changhui died.'

'How?'

'He was sentenced to what was known as "inch cuts".'

'What's that?' All eyes were focused. All ears pricked up. All noses smelling the flesh and blood.

'Inch cuts are just inch cuts. They cut him up in slices each two inches long and hang all the slices on the gate tower, with a sign that says these cuts are meant for watching only, not taking.' As soon as he said this, Ah Fong shut up, refusing to say another word, refusing to answer any questions.

'Let's do that to my fish.' A delighted yell caught everyone's attention. It was Ah Toy who had just caught a number of carp, silvery and flapping, all strung up by the gills on a thin blade of grass.

*

That night, inside a makeshift tent, made of the large and small gum tree branches with leaves, Ah Sin went on with the story he had only begun telling on board Land of Cakes.

> It's a very long story, about twenty pages when I read it. But I have to condense it so you guys don't have to keep awake all night listening to it. The protagonist is a man who is a good-for-nothing kind of guy. Does everything. Fails in everything. Turns 30. Has no wife. But a fortune-teller predicts that he is going to make it big one day. Who knows? Life is full of ups and downs, tides and eddies. That much one knows. This guy starts a business selling fans featuring famous calligraphy by famous calligraphers. He goes to Peking. He gets interested customers wanting to see what it's like. But his own face turns ghastly when he sees that the customer can't open the fan. Because the autumn in Peking is quite wet most of his fans get moistened and stuck together, and they won't open. After he sells the rest of the stock for a song, he is left with only one silver piece.
>
> It so happens that a few friends are going overseas to trade and they bump into each other on the street. When they ask him to come along, Wen Ruoxu, his name, agrees. He has no other choice. He either stays home doing nothing or going away to see the world with these new friends, to help them along the way, just so he has food on the plate.
>
> While his friends are loading the ship with their goods, Wen

casts about for something to take along with him. His eyes are lit up at the sight of the oranges, a kind that's known as Dongting Red. It's so cheap that with the one single piece of silver on him he can get 10 bamboo bucketloads of them and he does. When he goes on board the ship, he is ashamed of hearing his friends remarking how much 'treasure' he has found.

After sailing for a few days, they come to the capital of a country called Jiling. There, people are busy buying and selling. But anything that comes from China sells at three times its original price. Wen waits on board for his friends to come back from their business, while taking a rest by hauling a basket out from beneath the deck and taking an orange to sample it. The locals, fascinated by the fiery colour of something they've never set their eyes on, come over and watch, and wonder how much it is, too.

Something about the Dongting Red. This is a kind that is sour when picked but turns sweet after storing away for a few days, so when Wen tastes it, it feels just right, all its innate sweetness coming out. When asked how much it is, Wen doesn't understand. But his friend on board puts out a finger indicating that it is one silver piece per orange. That's decided. And soon all nine baskets except one get sold and he has reaped a heap of silver pieces.

The silver coins in this country range from the highest to the lowest, in different patterns of dragon and phoenix, people, animals, trees, and water weeds. Locals think they've got a good deal when they pay him in coins of water weeds. But, seeing his oranges disappear so fast, Wen decides to increase the price, so a local buys one for two coins, till a guy comes rushing in on a piebald horse and says to him that he wants to buy all the remaining stuff because he has to make an offering of them to his Khan. But Wen is not sure when the guy gives him one coin of dragon and phoenix, thinking it might not be worth much till the guy explains that it is worth 100 water-weed coins!

By now, all had fallen asleep, no one listening. Ah Sin crept out of the tent and raised his head, to see a huge moon, the size of a bamboo basket, hanging in the sky. He stood by the side of the lake, pissed into it and went back inside.

*

From Baohui's research notes: When it comes to the shoes, men in the Qing dynasty wore a variety of shoes, from *guanxue* (the officer's boots), through *fuzilü* (福-character shoes), *pingban xie* (flat-soled shoes), *longxue* (dragon boots), *qianceng di* (thousand-layered soles) and *yuntou* (cloud-head shoes), as later portrayed in anti-Chinese cartoons. But I'd like to get Ah Sin to wear *caoxie* (straw shoes) because these were the cheapest shoes and, from today's point of view, the most ecological because, once discarded, they merged into the wind, rain and the soil, becoming one with them, leaving no toxic effects like modern plastic products that were indestructibly lasting.

Chapter 7

Part of an email response from Stacey:

> Dear Baohui,
> This looks like it's going to be a very self-conscious novel. In the past, a writer was a maker of a product without worrying too much about the process. As long as he achieved his purpose — appealing to the maximum number of readers with the maximum impact — with his writing, making both his readers and his publisher happy, he was happy. The novelist today has to make a choice between what he writes or does not write about. Does he hand over the finished product of a watch to you that he has made or does he take it apart, put all the insides on the table and put them together for your scrutiny? If he chooses the latter, will he not be concerned with the fact that you as a reader may get bored and stop reading after a few pages?

And a reply from Baohui says, very briefly,

> Thank you for your thought, Stacey. Let me finish a couple of chapters before I send them to you and hear your comments.

Then, it's not till he finished the above, his finger hovering above 'Send', that he thought he must include a 'PS', with what he had been thinking thus far. He said,

> Can I say this that all ways of storytelling thus far are problematic? What is a plot, regardless of its dictionary definition? Does a life, any life, move along the lines of a plot? Or is it planned rather

than plotted? What about climax? Is that cousin to climate? Is a tsunami bound to come because it's forecast to be so or because it is bound to come regardless? Why does the climax have to be preceded by an anti-climax? Why can't it be preceded by multiple climaxes and followed by more? Why does the book have to remain so tame, so tied up by so many dogmas, dog/mas, cat/mas, tiger/mas, wolf/mas, donkey/mas, pig/mas, cow/mas, mice/mas, that it becomes overcrowded in a bookshop of no sales, on the point of closing down, at greatly discounted price, e.g. a dollar a copy? In a world where no readers exist but their replacement with fans and followers, who bothers listening to whose opinion in regard to what books are the best because most standard conforming to all requirements in say *The Complete Guide to Writing Fiction*?

When he finished the above, his hand automatically reached for a book that lay next to his right hand in which, after the turn of a few pages, including the word 'restrictions' in the Index, he quickly located the following,

> With regard to the exclusion policies, the first restriction Act was passed in 1855 in Victoria as 'An Act to Make Provision for Certain Immigrants'. This limited the number of Chinese passengers to one for every ten tons of registered tonnage, together with the imposition of a 10-pound capitation fee, which was followed by further legislative restrictions in South Australia (1857) and New South Wales (1861), all identical in nature and all suspended or dropped by 1867 because of their success in reducing the number of the Chinese in those three colonies.

As he went on looking for more info, he started wondering about the ways of doing a possible exegesis. He's sick of reading all the rest of the PhD-based novels or long poems, divided equally between a formal creative part and a formal critical part, almost like a brain formed of two hemispheres, one critical and, the other, creative. Can't I somehow merge them in one to an indistinguishable degree? If I divide the thesis into two, is that meant to make it easier to read and to judge for the future judging panel? To put it bluntly, is that meant to minimize the time they are going to spend in reading and grading it? If they are lazy about this, why can't I play a lazy part in just inserting stuff exegetically wherever I see fit? Isn't that more congenial with the life itself as it's lived, creatively or critically? Can I do the creative part in English and the theoretical part in Chinese? What if Stacey doesn't understand the Chinese part? As he thought so, he found another piece of information on the Australian restrictions of the Chinese,

It should be pointed out that at this stage the Chinese government began, for the first time in Chinese history, to pay serious attention to the welfare of its nationals abroad. As a result of the Second Opium War (1856–60), the Qing government had granted permission for the emigration of its nationals abroad, reversing all its previous restrictions, thus beginning a new period in which government policy turned from restriction to protection, and protection of Chinese nationals was seriously considered as 'the prime reason for the appointment' of officials abroad. Several events were significant. In 1868 China sent its first diplomatic mission, called the Burlingame Mission, to the United States, and, subsequently, other European countries, such as England, France and Germany. By 1874 the Chinese government had effectively brought the coolie emigration to an end. This was followed by the establishment of a series of Chinese legations in European countries as well as Japan for the protection of Chinese nationals there, starting from 1875. Moreover, in 1886, a mission led by Chinese Commissioners Wang Yung-ho and Yu Chun left for South-east Asia and Australia to investigate the general situation with regard to the Chinese nationals there. All these were signs of a growing concern with the Chinese abroad and increasing attention to international affairs on the part of the Chinese government, though they did not produce much effect; on the contrary, they were viewed with serious concern in Australia and were regarded as a precursor to invasion. The Chinese government's suggestion that they establish a consulate in Melbourne in the late 1880s met with strong disapproval from Great Britain because of the fear that it might arouse anti-Chinese feelings in Australia.[1]

Then this, in regard to the restrictions in the 4-eye countries,

> At this point, one should do well to bear in mind that anti-Chinese feelings and legislative restrictions are not exclusively an Australian problem but an international phenomenon. According to Li Changfu, all the countries to which the Chinese emigrated except North Borneo and Brazil adopted restrictive and exclusive measures. It is the rising fear of the 'Yellow Peril' that lies at the bottom of this widespread exclusion of the Chinese, particularly in European countries and English dominions. Each of the four countries—Canada, America, Australia and New Zealand—had its full share of legislative restrictions. The American Congress passed its *Chinese Exclusion Act* in 1882, New Zealand adopted the *Natal Act* to exclude Chinese in 1899, and Canada passed its first anti-Chinese bill in 1885.
>
> However, it is not in those white countries but in Australia that anti-Chinese, anti-Asian feelings turned into a unanimous national policy in 'White Australia' and helped unite the six colonies into a federation. The twofold significance of this cannot be over-stressed: first, that Australia as a nation was founded on the basis of excluding coloured people in general and the Chinese in particular; and second, that on a metaphysical level, the Chinese, along with other coloured races, were to remain the underground and shadowy counterpart of this 'white' Australia in its process of nation-building for a long time to come.[2]

One word that emerged out of this overwhelming drainage was the word *jin* （禁） for restrictions, which shares the same sound as that of *jin* （金） for gold. Whenever something happens in relation to gold,

1 Qtd in Ouyang Yu, *Chinese in Australian Fiction: 1889-1988*. Cambria Press, 2008, pp. 18-9, with slight variation.
2 Ibid, pp. 19-20.

it seems, restrictions are introduced, particularly when the Chinese are involved. And things seem to also work in reverse, too. For example, when restrictions were relaxed in China, letting as many people out as humanly possible, they were tightened in the receiving countries.

'I'll think these things over,' Baohui said to himself, 'and will probably work them into the novel itself as time goes by.'

*

In the eyes of a local, or any locals in Robe, for example, these people from the Celestial Empire had no distinguishing qualities other than their unifying features of shaven heads, shaven mouths, male queues, yellow-skinned faces, yellow-stained teeth, silly smiles, black or white gowns, baggy half-gowns and loose baggy trousers reaching only half-shins, thick-soled shoes in the shape of a sampan, and eyes that stare, gaze or simply look, in what seem to be shifty ways. A mass of unindividualized human flesh, with hearts that were unfeeling, minds that were unthinking, limbs that seemed to enjoy rather than dread hard labour, the way buffalos or horses do, and tongues that could only speak a foreign tongue that sounded barbarian, savage, unintelligible and animalistic. The locals stood there and watched them, fascinated. They had read about them arriving in Sydney, on board the *Ningpo*, on 2 October 1848, with 100 miners and 20 boys. They had also read about 4000-odd more arriving there in the four years between 1849 and 1852. They had remained unmoved and the news soon faded from their collective memory except the image of the same that remained, confirmed by the human spectacle they now saw. When they witnessed them arriving en masse, they could think of nothing better than the word 'invasion' to describe them as Thomas Drury Smeaton did when he was manager of the Robe branch of the Bank of South Australia. A man of kind heart, Thomas harboured no evil intentions towards these invaders. It was obvious that the celestials had no weapons of any sorts. And after he had a talk with Captain Miller, when he better understood the invaders' position, he was relieved to learn that they'd soon be on their way to the Victorian goldfields, with no one to stay behind. Part of the conversation he had over dinner that night with Margaret his wife went something like this,

'These people, the invaders, are driven by a desire for gold from thousands of miles away over the sea and Robe is certainly not their cup of tea,' said Thomas as he took a spoonful of the pumpkin soup.

'They won't stay, you mean?' Margaret walked up to the table and put down the cup into which she poured the freshly brewed tea.

'There's no way they're going to stay. No gold for them here.'

'Let them go wherever they can find it then.'

'Sure. They'll travel hundreds of miles to the goldfields in Victoria.'

'But how are they going to live like that,' said Margaret.

'Like what?' said Thomas.

'I mean, there's not a single woman among them as far as I can see.'

'Oh, yes, you are right. That's going to be a problem,' said Thomas, and on second thought added, 'potentially.'

'I'm pretty sure it is,' agreed Margaret as she sat down, her eyes full of love for her man and for their young toddler lying asleep in the cradle next to her. 'I got a feeling that these are a people bent on pursing the gold to the exclusion of anything else. So vulgar.'

'Meaning?'

'What do they have except their tools meant for digging for gold? What do they have in their brains except an overwhelming desire for gold? What do they want from Australia except gold?' As she said, she fixed her eyes on the piano they had in their possession near a corner whose colour of amber struck off an eerie light in the evening glow.

'Nothing I suppose,' said Thomas. Then he found himself quoting Pascal in a remark that went, 'All men's miseries derive from not being able to sit in a room alone.'

'I meant more than that,' said Margaret. 'Out of these people, would you think there is any likelihood that there will be a Shakespeare, a Balzac, a Charles Dickens, a Lord Byron, a Molière, a Miguel De Cervantes, a Wolfgang Amadeus Mozart or any one of any note, historical, philosophical, literary or musical?'

'By no means,' said Thomas, seeing the reflection of the piano in her hazel eyes. 'The glory of that nation was all in the past, thousands of years ago. All you end up seeing now are these dregs of society, pursuers of gold and wearers of shadow.'

'Oh, you are a poet,' said Margaret, with much admiration for her bank manager husband.

Chapter 8

Ah Ling was the first to fall in Robe. He had caught malaria. His whole person was shivering like a last leaf in winter. Despite the 40 degrees Celsius, 104 in the old measure, he felt as if he'd fallen inside an ice cellar. While everyone else was wearing their lightest clothes and still could not help sweating, he kept adding all the warm clothes with which he wrapped himself up till he was buried inside a mountain of clothes, feeling still chilled. Then, he began stripping himself until he was lying in shorts, his forehead scorchingly hot. I got worried watching him swinging between these two extremes and called in a nurse, by the name of Mrs Brewe. Her blonde hair and blue eyes impressed me deeply when she came in perhaps because I had not seen a woman in a long time, least of all a woman with fair skin. What followed was even more impressive because she handled her patient with patience and much dexterity, administering medications to him, with spoon and hot water which she blew lukewarm. I sat watching, fascinated. She was in white, in a clean summery dress that seemed to send forth wisps of fragrance. She wore white socks and black shoes, with what seemed the straps in the shape of an 'X' on the backs of her feet. I loved the look of it so much I found myself getting warm and had to look away for a minute, to reduce the intensity of the heat within me.

That night, Ah Ling breathed his last. We lay him on the ground, fully clothed, and sat in a circle around him. We took turns fanning the mosquitoes off him, with a fan made of broadleaves from the roadside trees. They were kind enough to relieve me of the duty by getting me to tell stories, any stories. I started off with something off the top of my head. Then I gave it up because it's a joke that might not match the feelings the circumstances required. I had meant to say that in my old hometown there was a rich man with many concubines. He was busy keeping them big with babies till one day when he found that one of the least pretty ones was also big with a baby. Then he thought to himself: But I don't seem to have slept with her for ages. How come? Perhaps it was, after all, true that a spirit had somehow entered into her in a dream?

I said, 'Listen. If you listen hard enough, you can hear a heart ticking away somewhere. Put that fan down and listen. No, it's not a mosquito. It's something more than the flying mosquitoes. I think it's Ah Ling's soul going on its journey faster than any of us to the goldfields, in either ABC or BBC. You don't know what ABC is? It's Ararat, Ballarat and Castlemaine whereas BBC is Ballarat, Bendigo and Castlemaine. It all makes sense to me as these four places match the four places in Sze Yap in Canton, that is, Xinhui, Taishan, Kaiping and Enping. Somewhere Ah Ling's soul will find for him the first pot of gold and take it straight back to China in his home village, Sanhe Village, which, if you really want to know, literally sounds like Sandhurst, the other name for Bendigo, because it is pronounced in my lingo, yours, too, as 'Sanho'. See what I mean, everything already pre-existing and pre-determined? The soul, with its gold nugget, will make his family happy, keeping them alive for the rest of their lives, whereas his bones won't have to travel literally back to his village as many of us would prefer.'

Ah Toy's voice came, interrupting me. 'But he said in his dying words that he didn't want to trouble anyone for taking his bones back as he would prefer to stay here.'

'That's probably the best one could do,' said Ah Fong. 'Rather than keep his death a secret from his family, we'd better write a letter and get a ketou, guest headman, to take it back on the ship's return journey, making sure that the letter arrives in his father's hands, along with a donation of money from each and every one of us, one shilling per person. How's that sound?'

'What about his remains?' said Ah Mao.

'Well, I think we can share them amongst us instead of either getting them taken all the way back to Sanhe Village or chucked outright.'

'That's a very good idea,' said I. 'But what about his burial tomorrow? That costs money.'

'Oh, I've got that sorted out, too,' a prepared Ah Fong said. 'With the money he's got in his possession, we can buy a headstone as well as a burial place, and pay for someone to carve his name, before burying his remains. It doesn't have to be much because he hasn't got much left. But anything that is left, will be put together with our donation, to be sent home.'

It didn't take long for these things organized and done, at 14 O'Halloran Street, a number that struck me as fatal and fatalistic, one that we would never use where we came from. Some of us, when learning about the number, refused to go, complaining that the number was simply too unlucky and that might trick more deaths. Ah Fong and I decided to go. Ah Toy and Ah Mao followed, after a momentary hesitation. With the help of a few locals, all from the church, we carried Ah Ling's body to the cemetery. It was not till it was lowered into the grave, the earth was shovelled in and the stone was erected that Father Ling said, 'But is he Irish?'

None of us could make head or tail of what he meant by that. But all had taken note of the fact that they shared the same surname: Ah Ling and Father Ling, without understanding where the connection arose and ended. Nor did they understand anything the priest said at the service. But as soon as the service ended, they set off firecrackers they had brought along with them, raising a hell of noise, to my embarrassment, because, for the first time, I realised how vulgar that practice of ours was. To me, the cemetery was like a garden where each grave looked like a luxurious mansion in miniature. And there was nothing death-like in the place. One almost felt that one had found one's happiness after one was buried. At heart, I said to myself, when I die, this is the sort of place I shall return to, the best if the place faces the sea, the kind like the Guichen Bay.

*

Insertion of Baohui's Writing Journal or what he refers to as 'Thought Bursts':

10.15am, 27/1: The hardest thing is to pin things down. How do you retrace the footsteps of someone who was alive more than 160 years ago? How do you pin them down to a particular spot in historical space and time? If it is a great personage, the traces might have been kept in writing. But if it is an ordinary being, as unknown as a bird, a lizard, or a tree leaf, without even a name, how can you do that?

But if you write historical stories in a way that historians find can't match the historical facts and say they can't be bothered with it, does that stop you from imagining and fictionalizing?

10.31.19am: Diaries. People kept diaries probably from when they first had the impulse to write. If they scratched on the sand with a branch, that was their first attempt to make a diary entry, even if they erased it afterwards. Even a bird makes diary entries when it flies across the skies, leaving that twitter and that transient shadow in its path. I'm not making poetry here. I'm just stating a fact because I'm thinking of my characters, Ah Sin in particular, as beings capable of doing such acts, if not feats.

10.42.37am: Technology is one way to measure authenticity. I want Ah Sin to keep a diary. But it is obvious he can't do it because in his time his people couldn't possibly write anything unless they used brushes and ground ink as well as large-sized rice papers. These were heavy to carry in large quantities. Still, wasn't it possible that he could have used a quill pen instead? China wasn't that isolated from the rest of the world at his time because the Second Opium War was raging across the country and even as early as the late 1830s, there were missionaries in Guangzhou, such as an Edwin Stevens. Well, even if nothing was available to him at the time, or he had forgotten to bring one with him in his hurry to aboard the boat bound for Hong Kong, he could have bought a quill and some stationery at Robe and he could have made his, or one of his entries after landing. It's all possible. History, if anything, is possibilities, and historians, limits.

12.10.16pm: I think I ought to attempt one entry, at least, for Ah Sin, with a quill pen and paper bought at Robe:

20/1/1857: Beautiful country. Lovely people. Except when it comes to money. We haggle. They not budge. We haggle hard. They unbudge hard. The weather so hot we have to leave a few things behind, taking only the essential, picks and shovels and bamboo baskets and bamboo shoulder-poles as well as bowls and chopsticks, chucking out a few woks and kitchen utensils as that reduced the weight and we could share the stuff for cooking.

It's getting more urgent I learn the gweilo language. Otherwise, I not understanding a thing. So awful.

I won't tell Stacey about my thought bursts. I got a feeling that she may not be hospitable to them.

3.57.34pm: You cannot fix history, spot to spot, point to point, dot to dot. It's all slippage, slippery. It's all breaths breathed. You want to catch a fingerful of the breathed breath?

Oh, yes, I'm driving and thinking, a thought caught as it burst out of my mind.

*

High summer. Hot. You could almost see the heat roll wave after wave in thin bluish veils across the fields of harvested wheat. The colour of the fields was all yellow, on either side of the road, lined with gum trees. In one glance, one could see that the heat was so intense that these trees had all shed their clothing, standing in the nude, some completely, others in patches, their trunks a motley colour of grey and brown, still others so black because burnt that they accentuated the whiteness of the naked trunks. The eye could take everything in all at once but couldn't take them apart, couldn't distinguish between them, found it hard to absorb so many things so strange with so many details so different from anything I and my fellow travellers had ever seen or lived with. Ah Fong surveyed the landscape, put the straw hat on his head, and said nothing. Then, his chin lifted up, he nodded in the direction of the goldfields, and beckoned all of us to follow, one by one, in a single file, each one spaced from the other by the length of a shoulder-pole. In fact, he was indicating the bullocky that was walking beside his bullocks ahead of us, a man by the name of Don, as bulky and heavy as one of his bullocks. Since Ah Fong was our unofficial team leader, we all did as he told.

As we walked, we uttered sounds in unison with the noise our bamboo baskets made on either end of the shoulder-poles. The weight would thus be greatly eased. If there was a god watching in the sky, he would see us not walking, but jogging, as if hurrying towards our destination, in a line that snaked, always ahead, kilometres apart from the other lines, formed of separate teams. He would hear the chanting we invariably made under the weight, so uniform and unique, that the bearded bullocky would sometimes turn his head back to look at us and shake his head as he spat out a fuck word before he turned back towards the road lying ahead of him, whipping his whip over the bullocks with a crisp crack. But the god couldn't see or hear what was going through my head. Perhaps I myself wasn't even sure what it was that was occupying my thoughts. All I knew was that I should congratulate myself for having come to a country of infinite possibilities where even the sun seemed kinder in its heat. This procession of shoulder-poles and bamboo baskets on human feet might have resembled one of crawling ants to the god in the sky but each and every ant was full of an energy never seen before.

Already, I began composing a letter in my head, to be sent by telepathy, or xinling ganying, to my family, as the words rolled flashing across my mindscape:

Dear Mum and Dad,
Thank God I have finally arrived after spending weeks on the sea. It is so hot here because we are at the other end of the world and it is summer.

We stayed in a tiny port town called Robe for a couple of days and have now got on our way to the goldfields. Most of us agreed we'd go to the nearest town called Ararat because it's less than 700 *li.*

Once we get there, I shall do my hardest to get as much gold as possible so I can pay off the debt, get married and help you two, together with my two brothers, live a better life.

As far as I can see, this is a good country. People seem kind. If you have money, you can do anything.

In my dream last night, I saw Dad ploughing the rice paddy, filled with water, with a grey water buffalo, his whip raised in the sky. But the buffalo refuses to move ahead perhaps because tired. I wish I could be home and give Dad a hand. My dream about Mum was a few nights ago when I heard her with our neighbour how to arrange marriage for me by finding a suitable girl in the village. But don't worry, Mum. I'm sure I'll find someone here.

I'll keep you posted.

Before I had time to sign a mental signature to this letter a shout woke me from my reverie. 'What is that?' The shout acted like a brake on the trotting procession, stopping it in the middle of its forward movement. The shouter was Ah Toy, who had spotted a group of kangaroos in the foreground, watching, and had so abruptly stopped dead in his tracks that his shoulder-pole had thrust almost right in the face of Ah Mao, who was trotting behind him. But for his quick tilting of his head, Ah Mao would have got a manmian kaihua, a full blossoming blow in his face. He cursed and cursed. But even as he kept cursing, he couldn't take his eyes off what had been pointed out to him and the rest of the shoulder-polers: animals, of a kind never seen, were running away, hopping and stopping, as they turned their little heads around to watch.

'It's not the rabbits,' said Ah Fong as he took the opportunity to get the team to rest. 'It's more like rats with bags. I think The Classic of Mountains and Seas, existing in the 4th BC, has made references to it, as something twin-headed. See.'

They followed his pointing finger and, sure enough, saw one of the kangaroos with two heads, one bigger than the other, which obviously was a baby roo, moving beneath its mother's head.

All the while, I kept mum. But I was observing. I could see how one of them stood, its front paws drawn to its chest, its head quite proud in its rotation, not fearful at all. The colour of this one, as of the other three, was dark grey, quite unlike the yellow-brown of the harvested wheatfield. All their eyes, even at a distance, seemed a deep dark, and had a penetrating power that reached the heart. I couldn't think of anything that could match the intensity of this experience, which simply struck me speechless.

And what I saw next was even more astonishing as a human shape, completely naked and black, as black as burnt, emerged out of nowhere, with a long spear, who hurtled the spear onto the bag rat and hit him hard on the head, with blood spilled out in an instant.

When I looked again, the shape disappeared, along with the roo. I wondered if this was a day dream. Because no one said anything about what I had seen, I didn't mention it but I was wondering if the roo would be cooked and if the meat was good.

Chapter 9

In the spirit of reconciliation I acknowledge the Traditional Custodians of country throughout Australia and their connections to land, sea and community. We pay our respect to their elders past and present and extend that respect to all Aboriginal and Torres Strait Islander peoples today. I also pay respect to multicultural Australia for giving me the opportunity to study and live in the country.

[A letter from Baohui to Stacey deleted as part of the editorial process.]

*

Ah Sin's story continued while others were taking a rest by the roadside:

Our hero, whose name is Wen Ruoxu and I'll simply call him Ah Wen now, spends time wandering alone on a deserted island on his way home where their ship stops by. To his delight, he finds an empty turtle shell the size of a huge bed. Strangely moved, he decides to bring it home. His fellow passengers are surprised and wonder aloud why he picks up such a useless thing. He says he likes useless things as long as they are rare, so they arrive back in the port they have left, staying in a hotel managed by a blue-eyed and curly-haired Persian merchant, who treats all of them as distinguished guests except Ah Wen until he realizes he's got something rare. When Ah Wen, at the merchant's request, shows the shell, the Persian is so amazed that he apologises to Ah Wen and sits him at the top of the table, inviting everyone back for another dinner when he proposes to buy the whole shell, asking Ah Wen to give him a price. Ah Wen is lost for words as he has hardly expected anyone to find such a thing useful and all his friends have been laughing at him. As he is unsure, not knowing how much the right price ought to be, not wanting to offend by asking for too much or to be held to ridicule asking for too little, Ah Da, the managing agent for the ship, gestures with five fingers between his legs. Prompted by that, Ah Wen says, 'Five thousand pieces of silver.'

The merchant bursts out laughing, saying as he shakes his head, 'You must be joking, you must be joking! That's absolutely too little for such a rare treasure.'

It's not till Ah Wen gives a figure of '50,000' silver pieces, after briefly discussing it with Ah Da, that Mabuha the Persian merchant very reluctantly agrees, grudging that it is a case of pearls cast before swine, then revealing that each of the 24 ribs in the shell contains a pearl, known literally as the Night-light Pearls or Luminous Beads, each worth 50,000 silver pieces alone!

Because the silver pieces are so heavy in ten barrels of forty thousand pieces, with the rest given away as gifts to the crew and the fellow traveling business partners, Ah Wen decides to stay in the seaport, get married and live a happy life ever after.

'Not very interesting,' said Ah Toy. 'But what's the moral of the story?'

'You need at least thank Ah Sin for his time and effort,' said Ah Fong.

'But we don't need that, do we?' said Ah Toy, winking at Ah Sin.

'No, we don't; we are good friends,' said Ah Sin. 'In fact, I don't like saying "thank you" all the time. It sounds like a lot of bullship.'

'Not "bullship", but bullshit,' said Ah Toy.

'Doesn't matter,' said Ah Sin. 'Want to hear the moral?'

Amidst a clamorous chorus of 'yes', Ah Sin said, 'There's no moral, really. But at the end of the transaction when his friends urge him to ask more from the Persian merchant, Ah Wen dismisses the idea as unacceptable, saying that one ought to be content with what one has, instead of asking for more because one's greed is an animal whose desire can never be satisfied.'

*

[646 words removed from this section, irrelevant—SA]

Chapter 10

Things went from bad to worse. Because of the hard walk, nearly everyone got blisters on their feet. And their shoulders were bruised from the constant movement of the poles rotating from one side to the other, with the baskets at either end seeming to grow heavier at the end of the day. Ah Toy and I fared better. Ah Toy did not have anything in the first place. He literally was an unburdened man, as free as a bird, although his face was as bitter as a bitter melon, never smiling, speaking hardly ever a word. I treated him as a younger brother, lending him my clothing, sharing everything between us. Because they liked the stories I told and knew that I had no money on me, they *dashang*, awarded, me in fits and starts, a few pence here and there, and, very occasionally, a shilling. As Ah Toy was younger and stronger than me, he insisted on carrying my stuff much of the way so I could make space in my head for the stories my people wanted to hear, during breaks or at night. An idea came to me while we were walking in that serpentine single file that there was something we could do for those that followed in days to come. After a discussion with them, it was agreed that I should be the one to carve the characters on the barks of the trees as directions to the new arrivals on their way to the goldfields. This was from an observation I had made when going past tree after gum tree. Some tree barks, to me, seemed to bear character-like cracks or scratches, resembling 十 (10) or 天 (sky) or 二 (2) , or a number of combinations. It made me wonder if I could write characters on the smooth, white bark. Ah Mao expressed concern that this might reduce our chance of finding gold or have the potential of causing us to have a smaller share of the gold found. Some agreed. But most others rejected this concern as selfish; the ancient idiom, *jianli wangyi*, forgetting moral justice at the mere sight of money, was not something to follow. As soon as someone mentioned that idiom, it gave me occasion to tell them a related story and a quick one at that.

I said, in a loud voice, as they were jogging past me, 'There is a rich guy who falls overboard in the Yanshui River and gets stranded on a mattress of floating grass. When he spots a fisherman rowing his boat to come to his rescue, he promises he'll give him 100 taels of gold if he rows him ashore, which the fisherman duly does. Instead, he gives him only 10. When the fisherman asks why he doesn't keep his promise, the rich man loses his temper and says that he ought to be content with what he's got as he can't even earn one percent of the amount a day. Many years after, in Lüliang Lake, the rich man has another accident that causes his boat to sink. It so happens that the same fisherman is nearby. Asked why he is not saving him, the fisherman informs of the broken promise about the 100 taels of gold. He rows ashore and watches the man drown from a distance.'

*

'In my research', Baohui noted, to himself, 'I have come across references to shamanism and how shamans in China, particularly the north-eastern part of it, relied on their own invented road signs carved on the tree bark. They used this "←" to mean go west, this →to "go east", this "↑" to go south and this "↓" to go north. And this " ⌐" meant to turn right and this, "⌐ ", to turn left. If they used this, "x", it meant the road ahead as impassable. (See Guo, p. 432) But there's a lot more in the book I am reading except that the signs, such as those indicating mountains, grasslands and rivers, are not available in the "Advanced Symbol" in my apple computer. I wonder if I should ring up AppleCare to seek technical support. But they may refer me to Microsoft Word after waiting for a long time on the phone. Eventually, I gave the idea up because while shamanism was widely practised by the Manchus it was not part and parcel of the Han culture among the Cantonese people, some of whom have found their way into this book.

*

'Have you noticed something?' said Ah Sin.

'No, not really. What?' said Ah Toy.

'We haven't had vegetables for a long time now.'

'Oh, yes, bok choy, wombok, gai choy, choy sum, en choy, chi qua, sin qua. I love them all. But where are they?' said Ah Toy.

'Not even the qua after my name,' said Ah Sin.

'Qua after your name?' Ah Mao chipped in. 'What's that?'

'Sin qua,' said Ah Sin, laughing.

'Then we must find a way to grow them,' said Ah Mao.

Ah Sin looked up in surprise at Ah Mao's face, a board of marks with two beaded eyes. But he knew him to be a kind-hearted man as he had helped Ah Sin in the water after he fell overboard and bitterly cried at Ah Ling's funeral in Robe. 'So, what is it that you are thinking of doing?' said Ah Sin.

'Oh,' their eyes met. But Ah Mao turned away in shame,

saying, 'I'm afraid I can't go on with you guys to the goldfields. For one thing, I'm not particularly interested in gold. I like the place better than gold. And I like doing stuff that I like, for example, growing vegetables. From the first day of our arrival, I have noticed how miserable a life the gweilo live, eating only BBBB and PPPP.'

'BBBB?'

'Oh, yes, bread, bacon, beef, beer.'

'And PPPP?'

'Plum pudding, potato, pumpkin,' sighed Ah Mao, saying, 'such boring and unhealthy food except perhaps the pumpkin, something we wouldn't even touch back at home because we had such a large variety to choose from.'

'I'm sorry I should never have brought this up or else you may not have been lured into thinking about staying behind doing something no one else wants to do,' said Ah Sin.

Ah Mao didn't say anything. He threw a meaningful look at Ah Sin and went back to dwelling on his plan, long harboured in his heart and ignited by today's talk. Something gentle reminded him that this place called Penola might be the right one for him to carry out his plan now.

*

Dear Stacey,

Yesterday I wrote something in the traditional way, then discarded it. I wanted to assume the position of Ah Sin, continuing the storyline in the first-person narrative. After less than 100 words, I found it impossible to sustain it. I could, though, keep it going by telling one lie after another, as I did below,

I lived before many of you, all of you, were born; you had to wait one hundred or so years before that happened. I was born in Xiaoma Village at the foot of the Caofeng Hill in Chixi. In my early teens, Dad died in one of the riots between the locals and the Hakkas. Not long after, Mum died of a broken heart. I was adopted by my uncle Ah Hua, a rich Hakka merchant who managed to survive the decade-long riots unscathed.

But I found it boring. I need to tell his story in a variety of ways. For example, I need to stand aside and apart from him, watching him as he lives the life I have imagined for him. And I need to get intimate with him, too, by addressing him as 'you'. I'll come to that. But the last thing I want to do is tell the reader who this 'I' is, where 'I' comes from, and whose son or grandson 'I' is. One only does that in a court if one is someone charged with a crime. In daily human interaction, people are moving castles of secrets to which little access is granted. Before I came to do my PhD in creative writing, I had studied in a Wuhan-based university, where I shared accommodation with two other schoolmates. We knew who came from where, got what academic qualifications, had or hadn't got a girlfriend. The tentacles of our knowledge never extended themselves into each other's families or family lives. A human being, at best, is an opaque object that requires careful study by himself if not by anyone else. And a writer these days is but a putter-together of information surrounding a being in an attempt to produce something saleable in accordance with all the literary requirements, which, in my opinion, is a mere producer with a mind full of market and a *shenti* without soul, 'shenti' being body. I know I have no right to criticise, being a PhD student. And I know, too, that only when you can make great sales with your book can you be regarded as a great writer. But I doubt that. These people that I write about were the lowest of the low. They were almost invariably losers in the truest sense of the word. You can call them survivors if you want to make it sound better. But that's as far as you can go. They came, they went, they disappeared, almost without a trace, with a few names here and there that evoke no connections to their individual pasts, that tell nothing about themselves, that do not even have a surname to date back to. Isn't a writer someone whose duty it is to mentally, spiritually, heartfeltly and imaginatively live their lives in an empathic and sympathetic way? I don't know. I have no idea. Perhaps I can never be a writer, let alone a good writer.

Educate me if you like.

Baohui

In the spirit of reconciliation I acknowledge the Traditional Custodians of country throughout Australia and their connections to land, sea and community. We pay our respect to their elders past and present and extend that respect to all Aboriginal and Torres Strait Islander peoples today. I also pay respect to multicultural Australia for giving me the opportunity to study and live in the country.

P.S.

Just an idea. This will probably be my way of writing an exegesis, not as something side by side with the main body of my 'work', like a growth, a tumour, a critical tumour, but as an organic part of the body, an organ of it, grown within, naturally and spontaneously. But, of course, if you don't agree, I can always gouge them, bits and pieces here and there, like an after-thought, a pre-thought, and put them together in what is officially and acceptably known as an 'exegesis'.

And I must remind myself to delete the bits about the market as it doesn't seem to sound right in an age where market is the new god that decides everything.

*

Is there anything that is not possible? No, said I to myself when I thought of what to do in celebration of the coming new Spring Festival, to usher in the Year of the Snake. Was it a problem if we were summer, not winter? No, I said. Was it a problem no one here observed the festive occasion? No, I said. Was it a problem if our dates didn't match theirs? No, I said. Our emperor's birthday is our national day. So what's your idea?

I told them of my idea, 'Let's handmake a dragon with branches found in the bush. Let's wrap the branches up with our rags. If they are not golden, it's not a problem as we can go gathering yellow flowers in the bush and cover the rags-based dragon with them. If there are no cymbals and gongs, we can use substitutes such as iron wash basins, bronze teapots, iron woks, and hit them with silver chopsticks, bamboo chopsticks, silver spoons, iron fire tongs and hard wooden sticks made of the local tree branches, as hard as we can to make celebratory noise. The worst problem is that we don't have any firecrackers. The ones some of us got have got dampened and discarded. Only one string of firecrackers is left. But we are not sure if they can be set off. We'll have Ah Mao see to it that they do. As for the food, we've got plenty except the greens. As far as everyone can see, the locals don't grow them, don't seem to know how to. Yes, the pumpkins can do. We do have the fish, the salty fish. We can also go looking for fresh ones in the creeks. Why not? Let's buy a whole sheep and roast the lot. Let's do that.'

On 26 January, the first day of Spring Festival, and of the Year of the Snake, we celebrated the occasion, not with Ah Mao's string of fire-crackers because they didn't work even when dried, but with the fire-works we bought in a local shop. No sooner had we got started, with the makeshift lion, lifted high above the heads, dancing on the main street of Penola than kids and dogs came over to watch. And, of course, there were adults, men and women who found the spectacle strange and rare, quite an eye-opener to something extraterritorial. One elderly man said, 'I've never seen a dragon like that. It looks more like a snake, a black snake.' A woman next to him said, 'Oh, no. I think it's artistic, covered in the little yellow stars or button flowers. I think they are quite nice.' While kids were weaving through the procession, I stopped them by giving them candies brought from Canton. Because of the noise our men raised by beating their woks, their washing basins, even their broad shovels hitting against their hoes, many of the onlookers, particularly the female ones, covered their ears. Ah Toy and Ah Mao, the two mighty ones, were the main props, one holding the head and the other, the tail. The rest of the people were holding up one part of the dragon body with handles of their hoes. As they came to the centre of the road, the traffic was held up, temporarily, as the black dragon became alive in their hands. Prompted and urged by the beating of the iron pieces, the dragon shot up in waves of agony and pleasure, drifting, skiing, jumping, leaping, and even lying low, at one stage, when everyone lay themselves prostrate on the ground, with the dragon lying on top of them as if to rest up. But only for a brief moment before the dragon took flight and shot into the air, with a whoop of the air pulled behind it, drawing everyone's attention but Constable Harris's.

'Hey, I say, this must stop!' said Constable Harris, yelling into the crowd, holding up his hand with a baton in it. Seeing that no one listened, he began hacking his way through the crowd till he stood right in front of Ah Toy, blocking his way.

I quickly went over and stood next to the constable in case anything happened.

'Are you an interpreter?' said the constable to me.

I didn't understand. But I nodded my head.

'Tell him and the others to move off the road,' said he, pointing to the bullocks beyond the crowd.

I got the hint and said to a bewildered Ah Toy in our own language, 'Let's end this show because the bullocks want to come down the road.'

Ah Toy told the same to the rest of them. Immediately after, they moved out of the way, not without muttering with expletives known only to themselves while I stood there, communicating with Constable Harris as if we understood each other perfectly.

When the stopped traffic got started again, with bullockies whipping their bullocks drawing carts carrying huge tree trunks down the road, the constable heaved a sigh of relief and said to me, 'What's your name?'

I told him.

'Where did you come from? Where are you guys going? What do you want to do here in this place?' a string of questions fell off his lips.

I looked into his blue eyes, as blue as the January sky, and shook my head. Then I took him to a spot, picked up a short branch, the length of a chopstick, and wrote down a few capitalized letters in sand: R, A, B, C, with an arrow that inter-connected them.

The constable looked up at me and smiled. Our smiles locked in that instant in which meaning sank in without a word said.

*

Dear Baohui,

Sorry I'm on holiday but have managed to read everything you've written so far. I have only one word for you: Stop!

I am concerned that after nearly 20,000 words the story is still not there. You must decide whether you want to shed the lot and start the story afresh or plunge into it straight away. I know you know the standing joke about the publisher's rule that they only read the first 50 pages to decide whether they want to read the rest or reject the manuscript. In a way, this resembles the early gold-diggers who come looking for surface gold nuggets, not the ones lying deeper than one can see in a glance. Although we academics don't believe that kind of bullshit, as we are convinced that true story may well begin after page 50, the same way tons of gold may lie at least 50 meters underground, there must be a cut-off line where we say to ourselves: But where is the story? And what is the story anyway?

If you want to write a 'masterpiece' as you said you would, in that MA piece you showed me as part of your creative writing portfolio when you were an MA student in Shanghai, find a few masterpieces to read and emulate, you might at least successfully complete this PhD instead of straying into something that doesn't resemble anything, least of all a masterpiece.

Perhaps we should meet and discuss this when I come back from holiday in two weeks' time?

Ciao,
Stacey

Part II

Chapter 1

I tell ya I'm no good prospecting, fossicking for gold. I'm better than that. I'm cut out for better things than mere gold. My arm is easily tired out when I pan the pan. And my eyes become weary staring into the sands for that tiny little golden thing that never turns up. A whole day may pass without me finding anything outstanding, not even instanding. But this is what I like, telling you stories. If you like what you have heard, please drop me a coin or two in this basin and I shall be pleased and tell you more interesting stuff.

Let me start with this one about Confucius and his disciples. Meng Wubo asks Confucius whether he knows if Zi Lu, his disciple, is a benevolent person. Confucius says that he knows Zi Lu can work and manage the financial affairs of a big country of thousands of chariots but he doesn't know if he's a benevolent person.

Then the question moves on about his next disciple Ran Qiu along the same line. Confucius's answer is that this one may have the ability to manage a small town of one thousand households but he still doesn't know if he's a benevolent person.

Now, I can see you guys are getting bored. Some of you are even leaving. I won't ask you back because you are going to miss out on the good stuff I'm coming to. How about a Mongolian girl, after her marriage to the king, falls in love with the king's brother?

This is the story I read and handpicked from The Annals of the Kingdoms in the East Zhou Dynasty, more than 2500 years ago although, I must say, human nature remains the same as nothing fundamental has ever changed. Agreed? I mean: A greed?

Basically, her name is Shu Wei. Very beautiful, an excellent horse-rider, and good at archery. She's married to King of Zhou but is not satisfied because he is over 50 and she is only slightly over 20. What is that like? Let me put it this way. The king is a fire, on the point of burning out, and the queen is another fire, in the middle of burning, brisk and bright. How's that for a comparison?

Pretty soon, the queen has exhausted the king, like a rag wrung dry. Forgive the metaphor. But she wants to go out. She wants to have fun, riding her horse and hunting for animals with her arrows and bow. That's exactly what the king has wanted. He wants his peace and quiet. He doesn't want to die in bed, fucked to death. Sorry about that. So he lets Shu Wei go seeking her own pleasure. On a fine day, she goes out with her entourage and comes running down the hill to a vast plain. There, she meets Gan Gongdai, the king's step-brother, a very handsome man with supreme mastery of all the skills required of a great soldier. They took a look at each other and their hearts lock, never wanting to leave each other again. She praises him for being a great warrior and he humbles himself by praising her as a rare beauty with the courage of a man. They hit it off straight away and spend the night together in a room next to the king's chamber.

Of course there are more details than I can enumerate. To put it simply, Gongdai sets his sights on a court singing girl who doesn't let him sleep with her. This makes him furious. He pulls out his sword and chases after her, intending to kill her. She runs to the king and tells him everything. That's when the whole thing is exposed.

'What are you doing here?' a policeman turned up from nowhere and said to me, in a voice that wasn't impolite.

My audience dispersed at the sight of the policeman. Only one man didn't leave even though he was also Chinese. He put a shilling coin in the empty bowl in front of me with a clink and stood watching.

'No savvy,' said I.

The policeman grinned, showing a row of tiny teeth. And he looked to the man who had given me a shilling for help.

'This man has done a very good job,' said the Chinese man with a square face, without looking at me.

'What did he do?' said the policeman.

'He's a street storyteller. He's just told his gold-digger audience a story of a love affair between the queen and the king's brother in ancient China.'

'Tell him not to do that anymore because a large gathering is not allowed in public. Know what I mean?'

'Yes, Mr McCoy,' said Ah Liu, the local interpreter, as the image of the Eureka Stockade flashed across his mind.

Afterwards, when Mr McCoy the policeman left the scene, I thanked Ah Liu for his kindness and admired him for his command of English.

'You have a great ability to tell stories,' said Ah Liu. 'It would be good if you could tell them in English.'

'That's exactly what I wanted. How and where can I learn it then?' said I, as I lit his pipe for him before I went on to light my own.

'I learnt it in my village in Taishan from an American missionary and found it immensely useful as soon as I arrived here.'

Then we started talking about Taishan and how we missed the great food there when he said, 'Do you go to church?'

'No, not really,' said I.

'I think it's time you did,' said Ah Liu, explaining how one could learn English there on top of meeting different people and learning about the scriptures.

*

She was there, standing outside the church. I spotted her in a crowd. I spotted her eyes, such black eyes, so beautiful. It made me self-conscious, aware of my own attire. Out of habit, I reached out for my pigtail, to put it in place. Then I realised, with a sudden pit-a-pat, that it was no longer there. I had shed it in defiance of the Qing law, putting my own life at risk because of the law stipulating about keeping alive with pigtails or dying without them. I was now living in a free country where no one else except my compatriots still kept the custom. But I was the one to opt out. I discarded the tail, I wore suit and tie, I cultivated a moustache. And now, I went to church to learn English. I thought I had attracted the girl's attention. But she didn't raise her eyes. She stood out from the others not because she was loudly dressed up. On the contrary, she stood in a plain grey dress, the colour of the morning sky with the sun behind the clouds. But her eyes captured me, captivating me in their dreamlike qualities, causing me to temporarily forget Ah Liu, who stood next to me.

The sermon did not begin till all of us went inside the chapel. When it began, I couldn't make head or tail of it, so, instead, I focussed my attention on my surroundings. I saw the light suffusing the coloured windows. I saw the faces of people, most of them women, bathed in the colourful light as if enraptured. I could tell that none of my people were there except Ah Liu. And I could hear the booming voice of the priest as he stood at the rostrum, his face small and lit, reading from a huge book. I whispered for Ah Liu to explain. But he shook his head, motioning me to shut up. I then let my eyes roam, from face to face and head to head, to stop at the face already familiar enough to me, like an old friend's.

'Will you stop roaming around with eyes like those of a hungry wolf please?' I woke from my reverie with a jump. Who was that directed to? Was it me that this voice was speaking to? What wrong have I done? I had no time to reflect upon these when Father Gargan went down the aisle towards me, his face looking so serious I had a sudden urge to stand up and take to me feet. But I held my ground because Ah Liu held my hand, in such a tightening grip I almost let out a cry in pain.

The man stood in front of me and let flow a string of words in total solemnity. He said, 'Brethren, in the primitive Church there was a godly discipline, that, at the beginning of Lent, such persons as were notorious sinners were put to open penance and punished in this world, that their souls might be saved in the day of the Lord; and that others admonished by their example might be more afraid to offend.'

I suppressed a strong desire to burst out laughing and, in a very low voice, said to Ah Liu, 'What was that?'

He simply said, in Cantonese, 'You are a sinner. You need to repent.'

Afterwards, when the morning service was over, and we all went out, Father Gargan came to us and said to Ah Liu, 'Tell this gentleman to mind his manners and pay attention when the service is being conducted, and if possible at all, try to get more of your fellow countrymen to come here.'

Ah Liu explained that he had brought me here because I had wanted to learn English.

Father Gargan turned around and took a hard look at me. I turned away from his stare and glare and heard myself murmur in answer to his question about my name, 'Ah Sin.'

'Ah, sin, a sinner you are, ah!'

I looked up in surprise, looking for any sign of amusement on his face. But there was none. Then I heard a deep booming laughter rolling out of his lungs and saw his eyes beaming in a kindness that relaxed me.

'What is that?' he pointed to the wall and said.

'Wall?' said I.

'No. Stone,' said he.

'What is that?' said he as he pointed to the sky.

'Sky?'

'Yes and no. Heaven,' said he. 'And what is that?'

I followed his finger and couldn't work out what exactly he meant.

'Air,' said he. Then he added, 'when you are alive, you live with air. When you are dead, you live with a stone on your back. But you can never live in heaven whether alive or dead.'

I nodded my head when Ah Liu translated the message to me and I said through Ah Liu that Father Gargan sounded like a poet to me.

That did the trick. Father Gargan agreed to give me lessons in English.

*

Many things had happened in the intervening time since my arrival. I thought I had told about the writing on the tree bark and in the sky. But I had only told myself that, not even Ah Liu. He had arrived from Melbourne before the head tax was introduced. As the saying goes, he was one of the lucky bastards. But I admired him for his good command of English and his ability to make friends with Chinese and Europeans alike. Oh, yes, the writing on the tree bark. It was my idea and I shared it with Ah Fong, our headman, so he let me do the writing for the rest of our fellow countrymen to follow our track to the goldfields.

I started with carving the character of 金（gold）on the tree bark with the metal blade of the hoe. Then, without knowing why, I found myself carving characters like 钱（money）and 人（people）, even 诗（poetry）, accompanied with an arrow sign, pointing to A, meaning Ararat. Nearly every tree was decorated with my handwriting. At one stage, I even carved a full English word 'Ararat' that I had learnt from a local newspaper. But I changed my mind and put its translation next to it：阿拉辣, the last character 辣 means hot, not weather hot, but chilli hot. Then, I changed my mind again. On the next tree, I cut out a new translation, calling it 阿拉腊, the 腊 means salty as in salty fish or pork. I know my fellow countrymen didn't like hot food. But they loved salty stuff.

Travelling and carving, travelling and carving, for days on end, led to my forming a new habit of writing in the sky. The minute my head hit a large pillow of wild grass pulled from around me as I lay for a rest and looked straight into the skies above me, I saw my hoe carving characters right into the blue, forming lines of their own, like a letter,

> Dear Mum and Dad,
> It's your son Ah Sin, lying down on a road that goes to Ararat. This piece of sky I'm writing a letter to you is the bluest I have ever seen. Your son is doing great. He's become a writer now, writing with a hoe, giving directions to his followers, perhaps hundreds of them on their way to the goldfields. I haven't seen a shred of gold. But already I'm tired of it all. We all like gold but does gold like us? They have, nuggets of it, been sleeping there for perhaps millions of years. Waiting to be disturbed? To be used? To benefit the finders?
>
> I don't know. But your son wishes you a wonderful year of the snake.

These lines of characters passed quickly before my eyes and were obliterated by a drifting cloud. But I enjoyed the way they appeared as instantly as they disappeared.

Why am I indulging in memory instead of getting to the point? Not long after I took English lessons from Father Gargan, gratis, I did something that surprised even myself. We were exchanging daily greetings when I found myself forming a question in my head before uttering it, 'Father, I know why people are all called "teens", including myself. They do so because there are words that contain it, or is that right?'

'Like what?' There was no smile on Father Gargan's face. He was as serious as ever although one never knew when he'd burst out laughing.

'It's this,' said I, launching into something much longer than I was able to in the last few months. 'We talk about teenage as from 13 to 19 that is because there is twelve and twenty.'

'Yes?' Father's face began breaking into something that looked like a faint smile.

'And all the words between 12 and 20 end in "teen". See what I mean?'

Father Gargan didn't say a word. Instead, he took my head in his hand and began examining it, turning it around, like a globe. Then, for the first time, that faint smile broke into a raucous laughter.

Bewildered, I broke free and wondered aloud, 'Why? What's the matter with you?'

'In the beginning was the Word, and the Word was with God, and the Word was God,' quoted Father Gargan. 'If you know the word, you know the world.'

'But isn't that true of gold? It sounds like "world". Doesn't it work backwards? That is, if you know gold, you know god?'

'Yes, god in small letters, god of desire, god of vanity, god of fall.'

That led to a long discussion about the pros and cons of gold-digging and its consequences. Even though I wasn't able to give it a full description here I managed to offer my own 19-year-old opinion of what I thought in fairly broken English. I said that my arrival in this new country had nearly changed everything I had thought about life. I said that to me freedom was, first and foremost, more important than gold. I said that I wanted to live a free life. He cut me short in my ramblings and said, 'But there is freedom to and there is freedom from. And you can't have both at the same time. You don't want freedom from freedom, do you?'

That was something that got me thinking.

[A mini comment by SA: Check this out about the origin of 'teenage': https://boundlesstheatre.org.uk/we-are-boundless/the-origin-of-the-teenager/ and make a necessary correction please.]

*

I, Bao Hui, am sorry that I have to break the flow of the Ah Sin story to insert my own story. This involves my recent reading of a novel, written in Chinese and published in 1905 in China, telling the story of a number of Chinese students' lives in America, mainly that of Huang Sun from Hunan. Even though I am less than halfway through, I am impressed, particularly where a total discrimination on the part of his American classmates occurs when they not only jeer at him for wearing tatters, looking like a beggar and smelling like one, too, openly calling him so, but also boycott the classes by vacating the classroom, leaving him in the empty room alone and chased out by the lecturer. The overall feeling I got out of the book was that he is a friendless Chinese student in America. Even though I live in a different time and space as well as a different country, I can very much share that feeling of friendlessness with him here, too.

I have an idea. I'd like to recommend to Stacey that I translate part of the story into English so she knows what is going on in the background. Even if she is not interested, I can enlighten myself with the resentment, buried all along.

That novel, by the way, is titled, Bitter Students, by someone with a pseudonym, Qi You Zi, based on the phrase 'qiren youtian', a man from the Kingdom of Qi who worries that the skies might fall in.

And, reminded by Stacey in her last email letter, I found my own 'piece', titled, 'No: A Self-hater's Elegy', and provided a fragment of it as follows,

...I have no ambitions, big or small. I'm not interested in anything, least of all in politics, not even in sex, increasingly less in books. I believe because everything has been done before, written before, felt before, thought of before there is no need to create more. I believe to live is but to waste one's life living. If I am a twenty-year-old, think such thoughts and say such things, it doesn't mean I deserve less living than the rest of you. It doesn't really mean anything. I strayed into a writing class because I thought it would be fun and also because I didn't have any hope in myself. I'm just one of the billions of people the world over and I have no reason to believe that the world would be either better off or worse off without me. If you insist I have hope so other people don't get depressed because of me, I'll imagine myself hoping that one day I'll write a masterpisssorry, I meant masterpiece before I kill myself, the great quality of a masterpiece only to be determined and declared after its author's death, I forgot who said that but I have no doubt about it.

I chuckled and said, to myself: You self-hater! I'd like to see you last but I can't promise how long that will be.

*

Monday was the day when the local court was open for hearings. I met Ah Liu outside the courthouse, a grey stone affair that looked solemn and austere. He had asked me in to have a look around to see if there was anything I could learn from while there. Immediately, I noticed that people turned away from me in disgust as if I was some sort of plague. By comparison, people in the church seemed kinder. This was Monday but I saw people in their Sunday best, men in suits and ties, women in modest dresses, nothing flowery. They were all whites. Why were they there? Seeing my puzzled face, Ah Liu whispered in my ear, 'They fight all the time. These people can't get along well with each other for long. That's why.' Up to that very moment, I had thought that it's my people that were best known for their indulgence in fighting, year in, year out, with fires of war raging across the country that were never put out for one moment. But for my opting out, I might have died a thousand times in my celestial empire. 'But these people look so refined. How come they—,' I didn't have time to finish my sentence when a 'shush' from Ah Liu cut me short. I went silent, aware of a few glaring glances thrown my way, and followed him into the court.

Because I was totally ignored, that gave me real peace and quiet and helped me get used to the sombre and serious atmosphere. Everyone was seated on the wooden benches. They were talking but one couldn't hear what they were talking about because they acted as if they were whispering among themselves. I was about to say something to Ah Liu when he motioned for me to keep silent. Then he excused himself in a very low voice, rose and went to sit in the front row, next to a Chinese man in white. I was left alone, staring ahead of me across an empty bar table at the desk on the stage and at the back of the Chinese man with a pigtail, wondering who he was.

The quiet containing whispering voices didn't last long before it was broken by the announcement of a man, wearing a black calf-length gown, who came into the court from a side door and said in a commanding voice, 'Silence. All rise please. The court is now in session, the Honourable Magistrate Graham now presiding.'

All stood up, without exception, with a noise that sounded like something scraping a vast cloth. I, too, stood up, even though I didn't understand the second part of the sentence.

Shortly after, a man came in, wearing a wig, with curls, and a black gown, blacker than the bench clerk, it seemed, and sat down behind the desk. Without looking at anyone, he said, 'Please be seated.'

Then they immediately plunged into work, with the plaintiff reading out the charges and calling a witness to give evidence. I found all this exceedingly boring. Already, someone by my side had fallen asleep. I thought of leaving. But I didn't dare as I didn't know if I might offend by so doing nor did I know what to do when rising to leave. I vaguely remembered people seemed to be bowing before they opened the door but I wasn't sure.

'Ah Mao, please stand up!' I gave a start when I heard the name. 'It is him,' I said to myself and repeated it at heart. A series of possibilities flashed across my mind: He had killed someone; he had raped someone; he had committed robbery; he had smoked too much smuggled opium without paying tax.

I was left in shock.

But it was nothing like that. He went to stand inside the witness box and Ah Liu stood next to him. Then the bench clerk administered oath to him, asking him what he'd like to choose, a bible or an oath, till he said, through Ah Liu, 'I need a cock.' His voice was so loud the audience was shocked and when what he said sank in they burst out laughing, mixed with giggling from the female audience members till the serious-looking magistrate wiped the merriment off their collective faces with a swipe of his hand.

A cock was brought in, cackling and crowing, onto a chopping block, placed on one edge of the bar table, to the amazement of all watching. 'Such blasphemy and savagery,' I heard someone muttering in a subdued voice. What happened next was sheer savagery, to the whites, though not to me, a common sight in my village, as the bench clerk dexterously beheaded the cock before he put its neck in a ready bowl, letting the blood pour out, thus completing the ritual of oath-taking.

I understood the whole thing from what Ah Mao said in answer to the questions, that he had stolen a dog which he said was a wild one roaming the diggings, and had skinned it and cooked it, turning it into a wok of soup, that he had done this alone, without involving anyone else and that even if there were witnesses who had seen him eating the soup they wouldn't be able to come as they were busy digging for gold, and that he loved eating dogs as they were nutritious food in his home village and were particularly good against the cold.

Without much ado, a disgusted magistrate ruled against him with an order that he pay £1.

Afterwards, when it was over, and Ah Liu and I walked out of the courthouse, I said to him, 'I know this guy.'

'Why didn't you tell me?' said Ah Liu.

'I can't have been of any use because we've lost contact for a very long time.'

'He's a dangerous person,' said Ah Liu, explaining how Ah Mao was getting more and more rebellious, vowing to take revenge, though he did not know against whom.

I wondered why and thought of my own joyful experience living in this new country, of the shadow of a tree lengthened in the morning in the sun and lengthened in the evening in the opposite direction in the evening, which set me wondering about my own shadow after my death. Would there be such a shadow left? Then who would see it? When I told him of what I had thought, he simply said, 'You think too much.'

'It's just a wandering thought,' said I. 'but I'll talk to him when I get a minute.'

*

I found Ah Mao behind his tent shared with the other diggers. While they were out digging for gold in the creek nearby, he did nothing, sitting idle and smoking his opium. I offered him mine. He shook his head and pointed at the pipe with his right index-finger.

'What happened?' said I.

'Nothing,' he said, not looking at me.

'I saw it all in the court,' said I, lighting his pipe up when it stopped fuming.

'Bah!' he turned his bloodshot eyes towards me. 'I won't pay. Yao-qian meiyou, yaoming yitiao.'

I knew what he meant. He was saying that if they wanted money he had none but if they wanted his life, they could have it for the taking.

I said, 'But you know the law here is tough. You can't fight it.'

'I won't fight it. Why would I fight it?' he puffed out a large cloud of smoke and spat.

'Then what do you want to do?' said I, thinking of all the possibilities for him.

'I'll run away,' he lowered his voice as he turned around to see if there was anyone eavesdropping on him.

'Don't worry,' I said. 'Even if you shout out loud, no one understands you.'

'I don't like the place,' said he. 'It's so bloody hard to find gold. When you find something good and think of doing a clean job getting the lot they jump the claim, those man-eating gweilo! They chased you off your diggings and they occupy them as their own. You were left working over the surface tailings, like rats burrowing into the dumped soil by the gweilo. I hate the place. I hate them.'

My impulse to say something in defence of the gweilo was reduced to silence. Then, I thought of something and said, 'Did you know what Confucius said about Ning Wuzi, a minister in the State of Wei in the Spring and Autumn Period, some 2500 years ago?'

He kept silent. But his ears were pricked.

'He praised Ning as someone who was both intelligent and stupid, intelligent under a wise king and becoming woodenly stupid when the ruler turned nasty. According to Confucius, it's easy to be an intelligent minister offering good advice to the king but hard to sham stupidity by not participating in the proper management of affairs of state because most people tend to show off their abilities for all sorts of reasons.'

'What?' he burst out in anger. 'You want me to be a fool?'

'That's not what I mean,' said I, defending myself. 'I was just reminded of this story regarding Confucius, so I thought of sharing it with you.'

'I want none of that,' said Ah Mao. 'I actually wish that I had stayed in Penola like Ah Ting. I heard that he's doing very well, managing a market garden, and is getting married to a white girl.' He couldn't help tittering as he said that.

'That sounds wonderful,' said I, recalling a white guy I had met, by the name of Eugène von Guérard. I told Ah Mao that, explaining that this was an artist, a failure in the gold-diggings, so much so that he left the place to pursue his passion for painting. 'The world is so big one can do anything as long as one likes doing it.'

'I might as well go roaming the country like a bushranger,' said Ah Mao.

'You mean like a bandit?' I said, staring at his pockmarked face, as a fleeting thought came to me: He might be one already.

'Why not, I mean? Better than working here bent double day in and day out. And when you strike something rich, you are riddled with fear, of being either pilfered by your own comrades or robbed by the white guys. I've lost my nugget, you know, my first one found ever.'

Before I uttered my surprise, he stopped me, holding up an open palm. Then he put down his pipe and went, with a bent back, towards a hole in the slope beneath a cluster of wild grass. I followed him closely. He 'shooed' me away. I stopped in my tracks and stood watching from a distance.

I saw how he picked up a broken branch, poking it through something while covering his nose and, with a cry of joy, he chucked the branch as he picked up something, with a strong smell lingering in the air. It dawned on me that he must have found treasure hidden in someone's shit. Already, there was trouble brewing.

Because there was lack of water, he pissed on the nugget he had found and buried it inside the soil, dry-washing it till it was clean, then dusting it. When he raised his head to look at me, I backed off, pretending not to have seen anything and waved him goodbye.

*

A short email reply from Stacey after I sent her Chapter 1 made me aware of an issue I had not thought of, mainly that of incongruity with Ah Sin speaking near perfect English while playing inventive language games with the English words. My reply, equally short, thus went, 'It is precisely because Ah Sin has a good command of English that he can afford to play with the language in all sorts of bad ways. After all, who knows what happened then? As a fictionist, all one has ever got from history is the fun one can have with it via imagination, not the tonnage of dead burying material.'

Chapter 2

Poetry was gathering, like clouds, inside my heart, my head, my head-heart, my heart-head, and rained, in words:

> He pointed at the place and said, *that used to be ours, now it's theirs*
> *That's ours, too, it's theirs now*
> *The Canton Lead, ours, theirs now*
> *The Skull Creek, ours, theirs now*
> *The Deadman's Hill, ours, theirs now*
> *The Murder Mountain, ours, theirs now*
> *The Tearful Creek, ours, theirs now*
> *The Dream Dale, ours, theirs now*
> Nothing ours is ours any more
> If there were eyes higher above, they must have seen all this happening
> Would He be a Historian keeping a record of all these happenings, this violence?

And I literally saw the words scatter around my place, planting in the earth like raindrops, unfindable hereafter.

Chapter 3

I wrote myself an email, saying, 'I wrote a poem for Ah Sin instead and pretend that it can count as a chapter.'

Ah Sin Says

History is nothing but numbers
how many arrived on such and such a date
how many got killed or wounded in an anti-Chinese riot
in such and such a place
how many women, how many men, how many kids
even though, I must say, history is not yet sophisticated enough
to take into account how many tons of piss and shit
these gold-diggers have dumped in the goldfields
and how many ounces of air breathed in and out
history remains shy, and puritanical
history tends to cite sources in footnotes or endnotes
history gets closer to the skin by getting further away in years
it is fiction that is interested in how I smell, how ugly my teeth look
how my face is a harbour of discontent that doesn't show
fiction is always keen on knowing what my sex life is like
whether I smoke opium while having sex or after having sex
with whom I have sex and how
and if it is a girl or post-girl that I have sex with
or even if it is a boy, and if so, how
if history is a calculator, fiction is a pervert
I can't be bothered with either
I live, and that is all

Chapter 4

Father Gargan taught me conversational English. He asked me to tell him about my family. He also asked me how I felt about this new country that was not part of the Great Britain as I thought it was but a colony of it. He taught me such idiomatic expressions as 'a sea of people'. Soon, I made my discovery in a way that was as thrilling as the discovery of gold. When it came for us to meet and talk English, I showed him a list of expressions that compared the English and the Chinese. I said to him, 'When you say, "a sea of people", you use one image. But we use two when we say the same because we say, "a sea and a mountain of people". That way, we create a perfectly balanced situation.'

I told him that our language was so balanced that while they said 'in two minds' we would say 'in three hearts and two minds', while they said 'a heart of stone' we would say 'a heart of iron and stone', and while they said 'made in heaven' we would say 'made in heaven and on earth'. But for his stopping me in the middle of it all, with a hand waving in front of me, I would have gone on reading the examples I had listed on a piece of paper.

He said, 'I like your "three hearts" and "a heart of iron"'.

I found myself blurting out, quite out of proportion with the situation, saying, 'but I constantly make mistakes. The other day, when I was in court, I heart the magistrate say two words that contain "money". But I couldn't find them in a dictionary.'

'What words?' said Father Gargan.

'Matrimoney and harmoney,' said I.

'Hee, hee, hee,' Father Gargan chuckled, in a small titter that revealed his heeing teeth, tiny and withdrawn. 'it's a good mistake because it somehow imbued the words with philosophy.'

'Feelowsofee?' said I, bewildered.

'Yes, because they make perfect sense, in a balanced manner that you proposed. Neither can happen without it.'

'It? You mean money?'

'What else? You can't maintain harmony in matrimony without money,' said Father Gargan with his eyes closed.

I thought it's his way of not wanting to see me; his way of wanting to see the physical shape of money in his closed eyes, the way he sees the appearance of a real God. Or perhaps it's his way of physically living the language. I have no idea. I couldn't express myself properly.

'I can't do either, then,' said I, feeling helpless.

'You need to look to God for help,' said Father Gargan, his eyes still closed. 'Your best bet is to believe in Him.'

My thought wandered to Confucius, again. Whenever God was mentioned, I tended to think of Confucius. And I found myself saying, 'I recall a story about Confucius.'

'Confucius?' Father Gargan opened his eyes, and his teeth-hidden mouth.

'He asked Zi Lu and Yan Yuan, two of his disciples, to tell him what ambitions they had. Zi Lu said he'd like to share his chariot and good clothes with his friends if he got rich and Yan Yuan said he wouldn't boast of his achievements if he made any.'

'What did Confucius say about himself?'

'He said he'd do three things, that is: I wish the old could live in peace, my friends could trust me and the young would miss me.'

'He'd wish,' he corrected me, saying, 'But this is good philosophy, as good as that of sharing and refraining from vanity, proposed by his disciples.' He said these last words with eyes opened and handed me a copy of the Bible, adding, 'Read this and learn your English from it as well. But tell me something.' He paused, focussing his dark hazelnut eyes on me, and resumed, 'Tell me why it's so hard to get your people to come to church?'

'Oh, they are too busy digging for gold to care about God, I'm afraid.'

'The interpreter said the same thing to me the other day.'

'Oh, yes, he even joked with me that the Church might have to think of paying them for them to come.'

'That's bullcrap!'

'And you know what?' said I, noticing his use of a curse word. 'We in China have many gods, too. We have God of Wealth, God of Earth, Kitchen God, Door God, House God, Well God – ,' Father Gargan cut me short, with a 'as many as our dogs.'

I didn't get the joke; I found it offensive. It's not till much later that I saw his play on words, reversing 'god' to 'dog'.

But I went on breathlessly, wishing for him to learn, 'We also have a female god, called Mazu, an ancestress of all

mothers, literally. It's with her protection that we managed to reach Australia without encountering any danger or difficulties at sea.'

'That's enough for the day,' I saw him say this with his hands holding his head as if in pain. As I rose, I said, 'See you around'.

*

I'm thinking of the woman. I'm thinking of her directness, as direct as her offered face. Unblemished, unadorned, a full-face impact. What you see is what you get: A girl, with a full face. Not a name yet. Not Gargan, no. Something plain? As plain as Briana or Cara or Ciara or Alyssa? How about Aoife? You like the look of that 'o' inside the word 'Aoife'? You don't like it because you don't know how to pronounce it? It sounds quite like 'Eva'. It's even more like 'Efa'. Yes, that's it: Eeffa, or Aoife. It looks different than it sounds. In that sense, it is Chinese, like Ah Sin（阿辛）. It has a story attached to it. But I'll let Aoife tell him that story. Meanwhile, Ah Sin went back to the camp to see his old friends.

'How are things going?' he said to everyone as soon as he arrived in their camp at Forest Creek by the side of White Hill.

Ignoring his greetings, Ah Fong said, 'How did you go?'

'Not bad,' realizing the sarcasm in his tone, Ah Sin added. 'not too bad.'

'That is to say,' said Ah Mao. 'Very good, so good.'

'Where is Ah Toy?' Ah Sin looked everywhere in the tent and outside it but couldn't see any sign of Ah Toy.

'Gone,' said Ah Fong.

'Gone where?'

'No idea.'

'Probably went to the city?' Ah Sin said, remembering how much Ah Toy loved to see new things in this new country as he easily got distracted.

'Don't know, don't know,' said Ah Mao as he went out of the tent and squatted next to a hole dug in the ground over which was laid a wok. From it, an aroma of the rice being cooked was rising. Ah Sin felt hungry.

'Stay, and eat with us,' said Ah Fong and he beckoned for Ah Sin to come inside the tent. The latter did and followed him inside.

Outside, it was a bare hill. Nearly all the trees were gone, used as firewood or building material for tents. A camp alive with burrowing people, an ugly sight that turned Ah Sin's stomach. Inside, there were what looked like beds, spread across the ground, made of branches, leaves, and earth. Perhaps there was gold? As soon as the thought arose in his head, Ah Sin suppressed it as if it were a crime committed. And the tree-bed was covered with a sheet of bamboo mat, on which their bedrolls laid open. In the corner was a makeshift table, with a single oil lamp. A late sun was quickly setting behind the hill as it was growing darker inside the hut.

'Things are not that fantastic here,' said Ah Fong, after Ah Sin lit his pipe for him, then his own. 'When we arrived, we already were late as tons of gold had been found and taken back to their home countries by the European miners, such as the Cornish and the German. They are better equipped with mining machinery whereas we can only use our primitive agricultural tools, and our hands. Occasionally, when you dig deep into the ground, you may return with bucketloads of gold. But that's a long memory ago. Not anymore. Our luck is running out.''As is mine,' Ah Sin confessed. 'I don't think my future lies with gold, of this kind.' He told Ah Fong how he had been going around the place, learning English or going to court with Ah Liu the interpreter. But he didn't tell him about the case involving Ah Mao.

'If there is a way, it must be that,' sighed Ah Fong. 'I was a failure in the war. And my stay here shows that I'm going to be a failure again.'

'Perhaps there is a way out, no?'

'Yeh, sure. I think Ah Ting did it right when he decided to stay in Penola. I heard he has gone into market gardening. Ah Mao was on the point of staying when he changed his mind.'

'How was he doing?' Ah Sin had a look in Ah Mao's direction and saw that he was coming in with a steaming bowl in hand, so he quickly shook his head for Ah Fong to stop talking about him.

Soon, three large blue and white porcelain bowls of rice were put on the corner table, with three sets of chopsticks. Ah Sin helped light the oil lamp. As the fire leapt, from blue to red, three faces were lit up, like three yellow halos.

'It smells so nice,' said Ah Sin, nodding his head with appreciation.

It looked as if there were no dishes of meat or vegetables. But Ah Sin knew that there were as these dishes were buried, like gold, in the rice. Sure enough, there were two pieces of salted fish and salted pork as well as pickled vegetables. They gave forth a wonderful smell and tasted beautiful when dug out, this being so particularly so because they smelled of home.

'Pity that we don't have anything fresh,' said Ah Fong.

'Exactly why Ah Ting did what he did, bringing fresh vegetables to the Australian mouths,' said Ah Mao.

'Lately, I'm being bothered by something,' said Ah Fong.

'Like what?' said Ah Sin.

'Why, all of a sudden, have we suffered such a downturn that we are never made welcome anywhere we go? We haven't done anything wrong; we haven't done anything bad.'

'That's right. We haven't,' agreed Ah Mao.

'Sheep haven't done anything wrong or bad. But they get killed and eaten,' said Ah Sin.

'Good on you,' said Ah Fong. 'you sound like a philosopher.'

'No, I am not,' said Ah Sin. 'I'm only telling the truth.'

'I'm going to write home to warn them against coming here,' said Ah Fong. 'Would you like to help me write one? I'll pay you one shilling.'

'Me, too,' said Ah Mao. 'Please write me a letter and I'll pay you, too.'

'I was meaning to entertain you guys with a story tonight,' said Ah Sin. 'I'll have to write the letters now. But no problem at all. Will do that first and if there's more time, I'll tell you at least one story.' After a pause, Ah Sin added, 'Actually, I'll put you to sleep first, with a story, before I write letters in the quiet that follows. How about that?'

Afterwards, when the darkness had fallen and they had finished their meal, each of them lying in their beds, smoking, Ah Sin began his story from The Annals of the Kingdoms in the East Zhou Dynasty.

'Did you know who Jing Ke was?' said Ah Sin.

'Oh, yeh, wasn't he the guy who attempted to assassinate Emperor Qin Shi Huang, the first emperor of a unified China?' said Ah Fong.

'Yes, I think I know that,' said Ah Mao. 'but I don't remember anything about it.'

'At least I know the idiom, tuqiong bijian,' said Ah Fong.

'What does it mean?' said Ah Mao.

'Oh, it means you hide a dagger inside a folded map. When you unwrap the map, the dagger is revealed,' said Ah Fong.

'Still, what does it mean?' said Ah Mao.

'It means—,' Ah Fong was lost for words.

'It means truth will out,' said Ah Sin. 'eventually.'

'Exactly, truth will always out, eventually,' said Ah Fong. 'We came here, thanks to the Opium War the Brits had fought with us and thanks to the Brits who had made it possible for us to be allowed in. But the tax they are exacting from us!'

'You want to hear the story?' said Ah Sin.

'Oh yes, please,' both Ah Fong and Ah Mao chimed in.

'There's too many stories about the famed assassin. Sin, see? We share the name in half,' said Ah Sin. 'But this one is a rare one, in regard to a beautiful woman.'

'Oh, I love beautiful women,' said Ah Mao.

'You do. I know,' said Ah Fong.

'Well, I'm going to sleep if you don't give me a chance.'

Silence. All quiet. Only the sound of firewood crackling in a nearby camp.

'Crown Prince Dan liked Jing Ke so much that he didn't stint anything as long as it pleased the latter. For example, when they went watching the fish swimming in a pond and saw a huge fish emerge, Jing Ke threw a broken roof tile at it when Crown Prince Dan offered him golden pellets. When they were out riding a swift horse, known as a one-thousand-mile horse, meaning that it could cover a thousand miles in a day, Jing Ke dropped a casual remark that the horse liver tasted good when an order was issued to kill the horse to get the liver. Subsequently, they had a dinner party at Huayang Terrace where they got beautiful women to play musical instruments to entertain the distinguished guests. Moved by the beautiful hands of a beautiful woman musician, Jing Ke couldn't help admiring it, saying, "What beautiful hands!" And you know what happened afterwards?' paused Ah Sin.

'Well, I'm sure he'll be entertained by the woman for his private pleasure,' said Ah Mao.

'I'm not sure, actually,' said Ah Fong, his voice heavy with sleep. 'because didn't he say that he loved her hands?'

'Which is what?' said Ah Mao, confused.

Chapter 5

When Ah Sin finished telling the story, the other two had long gone asleep. There was no moral in that story. There was only the Story, in which, near the end, when Jing Ke expresses his admiration for the beautiful hands of the dancing woman, the wondrous hands, neatly severed from the woman, are brought in to him on a blue and white porcelain plate, one of the rarest kind.

Before I go, before I let myself go and stop my ramblings, self-censored and deleted, I probably will prepare my readers with what I'm going to do next. I will, for example, conduct interviews with a number of hand-picked dead Chinese in the Chinese cemeteries scattered at ABC (Ararat, Bendigo, Castlemaine) or BBC (Ballarat, Bendigo, Castlemaine). One will tell me how he falls in love with a white girl and takes her back to China to meet his first wife, leading a happy life ever after. Another, actually not dead yet, but inclined to think he is, will tell me how he has been chatting with his cemetery mates 24/7 for over 150 years about anything and everything. It'll bore you to death or tears if you listen. The belief that once someone is dead he is forever dead is an inane one in that the believer has forgotten that he is also a daily dreamer, of things that never exist but that are always coming into existence, like clouds, unlike clouds. And yes there will be a she, lots of she, too, a very she she, if you know what I mean. The rest of the story, though, will remain a mystery that will only unwrap itself like a precious gift as time goes by.

Oh, gosh, I almost forgot something. Ling, yes, Ling, not Sling, not Ling It, but potentially could be either or both or all. Not even Dyson's Ah Ling. But just Ah Sin's Ah Ling who dies in Robe in my fiction and gets buried in the Robe public cemetery. It's a slip of writing memory, a writer's memory. As a matter of fact, his soul is buried there. But his bones are long taken back. I use the present tense because I'm telling his story as if I were quoting it from a piece of written fiction that I thought I had written but that I haven't. Righto, get on with it and chuck it all out, along the lines of what Pascal suggests: 'Imagine a body of thinking members'. Now, in Ah Sin's voice.

'We waited for his body to rot till only the bones remained. But that was not possible. It would take weeks or months for that to happen. Fortunately, we got a bone-scraping master on board the ship. His name was Ah Wong. It would have been a spectacle but for the fact that the privilege was denied everyone except Ah Fong and I. We watched with our own eyes how Ah Wong used one of his instruments from a set of them to pick his bones clean, removing all the rotting flesh, much of which was still fresh, even warm, as I imagined seeing crisps of steam rising from his parted flesh. The bones that were picked clean were so white that they somehow resembled the trunks of the gum trees whose barks were newly shed. There were rotten smells in the air. The bones carried a stench much like that of fish. And when they were put together, the bits and pieces, including the gouged eyeballs, the cut ears and nose, and the dug tongue, formed a stack that was quickly buried, hidden away from the eye. Then, into a leather bag, Ah Wong collected all the bones, including the skull, and put them, one by crisp one, till the job was done. All the while, a priest whose name I couldn't remember, stood nearby, praying, his eyes closed, not wanting to see or perhaps seeing all through his transparent eyelids.

'The bag containing his bones went back to his home village on a return journey by the same ship that had carried us all the way from Taishan.'

*

The night didn't end without a story about sex. That's how Ah Fong and Ah Mao made me understand because the Jing Ke story wasn't interesting enough. So, to amuse them, I told them something about Yang Jian, first emperor of the Sui Dynasty, about 1300 years ago. Because Empress Dugu (Solitude), his wife, of the Xianbei ethnicity, with her familial influences, had helped him ascend to power, Yang Jian vowed to never have kids with any other women, including a dozen imperial concubines he kept in his harem, just for show. Together, they ruled the country like 'two saints', a nickname given by the people in the royal court. On one occasion, though, Yang Jian spotted a pretty woman, grand-daughter of Yuchi Jiong, and had an affair with her. When Empress Dugu learnt about this, she did not confront Yang Jian about it. Instead, she had her murdered. This made Yang Jian so angry that he rode his horse straight into the woods in the mountain and into the night until his men found him and tried to bring him round back to the palace when he sighed and said that he had no freedom as an emperor. It was not till Gao Ying, a trusted minister, said to him that state affairs were more important than women that Yang Jian decided to return with them, arriving back at the palace at midnight, to an apologetic Empress Dugu. Poor Yang Jian had to wait years until Empress Dugu died before he had a chance to name Lady Xuanhua and Lady Ronghua his women of the bed chamber, serving him by turn every night. By then, he was 62 years old. One year after, he died.

'Why?' said Ah Mao.

'Emperors, as a rule, die young because they fuck too much,' said Ah Sin.

'But Yang Jian didn't,' said Ah Fong.

'Marrying someone outside your race may have helped,' said Ah Sin.

'But I heard Yang Yong, one of his sons, led a quite licentious life, or is that right?' Ah Fong said.

'Right,' said Ah Sin. 'He died in his early 30s, having fathered a daughter and a dozen sons, by five to six mothers.'

'Five to six mothers?' said Ah Mao.

'Mate, he fucked five to six women to make them give birth to more than a dozen sons,' said Ah Fong.

'Oh, I wish I had a life like that,' said Ah Mao.

'You'll definitely have that next life, or in a dream, if you dream hard enough,' said Ah Sin.

*

I am Charlie. Charlie Kut. I was born of Chinese and Aboriginal parentage. I was thus considered the worst of the worst, the lowest of the lowest. My dad came from China and he died of overwork while digging for gold in Castlemaine. I knew Ah Sin because Dad had worked with them. My mum was an Aboriginal, what they called a lubra. I don't know why they called them that. I suspect it's taken from the word lubrication. My mum died of smallpox in one of its epidemics that swept across Australia. When I first met Ah Sin, I had my face read by him. After it, he remained silent for a long time. That made me furious as I found myself yelling at him, accusing him of being a dickhead with no knowledge of fortune-telling. Without a word, he ingratiatingly offered me a pipe of tobacco from Canton,. I took it without thanking him. Then I heard him say, *I wish you good luck*. When I raised my head from the pipe with a large cloud smoke rising between us, I heard him say something else, in a low voice. 'What did you say just now?' I heard myself say to him. 'Say that again, will ya?' He said, 'I'm sorry. But what I meant was that you have a fierce intelligence, coupled with two oldest cultures in the world, your eyes so sharp and piercing they could peel centuries and millenniums back to their origins.

Now, that was that. I felt better after it.

*

Linden Tree Village, Taishan. A river ran quietly through it. A bridge across the river, connecting one half of the village to the other. Cocks crowing, one after another, their voices lifting on an upward sliding scale. Dogs barking. Occasional gruntings of a pig as it was getting fed in a sty. Sparrows twittering, as they flew from roof to black-tiled roof or to the crown of a tree. When the mail delivery man appeared on the bridge, the fish in the water darted about, hiding themselves in the depths, and the dogs started barking in unison, some welcoming, others with hostility. The man with a long pigtail walked straight to Grandma Chen, took off his pointed bamboo hat, made a deep bow and handed over a letter to her, saying, 'if you please.'

Grandma was all smiles, every fishtail line lit up. She grabbed a handful of grains and threw them far and wide, not too far, not too wide, just far-wide enough for the grains to spread in a neat circle in her yard before her door when her own hens rushed striding towards them, followed by a brood of yellow fluffy little chicks. Two waddling ducks, quacking, also joined them.

She opened the letter and took out the contents, a long slip of paper, with characters written vertically in a tidy manner. She put on her spectacles, unfolded the paper and read it from top to bottom and from right to left until she finished it and put it aside.

Although she couldn't understand a character of it, she would judge by its look that the news carried in it was at least auspicious. The paper inside was clean, crisp. The ink was fresh, black. When the letter was slipped inside and the envelope was closed, it was fat and pregnant to the touch.

She didn't know a word, not a single character. In her 80s, she did not have a day of schooling. After the grandfather died, she would have to wait till her grandson's daughter came back with her child from the field and she would get her to read the letter for her. Any news, good or bad, would be tidings to die for after a long absence.

The letter, written by Ah Sin for Ah Fong, went as follows,

Dear Grandma and Grandpa,
I hope this letter finds you both well.

I have been away for more than a year now and have been in this country for about six months, too. There are many people here, digging for gold. They come from all over the world. People here are nice, after a fashion. We have suffered enough. But we don't seem to have come to the right place. Gold seems to have been washed clean off the hill we are occupying. Big nuggets are all gone. We end up picking sesame-sized gold sands, in places deserted by the European miners. The government clamped down on us with all sorts of tax and we tried hard to dodge them, not paying or paying as little as possible. Why just us, of all the other people?

But don't worry about me. I am strong. I have got enough meat and rice to eat. If we run out of food, there are always kangaroos to catch and eat. Their flesh is a bit tough but is good enough to eat if well cooked and added with the right ingredients.

I hope Grandpa keeps fit, and Ah Min is well with our child.

I'll come back to see you all very shortly with all the gold I've found.

*

I, Baohui, wrote a letter to myself, in the cinema where I was watching a film alone. I wrote the whole thing on my Nokia phone, then copied and pasted here below. I wanted to remind myself who I am and what I am:

Baohui, I don't think you are good enough. You never are. I think what is uppermost in your mind is this thought that you are thinking of. You want to give up. You can't write a novel. You can't write it properly. You can't reach perfection because there is no perfection in this world even if you think there is. A novel, you believe, is an imperfect thing in itself and for itself, like a human being. You can think the most beautiful thoughts, dress yourself up in a most beautiful way, speak a pure language without using any expletives, make yourself up perfectly even if you are a male, do everything by following the ancient codes of conduct passed down for generations and centuries, but you can't escape from the feeling that you are a mass of imperfections. Just one fact suffices: you eat a beautiful dinner today and by tomorrow morning the first thing you do is shit and that is the opposite of what you eat. Then why do you entertain yourself with the idea of perfection or perfections? Why can't you live with the comfortable idea of what you are and who you are without pretending on a daily basis and even wordly basis?

Baohui, you must write to Stacey to tell her the same thing that you are no good, that you can't carry on with this fiction, that you have to give up on it all because nothing is good, not good enough and that all you really need is love.

You need to fall in love. Simple as that but the strictures of fiction require that you can't tell your side of the story. How absurd is that?

I hate you, I hate you, I hate you!

Chapter 6

As the number of my days in the goldfields grew, my command of English grew, too. I became more and more interested in liaising between my fellow countrymen gold-diggers and the white people representing law and order. And I read newspapers like *The Age* and *The Argus*. One morning, I stood against the wall. It was cold. But I liked it because I could stand in my newly brought second-hand overcoat, a tad show-offish, and in my brown boots, also second-hand. The good thing about the new country was that everything came in second-hand and cheap. The sun was rising above Bourke Street. A horse-drawn carriage went down the street, carrying stacks of sheep skins. Another followed. People appeared from nowhere, popping up as if from underground. Wearing their winter coats and hats, they looked ahead of them, grim. White faces of seriousness untainted by smiles. An occasional lady went by with a dog. A thought went through my mind: Should I keep a dog? Then it dismissed itself: I don't have time and money to keep it. Perhaps one day I will.

A man came to a stop in front of me, looking at the sign I had put next to me, with these words: 'Story for Sale'.

'You telling a story, aren't you?' said the man, wearing a tall hat and a long, black overcoat, a grey suit underneath.

'Yes, sir,' I held his eyes steady in my eyes, and said. 'What would you like to hear?'

'How much do you charge per story and for how long?' said the man.

'As long as you like and as much as you like, too. But you don't have to pay anything if you don't want to hear or if you find it boring. You can leave anytime if the story ceases to interest you.'

'Carry on,' Ah Sin heard the man say and detected no sign of him leaving.

'You know how old I am?' said Ah Sin, looking at the pink face of the man.

'I don't know. Maybe 1 year old?' muttered the man.

'Thank you for your compliment, Mr – oh, sorry but what's your name?'

'Ling. Call me Mr Ling,' said the man, his eyes turned towards another horse-drawn cart running clattering down the road.

'But that's a Chinese name? Are you Chinese?'

'Irish.'

Supressing an instant impulse to express further curiosity, Ah Sin simply said, 'I'm 5000 thousand years old.'

'You must be joking,' said the man.

'Or at least half that age.'

'Are you crazy or something?'

'Yeh, that's what you think of us, don't you?'

'What do we think of you?'

'Oh, that we are like women, wearing pigtails and coolie hats, that we yell instead of talk in a proper manner, that we don't bring our women with us, that we smoke opium, that we eat rats, cats and dogs.'

'Is that not true?'

'You know what people back in our old country think of you?'

'No.'

'They call you people white devils. They describe the English people as having long legs that can't bend nor run and they are people with blue eyes that can't open under the noon sun, and that when they come to China they cut open children's brains and cook them to get the oil. In the Chinese eyes, they are extremely ugly because they have sunken eyes and hook noses. Chinese people watch them like watching a show of devils from hell.'

Before I finished my words, I heard the clinking sound of a coin in the iron bowl laid in front of him. A shilling. My heart gave a leap.

'But I haven't even begun my story yet,' said I, apologetically.'Don't you worry,' said Mr Ling. 'I like what you said. But I haven't got all day. Here's my address.' He tore a piece of paper from his notebook and scribbled something on it before handing it to me.

I thanked him, watched him go and then took a look at the paper. On it was written, Ling & Co., Barristers and Solicitors.

*

'I have something to ask you,' he said to me as soon as I stepped into the grey granite building in which Mr Ling's office was located.

'Like what?' said I.

'Do you people have multiple wives?' said he.

'My people?' I was confused.

'The Chinese people from the Celestial Empire, I mean,' said he.

'Oh, yes,' said I, launched, as it were, into an immediate recount of how it was customary for the rich men, usually merchants, to have multiple wives.

'Wait, wait,' impatiently, he cut me short, saying, 'I know all that. Note that I used the word "from".'

'I see. You mean the celestials here who originally came from China?'

'Exactly.'

'No,' said I. 'Not really. How can they afford them, I mean? Women cost money.'

'What if they get married here while keeping wives at home?'

'That is quite possible, even likely,' said I, recalling how an acquaintance of mine, a merchant, running a shop in Ballarat, had married a European woman and was said to have been married with kids back in China.

'I want you to tell me,' said he, 'how these people manage their financial affairs.'

'That, I really don't know.'

'Have you ever thought of jealousy as an issue?'

'Jealousy? What's that?'

'Well, if someone is better than you, you hate him. That's jealousy. Don't you ever have that feeling?'

'Oh, yes, I know, I know. That in our language is jidu or duji. Everyone has that, expecially women,' said I.

'Especially,' said he, correcting me.

'Especially,' echoed I, wondering why he didn't give me a chance by picking up my word or else I might have a chance to correct him.

'Let's get straight to the point,' he said to me as he began telling me a story of how a local celestial merchant would like to bring his wife and kids from China to join his Australian wife in Melbourne and whether jealousy might be a major problem preventing that from happening.

'What do you think?' he said after he finished his words.

'Well,' I drawled, 'perhaps the best thing is tell you a few stories, very short ones.'

'No,' he said, his hand shot up, like a fan. 'I don't have time for that. Can you do me a favour, though?'

'Like what?' said I.

'Go and buy me a coffee and bring it in. I'm badly in need of one now.' With that, he put a few coins in my hand and waved me out.

*

I went down Little Bourke Street, wondering which coffee shop I should go to. As I passed restaurants, teahouses and opium houses, I had a sudden realisation that there was no coffee shop in this street as no celestials of my kind drank coffee, opium being a much better tranquilizer than a coffee stimulant and tea a beater of it all, so I turned left into Bourke Street. There, just around the corner, loomed a café with these words written above, Dinkum Café. I paused, because the word 'dinkum' caught my eye. For a fleeting moment, I thought I saw a Mandarin word. Something vague swept across my mind. But, finding nothing that made sense, I failed to make the connection. I went in regardless, ignoring people who looked up in surprise when seeing my strange attire and my somehow always distinct face, like a crane in a herd of cows.

The man, a young white man of twenty something, behind the counter said, 'What would you like, sir?' The word 'sir' was only half voiced, stopping short of pronouncing the 'r'.

'Just a coffee please,' said I as I put a handful of coins on the counter.
'Coffee?' the man laughed.

A tittering arose among the coffee drinkers in the semi-darkness of the narrow bar. I was suddenly made aware of myself as a spectacle. And I was struck tongue-tied.

'Go and have tea in one of those bloody teahouses next door in Little Bourke Street, Mate,' a voice came from nearby.

When I threw a look in its direction, my heart gave a leap because I thought I saw Captain Miller, a heavy man with a heavy moustache in a heavy overcoat whose voice was sonorous and brusque.

I gave him the go-by and said to the boy behind the counter, 'Just a latte, please.'

With my back towards the heavy overcoat behind me, I had a swift illusory feeling that the man was jumping out of his seat to pounce on me, slapping me hard across the face and throwing me out doors.

Nothing like that happened although the waiting seemed to take for ever in which the heavy, oppressive atmosphere reduced me to sweating.

I paid, got my latte, went out, feeling the eyes follow me, and went back to the bluestone building. Seeing that Mr Ling's door was closed, I went over and tapped on the door.

He came out, with a surprised look on his face.

'What did you get?' his voice was harsh.

'A latte,' said I.

'But I don't want a latte. I want proper coffee.'

'What's proper coffee?'

'I want a short black,' said he.

'But you said you wanted coffee.'

'Oh,' the man rolled his eyes and spread his hands, in a gesture indicating his frustration and disappointment. 'You have it then. I don't want it.'

I was about to blurt out saying that he hadn't specified what exactly he had wanted when my mother's words rang in my ears, 'Don't antagonise people, particularly elderly people and your superiors, least of all gweilo.'

I wasn't happy at heart. I probably looked it because Mr Ling relaxed his face, forcing a smile, and said, 'Don't worry about it. Come back some other day then.'

As he said so, he closed the door behind him, leaving the half-warm latte in my hand.

*

A note to myself that I may have to change the word 'latte' to something else after a friend pointed out that it might not be the right drink in the times I wrote about. But who cares? I am just a student, allowed to make as many mistakes as possible, only for the supervisor to correct or point out for me to correct. And don't mistakes have the effect of a stimulant such as coffee to induce the urge in us to correct them?

*

In the instant in which the door was opened and closed, I glimpsed a Chinese man sitting inside the office by the desk, covered with heaps of yellow files, each bundled up with a dark-pink ribbon. Even though I could only see a profile, I could tell that this was a man without the pigtail that most Chinese men wore. He was wearing a dark suit, with dark-blue trousers to match, and a pair of shiny black leather shoes. He quickly glanced at me and instantly took his glance back. But it was a telling glance that suggested many things, all at once: a rich man with a future, deeply rooted in the past. I had a vague feeling that his presence there had something to do with what Mr Ling had asked me about. But because I stood outside the closed door and was obviously unwanted, I went away. Aware the coffee in my hand was getting cold, I began sipping from it as I stepped outside.

The morning had just begun. People walked in all directions. No one paid attention to me. I had not planned what I'd be going to do for the rest of the day. My random idea, frustrated now, of possibly getting a job from Mr Ling, I thought of finding a spot somewhere and carrying on with my business of telling stories. I wandered back across

Little Bourke Street into Lonsdale Street till I stopped, not far from St Francis' Church, an awe-inspiring mass of granite, near the corner of Lonsdale Street and Elizabeth Street. There weren't many people there but I might catch the attention of church-goers who might be interested in hearing a yarn or two from me. As soon as I put my sign down against the wall, an old pedestrian came to a stop right in front of me, eyeing me from head to toe, before he uttered these words,

'Lad, what are you going to tell me if you have any stories?'

'Oh, plenty on order, plenty,' said I, jocosely.

'Perhaps something about China?' said the old man, his hair snow white, in a black gown.

'What about jealousy?' said I, recalling my conversation with Mr Ling.

'What about it?' the eyes of the old man sparkled.

In as few words as possible, I told him of what had happened between Mr Ling and I, carefully concealing his name and his profession.

The old man cut me short, with a curt remark, 'Go ahead.'

In a modified form, I told him of a Mr Hu, in ancient China, some 500-odd years ago, who, married for many years, spent a large sum of money buying a concubine, decades younger than his own wife, bringing her home, only to find his jealous wife hating her guts, not allowing her to come inside the house so that the old man had to set her up in a wing room.

'What about the young one? Did anything happen between her and the old one?' the man said, his eyes fixed on me, prompting an instant wonderment in me how blue they were.

'Nope,' said I. 'the old wife didn't sleep with the old man. She didn't allow the concubine to sleep with him, either. And the young woman didn't allow the man to sleep with her, too.'

'That's interesting. But why?'

'Because the old wife would kick up a terrible row if she saw them together. In fact, she taunted and abused the man's concubine day in and day out. The concubine never talked back. Even when the old man made numerous attempts to have her, she refused.'

'What's supposed to be the moral?'

'Moral? What did you mean?'

'What are people supposed to learn from this story?'

'Oh, that. But I haven't told you the rest of the story yet.'

'What's it then?'

'But you probably don't have time to hear it out as it may take hours to relate it, too involved.'

'Given that is the case, why don't you come over and have a look?'

'A look?' I was taken aback. 'A look where?'

'You done a good job,' said the man. 'Now take this.'

I opened my eyes and saw the coin lying in his open palm. But I didn't recognize it.

'It's a Spanish dollar,' said the man.

'Spanish dollar?'

'That's five shillings.'

'Oh, thank you so much,' said I as I picked it up and weighed it in my hand. It felt nice and heavy.

'What's your name, by the way?'

'Ah Sin.'

'Ah, sin that begins in our heart.'

'I'm sorry?'

'Ah Sin, ah, you miss the mark.'

'Miss the mark? How did you mean?'

'Didn't you know what the original meaning of sin is?'

'Nope.'

'It means missing the mark or the target. If the soldiers in ancient Israel slung stones right on target, they were said not to sin. Get that?'

'Got it and what's your name please?'

'Call me Father Henry.'

'Father Henry, pleased to meet you,' I held out my hand.

We shook hands and he said,

'If you like, come with me to my church,' said the man, turning to go, in the direction of the grey building across the road.

*

I, BH, refrained from telling other stories of jealousy by putting them in Ah Sin's mouth. Emperor Yang of Sui (569-618 AD) was a man of sort of letters who dabbled in poetry and because he was the emperor, he considered all the other men of letters beneath contempt and got rid of those who didn't sing constant praises of his work. One such person was Xiao Daoheng, much admired for his poetry of exquisite beauty. When he was sentenced to death on trumped-up charges, the emperor said to him, 'Can you still produce something like *kong liang luo yan ni*?' He was referring to a most famous line by Xiao that goes, 'the swallow's mud pellets drop out of an empty house beam'. Yang Guang, the emperor, did the same with Wang Zhou, another well-known poet. When he had him executed, he confronted him with a similar question by challenging him to write a line equally as good as this, *ting cao wu ren sui yi lü* (The grass in the courtyard was greening at will and random when no one was there), Wang's best-known line. History does not record how the two poets replied. But if it were me, knowing I was going to die anyway, I would simply tell the emperor off by saying to him, 'You can't even write half as well as I did, why would I be bothered writing better than my best?'

One thing I keep wondering to myself is this: Why are people in powerful positions even jealous of people with talent but that are in inferior positions? Why do they want admiration from them? Why, for example, do the whites want admiration from people of colour they consider racially inferior to them?

Chapter 7

Readers are warned that this chapter is going to bore as it breaks the flow of the narrative with my musings on fiction and relevant things, and they are advised that they can skip the chapter if it is their wish to do so. In Chapter 8, I'm going to write about Ah Sin in love, so please don't hold your breath and go straight there. If you know how to skip sections based on the instructions given on a form, you know what to do.

In the middle of writing, I often experience a feeling akin to death. I feel that fiction is somehow depriving me of my right to live and to live properly. While the world is alive with activities, e.g. a retired worker is fishing in a dirty river surrounded with flowering trees, a poet is playing Mahjong with his non-poet mates, saying he often derives a different pleasure from them than from his fellow poets, and a calligrapher has just posted in the WeChat Moments a number of calligraphic works he produced with a poet, in a bilingual manner, featuring these three Chinese characters in the traditional Chinese way, that is, from right to left: "家享诗", alongside which the poet wrote three English words underneath, also from right to left: 'Home Enjoys Poetry'. While the words found their way to the computer screen from my fingertips hitting the keys, my life was ebbing away. And I was acutely aware of the quietness around me, like a shroud wrapping me up even in a country that was not Australia, surrounding me like an army of silence. The price of modernity, believe it or not, is the ultimate death-like silence, in which one man performs his writing ritual, squeezed between his desk and his bed, half of which was covered with books. And this man, that is me, Mr Zhang, as they call me, killing one cigarette after another as if their deaths might help bring back lives that didn't exist in the first place except in the soil of one's mind?

I went to watch this show, presented by a woman dancer and body painter from New York the other day. I can't say if I liked it much. But I liked the way the student actors threw rags, sodden with black ink, and red, onto strips of standing white boards, creating random nonsensical pictures of blotches, splashes and smashes. When I was asked to make comments, like the others who had only good things to say, I declined. Life, if anything, had little good to speak of. It was just a day-to-day stream of unconsciousness, brightening up when the flowers flashed, or flower-like faces appeared and disappeared, or when the setting sun or rising sun assaulted one's numbed sense like in a burning fire. Everyone's head was lowered, over the mobile phone in their hands. Even a motorcyclist did that as he sped away through the thronging crowd on the street. On more than one occasion, I thought of giving up on pursuing the degree. Can someone from a non-English-speaking country have a future as a writer writing in English for an English-speaking audience or readership? My mini-research returned very few engaging in this non-profitable business. And the ones who did obviously didn't do well, by comparison. So, the point?

Stacey is probably right when she said not to worry about the point, simply because there wasn't any point, the worrying itself probably the point. The point of a cigarette, for example, is that it gets smoked to its ashes, then dumped, making the time in between well spent or seemingly so, quite like a book, read then put aside, never to be read again, spending time so that time is spent. Following is a fragment I wrote after meeting the dancer, as part of my musings:

> She told you that she went to Australia in 1983. Nothing impressed more than the smiles. The smiles of people. The smiling people. The kind of smile she'd never seen in her own country. It was so pure, she said. In her country, people were not encouraged to smile. Smiling was regarded as decadent, indulgent, self-indulgent, open to interpretation, bourgeois, petty bourgeois, revolutionarily unacceptable. Her parents never smiled. Her father's face was stern, unforgiving. Her mother's face was relentless, never showing emotion. Everyone was so serious-looking. It was always criticism,

self-criticism, self-loathing.

'Australia,' said she. 'It was fantastic. The girls' smiles in particular, pure beyond imagination. It's like they've never suffered, happiness from the very start. Innate. Born with it. It's like the country overflowing with such smiles, to the point of enrapture. It's my first time in there. That's what impressed.'

The man, the ageing man, sitting across the tea table from her, remained silent, and he thought: But that's not my experience. When I first arrived, I saw no smiles. Indeed, smiling was an act that I did not see happen on any faces. Was I blind? In the car Alex drove me from the airport, I saw brownish masses dotting the roadside and I asked what they were. He said he didn't know. Never even noticed them. Looking out of the window in the airplane, I saw a landscape of colours dominated by grey or brown or grey-brown. Perhaps that's because it was almost a decade from when she first saw those rapturous smiles.

'And things had perhaps drastically changed,' said he, blurting out the words that took himself by surprise.

'Oh, is that right?' the woman artist, also a dancer, said.

The ageing man made a single remark, then went silent, never to be drawn out again. He said, 'I still remember an American expert on hydroelectricity. In his first visit to China, he told me, he never ceased to be amazed by the number of smiling faces on the streets and he would stand by the roadside looking at the smiling faces for hours.'

She told you yesterday.

It's not 'yesterday'; it's actually many days ago. If you don't give it a date, it remains 'yesterday' or yesterday.

*

'Let's start with the Japanese', the man said, without looking at anyone. 'They beat us in the war. Everyone beat us. The Russians. The Brits.

The French. The Germans. But the Japanese, they were Asians, Far Easterners, like us. They beat us. That's insufferable, most insufferable. These other nations did nothing to intervene. They had their treaties signed with us. They got paid in huge amounts of war indemnities. They chopped up our land like cakes. They carved it up like water melons. Haishenwai was ours. But it became part of the Russian territory, called Vladivostok, 600 square kilometres. Boli, also our territory, became part of the Russian land, called Khabarovsk, 800 square kilometres. Jiangdong liushisi tun, the Sixty-four Villages East of the Heilongjiang River, our territory, became part of the Russian land, 3600 square kilometres. No, not "became", but were forcibly taken by them. In total, they took 5 million square kilometres of our land, from 1689 to 1944. What about the Japanese? What about them? They beat us, the little Japs. First, the Brits weakened us with opium. They had it flowing into the country. They had white silver and yellow gold flowing out of the country into their pockets. They fought two wars with us. We lost both of them. We were perpetual losers. And we thought we were peace-lovers. We didn't want to fight with anyone, propped as it were by the dictum that *he wei gui*, peace is the most treasured thing, so we ended up giving our land to them, giving our women to them, giving our money to them, giving our minds to them. A Christian missionary went so far as to suggest that foreigners must be installed at every level of the government. Don't ask me what his name was. I don't remember. It's the historian's business to remember the dates and the names. Because we were big, we were bound to become small, smaller. That's the rule of the game. The 19th century was a white century, a century of white supremacy. They went everywhere and left colonies in their wake. They got Indonesians to speak Dutch. They got Algerians to speak French. They got Brazilians to speak Portuguese. They got South Africans to speak English and Dutch. They got everyone to abandon their own languages in favour of speaking someone else's languages. They fucked things up. They fucked people up. They wiped things out. They whited things out. They were the proud people whose sun never set. Then they fought among themselves. They killed one another. They killed each other. I know I'm repeating myself in different words.

But that's what they did. They killed, then they said sorry. Then they killed again. They always say sorry after they commit atrocities. That's because they are more human than humans or think they are. Oh, yes, the Japs. In the First Sino-Japanese War, 1894, they took only one year to vanquish China. The Chinese armies were said to be *wangfeng ertao*, watching the wind and running away with it. The ones who fought against them died. The ones who didn't prospered.'

The man in the madhouse said.

*

Diary entry (17/4): I have not written a single word. Things pile up, which is not an excuse. I urge myself to write at least a word each day and every day. But, at the end of each day, when I go to bed, I hear myself say, to myself: Forget it. I just can't write anything. Nothing moves. Nothing seems to move. I keep reminding myself of the graves scattered over the land, ignored, neglected, wind-swept, rain-washed, sun-dried, bird-shat, mud-covered, people-passed, history-listed, name-unmatched, rarely visited, hardly remembered, sun-drenched, wind-kissed, leaf-touched, thought-glimpsed, night-merged, kangaroo-leapt, season-flowed, star-struck, God-forgotten, sense-numbed, smoke-soothed, none-loved, death-dealt, dawn-donned, sun-tanned, sun-shuied, sleep-soothed, dream-drunk, rock-hardened, song-softened, prayer-said, nothing achieved, gold-departed, never coupled, never reunited, never comforted, never apologized for, solitude-infested, heartstring-broken, hearthoughts-forsaken, brain-burned, sky-canopied, tree-accompanied, earth-bedded, word-unuttered, letter-unsent, bone-unrepatriated, mouth-abused, head-bashed, pigtail-pulled and cut, past-belittled, future-ungiven, holed, holed, holed.

I shall ask the editor not to correct my self-created words, such as 'sun-shuied' and 'hearthought-forsaken' if this book is ever published.

Chapter 8

The church was nothing like anything I had seen back in my hometown. Over there, it was a hut, and a thatched one at that. When the flood came, it carried it away, all straw and sticks, floating down the river. Then they built it again and it flowed away again, year in, year out. This church here – what should I say? – was a mass so indestructible that it seemed to have become part of the sky.

My arrival was met with curious glances and quick head turns, to which I nodded my head and smiled. As far as I was concerned, I kept a positive profile, I offered a smile to the world, I ignored negativity that came my way, and I survived. Didn't I hear someone muttering something about 'a heathen'? I ignored it or I pretended that it was aimed at someone else, having nothing to do with myself. Besides, I had an opinion of my own, which I kept to myself because I wouldn't share it with anyone else unless he or she was sympathetic or open-minded enough.

I picked a place to sit down. Immediately, people on either side receded from me, like a tide receding from a dangerous sea animal. I took note and kept silent, looking straight ahead of me. As it was, Father Henry was walking down the altar, with a silver plate in his hand, out of which he was distributing something to the people in the front row, one by one. A wave of music rose, softened and moving. People stood up to receive the little white thing. When he came and stopped in front of me, I received it likewise. It was like the biscuit I had had back in my home village. But it was whiter, thinner and less tasty. As I ate it, following the example of the others, I raised my eyes in thanks to Father Henry. But he had already moved to the next row. I was in time to catch a glimpse of his black-robed back and his greying hair.

The upshot of this visit was an absence of verbal communications with anyone, let alone the priest, in my first holy communion experience, as I lay in my bed at night, thinking of what had happened during the day. The more interesting thing happened afterwards when I came out and met someone at the entrance to the solid grey structure.

'Hi, Brother,' the man accosted me in a familiar tone.

'Oh, it's you,' I said. 'We've met somewhere before. But I've forgotten your name.'

'Hahaha, exactly like what the saying describes: A rich man tends to be forgetful,' the man said.

'No, no, no,' said I. 'nothing like that.' Then, 'Did we meet in Vaughan by the Loddon River?'

'We could have,' the man laughed, in a small laugh afraid of making itself audible, 'if we were lovers.'

'But where? Can you remind me?'

'It's on the ship, remember?'

'Oh, the ship! In Robe?'

'That arrived in Robe, yes.'

'You must have belonged to a different group, staying on a different level under the deck. And took a different route to the goldfields. No?'

'Whatever the case may be, we met on the deck of the ship, called something like A Piece of Cake.'

'No, not that. It's called Land of Cakes.'

'Exactly!'

We talked as we walked. By the time we worked out that the ship was not a piece of cake but the land of cakes we had arrived at Small Smoke, an opium house in Little Bourke Street, and found ourselves a vacant seat, with two wooden recliner chairs sandwiching a combination tea and opium table. Vastly different from the church in every way possible, the place was also full of people who were smoking or sleeping. There was loud-mouthed talking or laughing; there was also snoring, so much reminiscent of my hometown that I started missing it. But only for a second.

'What are you doing now?' said Get, Ah Get.

'Not much. Just mucking around,' said I, and added, 'And what about you?'

'Trying to be a priest,' said he, then adding, 'or learning to be one.'

'Like me,' said I. 'trying to be or learning to be an interpreter.'

When the set of opium tools was brought in, the paraphernalia as it were, we each took a pipe in hand, stuffed the ball of opium in it, pressing it down till it was nice and tight, lit the opium lamp, from which we further lit the pipe. It had such a powerful effect that soon I was dizzy with hallucination, thinking I had wandered into an aquarium full of women turned fish. And I half-heard him say that he was going to have his first mass and was mentally preparing to talk up a storm with his first sermon.

'What are you going to say?' I heard myself say.

'Not really sure what,' said he. 'You got any ideas?'

'No. I would blunder through the whole thing.'

'What would you say then?'

'Oh, I'd say – please forgive me if I say anything wrong as I'm heavily under the influence of the opium – God is gold but fake gold. You can't buy anything with that gold. But real gold is hard to come by. It easily comes by death.'

'True. I've seen so many deaths I don't even want to talk about it, them.'

'I'd rather die smoking, in the smoke, wrapped up with the smoke, than working bent double digging for gold that was never there or that was there but that was snatched away or stolen when you were asleep. It makes one stupid lying sleepless on a pillow filled with gold night after night as it happened to me.'

'But it's stupid to do that, you know?'

'I know. I was only joking. I actually like gold; I like it a lot. It's like women. The only two things that matter in this world and this life.'

'Two things only?'

'Two things only: money and women. Or, simply, womoney.'

'Ah, both in one. What a wordsmith you are!'

'Don't say that. I'm just a wordplayer. That's all.'

'How are things woman-wise?'

'I see them.'

'You see them? Where?'

'In my pipe.'

'You fancy them?'

'I fantasize about them. They appear as I smoke. I smoke them out, it seems.'

'What are they like?'

'Most beautiful, china-skinned, rainbow-coloured hair, big dewy eyes, fantastic bodies, lethal. They killed so many ancient Chinese emperors.'

'Oh, yes, I know that.'

'Anyone specific?'

'Not really. I hardly read. The only book I read is the Bible, a translated one in Chinese.'

'What about Nan Zi?'

'Never heard about it.'

'It's a woman.'

*

'A beautiful woman,' I said.

'Oh, yeh?'

'Long dead, she's the wife of Duke Ling of Wey. She has numerous love affairs with other men. Eventually, she dies of sex, or a surfeit of it.'

'I see, not very inspiring.'

'Oh, yeh. She meets Confucius.'

'Confucius the Saint? How does he handle that?'

'He handles it with dignity despite Zi Lu, one of his disciples' sharp criticism. Nan Zi wants to meet Confucius because of the latter's reputation as a sound political advisor. It is said that Confucius enters the palace, sits down and kowtows. Nan Zi, fully dressed, sits behind a screen and does the same. As she does so, her jade pendants fill his ears with a beautiful sound. History doesn't say whether they've made love. But Zi Lu, one of his worst-tempered disciples, attacks Confucius for meeting a lascivious woman when the latter exclaims: Oh, no, no. If I had done anything wrong, let heavens punish me!'

'Interesting.'

'See. That's what I do, to be or trying to be an interpreter and a storyteller as well.'

'But there's no money in storytelling or is there?'

'Yes, there is but not much.'

'How about become a priest?'

'No, not interested. Why would I do that?'

'There's money, plenty of money.'

'I know. But I'm not interested.'

'I'm joking. I meant spiritual money.'

'Spiritual money?'

'Come to my first day and you'll know what it is.'

*

It's a hut, this one, called Our Lady of China, a catholic 'church', found in a hut by the Yarra River. A mud hut woven of the wattle, with yellow flowers here and there peeping out of the cracks, so humble one could smell the mud and the leaves and the water outside in the river. I was there early, wearing my suit and tie. No pigtail. Get Sling, all in black, black-haired, black-eyed, black-gowned and black-shoed, arrived nearly at the same time. It was his day. When others arrived, my fellow countrymen all, and one woman only, a white woman whom I realised was Get Sling's wife.

Without much ceremony, Get Sling plunged into his work straight away. He began by praising God Almighty in as few words as possible before he produced his own interpretation in what I thought and re-membered his literal wording in Cantonese,

> Who do you think God is? He is nothing but a bin. God's bin, God that's bin, God that's a bin. Why bin? Because beings need a bin; beings need bins. God is a collective bin for all. When you feel bad about something that you can't tell anyone else, when you are miserable without knowing why, when you are rich enough to feel sad, when you go through brainstorms and heartstorms to experience the unspeakable, when you find your mind and your

heart clogged up, with things you can never sort out, it is time to go to God and dump them in his bin, the Bin. Then you come away cleansed, cleaned up, completely gratified with the absence of sins because God will get rid of them for you. But if you store them up inside you and never take them out like the garbage or rubbish in your household, they'll rot away until it gets to a point where you are reduced to a bin yourself, bursting with the unwanted stuff.

When I looked away, feeling ashamed of the God-bin comparison, my eyes met the woman's eyes and they locked, in the shortest time possible, before they came apart. In that instant, I saw an apologetic smile, one that seemed to suggest more than a mere apology. Slightly resentful, I think. But, I thought to myself: I don't even know what her name was. How do I know what was going on in her mind and behind her eyes?

*

On my way back to my tent, shared with a few others, I heard the man's voice again. He pointed at me, his index-finger like a dagger, pointing at my nose, jabbing, and said,

You are the worst, of all the people in the world. You swarm our country like flies, locusts, mosquitoes, wild rabbits, rats, maggots, worms, horrible, horrible things. You dream only of money; you live for money; you die for money; you have only one purpose in life: make as much money as possible in the shortest possible time. You have no respect for any religions. You only respect money. You believe in nothing but money. Oh, yes, you do have a religion. It is called Money. Your God is money. You are ugly. Everything about you is ugly. You eat and make noise, like pigs. You look so vastly different, differently ugly, that a glance at your face makes one want to vomit. And you lie, born liars, you lie all the time. Nothing you say is believable. Nothing you do is decent. You are chicken, too. You don't fight; you can't fight; you give up easily and run away at the first opportunity. You have absolutely no heroic qualities. The only qualities you have consist of eating and drinking, qualities of a pig. Your brains are fit not for thinking but for thinking of money. You are the worst, the most inferior people the world has ever seen.

I looked back at the man, at his pointing finger, at his hoarse yelling voice, and I smiled, a not easily detectible smile, as the story of Goujian came to mind.

*

That night, I invited the man – Harry I think his name was – to Small Smoke in Little Bourke Street. He was surprised that I didn't take offence and he was more surprised by the ease with which people treated him. The celestials, full of smiles and pigtails, paused over their pipes, glanced at me entering the house with a white guy and uttered small cries of pleasant surprise before they returned to their pipes, as if nothing had happened. Ah Tong, the head waiter, made a deep bow, with an extended hand to indicate where the opium table and reclining chairs were. When we settled in, he brought us a tea set, with a tea pot and two teacups, filling them with hot tea. While I sipped it from my cup, Harry took a gulp from his, downing the hot tea in one go and spewed it out immediately after, a series of exclamations tumbling off his tongue, 'Oh, God!', 'So bloody hot!', 'So fucking scorching!' 'It's killing me!'

Ah Tong quickly came over, with a hot towel, with which he cleaned up the watery debris and was about to pass Harry a clean white towel to wipe himself when Harry rose and spat, right onto Ah Tong's face, along with a yapping curse word.

That did it.

Ah Tong, a minute ago an urbane, humble, courteous gentleman mastering all the civilised and polite manners in the world, was now turning into a lion. He put both his hands out, grabbing hold of Harry's shoulders one at a time, pulling him out of the opium chair and, lifting him up like a sack of flour, dumped him on the floor, with a heavy thud. Then he went over, one knee pressed on his belly, pinning him down on the floor and staring down the barrel of his face.

'You want me to give you one back?' said he as he cleared his throat and gathered his phlegm in the mouth.

'No, no, sorry,' said Harry.

'I'll pianyi le you this time round,' said Ah Tong, coughing out a thick blob of spit right next to Harry's neck, barely missing him, as he chucked the white towel to him, commanding, 'Wipe it clean. Do it!'

Meekly, Harry wiped the phlegm off the floor and struggled to his feet.

I watched the whole scene without saying a word and it was not till Harry stood up, swaying from side to side, on unsteady feet, that I went over and supported him back to the chair and plonked him down in it.

Utterly subdued, he sat there silent, for a long time, while I showed him how to sip tea from a cup, slowly and patiently, one sip at a time, and how to taste, and enjoy the taste, of hot tea on the tip of one's tongue, turning it around on the roof of one's tongue, before mini-swallowing it the way one swallows an unspat chunk of spit. 'Every-thing that comes with tea,' said I, 'is civility, civilisation.'

Ignoring all that, he said, 'But how did the fucking guy have that strength to pick me up and throw me down?'

'Oh, that is a skill,' I said as I started telling him about martial arts when I thought of something and said, 'Sometimes people don't need any force to work their magic. Once there was a guy who was behaving quite rudely in front of everyone in a shop when the shop-owner came over and patted him on the shoulder, quite gently, and said, also in a very gentle voice, "If you behave yourself you'll have all the respect in the world." The rudely behaving man didn't say anything. He took a look at him and went out. Shortly after, he fell in the middle of the road, like a heap of wet mud. The doctor who saw him could not work out what was going on till he told of the gentle pad on the shoulder when the doctor realised it was an act of magic, something only a well-practised martial artist could achieve.'

'Will you do that on me?' said Harry, his eyes filled with fear.

'No. I love martial arts. But I didn't receive much training and my interest lies elsewhere.'

'Where?'

'I tell you what,' said I as the story of Goujian came to mind, along with what he had yelled into my face the other day. 'There's this king of the State of Wu by the name of Fucha, about 2500 years ago. When his army defeated the army of the State of Yue, Goujian, its king, was taken prisoner. He spent three years living in a thatched hut with his wife by the graveside of Helü, Fucha's father, raising horses. One day, when he heard that Fucha was down with a condition and couldn't be cured, he offered to have a taste of his shit, saying that he had once practised as a doctor. As it happened, he put his hand into Fucha's honey bucket and came out with a handful of honey, or shit, you know, then had a good bite. It was so horridly smelly that Fucha's ministers all covered their noses. After chewing and tasting his honey-shit for a good while, Goujian comforted Fucha by saying that there was nothing serious as the taste of the shit-honey indicated a change of seasons and Fucha would soon recover from the condition. Fucha was so moved and impressed that he said that not even his own son would do things like that. Wu Zixu, a general and political advisor of Fucha's, was not impressed or convinced. He cautioned Fucha that there was trickery in the very act of shit-tasting and that if Fucha was too lenient towards Goujian, he might one day find himself vanquished. Sure enough, 18 years after Fucha set him free, Goujian, King of Yue, wiped out the State of Wu.'

'A typical case of the weak extinguishing the strong?' said Harry as he yawned, and coughed over his pipe.

'Is democracy really democratic?' I thought of the question short of blurting it out.

*

A thought burst by Baohui (3.59pm): Vaguely, I recall having come across a reference to a gold-field Chinese miner as a hero. But, in my busy search for items of the moment, I lost it. Then I thought of the story, 'The Ring Valley'. When I found the book that I thought contained the story, I was disappointed to find only two references to a Loong Hai-Peng, an 'England-educated Chinese merchant...regarded "with highest consideration" and "courage of the highest kind". [Fitzgerald, p. 20 and p. 36]

This made me pause and wonder: Was it because he was a merchant that the word 'highest' was used twice?

A cautionary remark from Stacey in one of the coffee conversations we had on campus, 'Don't know if I need to tell you this, something you would do well to keep in mind. In this country, if you are a male from Asia, choose to write fiction in a foreign tongue, in your case, English, and to pursue a literary career, ten to one you will never get anywhere unless you get a white native speaker to ghost write your personal story, or you revise your story multiple times till it is no longer revisable, taking a decade or so, or you only write an autobiography to give the white Australian, particularly women white Australian readers the pleasure of voyeurism into a total male Asian stranger's life or you give yourself a pseudonym disguising yourself as a woman, which I strongly advise against, and, by all means, kill the male protagonist by creating a female one, or better still, tell a story in the tradition of Yung Chang with mothers, grandmothers and daughters, all in one go. Or else you'd corner yourself till you are left with no readers. But, of course, you don't have to mind it because, after all, you are the writer, not I.'

When I wrote it, I realized she had made a mistake with 'Yung Chang', which really should be 'Jung Chang'.

Chapter 9

Stacey,

Hope this email finds you well. And please find my two recent chapters attached for your perusal and comments. A no hoper myself, I shall try my best.

At the moment, I'm reading another ancient Chinese novel. Titled,《封神演义》, it gives me a pause in translation. The first half, 'fengshen', could be rendered as 'apotheosizing'. But the second half, 'yanyi', is a hard one. If written in the traditional script, the simplified "义" would be "義" and the meaning is more apparent as there is a "我" (I or me) underneath a radical indicating half of what forms of the character for 美（beauty）or 羊（sheep）. Confusing? Yes. But not enough to make no sense as 演（yan） means performing. Hence a performance of 義 in the process of apotheosizing. Or further: a word performance of I-related process of apotheosizing.

So much for this almost meaningless *yanyi* of something untranslatable. For your information, a translation of the title, *Investiture of the Gods*, is findable online at: https://en.wikipedia.org/wiki/Investiture_of_the_Gods

As I know you are learning Chinese, this explanation about the expression 'yanyi' as a word for 'fiction' in its broadest sense is findable in this Chinese-language site here: https://baike.baidu.com/item/演义/2458048

As Ah Sin's story gets in the way, I'll have to give way and let him carry on, my email for later, much later.

Chapter 10

Love hit me like the lash of a whip. With it a mishmash of images flitted across my eyelids: a white face atop a black gown by the side of the little white chapel; a vast plain of golden hairs in summer waves; a boat, a woman, a sea; a carriage piled high with luggage and diggers, with a blue-eyed lass whose eyes were averted; a food stand selling bread and milk behind which she stood in a florid flower dress, in Four Mile Flat, near Avoca; the girl whose name I think was Avoca.

'Are you Avoca?' said I to her, in a bar, after having done a whole day of interpreting at the local magistrates court.

'What made you think of that?' the girl, alone, said to me from across the table.

While I was amazed by my own boldness, having never

spoken more than two words to a woman in my life, let alone a white woman, about my age, I kept wishing that this wasn't just for fun. I stole a glance around me and saw that no one was watching.

'I thought you were because,' said I as I recalled seeing a white girl doing the laundry by the side of the Avoca River.

'Because of what?' the girl said.

'Because of what I don't know,' I said, then added, 'No, I withdraw that. Because of what I dreamt in a dream.'

'Dreamt in a dream?' the girl narrowed her eyes, looking at me through her long lashes. 'But dreams are boring.'

'You think so?' in one glance, I saw she had drunk her coffee to the dregs, so I offered, 'Can I buy you another one?'

'Oh, why not?' said she, not looking at me.

Did I look too keen? I posed myself a mental question and answered it with Ah Fong's voice: You can't afford to show too much passion in the face of love. If you are too enthusiastic, the other party will turn cold, even indifferent. You hold the fire within. You don't even allow the smoke to come out of your eyes. Just observe and take whatever action that suits the occasion.

I ordered a latte for her, the same one I had seen her finish, and ordered myself another long black. While waiting, I held my tongue and looked straight past her letting my eye fall on the passing pedestrians outside the café in the gathering darkness.

'What are you looking at?' said the girl.

'Nothing.'

'No, you are not telling the truth.'

'I am. It's just nothing I'm looking at.'

'Why Avoca, of all the places?'

'Because I lived there once.'

'You did?'

'Yes, digging for gold by the river.'

'You must be a rich man then.'

'Who? Me? No, not me.'

'What do you do for a living?'

'I'm an interpreter.'

'Oh, that.'

'What about you?'

'I'm just a girl, a maid.'

'Not the kind of servant girl working for a rich family, I suppose?' the words stopped short of being blurted out; instead, I said, 'Good on you!'

'What's good about it being someone else's servant?'

'Oh, you are?'

'What about you? Where did you come from?'

'Taishan.'

'Where is that?'

'Far away, on the other side of the world.'

'Like me.'

'Where?'

'Galway.'

'Never heard of that.'

'It's in Ireland.'

'Ire, a land of ire?'

'Don't know what you are talking about.'

'Forget it. I didn't mean it.'

'You speak good English. Your English is better than mine.'

'Oh, no, that's not true.'

'It's true. I didn't used to speak English. I spoke Irish. I still do.'

'What language is that?'

'It's my mother tongue.'

'I have my mother tongue, too.'

'Your mother tongue?'

'Yes, Mandarin, and, more specifically, Cantonese.'

'Well, it all sounds very interesting,' said the girl as she took the glass served, put a spoon of brown sugar in it and was about to take a sip when she said, to herself, 'Oh, no, I have to go.' She shot me a quick glance and went to get a cup.

'Then, I'll see you around?' said I.

'I don't even know your name.'

'Sin, Ah Sin.'

'You come here often?'

'Only sometimes.' Then I told her to drop in on me outside Small Smoke in Little Bourke Street where I'd regularly tell stories.

Her eyes lit up with delight, she said, 'Oh, that must be nice.'

I watched her youthful legs briskly stepping out of the café, my heart as placid as the lake we had once gone past on our way from Robe to the Castlemaine goldfields.

*

I found a place, not far from Small Smoke. I wouldn't mind people seeing me there, people I knew. The more they knew, the better because words travelled. And I needed that. This was a Saturday morning, after a huge downpour the day before that flooded the Melbourne streets and lanes, so much so that there were tiny ponds here and there, small skies on the ground. I shook my bell to catch attention. It's still early. There was only a little boy and a little girl, who appeared as if from nowhere. Both white, both big-eyed, both serious-looking. I thought I was in a dream. I stared hard and they were there, staring back. Pure white, not a trace of anything else. They stared and took their eyes elsewhere before wandering back, to meet my stare again. I smiled. They didn't. Instead, their faces registered the slightest shade of disgust. This fight of staring between us lasted no more than a few seconds when I burst out laughing, pointing to the boy's shoe and exclaiming, 'But the mouth's open and the toes are out!'

The boy looked down as a scarlet cloud crept onto his face and spread all over it in no time.

'Please don't laugh at him, please, will you?' the girl said, looking worried, stressed.

I beckoned the boy to come over and have no fear. When he did, I asked him to sit on my lap, took out my sewing kit and, with a few stitches, quickly sewed the broken toe-part together. Then I put him down and let him walk a few steps.

'No more peep toe, no more peep toe,' the girl cried out, jumping for joy. Then she saw me and all the smile went out of her blue eyes as she was downright serious again.

A middle-aged woman came and removed the two kids from the scene despite their reluctance. I could detect her eyes suffused with disgust as she left as if I were a leper.

*

This is not my (BH's) thought burst. It is part of my exegesis involving my daily desultory reading, e.g. of a novel by a woman with a man's name, Henry Handel Richardson, 'for mixed motives' (http://adb.anu.edu.au/biography/richardson-ethel-florence-henry-handel-8202), a trilogy too long to finish. But I caught its description of the kids' view of the Chinese as bogies in the early days, as contrasted with my view, in the following passage,

The Chinaman jog-trotted towards them, his baskets a-sway, his mouth stretched to a friendly grin. "You no want cabbagee to-day? Me got velly good cabbegee," he said persuasively and lowered his pole.

"No thank you, John, not to-day. Me wait for white man."

"Me bling pleasant for lilly missee," said the Chow; and unknotting a dirty nosecloth, he drew from it an ancient lump of candied ginger. "Lilly missee eatee him...oh, yum, yum! Velly good. My word!"

But Chinamen to Trotty were fearsome bogies, corresponding to the swart-faced, white-eyed, chimney-sweeps of the English nursery. She hid behind her aunt, holding fast to the latter's skirts, and only stealing an occasional peep from one saucer-like blue eye. (Richardson, p. 171)

However bothering these descriptions are, I remain unmoved.

*

I know I was supposed to be happy. But when I saw her, the woman I called Avoca, I felt sad. There was, I think, a river flowing in her eyes from a faraway place, further away than China. A few years ago, there was a murder case in Avoca, involving Ga-Poo at Donkey-woman's Gully. When his body was found, his head was bashed in, swarming with maggots. How could I even begin to tell the story to this innocent woman? And there was also the Blood Hole Massacre that took place near Avoca at Middle Creek, involving a number of Aboriginal deaths. The news had it that they were shot dead one by one in a waterhole as they came out of the water for air. My memory was so full of bloody stories that I didn't want to think of them.

Looking into her eyes, I said, 'Good to see you here again, Avoca.'

'Ciara,' she said, almost soundlessly.

'Ah ha, Ciaravoca,' said I, in jest.

'Don't do that?' she made faces at me.

'Sorry,' said I. 'I didn't mean it.'

130

'Tell me a story as you told them,' she commanded.

'I tell a story and you have it,' said I as I plunged into something that came straight to my head:

Eric came to Australia by ship, an overcrowded ship that stunk with human excrement. In the beginning, he wasn't used to it. As time went by, he got used to it by spending as much time as possible on deck, enjoying the seascape. One evening, as the sun was setting, he was strolling near the stern when a wave came and was about to engulf him, rolling him off board, when he thrust his right hand into the sea water and felt as if everything became frozen in that instant.

The wave, instead of dragging him down to the sea, pushed him back on board, throwing him down on his back, facing a whole sky, a moment he later described as the most significant in his life because he had never so fully stared into the sky till then. It was a totally new and rewarding experience as the emptiness of the sky was so filling, fulfilling.

That night in bed, he kept thinking back on the sudden feeling he had had during the day. Apparently, the cold hand in the sea that grabbed hold of him, while saving him, made his own hand cold, so cold it felt like a long bar of ice. Then, he walked straight into a dream in which he fell in love with a thousand-year-old fox.

Ever afterwards, he walked on the new land of Australia with that cold hand, the blood in it so cold that it would serve as cold drink in high summer if it was drinkable. One day, he went to the local court in support of a mate charged with recklessly damaging private property on account of uncontrollable anger. By the time the case was finished and everyone came out of the court, the plaintiff, a white woman, fainted on the steps as soon as she started walking down them. In a quick glance that saw it all, Eric went up and held the woman in his arms with his right hand. This was a devastating moment that astonished all, as angry, disgusted white glances were shot at Eric from all around except Ah Zhu and his supporters.

But just when a big white man, obviously the woman's husband, was about to intervene, something magical happened. The woman woke up in Eric's arms, held by his icy-cold right arm. And, in a second, she recovered herself and returned to normal, grateful that the strange Chinaman had somehow worked wonders.

The crowd burst into applause, cheering Eric for what he had done. An instant fan went so far as to produce a notebook for Eric to sign his name in. When he did, the fan saw the words come out in a sweeping flow: 'Eric Chong the Magician'.

*

'But why did you say "white"?' afterwards when we met again in a nearby café, she said to me.

'That's nothing derogatory; it's the truth because they were white,' said I.

'You don't like the whites, by the sound of it?'

'Yes and no.'

'Meaning?'

'Well, I like white women,' I drawled out the word 'women' and, then, I said. 'I like you.'

'What do you like them about?'

'What do I like you about?'

'Well, yeeees.'

'I like your golden hair, so golden it reminds me of a summer plain. I like your eyes which are two stars twinkling in the sky of your face. And I like the quick way you smile, almost as if you've only smiled the shadow of a smile.'

'Enough. I can't stand such glib flattery,'

'But I mean it. I've never seen so many beautiful women in Australia. It's so full of them here.'

'You can't love them all, can you?'

'No. And I don't want to do that, either. All I want is to love one woman, to love her and to have her love back.'

As I said this, I held her in my gaze. She returned the gaze. Our eyes

Chapter 11

Stacey,

[from part of the last email sent]

I want to plunge into love full on, I mean love between Sin and Ciara. I'm almost on the point of merging them into one, called Ciarana. But I break off with Chapter 11. That's my way, my textual coitus interruptus. I can make a recommendation to my future publisher, though, that he or she may remove these passages or paragraphs of coitus interruptus at their own discretion should they feel that the interruption or disruption of the story flow might help lose their readership affecting their sales.

Fact is, I'll make them – Sin and Ciara – make love throughout the next chapter. Hold your breath. Now, I think I've lost track of what I was intending to tell you in this part of the email. Oh, yes, I remember now. I was going to tell you about the happy history bit. I recently met a social worker, whose name is Shane. He told me how he had to take notes every day after work with violent families, families with a history of domestic violence, towards the wives, the kids and the men themselves, and of abuse, alcoholic abuse, language abuse, emotional abuse, financial abuse, sexual abuse and physical abuse. After a few years, he was tired out, so tired in fact that he decided to move on and found another job having nothing to do with the violent families and people, vowing never to put down a single word about the shitty lives.

'You see,' he said, looking at me with his big blue eyes. 'That's why I can't stand being a writer. The more you write about the negative things, the more negative you become until you are negativity yourself. Thing is, you can't hope to change people, not even yourself, by constantly complaining, constantly being

unhappy.'
Let me know how you go.
Best,
Z.B.H.

Chapter 12

In bed, after we made love, we watched the sky. Lovemaking, I must say, had always been shrouded in mystery. Kids were born and no one else knew what had happened, not even the kids themselves, least of all them. But why did I dwell on this? We looked into each other's eyes. We held hands. I was beginning to melt, by her smell, by her softness, by the enchanting way she talked. I was so close now I could see the tiny mole on her upper lip to the left, like a black sesame embedded in the flesh. Fingering it, I was about to flip it like a breadcrumb or a grain of rice when I realised that it was part of her the way her eyes, her nose and her mouth were part of her. We – Sin and Gin: Sina. Sinic. Sinary. Sinsational. Love, at its intensest, was nothing short of swallowing.

'I wanted to swallow you whole,' I said to Ciara.

'Why swallow? Isn't that a bird?' Ciara said.

'In Chinese, swallow （嚥） is also a bird, it containing the bird.'

'Swallowing a swallow that is wallowing in a wallow.'

'You are a poet.'

'No, I am not.'

'I just want to swallow you and melt you inside me.'

'No, you won't.'

'Yes, yes, yes.'

'No, no, no.'

'Is this a corset or cover?'

'No idea.'

'What about this, the girdle?'

'No idea, either.'

'Oh, but nothing underneath.'

'Don't know.'

'Oh, but there's so much water, so wet.'

'Don't ask. Don't say.'

My cock, hot as hell and as hard, went past layers of clothing she had on and thrust itself blindly inside her as her tongue shot into my mouth, filling it with her language, her language of flesh, momentarily stopping me from breathing. Her vagina was so warm and wet and tight it wrapped me up deep and dark and warm. Without realising what I was doing, I eased her into a sitting position by holding up her legs, letting her ride me like on a horse in reverse.

Afterwards, we lay side by side in an abandoned barn and watched the sky through the cracks in the roof.

'You know what?' I said to Ciara.

'What?' Ciara said.

'I love you.'

'I love you too.'

'I haven't told you yet.'

'Told me what?'

'The golden hut.'

'Like this one?'

'You wish. And I wish.'

'What is it?'

'It's a hotel built of a mudbrick structure, owned by an Irish couple. It went on the market but no one made an offer. As there were no guests to stay there for a long time, the couple decided to abandon it and went in search of gold in the goldfields. A Chinese gold-digger and his Irish girlfriend went there to shelter from the rain one night. They made love lying down. The girl got hurt in the back by a brick. The Chinese man grabbed hold of the brick from underneath her waist and hurtled it towards the wall. The brick broke in half. But they ignored it and kept making love till it was done. Then they slept. The next morning when the man woke up, he found the empty place flooded with golden sunshine that came through the window, the light particularly golden and strong where the brick lay broken. Careful not to wake up his girlfriend, the Chinese man stood up and went to the broken brick. He was thrilled to find that what was shining was the real gold nuggets, big and small, that lay spilled and scattered from the broken brick.'

'What happened then?'

'No idea.'

'Not true. You made it up.'

'Well, it could be true. A few possibilities: 1. The Chinese man walked off with the gold nuggets. 2. He and the Irish girl identified that the place was full of gold-filled bricks and they went in search of the Irish couple. 3. The girl was in fact the daughter of the Irish couple. And, as the result of this discovery, they made her and her China boyfriend heirs to the fortune.'

'You dream.'

'It's only by dreaming that we can make things happen.'

'No, you can't, not in my case.'

'How you mean?'

'I'm an orphan. I don't have parents. I don't know where I came from. Not even in my dream do I meet my parents.'

'Sorry I touched a sore spot.'

'No, you didn't. I have long meant to tell you all that. For someone like me, there is no future. I'm just a maid and I can see no way out.'

'That's not true. You have me. And you have my land behind you, too.'

'Your land? Flower land?'

'Haha, yes and no. Flower land and celestial empire. Don't you know that once you are married to a Chinaman, you are married to his family and even his country?'

'Oh, no. What a horrible idea is that?'

'It's just a saying, nothing serious. We must get married, shall we?'

'No. But are you serious?'

'Look at me,' said I, looking into her blue-sky eyes. 'Avoca, we must get married even though you don't have parents and I don't have money.'

'Stop calling me "Avoca". But, actually, I start liking the name.'

'You do? Great. When two nothings come together, they make everything.'

'Agreed.'

'Agreed? That's the first time you haven't said a no.'

'No, the second time.'

*

'You know what I dreamt of, Avoca?' I said on another occasion when we met and made love.

'No. How do I know?'

'In the dream, I see myself turn into a bar of gold, my whole person. An entire piece of gold, head to hips, teeth to toe.'

'Why? Isn't that head to toe?

'Boring. English is so boring a language you feel like wanting to make it new all the time.'

'Well, that's how I feel myself sometimes because you know I speak Irish.'

'How do you say, "I love you", in Irish?'

'Is breá liom tú.'

'Oh, no, that's so difficult. I can't say it.'

'And how do you say, "I love you", in Cantonese?'

'Ngo oi nei.'

'Oh, oi nei, oi nei, love you, love you?'

'Om tú, om tú, love you, love you?'

'Yeh-no, yeh no. But yes, yes, push it harder, harder, oh, I'm coming, I'm coming!'

'And I'm coming, tú!'

Afterwards, when the tide of love subsided, I told her of Daji, Minister Su Hu's beautiful daughter that King Zhou of Shang set his sights on and wanted to take as one of his imperial concubines, possibly the chief concubine. As Su Hu rejected the king's offer and took it out on him by writing an angry poem on the wall, he was sent into exile. But Su Hu rebelled and fought back against the king's troops. There were victories and losses on either side till San Yisheng, a military advisor, appeared. He wrote Su Hu a letter arguing for an end to all the conflicts. The letter struck Su as so convincing and rational that he decided to let the king have his daughter. In the middle of the night of his decision, Daji, his daughter, issued a loud cry in her tent. When people came to

138

her aid, she said that nothing had happened except that she had seen a fox. No one believed what she said as there was no trace left of the fox. But, as a matter of fact, Daji died on the spot. In her stead, there was the spirit of a nine-tailed fox, nine hundred years old, because it would take one hundred years at least to grow a tail. The fox thus inhabited her and made her the most beautiful woman ever, with the intention of killing the King Zhou because he was the cruellest and the worst king in history. The story has it that when King Zhou set his eyes on her, his heart became so wildly excited that he couldn't take his eyes off her, dismissed the session with his ministers and went to bed with her straight away. And, for many months subsequently, he did nothing but spend every day in bed with her, making love, and nothing but love, to the great chagrin of all the ministers because he gave them no audience and totally ignored the current political affairs, which explains his eventual downfall with his suicide by self-immolation.

'What is that, self-immolation?'

'He set fire to himself, burning himself to death.'

'Pugh.'

'And it's said that Daji was caught immediately after and taken to the execution ground. But she was so beautiful that the executioners fell in love at first sight and would rather kill themselves than hack her head off.'

'Disgusting.'

'But what is interesting is that King Zhou, when in power, let the woman have the upper hand. He followed her advice and let her have her say and her way. For that, an expression found its way into existence, pinji sichen: Let the hens manage the morning.'

'Meaning?'

'Instead of having roosters crow to usher in the morning, he'll have the hens, or the Hen, do the job.'

'How did that go then?'

'Well, it's only metaphorically speaking. One example suffices. When Daji saw ants crawl onto the fire basket and get scorched to death by the heat, she told the king of it. The king then invented a clever way of punishing the prisoners by having them hug the copper pillar burned hot from inside. That is known as paoluo.'

'Why do I have to know all that?'

'Because it gives women power to know that they were once power-ful.'

'No. But I'm not bad even though I'm not beautiful, either.'

'You ARE beautiful.'

'And you are good, too.'

'Oh, am I?'

'You are.'

*

A memory of something father and mother had shared with me a long time ago as a warning against any literary pursuits. The gist of it, not to dwell on a long drawn-out splash of all the aspects of it, was that, during the Cultural Revolution, scores of men and women of letters, e.g. poets, novelists, literary translators, musicians, artists, historians, philosophers, playwrights, pianists and university professors killed themselves as a result of persecution, some because their work was clas-sified as a big bunch of poisonous grass, others because they had writ-ten anti-Party, anti-Revolutionary stuff and still others because they had translated masterpieces deemed bourgeois and reactionary. They killed themselves in many ways, by domestic gas, by wrist-cutting, by jumping off a tall building, by taking poison, by throwing oneself into a lake or a river, by being beaten to death, by taking large dosages of sleeping pills, by jumping into a well, by hanging themselves, by star-vation, by purposefully going missing, by cutting the femoral artery, by throwing themselves headlong into an oncoming train, by lying across the railway lines and being crushed into pieces by a rushing train—the list went on till I said today, 'Would a fortune-teller see if someone was about to commit suicide by a simple look at his or her face?'

Both Mum and Dad burst out laughing, finding it so cruelly irresist-ible that a boy like me could be so funny. Mum said, rushing ahead of Dad, 'You have a head full of weird ideas, which is good for one who wants to be a writer in the future—' Before she was able to finish her words, Dad cut in, saying, 'I don't think it's a good idea. The past is a mirror in which you'll see your future when you grow up.'

I was glad that I had recalled that incident. Although I didn't remember any names of those people, I had somehow learnt about the ways of self-killing, which, in a way, was much more interesting than the names.

The second the word 'self-killing' entered my brain I was like an engine ignited. I immediately went online and checked things out. Things seemed to have relaxed after the Port Arthur Massacre as a lot of websites in this country did sell guns. I quickly settled for something not too cheap nor too expensive, a Smith & Wesson Mod 17-6 Revolver, with brown wood grip, a six-shot double-action revolver, and a used one at that, my toy gun for the moment. When it was delivered and unwrapped, I held the thing in my hand. It felt cold and totally impersonal but it scorched me the second I touched its body, so I instantly put it down and waited a long time before I picked it up again. I did not put down thoughts that went through my mind in that pause, that wait. But if I did I would have had to use words like stunning, amazing, and all the usual suspect words.

*

'You know what I like about you, Sin?' said Ciaravoca, a name I called her whenever we met and now we met for a third time and made love again. In fact, that's what we always did, first thing.

'What?'

'You don't know that yourself?'

'No,' I said and paused. Then I said, 'But I can guess.'

'You can?'

'Well, you like me because I'm rich, my body a bar of gold, even my eye.'

'I know. I remember that story of yours.'

'The eye? Oh, yes, the eye. The Chinaman who went back to China after spending a few years digging for gold in Ballarat and when he left Australia he had nothing on his back, just a roll of rotten clothes and sheets and he went blind in one eye.'

'No, stop. Don't tell me again.'

'Then he went home in Taishan perfectly safe and sound because he was so poor no one would touch him. In fact, the bandits wouldn't even look at him. When his parents saw him they were horrified by the sight of him. His mother wept uncontrollably, both because of the pleasure at the reunion and sadness at the sorry sight. His father, though, wasn't particularly convinced because he saw a faint smile on the son's face. It was not till both of them calmed down that he dug the eyeball out of the eye socket. He got his mother to fill a big bowl with clean water, in which he washed the ball, then wiped it clean with a rag till it shone. It's a ball of gold, weighing nearly a kilo! And the rags on him contained thick foils of gold, too.'

'No, you never told me that. And it can't be a kilo or else it would have long sunken into his guts from the socket.'

'What does the weight matter? It's a legend, isn't it? All it means is that this guy is clever and knows how to take advantage of the harsh circumstances.'

'And what else?'

'Oh, yes, I have powerful connections back in China, so powerful that they can make the English king kowtow to them when they go there to pay them respects.'

'And?' said she, with an audible yawn.

'Of course, I have women, women over here and over there, women galore — ouch, why did you pinch me so hard? It's sore.'

'Say that again! I'll give you another pinch, harder, and I'll slap you across the face, too.'

'I'm only joking. But why are you so jealous?'

'Because I love you, Idiot!'

'Well, it's all your fault. You asked what it is that I like you about and I told you.'

'But none of what you said is true. You have little money; your family is poor, and you have no more women than me, if that's what you want to know. Still, I like you for your honesty because you said you were beaten up in a group attack by the whites and that you were afraid of them. You could have pretended that you were afraid of nothing; you didn't. I like your way with words. I think I'll learn English from you, too. But, most important of all, I love the way you are who you are, not someone else because you can't. I think we must live together and start having kids. What do you think?'

'Done, done, done,' said I, emphatically, and then, 'You know what that sounds like in our own language?'

'What?'

'It sounds like the gong when struck, on celebratory or festive occasions, in my home county. It gives the sound of "dang, dang, dang", very loud and resounding.'

'Where shall we find a place?'

I told her my idea.

Chapter 13

I, Baohui, to myself: I have decided to change my mind and delete the whole thing with strikethrough, beginning with these bits: 'D̶i̶a̶r̶y̶ ̶e̶n̶-̶ ̶t̶r̶y̶ ̶(̶1̶7̶/̶5̶)̶:̶ ̶S̶h̶e̶'...[503 words removed]

Mini-diary entry (10.50.44am, same day): I'm thinking of where to get Ah Sin to live with Ciara O'Reilly, not her real name but her name anyway for the time being. I'm thinking of settling them in a hut built on the Yarra River, somewhere near Richmond, after a style Ah Sin prefers because it resembles the monk in *Investiture of the Gods*, in which he lives a life of picking the fresh flowers to decorate his hat and gathering the wild grass to lawn his bed. The life itself is simple enough to be ignored. Who is interested in a life spent getting up before sunrise, setting fire to a small woodpile, cooking the breakfast, going to the loo, coming back to wash, man going to the city to make a living and woman staying behind to look after the hut, especially when it is daily? Of a million and one details, I have one that insists on me writing about. I remember from my imagination that, on a May morning, suffused with a soft sunlight that makes the golden more golden and the green more green in the surrounding areas, he bids goodbye to his new wife and goes on his way to the asylum to see his good friend Ah Mao, now a mental patient housed permanently in the mental home.

*

When I arrived at the asylum, I said to myself: What a beautiful place this is! A white solid building of three-storeys occupied the central position behind the main gate. Part of the Yarra ran quietly outside the solemn wall, underneath the thick leaves of a large-toothed poplar and a huge oak tree, its spreading branches and darkening leaves provided a canopy for the morning entrance. I was stopped by a man who eyed me suspiciously and asked what business I had there. I told him that I wanted to see Ah Mao because he was an old mate in my gold-digging days. He asked me to put down my name on an open book, with the time and date and the name of the person I wanted to see, which I duly entered. I paused when I saw the blank space for 'Occupation'. 'A story-teller?' No, I said to myself silently. Instead, I put down 'Interpreter'. The guard looked at me again, this time with more respect, though still grudgingly. Before he let me in, he asked me to open my cloth bag. I showed him. There were three purple potatoes, white-skinned and purple-fleshed, a bunch of red, hot chilies and a number of small oranges I picked from my tree in the morning.

The guard waved me in.

After more stoppages and book-filling, I was shown in a side room and told to wait.

This was, as I could see, a bare room with only two chairs sandwich-ing a table. Through the window, I could see a gum tree with a half-burnt trunk oozing sap that looked like dark-brown honey. It would conveniently serve as an interview room in a police station if two more chairs were pulled in. I thought of the interviews I had helped the police with. One in particular stood out. The man was charged with molesting a boy because he had touched him on the top of his head and on one of his cheeks. Apart from interpreting for both the policeman and the Chinese man, I gave an explanation about how this was far from molesting; it was an act of endearment that very much accorded with the ancient tradition in which the elderly showed caring love for the young. The man walked off after he was given a warning.

My train of memory, or memory-thought, was interrupted when the door was swung open. A man was led in whom I had difficulty rec-ognizing: a mop of straggly hair covering half of his face and a beard that was dense and long, with clothes hanging loose on him. It was not till he opened his mouth and uttered something close to my name that I recognized the tone of his voice and saw the pockmarks on his face.

I *zuoyi*ed, making a bow with both hands folded in front of me. He didn't *zuoyi* back but just slumped in a chair. The doctor who took him in said to me, in a cold voice, 'I'll lock you two in so he can't run away.'

Instinctively, I took a look at the window and saw that it was barred.

'Why do I want to run away?' the man who was supposed to be Ah Mao said. 'The bloody place is so safe.'

'How are you these days?' I said.

'No idea.'

'Good food? Good sleep?'

'Awful food. Sleeping all day.'

'How's the other inmates treating you?'

'_____'

'And the doctors and nurses?'

'Don't know.'

'Tell me what happened.'

'The fucking gold. It's all having to do with the fucking gold. I carried off with that piece of shit and went north.'

'You did?'

'I did *ge pi*. I just wanted. I wanted to do bushranging.'

'That's risky.'

'I don't care. I wanted to go home. With my piece of shit gold. I wanted a woman. I wanted good food. I wanted comfort. I wanted everything I had at home.'

'But you can get them here.'

'In this country? You've got to be joking! Only sunshine. Down to earth, into earth. Up with shit. Then taken. Rushed and taken. Raided and taken. Beaten and taken. Tailings and very little.'

'What about bushranging? Faring better?'

'I got bushranged and I got bushranging. They robbed me of the piece of shit. I robbed them. I ate leaves. I ate grass. I ate leather. I ate tree bark. I drank my own piss once, when cornered. I drank from the creeks. I did stuff with a kitchen knife. I didn't kill. I just struck fear.'

'Poor Ah Mao,' said I, and as I said so, I opened the bag for him to see. 'A bag of small gifts for you.'

He didn't so much as glance at it but went on, 'They caught me and put me on trial. But nothing I said made sense. They got a doctor. The doctor said I was mad. They didn't put me in jail. They put me here.

They got me a priest and made me believe, so I believed. You think I'm mad?'

'Of course not.'

'I am mad. If they say you are mad, then you are mad. It's good to be mad when you are not because you get everything for free. You don't have to work for the rest of your life. You just eat, drink, piss and shit. Then you sleep. You are finally home. Mental home is a right description because you are mentally home. You have birds singing to you every day, in bird language you are not forced to learn. You eat medications like you eat food. And you see how I tremble? I tremble like I'm dancing. Am I not artistic?'

'No, you are not.' My heart was pinched in that moment, twisted like with a dagger.

'Yes, I am. I sing, too. Why, I mean, isn't this a great country where gold is aplenty and aplomb, where some will always make sure they dig more than you because the rules of the game make sure they do, and where if the rules fail the fists win.'

'But,' I stopped short of trying to say that the word 'aplomb' wasn't an adjective.

He ignored me and went on, 'It's a country of imagination, do you understand, where anything is possible. I am the king of this home because I rule myself to be a madman. I do all sorts of things. I sing to the birds in my own lingo that no one understands here. That no bird understands, either. I dance on the strength of the medications. No one dares get near because my dancing limbs might thrash and crash onto their faces or bodies smashing them. And I sleep and dream. More than once I meet the Chinese emperor Xianfeng in my dream, who asks me to keep peace in Australia. When I wonder when he'll pay me a visit, he says he has no interest in a foreign country on the fringes of civilisation, least of all in a convict-ridden place. When I woke up I found what he said is true. No emperors of China since 1788 have ever visited this country, not Emperor Qianlong, not Emperor Daoguang, not Emperor Jiaqing, not Emperor Xianfeng, and I doubt if any afterwards will do. They are content with sending the lowest of the low as their representatives.'

'The lowest of the low is sometimes the highest of the high,' said I, blurting out the unthought thought, the instant one.

'There may be something in what you said,' said Ah Mao, hit hard by the undertone.

Both of us said nothing for a long time afterwards. He looked down at his own toes and I looked down at the opening of the bag, the peeping chilies, oranges and potatoes. It dawned on me that I should serve him an orange, so I picked up one, peeled it and passed the peeled one to him, watching how he would take it.

He brushed my hand aside with the peeled orange, then bent and took a red chili from the bag and began chewing on it. I was horrified to see him swallow the chewed lot as beads of sweat stood out on his forehead.

'Are you okay?' I asked with concern.

'Don't you worry. If I don't do so, they won't believe how mad I am. If they want me to eat shit, I'll eat it for them, too. To their face, in their very presence.'

'Better eat the hands,' said I.

'Hands? What hands?'

'You remember Jing Ke and the beautiful hands of the woman?'

'Oh, that. Yes, if I were him I'd order for the hands to be cooked and eat them.'

'Oh, no,' said I, groaning in disgust. Then I thought of something and said, 'How about the other mates we were digging together with?'

'No idea. No one came to see me.'

'Where are they now?'

'No idea. Don't ask me these questions. Don't want to know. Who wants to see me, as insignificant as an ant and as mad as a hot chili?'

'Ah Kut did express his wish to see you.'

'Ah Kut? Who's that?'

'Charlie Kut, the Chinese-Aboriginal half-caste, you remember?'

'No. I don't.'

'I read his face in your presence.'

'Well, very faintly I can recall something. You did read but you didn't say anything. And he got upset.'

'That's right because he's got all the bad signs of having a small and sharp head, and a long neck, signs of abject poverty, as physiognomy books told me. But I didn't dare tell him the real truth, which is why I offered him tobacco. Now, his nickname is the philosopher.'

'Oh, yes, the philosopher. I seem to remember. Half face yellow, half face black, eyes more white than black, and facial skin like an orange peel.'

'You've got such an amazing memory!'

'I think he owes me a meal.'

'Oh, don't worry about that. He couldn't afford it anyway. We always give him free meals whenever he comes to our camp.'

'Did he always stink?'

'Yes and no. But he stank with thinking, thoughts, I mean.'

'You mean? What you mean?'

'It's you, I think, that gave him the nickname "the philosopher" because he was single, vowing he'd remain single for the rest of his life, like most of the philosophers we heard about, such as Lao Tzu, Chuang Tzu'

'No. That's not right. You think I've gone crazy? I am saner than all of you put together because I know and I remember that Chuang Tzu was married. When his wife died in his arms, he burst out laughing and went out onto the street, singing in a loud voice as he kept knocking on an empty basin. Why? Because he was happy and because he believed that his wife, on her death, would turn into a spirit, merging into the air, the earth and the clouds, which is why he was happy and he wanted to congratulate her on such a wonderful transformation.'

'Well said, Ah Mao, well said! In a way, you are more philosophical than the philosopher.'

'Why did he mention me?'

'Because he said that you represented the failure of the society in which we are living.'

'Is that it?'

'And also because he thought that there is no place in this society for people like us, like you, and like him, even less likelihood for people like him as he didn't belong to either blood, Aboriginal or Chinese.

Rejected by both, he has only his mind to explore for the thoughts that would not visit either.'

'I'm listening.'

'Whenever he comes to visit us in one of his walkabouts, he brings a little notebook with him, in which he puts down whatever that goes through his mind.'

'Yes?'

'I think he has an enormous contempt for gold and the craze for it. He told me that he would never spend a single day digging for gold. Why bother fighting your lives over a rotten piece of stone? His father's teachings about spiritual freedom may have had a lot of influence on him and his mother's dreamtime, too, would have been strongly at work in his general views of the world.'

'I'd like to see him one day, again.' With that, Ah Mao held his head in his trembling hands, complaining about a fierce headache as I rose to say goodbye.

*

A reminder to myself [BH]: Don't you forget that although there is little gold to dig for anywhere in Australia today much gold can still be found in history if one works hard enough and is prepared to work hard enough to dig into the past, the gold of thought, of buried breaths, and of untold tons of unspoken words. And also the fact that I have to shed the 'huge tree' image as not befitting the times, as suggested by S.

*

[499 Chinese characters cut, with the BH translation that follows in the next section—SA]

There was a creek at the foot of the hill. It didn't have a name. I said: Let's call it Dengtong Creek! Our team had a habit of giving everyone the right to name a place if it didn't have a known name, whether it was a hill or a creek or a stone and whether they used their own names or the names of their own home villages; they could even name the place after a meaning they had in mind. In any case, everyone had the right to do the name-giving by turns, like playing a game. Old Man, our teammate, called it Soul-broken Hill because the hill looked like something that would make one lose his soul. Old Man wasn't old. He was only twenty-five or twenty-six years old. But he looked like someone in his fifties or even sixties. This was because he had deep wrinkles on his forehead and had lost a few teeth, probably as a result of fighting. Hence his nickname 'Old Man'. While no one was watching, I went to the creek, just to have a look whereas in fact I was meaning to take a crap. The creek was wide, with a sluggish waterflow, with shifting sands and pebbles everywhere. In a broken bank where there was some coverage, I took off my pants and squatted, shitting as I watched the water meandering as it flew away into the distance. Occasionally, there was the sound of a plonk somewhere. I could tell that it was the swimming of a fish and, by the sound of it, the fish was quite big.

The air here was so fresh and one had an eyeful of greenness, the sky transparently blue. I had a smooth shit and was quickly done. Because I didn't have any straw paper with me, I went to the creek side and squatted again. I scooped the water with my right hand and washed between my buttocks, then washed them again, and again — hey, what's that? Something so heavy in my hand! I raised my cupped right hand beneath my nose and was stupefied: as water drained from my fingers, there was a huge heap of sunshine! How did the sunshine get on my palm? So dizzy, I didn't know what was going on. I smelt my hand. It stank. I 'oh'ed and put it down because I realized that there was shit in my fingernails, not washed clean, at the same time when I noticed that there really was a stone in my hand, a stone that shone golden. It's not the sunshine; it's the shine of gold. Make no mistake! It's the light of gold, real gold. 'Aye, aye, aye!' I couldn't help calling out, in a loud voice, till I drew all the attention from them when Old Man and Ah Gui rushed running over, wondering what had happened. When they got near, they were delighted: Ha, there is gold!

Holy shit, wasn't this a gold creek! Everything was gold except the running water. If you dug your hand into the mud on the creek bed, came out with a handful of mud, then let the water wash it away, soon your hand would be left with nothing but gold, the size of a quail egg or a pea. As soon as the news was out, the team went wild with joy. They all rushed in and did not stop till the moon reached the top of the hill. Even under the moonlight, the gold shone, with a mingled light of gold and silver.

Chapter 14

[Continuation of an intermittent email, never sent, from Baohui to Stacey].

[Unfair and unfavourable remarks on Australia and its culture, 315 words cut—SA]

For fear of a backlash, I didn't venture to make my characters suffer worse. Ah Mao, for example, was at one stage put in a straitjacket because he was rebellious. The doctor-in-charge, Dr White, said to the other nurses: 'Teach the Chinaman a lesson and put him in the jacket.' Despite his struggling and yelling, Ah Mao was eventually reduced to a mass of trembling flesh and bones, pinned down with the bed restraints, his mouth gagged and all his limbs tied up tight, all because he had only uttered a single remark: I hate this place like hell!

'If you hate,' Dr White said. 'you get what you deserve.'

Ah Mao was psychologically and psychiatrically correct when he mispronounced the word 'history' as 'hatestory', steeped in hate that turns into erasure.

Then, on another occasion, when Ah Mao was captured by the guards in a failed attempt to run away, he was chained to a tree, a naked gum tree standing in the middle of the hospital grounds, his mouth again gagged for fear of him uttering any unpleasantries, even in his native Cantonese. When they bound him up, they did it in such a way that he was holding the tree face in, like he was hugging it. I hate to tell you this but please forgive me if you are offended. In that hugging state in which he, gagged, could do nothing but maintain the hugging position he got a hard-on and rubbed himself against the trunk till he ejaculated, wetting his pants, in full view of the audience, the hospital staff and the motley crowd of the patients, some of whom burst into an uncontrollable laughter watching the semen-stained spectacle.

I practiced self-censorship by not allowing it in the main stream of the story.

You'll probably remember if you have read where Ah Sin mentions the word 'paoluo', in that conversation he has with Ciaravoca. The way Ah Mao is chained to the tree echoes the way people were put to death in King of Zhou's time when, for example, Mei Bei, an old stateman who had served three different emperors, was put to instant death because of his sharp criticism of the king for indulging in too much sexual pleasure with the imperial consort without attending to state affairs by having him hugging a copper pillar burned red hot from the inside, an idea Daji, King of Zhou's favoured royal consort, had when she spotted ants burnt to death when they crawled up to a fire basket. The ancient line of thinking always puts the blame on the women by suggesting, based on a Chinese expression that goes, 'zui du moguo furen xin' (nothing is more poisonous than a woman's heart), that women are capable of the worst things or thoughts possible.

I showed my correctness by not following that line. And, curiously enough, another cautionary remark, made by Stacey in another coffee conversation on campus, emerged deep from my memory, to the effect that to be experimental is to be mental (see the word already containing it 'experi/mental'), something essentially at odds with neoliberalism and liberal democracy whose essential values are money-based whereas anything wildly experimental is basically a self-pleaser, like shoes with impossible heels. Fiction, by its nature, does not sit comfortably with experimentation. If you think you can experiment with coffee-making until you produce something undrinkable you'd have to drink it all by yourself because no one else would. To write a work of fiction is to produce something drinkable, simple as that. Or you'd end up in the sky because sky would be your vastest reader, like it or not. Just leave your book open in the open and let the sky look down on it or overlook it or both.

*

I, as usual, went to Eastern Market to deliver my morning stories to whoever was willing to listen and pay. To save my breath, I'd quote a passage about the market written by a reporter from the Argus, who compared it to London's Covent Garden, saying that produce from,

> many acres of land, within an easy distance of the city (that were) under cultivation by market gardeners – at Moorabbin, Dandenong, the Plenty, Victoria, Heidelberg, Northcote, Merri Creek, Kew, Hawthorn, Richmond and Keilor. Our market site is within one-fourth as extensive a site as Covent Garden and when, as on a brisk market morning, it is attended by 700 drays loaded with produce, it affords a pleasurable surprise to any visitor who was previously unaware that a market of like pretentions was to be found in Melbourne. Some details of the quantities of the principal items may not be uninteresting... In the season about 1,200 loads of vegetables come into the market weekly (about seven or eight hundred weight each), consisting of every variety of vegetables known to Europeans, and the greater part of them in greater perfection than in the London markets; 500 geese and turkeys, 1,000 ducks and fowl, 1,000 dozen eggs, 100 suckling pigs, with an altogether unascertained but very appreciable number of rabbits, wild fowl, guinea fowl, pigeons, &c.; nearly half a ton of fresh butter is sold here every week, and honey in considerable quantities is brought through this channel before the public.[1]

I found a place near a fruit stand by the post and laid a silk cloth on the ground with a white porcelain bowl, with a few coins in it, suggesting payment. I didn't wear my western suit and tie. Deliberately, I put on my fake pigtail, my melon hat, my long silken gown and my pair of thick-soled black short boots, a prototype of a celestial from the Celestial Empire. Then, without further ado, I started chanting to the people who went in and out of the market, my voice not too loud but audible enough for people to hear what I was on about: 'Come and

---

1 Quoted from this link: https://en.wikipedia.org/wiki/Eastern_Market,_ Melbourne

hear my story of an ancient country, a country larger than any in the world, with the largest population, too. But their stories are as small as our own lives here, with plenty of tears and much laughter. If you care to listen you'll come away with more than you actually carry from the market.'

I waited, till there were three people who stopped to listen, a woman in them, then I started telling this story of love and judgement:

Once upon a time in the Song dynasty, about four or five hundred years ago, there were a man and a woman in love. Their love soon led to lovemaking. When they reached the highest intensity of love, the man said to the woman, 'I shall love you forever till I die and shall never think of leaving you for someone else.' The woman said the same, vowing never to break up.

They got married and had two sons. About 10 years after the marriage, the man died. The woman, with their two sons, lived with the man's parents.

Soon, matchmakers came to the door, offering ludicrous deals to the woman who was still relatively young. To her mother-in-law's surprise, she showed no reluctance in considering their offers and actually invited them to show themselves.

Despite repeated objection from her mother-in-law, the woman eventually settled for a lucrative deal by marrying a local tycoon and walking away without her kids.

She had the time of her life on the wedding day and the subsequent week, her box filled with gifts from all the guests. On the eighth day, though, her husband went on business, leaving her alone at home, feeling quite sad and looking forward to his return, when a young man came and hand-delivered a letter to her. On opening it, she received a shock because the letter was from her dead husband.

There's nothing but a poem in the letter. Because I guess no one likes poetry, I'll simply tell you the gist of it. The dead man basically accuses the woman of betrayal, not only to herself and to him but also to their two sons, adding that he has been to the court in the netherworld where a judgement has been made against the sinful woman to strip her of all her riches and reduce her to abject poverty.

'What happened to the woman?' wondered aloud the woman in the gathering audience.

'Oh, she couldn't eat or drink anything for days, her heart full of repentance, wishing she had never committed the sin. And she died shortly after.'

'That's not fair for her,' said the woman.

'Well, she deserves it, doesn't she?' a loud voice interrupted her.

I opened my eyes, and saw a big man in blue overalls throw a dirty look towards the woman by his side before he set to go, with half a sheep's leg wrapped up in a cloth bag.

'You know what you need to say when you talk about the woman in "abject poverty"'? the woman ignored the man and said.

'What, madam?'

'Just use the word destitute', said she, adding, 'but how cruel the man is!'

I wasn't sure who she was referring to, the man in overalls or the dead husband in the story.

*

The next day, after I assisted in a short interview with the police, in which a Chinese shop-owner was bashed up, his goods stolen by a white guy, I went to see Ah Fong, who was now running a restaurant near St Kilda Beach.

After we parted company in the goldfields, we had not caught up for quite some time. I missed his talk about politics and wars. I recalled something he said at one stage about Australia: This is not a country. It's only a colony. It has minds from everywhere but its own. Who wants to stay in this colony for long? I won't. My home country is infinitely better. Good food, good women, good fun along the way, and good everything. Even fighting a war is more interesting than simply fighting for gold.

'Why did you come in the first place then?' I recalled Ah Toy saying.

Afterwards, a long silence, in which birds were heard. No one spoke till eventually Ah Fong said, 'You don't ask why the rain rains and where the rain originally comes from. Things just happen and one doesn't really know why. Do you know why you were born in China, not in England?'

When I reached Feesh and Cheaps, Ah Fong's shop, it was noon. As soon as he saw me, Ah Fong gave out a cry of delight.

'Hi, old mate, long time no see!' he exclaimed.

'Wow, now, you've struck it rich, mate,' said I.

'Oh, no, no, no, far from it.'

'I like the name of your shop.'

'Just a wild thought, you know.'

'Fee in fish, hee hee.'

'And cheaps.'

He poured me a mug of red tea as I sat down and scanned the fish he had underneath the counter behind the glass: flathead, flake, whiting and snapper.

'Better than gold, hey?'

'Well, at least plenty in the sea. You never run out of it.'

'Oh, sea, oh, sea.'

'Want to go out and have a see-see?

'Maybe afterwards? I'm a little hungry.'

'Oh, sure, you'll have heaps to eat here.'

He made busy preparing the meal, putting a fillet of flake in the wok to deep-fry it while scooping up the deep-fried chips, all sunny, into a large basin. Then he came to my table with a large plate divided into one part of flake and one part of chips, sprayed with dark-red tomato sauce, a bit of salt and a bit of pepper, before he went back behind the counter to serve the other customers.

I set to and ate everything up in no time. As I ate by myself, a sound became familiar that was at the same time strange because people seemed to address him in a different appellation from the one that I had been used to. It sounded more like Affan than Ah Fong. I lit up a pipe of tobacco, mixed with a tinge of opium, and waited for the shop to get less busy. But it never did, so I decided to go out for a stroll on the beach.

This was a day in late May, not too cold nor too hot. The sun felt good on the face. The breeze also felt good as it came blowing from the sea. What amazed me was not that I was once again at the seaside after about a decade spent chasing after the gold, in the goldfields, then in the city, but the absolute blueness of the sea water, in wavelet after wavelet that kept pushing one another as it rolled towards the beach without stop, breaking into transparent flowers that died instantly as they receded. I went to the edge of the water, and, dipping a finger in it, I sucked on the fingertip. Instantly, the salty taste reminded me of my first arrival in Robe years ago when the future appeared so bright and everything seemed possible. Now, I looked down at my own shadow in the water and said to it: You are but your older self and getting older.

After wandering aimlessly around the beach, looking up and down at the sky, the sea and the horizon, I came back to the shop.

'How did you go?' said Ah Fong.

'Not too bad,' said I.

'Meaning you didn't like it much?'

'Oh, I like it a lot. But I just got a feeling that nothing much is going to change and we are in a fix.'

'As a much-maligned race, that's your fate and that's your destiny.'

'Mine only, not yours as well?'

'Good question,' said he as he lit another pipe and took another sip from his mug of tea. 'Did you know that Ah Toy is dead?'

'Oh, no. What happened?'

'He left us in Castlemaine and went onto Ararat. They struck it rich there, with what was known as the Canton Lead. Not long after, their tent was raided by a gang of thugs in the middle of the night, who took their possessions, set fire to the tent and when the Chinese diggers hit back, one of them received a blow to the head and died subsequently.'

'I'm sorry to hear that, really sorry,' said I, with a rising lump in my throat, my eyes moistened.

'I've contributed 10 pounds to the local community to part-cover the funeral cost.'

'That's very generous of you. Has the funeral already been done or is it going to happen? I might contribute something.'

'No, done already.'

We lapsed into a silence. I smoked and looked at the burning tobacco send forth a plume of smoke, and he did the same. There was only the sucking noise in the air. The atmosphere was so oppressive I felt the need for a change of topic.

'Have you found a partner now?' said I, knowing that many of our old mates had.

'No, no luck with either gold or women,' said he.

'I don't believe you.'

'Well, there once was one and we loved passionately, only to find that she left me for someone else.'

'A white girl, I guess?'

'Oh, yes, an English girl.'

'Any particular reasons?'

'Nothing in particular except that she seemed to have a preference for women, not men.'

'Oh, I see. A bit strange.'

'Not really. It happens even if it is one in a million as the case may be.'

'Now, you seem to have changed your name because I heard them address you as something different from Ah Fong, right?'

'Yes, it's Affan now. Easier for them, you know.'

'I think it sounds better. And it prompts me to have a rethink on my own name, possibly not Ah Sin any more but simply Ahsin. How's that sound?'

'Perfect!'

I couldn't help smirking when I saw an uncontrollable laughter emerging in his slit-eyes and bursting out of his nostrils. I laughed along with him, too.

*

[Part of the long email continued from the previous one]:

If Affan appears faintly familiar, it is because you may have read it somewhere. It is, to be more exact, salvaged from literary memory of a piece of writing by a very obscure writer whose name is almost on the edge of extinction: Elinor Mordaunt. In one of her stories, she depicts love at first sight between a Chinese man by the name of Affan and a white girl. I quote two salacious passages below for your appreciation,

> Talk of love at first sight! It was love and life both together in a flash. He [Affan] remembered the way that during a single night, the willows had sprung into leaf along the streams near his house in Southern China. Bare wand, and then, in a breath, as it were, that wonderful silken fringe of pale gold leaflets: life a stark rod, and then, of a sudden, clothed, most wonderfully clothed. That was Rosie Pye, the first bud on a bare bough, and all the sap of his being drawing towards it.[1]

And her response is equally enthusiastic:

> The way in which Rosie bloomed under the persistent, beneficent, mild beams of such a sun of love, was almost beyond belief. She must have literally fed upon it…her figure grew fuller, showing more delicate curves, and firmer, whiter; her lips deepened to the colour of a japonica bloom; her cheeks flew a faint flag of colour, her hair was bright as corn. She moved with assurance—the difference between somebody's dog and a stray whom nobody wants; little airs of innocent coquetry burgeoned about her; she held her head high, as all well-loved women have a right to do; while if she was the Moon of Affan Ming's Delight, swaying the tides, the many-tempered tides, within him—he, Affan Ming, small and slant-eyed John Chinaman, was the sun of her existence.[2]

---

1 'The Ginger Jar', in *Old Wine and New Bottles*. London: Hutchinson, 1919, p. 209.
2 Ibid, pp. 211-212.

There you are, Affan for my own purpose, and a footnote to literary history: a literary movement backwards, the possibility of a dream put a hundred years back in the head of a dreamer long dead. And what happens with the woman who left Affan is witnessed in an episode from *A Land of Gold-diggers* I hereby provide a translation of,

She lay in bed, side by side with Rose, both exhausted by their own lovemaking efforts. One of them had a skin as white as snow and the other, a skin as black and smooth as silk. The one's nipples were big and round and the other's, as tiny as the seeds. One plump-bodied and the other, muscular; one with eyes as those of a deer, and the other, as slitty as those of a bee. One from Ireland and the other, China. One abandoned, and the other, self-abandoned. One twenty-eight and the other, twenty-four. One in love, and the other, also in love. She, Ah Ru, by now could talk about her views and what she thought in clear enough English and could also briefly describe her own experience in English. Moreover, she could tell all sorts of ghost stories she had heard back in her home village when she was a child. After they finished making love, she went to the window, in all her nakedness, and pulled the curtain slightly ajar, as a soft sound reached her ears: Put on your clothes and don't catch cold.

When she crept back into her quilt — not really a quilt but a sheet on top of a blanket — Rose turned around, and, with a naked arm encircling her head, kissed her on her mouth, saying, 'Baby, I love you.' Ah Ru put out her tongue for her to suck as she said, 'I love you, too, Baby.' Every time she said that, she experienced a sense of discomfiture, not particularly happy with herself. Can't I go without the word 'too'? Even if it was a very insignificant word, it's something one couldn't overcome, like a barrier, for it's the basic element of a response, without which the whole thing would sound fake. She would very much like to share this thought with Rose in English but her thoughts, clear enough, were not possible to be clearly put in the language. She gave up. Just then, there came the ethereal calling of a rainbird outside the window, which made her giggle. Rose wondered what it was that made her laugh. She said: The bird seems to be speaking Chinese as every time it sings there are three characters in the song, 'jiao jiao wa' (delicate, delicate girl), or 'qiao qiao hua' (secretive, secretive flower), and sometimes more like 'qiao qiao ta' (see see her). In any case, it sounds different each and every time.

Rose was someone who could talk with her body. When she heard what she said, she didn't say anything; instead, she held her body closer to Ah Ru. The latter's body couldn't help trembling despite itself, her legs naturally parted and a spring started oozing out of her valley, never touched by a man, moistening the dryland around, waiting for Rose to explore it with her mouth, her tongue.

When the common expression refers to women as the long-tongued, it ignores another side of them. Take Rose, whose long tongue was wordless, languageless, like a long snake right now, curvaceously exploring the abundant valley of Ah Ru, playing with her labia majora and minora as she swallowed the yin-liquid surging from it like a spring while pushing her own hot waves into Ah Ru's night channel. In the orgasm-after-orgasm storm, Ah Ru died and came to life, again and again, and worked to bring Rose to the peak of passion. The whole night, including that morning, they, in the carnival of sex, met their demise together and returned to life in the house-falling and mountain-collapsing catharsis, to the exclusion of everything else in the world, entering into a space of two in extreme pleasure above and beyond worldly concerns, exactly the same way the two Himalayan silver firs, the only two in the whole of Australia, stood side by side on the peak of Mount Macedon.

*

After we moved into a hut on the bank of the Yarra, not far from Yarra Bend, Ciara and I lived as man and wife. There was no wedding ceremony. We couldn't afford it. There weren't friends. We didn't have any. Love was our friend, our best and only friend. That was enough.

With love for company, we spent every night in each other's arms. We slept together, completely naked, if you don't mind me telling you. That was our way. That was her preference, too. With her head pillowed on my right shoulder, my right arm holding her naked flesh, my right fingers caressing her right nipple, and my left fingers caressing her left, her tongue sucked in my mouth, she was quickly turned on. There was a crowd of frogs outside by the river or in the river. One loudest-mouthed croaked, then stopped, then croaked again. And he seemed to be doing this to the accompaniment of my thrusts into her love hole, so deep and nourishing that I came and came to in no time, often arriving at the climax together, when she would shiver all over in a spasm of pleasure akin to death. In fact, on one occasion, and by the dim light of the oil lamp, I saw her, in one of her ecstatic moments, rolling her eyes as if in pain. I was scared, so scared that I meant to stop. But she, as she rolled her eyes, showing the white of the eye, uttered a row of 'no's, stopping me from stopping. Afterwards, when we finished and cleaned up, I said to her,

'Did you feel anything in particular when you came?'

'I felt like I was going to die at any moment.'

'That's how I felt, too.'

'What if I did?'

'No, you won't.'

'Answer: what if I did die?'

'Oh, how do I know an answer to something that hasn't even happened?'

She made a grunting noise of discontent and turned her back towards me. I cajoled her, I cuddled her, I tickled her, I even bit her, softly on her shoulder. But she remained unmoved, until I said, 'If you died, I'd also die.'

'Really?' she turned around and sat up, looking at me in shock, as if I were a total stranger. 'No, you wouldn't.'

'I'm not joking. I'm serious.'

'No, you can't be. If one of us dies first, the other has to find someone else to fill the void. Or else life is meaningless.'

'How about I tell you a story?'

'Oh, Sin, you are so boring,' said Ciara as she fell back and turned to the other side, with her naked back towards me again.

Ignoring her feigned coldness, I started the story anyway, saying, 'Rui was a handsome young man who took a journey of one thousand kilometres to Chang'an, to seek his uncle's patronage. But misfortune struck as his uncle was involved in a scandal and put in jail. Rui had to retrace his steps returning home but he ran out of money. Alone, destitute and hungry in a hotel room one night, he burst into tears, thinking about his misfortune, when someone, disturbed by the crying next door, came over and asked what the matter was. When he found out, the man bought him a meal, paid off his cost of accommodation, took him home, put him up for the subsequent nights and was kind enough to marry his daughter to him, covering all his tuition cost by selling part of his acreage till, four years after, Rui successfully passed the civil service examination, winning the title of Zhuangyuan (the number-one scholar).

'By now, the wheel of fortune had turned in Rui's favour. He'd got everything, a beautiful woman, a great title and a bright future. Soon, his fortune got even better as he met a native of his own village who invited him to return home in silken robes, as the ancient saying goes. He did. Everyone came to pay their respects to him. In particular, the county magistrate set his sights on him as a possible marriageable candidate for his daughter. In fact, he insisted that he marry her. Unable to resist such temptations, he married her and started living in a lavish lifestyle, for more than a decade when, all of a sudden, his own wife appeared. She told him that her father had died and they had run out of luck and fortune so much so that she was destitute. She would like now to work as a cleaner to eke out an existence in his household. Fortunately, his new wife was so generous that she agreed to her being Rui's concubine, treating her like her own sister. In the first few days, the man was quite shy. But he relaxed and eased into it a few days after when he agreed to pass the night together with her. The next day, when they pushed the door open at midday, they found him lying on the floor, in a pool of blood, the other woman gone. On the night that followed, Rui's former wife came to his second wife's bedroom and told her what had happened. She had been dead for many years. In a court run in the netherworld, the judge ruled that the man, devoid of gratitude, deserve death. When the woman woke up, she realised that it was a dream.'

'Is that a real dream?' said Ciara, impressed.

'Who cares as long as it's a good story?'

'Admittedly it's good. But what do you mean by "destitute"'?'

'Extremely poor.'

'And what about the "concubine"'?

'It must have come from the word, "combine". By inserting "cu" – which might imply "cunt" between "com" and "bine", they created this word for the second woman or the third in the house.'

'Don't you ever use that dirty word, will you?' As she said so, she turned around and sealed my mouth with a wet kiss that caused me to have another hard-on.

Chapter 15

[Four 'Thought Bursts, of 487 words cut because irrelevant and harshly critical—SA.]

[Baohui, a self-musing, to himself]:

I'm not sure if I should put this in my diary or in that extended email not yet sent. But I do have a concern. My concern is I write like someone dead. There's no one watching how I write, putting one word down after another, or listening to the noise my fingers produce when they hit the keyboard. In a moment of wild imagination, I thought of standing a 360-degree video camera in my study so everything I do is captured as it is, thus made eternal, everlasting, undead. I even had a dream of holding my beloved in my arms, her naked back towards my naked bosom, my yang tool inside her yin tunnel, in a sitting position, both of us facing the computer screen, while I was typing away on the keyboard as a poem unfolded itself on the screen.

I was a little ashamed of myself when I woke up. Talking about shame, there's a lot to be ashamed about. Take my father. I've never revealed to anyone the fact that Dad is a billionaire, a fact that puts me to shame and explains why I rebel against it by choosing to go down the most unpromising, the most-failure prone and the least-chosen path of literature. Similarly, that is also why I decided to choose Australia over other countries, such as the UK, the USA and Canada. I have wanted to come to a place of failures and I am glad that Australia as a country seems to fit that image, as I later found. What's more, the Chinese in this country, or should I say, in that country, fit that image even better. Few films in this or that country are international enough to be world-famous; they are much less famous than the actors the country has produced. When a war is initiated by America, this-that country will do its bit by providing its cannon fodder, or paohui (cannon ashes) in Chinese, Gallipoli a quintessential, unforgettable example.

To put it in a nutshell, I didn't want my father's money. I paid my own way to do a PhD in creative writing in this-that country of failures and I covered my own tuition cost. And in doing so I lifted my game from shame. Now I work 20 hours a week in line with the government regulation for overseas students. I pay my own accommodation and my meals. So much for the boring bits of my life. 'What work?' I hear you say. Let me imagine one. A construction worker. Or a cleaner in a brothel.

*

'Hi, guys, I'm Sin, Ah Sin. Thank you for coming to hear my story. What I've got on offer today is a story of a murderer who turns into a deity.

'The man is Ah Gui. He is 25, lives with his blind father in Cowhide Street by the river and works in a herbal medicine shop. With the help of a matchmaker, he marries Ah Jin, 20 years of age, daughter of an umbrella-maker. What he does not know is that Ah Jin has already had a man by the name of Ah De, in his thirties, unmarried, who prefers to have affairs with women of his own choice.

'Things don't happen when they don't. But when they do, they happen one after another. On the 18th August, the big tide day, the city turns out to watch the coming of the tide. But Ah De quits in the middle of it all, paying a visit instead to his lover.

'Ah Gui's blind father is home, praying to Buddha, as he does on a daily basis. Ah Jin, his daughter-in-law, stays upstairs, feeling exceedingly bored. When Ah De, the man, knocks on the door with the handle of his fan, the old man opens it and asks what he's after.

'Ah De tells him so that he tells Ah Jin. Ah Jin is overjoyed and takes Ah De upstairs. They make love then and there. There's a poem describing this in the story, which, in part, goes,

It is a harmonious love that finds them together
Hugging the shoulders, cheek to cheek
A hand twisting the nipple
And finding it so wondrously soft
Before the pants are taken off and the silken shoes are removed...

'Listen. Don't be alarmed for love, and love made, it's common enough among lovers or else we wouldn't have kids.

'Ah De doesn't come back for quite a while because he is involved in a court case. When that is finished, he comes back again one day, with a roast goose in his sleeve, and, as soon as he greets the blind old man praying to Buddha, he goes upstairs, shares the goose with Ah Jin and goes to bed with her, spending the rest of the time with her till the old man is hungry and angry, getting impatient for a meal.

'The woman serves her father-in-law reluctantly and goes back to bed with Ah De till quite late.

'When Ah Gui comes home after work, his dad tells him what has happened and of his suspicion about a love affair going on, cautioning him to be careful.

'Ah Gui is enraged. He rushes upstairs and demands to know what has happened. Ah Jin, his wife, gets so upset that she accuses him of wronging her. She throws tantrums, she screams, she beats her chest, she raises hell, till Ah Gui gives in. Then she softens and throws herself into his arms. We all know that when a woman does that, a man finds it hard to resist her advances. Simply put, when a woman goes soft, a man goes hard. Afterwards, they have a wild night, enjoying themselves to the tilt.

'Everything is back to normal again until Ah De comes back. This time he comes in and goes upstairs directly. When they finish making love, he tells Ah Jin of what to do next in a stratagem that he's worked out. Ah Jin should go and get a cat. Let the cat scratch her breasts and leave bloody scratches. When Ah Gui comes home, get Ah Jin to show him the scratches and says that his blind dad has done that in an attempt to rape her. Then, demand that she go home and rest for a few months so Ah De and Ah Jin can enjoy themselves on a daily basis.

'Which is exactly what Ah Jin does on Ah Gui's return. Guess what? Ah Gui is totally convinced, to such a degree that he doesn't even go and check with his father! I don't know if that is true. But, hey, this is the story, in which anything can happen.

'As a result, Ah Gui pays for a sedan chair to carry Ah Jin home to her own parents. There, as you can imagine, she and her lover Ah De have the time of their lives. It's sex, sex, sex all night till Ah Gui turns up.

'That throws the household into chaos. Everyone is trying to find a place to hide. Ah De is hiding himself in the toilet. Ah Jin is the only one who keeps her cool. She asks Ah Gui why. Ah Gui says that he's worked too late. When he comes back the city gate is down. As it's too late to go back to the shop, he has to come here to stay for the night. As he says so, he goes to the toilet. But someone is holding the door without letting him in. Then the man pushes the door from inside, throwing him onto the ground and giving him a sound beating while calling out loudly, 'Catch a thief!', before running away.

'After this false alarm, Ah Gui lies in bed, sleepless, thinking long and hard about the whole thing, and rises early. When he arrives at the city gate, there is a crowd of street-peddlers with their shoulder-poles and baskets of fresh produce and local products, chatting while waiting.

'One man in particular is talking about the daughter of an umbrella-maker, how she is having an affair with another man without her husband's knowledge, how she gets away with it all by falsely charging her blind father-in-law with attempted rape, and how her husband gets bashed up as a burglar by the home-wrecker inside the toilet.

'The audience burst into laughter, dismissing the man in question as a complete idiot. One person goes so far as to say that if it were him he would go and buy a sharp knife and hack the two in half.

'Now, that does it all. Ah Gui goes to a shop and buys a sharp wrist knife. Then he pays a visit to the local Yan Temple, with a white cock, a bunch of fragrant incense and paper horses. He burns the incense and prays, telling the deity of what has happened. Then he says, to the god: I'll behead this cock. If it jumps once, I'll kill one person. If it jumps twice or thrice, I'll kill three.

'As it happens, he cuts the cock's head and it actually jumps four times on the ground before it takes a big jump onto the beam, doing it for a fifth time.

'Many things have happened in the intervening time. Let's skip all the details and just focus on the night when he goes to his wife's house. It so happens that Chun Mei, the maid, opens the door to buy the clay-over rolls from Old Wang who is hitting his bamboo tube with a thin piece of bamboo strip, to attract attention. Ah Gui takes the opportunity and slips in, heading straight for her parents' bedroom. Seeing that they are both asleep, he cuts their heads one by one before he goes upstairs. On his way, he runs into Chun Mei who's walking back into the house. Before she realises what is going on, her head is already cut and falls rolling on the floor.

'Having heard the noise downstairs, Ah Jin is petrified, so as soon as Ah Gui gets into her bedroom, he cuts her head off without any resistance from her. By now, Ah Gui has cut four heads. It dawns on him that there is one more head to cut. He starts looking everywhere until his eyes fall on a naked Ah De, lying on his belly on top of a beam overhead. Ah Gui launches an attack on him by hacking at him on the head, on his back, on his limbs and legs, till he rolls off the beam, and then thrusting the knife into his heart, finishing him off in one go.'

I stopped, breathless, to take a gulp from my tea mug. Already, I had heard the jingling and clattering of the coins that were dropped, like a cascade, into my bowl. My audience seemed to be riveted in the story, so much so that one young man, about 25 himself, said,

'What happened then?'

'Sorry,' said I. 'I can't tell you until tomorrow when I come back.'

'Do you have a book? Can I buy a copy?' said a man with a cap very low on his brows.

'No, sorry, I don't have a book. I write with my tongue,' said I.

Chapter 16

Since Stacey never replies to my multiple emails, I might like to give myself a mini creative holiday, to indulge in a number of things: checking out porn, sorting out my long and hard thinking about history, and going to the movies.

I won't record anything about my pornographical experience. It suffices to say that in my last visit back home in China I found porn easily available online even though you had to use a VPN to access anything outside China such as Twitter, Instagram, Facebook or Pinterest. Although China is placed on a par with North Korea and Eritrea in its internet censorship you would be surprised that porn is so easily available, either on your computer or on your mobile phone. I'm ashamed to say that I did once masturbate myself successfully in my hotel room while watching porn on my mobile phone. At the time I thought: if all the people spent their time watching porn or practising porn, the government would have a great time engaging in their own politics of money laundering, money pinching, money grabbing and money growing since the eyes of the public had gone blind, obsessed with its own pleasurizing.

I had a fleeting thought that I'd share this porn info with Dad but thought better of it. Politically, he was censored because, like the rest of the Party members, he had no access to a range of foreign-based social media such as FB, Twitter, Instagram and stuff, and if he was caught accessing them via a VPN he'd lose his Party membership and his job, and, sexually, I thought he might be more in need of stuff available on all those Western social media outlets without knowing that it was easily available on Baidu. But it was so difficult to bring up the matter that I had to stop short of doing it and start empathizing with him, sympathizing with him and taking pity on him. Still, I said to him that there was so much bullshit, sheepshit, dogshit and humanshit on those social media that it's more like an open toilet where anyone can go shitting, pissing, spitting and dumping, and, to cap it all, sharing them indiscriminately. Or what is indiscriminately? I don't give a fark. Ignoring Dad's criticism of my use of dirty language that must have been a direct result of my acculturation in Australia, a convict-stained and sustained country, I suggested that Mum do it via VPN as she was living in retirement and under less restrictions and I told her of the pleasures of watching all the mini-videos on FB from deep-sea fishing, through reaping in mouth-watering fruit of a great variety, tips on how to use the phone to chase up a guilty couple on their way to make love in a hotel room, extraordinary babies able to speak at least three languages including French, and a Cao Cao who was an American speaking impeccable Mandarin about current affairs in America, when Mum gave me a slap on the wrist, saying that she wouldn't want to be corrupted by all that as what was available on Chinese TV was much more enriching and lasting.

As usual, after I did my daily ration of writing, about 1000 words or so, and it took me a whole day to do that, I went to bed at around 12 midnight and fell asleep right away. Sometime in an unearthly hour, I woke up and went to the toilet. When I came back, I couldn't fall back in sleep again. A thought kept bothering me, one that came from nowhere, like a cloud that came upon a cloudless sky, a quite trite image that nevertheless is often the reality. Fiction, country, history, rules, regulations, one's own country, till words strung themselves together in a flow that sluggishly swept across the mindfield.

Yes, that's right. One writes one's own work of fiction the way one builds one's own country, a one-man's country, a country beyond the countries, over and above all the other countries, in which one makes one's own rules, issues visas only to those who are intelligent enough to read along intellectual, innovative and inventive lines, the i-i-i lines, and bars anyone who applies standards of the dead when it comes to works written for the next century or centuries. One ought to apply the imagination bar, akin to the old colour bar. One who has little imagination should be barred from reading the same way people of colour were barred in the past. A country in which readers who wander in follow the rules wherever they go and one of the rules in this country is that they can begin anywhere, at the beginning, at the end, in the middle, or on a randomly selected page. They can even choose to skip all the pages and only read the author biography or the copyright page. It is a country of fiction or a fiction of a country, meant only for the people bored enough with the same kind of food, called stories, cooked along the same a-b-c-d-e-f-g-h-i-j-k-l-m-n-o-p-q-r-s-t-u-v-w-x-y-z line, the same tedious pattern of characters, setting, plot, conflict, resolution, climax, anti-climax, even mood, and so on, served meal after meal, day after day, year after year, till the new technology, like 3D printing, AI, cryonics, and so on, makes it finally possible for no one to read except the shredding machine that does the most thorough reading of all.

*

Now, about what I said regarding history as fiction. I remember reading someone, a historian, on Twitter, making a comment on Billy Sing as a book she couldn't read because it didn't tally with her view of that part of history. I haven't read the book but I question the validity of her remark. History, as far as I am concerned, is anyone's business. I agree with Ambrose Bierce when he says that history is 'an account mostly false, of events mostly unimportant, which are brought about by rulers mostly knaves, and soldiers mostly fools.' (The Devil's Dictionary, p. 119.) But I have more to say. I have recently bought and read a textbook, in its fourth edition and sold for millions of copies in China, which has won First Prize for the Best Teaching Material in the Third National Education Commission. I managed to get halfway before I decided to ditch it for a simple reason. Between 14 and 24 September, 1937, Division No. 115, under the leadership of Division Commander Lin Biao, won the Battle of Pingxingguan, killing over 1000 Japanese soldiers, destroying 100-odd enemy trucks and capturing more than 1000 rifles, among other things. But, apart from one single mention of Lin Biao, his name is absent in the narration of that section of history as if the history or the victory had nothing to do with him. I was totally disgusted with the way history can be tampered with and, worst of all, taught to the university students like that. Because Lin had a fight with Mao, fled the country afterwards and died in a plane crash, his memory as a victorious general at a young age of 29 has been erased forever in the official accounts of the history although it is kept alive in the unofficial ones, on and off the internet.

Which goes to show that history is nothing if not fictional, a kaleidoscope that changes its view from person to person, a whip held in the hands of the powerful to whip anything into the shape they are after, a game in which the present rulers set the rules, only to be overthrown when the next regime change takes place, and a void and silence that is kept by the current government for as long as it thinks it safe to maintain its life without breaking the political ice, like the June 4th, thirty years now, ice that has turned into an iceberg, and an iceberg that threatens to turn into a glacier, growing bigger each decade despite climate change.

There is a secret I want to share, to a certain degree, though, that involves Mr Hua, an old friend, suffering from lung cancer, who realises that he is close to death. He called me in the other day and wondered if I had time and interest to do work for him. I said like what. He said if I could write his biography as his ghost writer. He sat behind his desk, with a tape-recorder beside him. His head was covered in snow-white hair. His face was wrinkled out of shape. He, though, wore his clothes in a fashionable style. He offered a few titbits for starters, saying that he had arrived from Penang in the 1950s as part of the Colombo Plan to pursue financial studies, settled and got married.

I listened and watched his eyes peering at me through the thick glasses. When he said, 'But you know, I have many women in my life', I held my breath. But he stopped and said, 'You have a think about it, okay? We'll talk more next time when we meet.'

But there is no next time. I was overseas on a research trip in Ireland when news came that he had died in hospital. I couldn't even begin to write a letter of condolences, because if I sent it to his email address, he wouldn't be the recipient. Besides, I knew no one of his family, least of all his many girlfriends, so I left the matter there, without bringing it up again.

Chapter 17

Lying in darkness, side by side with Ciaravoca, I listened to the beating of her heart and the beating of my own, less audible than hers.

Or was it the other way round?

'How's your day today?' said I.

'Everything's the same, day after day, week after week, month after month.'

'As long as there's money to make, I gather?'

'No. That's not what I want. I don't like to be bossed around, ordered around and tossed around. I don't like to be told what to do and what not.'

'Fair enough, Gin.'

'Gin? Is that how you call me?'

'Yes, it matches Sin.'

'Oh, no, that sounds like dim-sim.'

'Even better.'

'Anyway, I'm thinking of quitting my job as a servant. To be honest,' she paused and said, 'Do you find me dirty, Sin?'

'Dirty? Who said that? I never think you are. In fact, you are an epitome of cleanliness.'

'And am I a habitual liar, too?'

'No, Gin, you mustn't be influenced by people bad-mouthing behind you. People talk. They will always run you down, behind you if not in front of you.'

'They don't do it behind you. They do it openly. Didn't you see notices like "No Irish Need Apply"?'

'That sounds like a Chinaman's chance. Or, more, a china bowl's chance.'

'What's that?'

'If it's a Chinaman's chance, it's no chance at all, worse than the ads against the Irish.'

'Aren't we in the same boat?'

'Yes and no. We are more in the same bed.'

'The worst people, ha.'

'No, the best that are treated the worst, as the worst. Let's make love and take it out on love.'

'On love?'

'Take it out on them via love.'

Afterwards, we lay exhausted and I heard myself say,

'Even before we set out on our journey to Australia we'd heard how bad the situation was in America. When a white murdered a Chinese man, the other Chinese men who had seen it with their own eyes could not act as witnesses in a court because their words were not believed, so their evidence was regarded as useless. The reason? All Chinese are habitual liars whose words can't be believed.'

'What a load of crap!'

'Honesty, ever since I was born, was inculcated in my mind and heart, time and time again. It's one of the five virtues Confucius promoted.'

'Who's that?'

'He's our great ancient moral master, born more than 2000 years ago.'

'And the five virtues?'

'Gong, kuan, xin, min, hui.'

'Go on.'

'Gong means respectful, kuan means generous, xin means honest, min means diligent and hui means kind.'

'Wow, you seem to have embodied all these qualities in you already.'

'Actually, you do, too.'

'People are forced to be bad, don't you think?'

'That happens. Did you do something like that?'

A long pause, then, 'Yes.'

'May I know what happened?'

'I'll tell you some other time.'

'No worries.' Our conversation meandered until I thought of Ah Toy.

'You know what?'

'What?'

'Did I tell you about Ah Toy?'

'No. Who's he?'

'He's a good friend of mine from my gold-digging days.'

'And?'

'But he's gone missing. Don't know if he's gone back to China, moved on to America or gone to one of the goldfields in New South Wales. I mention him because of an old man who came to my storytelling session this morning. The guy wondered why I didn't find a decent job making money and maintaining a family with kids. He said that the only thing that mattered when a person was young and energetic was pursuit of money for the purpose of living. He's a white man, of course. He said that other things, such as arts and literature, could come later, much later, till one retired, for example, because they couldn't possibly be serious, just hobbies.'

'That sounds like a pig's philosophy.'

'Only in a colony like Australia can you find people like that. In my home country, people grow up with a constant trained sense of arts, calligraphy, painting, poetry, drama, music, and all sorts of things related to literature. Even a peasant is aware of their importance.'

'In my old country, too.'

'Which is why I thought of Ah Toy because I think he's a poet. Whenever he spoke, it sounded like poetry. Although nothing was recorded in writing, I tend to catch bits and pieces and save them onto my memory. Take this one that goes, "I spat on the gold / And I wiped it clean / With my spittle" '.

'I spat, too.'

'You did?'

'I broke a bowl the other day, an antique china bowl, that Missus said her husband had brought from China where he had lived for a few years as a missionary. She was very upset and started blaming me for always doing a bad job. I asked how much and said I'd pay. She said it's priceless. Then I got upset. And I spat.'

'You did? Good on you. Did you spit into their food?'

'No. I was picking up the broken pieces when I heard what she said and then I spat.'

'What did she say?'

'She said: you pay? Not till your parents are resurrected and restored to you.'

'Oh, she's so cruel. Awful.'

'And I quit after that.'

'You did? Good on you!' as I said so, I kissed her again and again, congratulating her on her boldness and decisiveness.

That night, we made love at least three times and talked till daybreak.

*

And in approaching that bit about Sin and Ciara sharing their racial grievances in the lead up to their lovemaking, I, B.H., thought of Lawson and Dyson but found them too young for my purpose, one 1867-1922 and the other 1865-1931, despite the former's Ah Soon, Ah See and Ah Soo and the latter's Sin Fat, much worse represented than the former's three 'Ah's. Lawson was a tortured man, torn between his hate of the Chinese and his desire to do them justice. He wrote a poem to express his disgust with mixed marriages,

> I see the stricken city fall...
> The pure girl to the leper's kiss
> God give us faith, for Christ's own sake,
> To kill our womankind ere this[1]

But he balanced that with this remark, possibly years after, in 'Ah Soon' that goes,

> I don't know whether a story about a Chinaman would be popular or acceptable here and now, and, for the matter of that, I don't

1 Qtd in June Duncan Owen, p. 13

care. I am anti-Chinese as far as Australia is concerned; in fact, I am all for a white Australia. But one may dislike or even hate a nation, without hating or disliking an individual of that nation. One may be on friendly terms; even pals in a way. I had a good deal of experience with the Chinese in the old years; and I never knew or heard of a Chinaman who neglected to pay his debts, who did a dishonest action, or who forgot a kindness to him or his, or was not charitable when he had the opportunity. [Leonard Cronin, p. 500]

*

Soon, it was nearly a decade after my arrival. Signs of a new life, with the coming of another spring. Gin was now pregnant. She walked with difficulty. She retched often. She had sleepless nights and that affected me so I had sleepless nights, too. She had many questions about the baby. Would we have a boy? Which should I prefer, a boy or a girl? What name if it was a girl? How to bring up the child if we had no previous knowledge of how to do it? What sort of a future we'd like to give it to him or her? Talking about that reminded me that my own parents never seemed to have entertained any idea of my future. All they ever said to me was: We hope you grow up into a healthy, happy and good man. To be a good person, that was their idea and that was their ideal. Whatever you do, be you a peasant farming the land or a soldier fighting in a war or a fisherman out fishing in the sea or whatever, you'll be fine as long as you are a good and kind-hearted man.

On her part, there was no such nonsense. She didn't have parents to bring her up in that belief. All she could retain was a faint memory of a past spent in a workhouse in Cork, sewing or doing household chores, such as the dishes. She didn't want to recall the miserable days wasted in the grey, death-like building of a workhouse, surrounded by the sub-divided, chopped up fields encircled with stone walls. There was one overriding hope: to get out, to go away and to get as far as one could go, and never return. As for whether one could grow up a good person, it all depends, because, in her view, one always, and already, is a good person when one is born but one is subject to changes and the surrounding circumstances, like a sapling. It wants to grow straight and strong. In most cases, it does. But sometimes it breaks in half in a storm or gets burnt down in a forest fire. 'Let's follow our instincts and you won't go wrong,' was what she would often say.

'It very much tallies with what the first line in The Three-Character Canon says: ren zhi chu, xing ben shan.' We were taking a slow walk after dinner outside along the Yarra River. This section of the river was quite wild, with dead trees fallen on the bank slopes, or lying across the standing trees, all gums. The water, of a muddy colour, wound sluggishly through the hills towards where the sun was setting, its glow setting bunches of leaves suddenly ablaze before it moved on to work instant wonders on other leaves, other trees and other green slopes.

'Dead trees and what did you mean, just now?'

'Oh, I was saying that the saying goes, "When one is born, one is by nature good".'

'That's what I said, no?'

'Yes, even though the Bible says the opposite.'

'I doubt it but I won't say anything because the Church is so powerful, too powerful. They'll stone you to death if you disbelieve.'

'Take stones,' I said as I followed my line of thinking. A stone was born just like that, in front of us, lying across the path, with no intention of hurting anyone, indeed with no intention at all because it is a stone, until it is picked up by a living person, to stone a Chinaman, for example.'

'Why Chinaman?'

'Because it is fun to stone a Chinaman.'

'For the whites you mean?'

'Exactly and in the goldfields. I was hit quite a few times. A friend I met who came from Lambing Flat in New South Wales told me of what had happened there.'

'It's an old story, isn't it?' she said as she stared at the flowing waters.

'Yes, as old as the flowing waters. The strong always bully the weak.'

'But the weak will grow up strong, stronger.'

'Like Huang Chao.'

'Who's that?'

'A peasant hero, a rebel near the end of the Tang dynasty, a thousand years ago.'

'What happened?'

'He led a peasant uprising but it was vanquished in the end. Halfway through, he found himself facing a cliff-face deep in a mountain valley. The locals told him that the smooth cliff-face was as shiny as a mirror that could reflect his previous life. When he went to have a look, he saw a monkey in it. That made him so angry that he had the cliff-face burnt out of its shape.'

'That's not nice. But why all of a sudden this guy?'

'I had told my friend of this story advising him against rising in a rebellion against the local whites because the best policy in a foreign country is to bide your time, make as much money as possible, keep safe and healthy, and as soon as the opportunity arises, pack up and leave.'

'Is that what you said to him? You are a smart guy.'

'Yes,' said I, thinking of our baby. 'What do you think of Na Za as a name?'

'Ah Za, I'm sorry?'

'N-a, z-a,' I said, laboriously, spelling it out, letter by letter.

'It sounds like Lazarus.'

'What's that?'

'I don't know exactly. Maybe Hebrew or some such thing.'

'I'll find out,' said I as I began telling her of Na Za, a fictional character in that ancient novel called The Making of the Gods. In it, this woman is pregnant for 42 months without giving birth to her child when she has a dream in which a deity orders her to give birth, which she does the next morning. The father, a general, on his return from the war, happens to be there at the exact moment of birth and is shocked to see a red burning ball rolling about. He is so angry that he smashes it up with his halberd when a brisk baby bursts out of the ball, in all his nakedness, and stops the father from killing him by going down on his knees, with a deep bow, almost touching his head on the floor, calling them in a loud and clear voice, 'Mum and Dad, your son has now come to this world! Thank you so much!'

I thought this might interest her. But Gin's face pulled in a wry smile. And she frowned. I got closer as I wondered what the matter was and if she didn't feel unwell. She said no and that everything was fine. Then she said, 'I'm not sure. But I'd more like to have a daughter. Men, at least men from my part of the world, are so rude, boisterous, aggressive towards their women, and easily get drunk and abusive. I don't want to give birth to a man. I've had enough of them. I want a daughter.'

'Fair enough', said I. 'I think calling a girl Na Za is even better if you know what happens later in the story.'

*

BH to himself: My only way to keep something in memory is to turn that into a found poem or else I'll forget it straight away. May I be allowed to make an exegetical comment by way of a found poem I just 'founded', 'found' as a verb as in 'I founded a poem', as follows:

> The white stereotype
> of the acceptable
> and unacceptable Asian
>
> is utterly without
> manhood. Good or
> bad, the stereotypical
>
> Asian is nothing
> as a man.
> At worst, the
>
> Asian American is
> contemptible because he
> is womanly, effeminate
>
> devoid of all
> the traditionally masculine

qualities of originality,

daring, physical courage
and creativity...(pp. 16-7, Aiiieeeee)

    I haven't thought of a title for this poem of three-word lines. But I'll leave it for the moment. In a way, I quite agree with the sentiments expressed there. I, for one, is without manhood, not even womanhood. It doesn't matter, does it?

*

In a dream, I met my old friend Ah Toy, who told me of what had happened to him at the Buckland River:

> The other day, when the whites came, it was my turn to cook. I was busy working in the work tent, washing and picking the rice, cutting the vegetables and meat on top of kneading the dough in order to pull it into strips for noodles. I was very good at that. I had a white apron on and wore a white chef hat, with my pigtail wound up inside it to avoid it being seen. The work tent was built half of a board woven with wattle (which I later learnt was called 金合欢花 [golden happy together flower] in Mandarin), about as high as my neck. When you looked out from above it, there was a wonderful scenery around the bend of the river, meandering and shining under the sun. The water was now boiling, with much steam. When I looked through the steam, the scenery was even better, looking as if a colour cloud had descended, flying into our kitchen tent. Our team wasn't big, just a dozen people. But if you added the river-flat and the surrounding valley, it would be as good as two thousand, twice as many as the Europeans.
>
>   I pulled out a few large chunks of wood from underneath the stove to reduce the intensity of the fire, and, with a redwood scoop, flanged with copper, I scooped a bit of rice soup. I used the scoop, meant for the raw rice, not the spoon, because Ah Mu, in a

fit of temper, had broken it last time when he smashed it against something hard. The rice soup was nutritious and would keep you fit. When it was time for lunch and they all came back, a bowl of it would revive the spirit. Just then, a faint yelling sound came from afar. A black magpie in a tree seemed agitated and burst out squawking. From the steam tapering as a result of the reduced fire, I could once again see Ah Mu and others busy on the river-flat. The dark-grey bamboo hats they wore created something anciently poetic in the hills and waters of the Buckland River.

The noise became louder. A din. A commotion. A bit like people going to a temple fair or a market fair. Then it didn't sound like anything but a crowd of animals that came blotting out the sky and covering up the earth. The magpie in the gum tree next to the kitchen tent went suddenly silent, soundless, before it fluttered its wings, flying away.

The sound did not come from one spot, but from all directions. Concerned that the rice might get burnt, I pulled out the remaining burning firewood and buried the heart of the fire with the ashes on the edge. Then I raised my head to see what was going on. Immediately, I saw my brothers, who had been busy panning for gold by the riverside, now running back towards the camp, bamboo hats in hand, despite the scorching sun overhead. Ah Mu ran so hard his pigtail fell loose, a sight I had never seen before. He ran the fastest and, as soon as he arrived, he said, breathlessly, 'Run for your life! Gweilos are killing people now!'

I wanted to know what was really going on. But he ignored me. He came straight into the tent and began ransacking it, gathering his own stuff up and starting to run, shoulder-poles on his shoulder, followed by a few others who did the same. In his confusion, Ah Xian overturned the tent, which fell on top of him and he couldn't get out of it. With a loud yo-heave-ho, they pulled him from underneath the fallen tent. But there was little time left because a dark mass of people was pressing down, all of them white miners. They were holding a flag, with words streaming across it: 'Roll up! No Chinese!' And they were yelling as well, a sound of devils and wolves: Roll up! Roll up! Their voices formed into a muddy wave so high it touched the sky. I was so scared that I put down my rice scoop and abandoned the cooking rice before I started scrambling to my feet and ran.

It was too late. Like a nightmare, a crowd of white miners appeared wearing felt hats, shirts, canvas pants and big-headed boots, with shovels, spades or sticks in hands, blocking my way, like a pack of wolves blocking a lamb's way, their faces furious, their eyes wide open, each face with a black hole in it because of the effort in shouting the 'Roll up' slogan. I was about to run. But once I saw this, I stopped and stood my ground. I picked up the scoop again and, unhurriedly, I went to the rice barrel, filled with the rice soup. I filled my scoop and began taking small sips from it, smacking my lips as I did so, appearing as if I were very content.

A big man stood out of the crowd. I knew him. He's Henry. If he's not German, he must be Irish. When he saw that I showed no fear, he raised his shovel and brought it down on my head. I dodged it and shot the scoopful of rice soup in his face, turning it into a full blooming face flower. The heat was such that he held his face in his hands, howling like hell. Then, with a force I knew not where it came from, I took the barrel of rice soup in my arms, raised it over head and poured it out, scorching the hell out of the white bastards. A few who didn't run quick enough were covered with it like dog blood, thoroughly drenched. The upshot of this confrontation was, of course, my utter defeat, my head receiving a hole from an iron bar in the hands of a white man. But for the meticulous treatment from my Aboriginal brothers with their bush medications, I would have died a long time ago. But that's another story.

*

My exegetical note to myself: 'My desultory reading brought me to an Australian classic, *Such is Life* by Tom Collins, an exceedingly boring book that I found I could hardly read. Flipping through the pages, I was about to put it aside without picking it up again, ever, when my eye caught the words "five mounted Chinamen", with someone called Sam Young, followed by a nasty description that goes,

> Then, addressing the Turanian horde, and adapting my speech to the understanding of our lowest types: "My word!" I exclaimed admiringly, "you take-um budgeree rise out-a whitepeller, John! Merrijig you! Borak you shift-um that peller bullock; borak you shift-um that peller yarraman. Whitepeller gib-it you fi' bob, buy-it opium. You savvy? Bale whitepeller tell-um boss. Bimeby white-peller yabber like-it, 'Chinaman berry good'yabber like-it, 'Comenavadrink, John'yabber like-it, 'Chinaman brother b'long-a whitepeller.' You savvy, John?"
>
> "Lak-hi-lo-hen-slung!" carolled a third Chow disdainfully.
>
> "You go hellee shut up! Eulopean allee sem plully whool! Lum-la-no-sun-hi-me!" And the raiders went on their way, warbling remarks to each other in their native tongue, while the discomfited foreign devils hurried toward their camp, to give the alarm. (See Collins, pp. 248-9)

If anyone could hear me right now, he or she would be able to hear a chortle full of mirth from me as I found this imitation of the Chinese talk so childish and funny and the 'alarm' so insidious. But the rest of the book just didn't make sense for me.

Chapter 18

I wrote an email to Dad.

Hi, Dad,

I'm pleased to tell you that I probably don't have to rely on you for financial support for too long now.

I have recently got in touch with Immediate Edge via James Packer, a billionaire in Australia. I don't know him personally. But I have read an article about him: https://beckeriffs.com/karlbreaking.html and I am intrigued. I have made initial contact and the evidence shown by the people who have made money seems quite encouraging and promising. If I regularly make four to five thousand Australian dollars per week, which is about 25k in Chinese currency, I don't have to live a life as I do now, living in a small rented room, paying bills regularly, more paid than earned, nothing incoming, all outgoing.

I can't tell you more except to say that I am proud of myself for not having to rely on a rich dad even though, from the very beginning, I had deep doubts about creating a literary path in a country that is not my native land and in a language that is not my native tongue. How many of them have managed to survive these two things and still succeed?

[Too much talk about racism. 378 words cut—SA]

So much for that. Now, to answer your question about the most important matter of my life, I have to say that nothing much has been achieved. I did have a girlfriend. But unable to bear the distance between us, she in Shenzhen and I in Melbourne, she decided to leave. Hence my micro-theory about love that leaves even though, this much has got to be said, she stays in my memory for always. Right now, there is a long period of drought. It is not that I don't have people approaching me, mind you, but anyone who comes to me and offers herself because my dad is a billionaire is immediately out of my orbit.

I'm not even sure if I can easily love someone of the opposite sex as I find young males equally beautiful if not more. In fact, they have more energy and less appetite for material things. I kind of admire Christopher Isherwood and Don Bachardy in love, the way Christopher would wait patiently for Don's return after a short-tempered fallout and would not say a thing on the latter's return.

The other thing is, I feel more and more both male and female these days, so much so that I am kind of my own girlfriend or my own boyfriend, both at the same time. Enough said.

I don't know what more to say. But I wish you and mum the best of your health and a happy life together.

Regards,

BH

After I finished the email and decided not to send it—many of my letters remained that way, letters being letter-bombs meant to implode—I found my revolver, in Chinese, a *zuolun shouqiang* (left-wheeled handgun). This I took in hand, a bit like my penis, albeit a constantly erected one, and aimed at a portrait hanging on the wall. Then I pulled the trigger and felt happy about it when I heard a crisp click. Oh, is that how the word 'trigger-happy' came about? Was the trigger happy or the person who pulled the trigger happy? I then thrust the mouth of the gun into my mouth. Instantly, a sense of pleasure swept over me, coupled with fright and a post-life conjecture of what must have been: a room splashed with bloodstains, if the trigger was happy or the trigger-puller was happy. Then, there was the wonderment how she must have felt when she put my guncock inside her mouth and ended up shooting. It must have felt like now when I was taking it so hard and open. If there were a bullet, it would happily go through my brain and the rest of it would be all talk afterwards.

It was not till then that I realised that I was aiming at myself, my self in the portrait that an artist friend had done for me, because I thought he was the devil, one who was at constant odds with the world, the rest of the world, one who would never want to travel down the path the world had chosen for him or advised him to go down, one who would not write fiction that followed the successful patterns and one who, ultimately, did not at heart recognize anything so far, including himself.

*

Today, a Sunday. I have to address a few issues that Stacey has raised. In a recent Whatsapp message, she said: 1. You need perhaps to rethink how you approach history, as a line to follow closely or to remake regardless. 2. You need to engage in more theoretical thinking. 3. Not too much indulgence in self.

*

Point by point, I now address the issues raised. But, first, I must address my own mental issues. I find I talk more and more to myself. I detest social media. I have removed myself from all the SM outlets. Social media is indeed SM or S/M. People who will never meet this life post stuff to gather praise. After I decided not to post a single thing, I felt better, and I felt better with each passing day because I do not get tortured by a sense of being ignored, not accepted, not praised, not recognised. I live my life as I need be, as I should be, as I ought to be, and as I must be: an individual living with himself, theyself, like no other, with no other. This morning I had the illusion, an imagination of a baby that offered himself to me. He's born in my household. He refused to speak to me even when I spoke to him. But when I went to the side room, I heard someone talking. It was him, talking to himself. Would he grow up only talking to himself? Why not, I now think to myself: He can very well buy an AI for himself and talk to him or her or him/her. Perhaps when we talk about the future as something wonderful, beautiful and hopeful, we are talking about that: an AI, or a number of AIs, for company for good, multilingual in the extreme.

Talking or self-talking about that, I think I do need Dad. I need money from him so that I can buy a Japanese sex doll, which is not much, only a couple of thousand American dollars. I may buy a few of them. I think I'm gradually losing interest in real human interaction. I'm not sure to what degree this state of mind will affect my fiction. Or is it true that an author has nothing to do with his fiction as his fiction grows up by itself?

To empower Ah Sin, though, I have been fruitlessly searching for goldfield heroes in nonfictional material, such as Chinese Cemeteries in Australia by Dr Kok Hu Jin, Tracking the Dragon, by a local Chinese organization, An Angel by the Water, edited by Mike Butcher, and Sojourners by Eric Rolls, stuff I found hard to swallow, until I found a Jimmy Ah San. Should I model my Ah Sin on Ah San? Let me quote a paragraph to remind the forgetful me to see if it is workable. After reading the story again, I decided to include the entire chapter:

CHAPTER III ~ JIMMY AH SAN

Consternation was depicted on the faces of the men. And they all began to question Jacky at once, until Grainger appeared, and then the black boy gave them farther particulars—the Chinamen, he said, were all on foot, each man carrying two baskets on a stick, but there were also five or six pack-horses loaded with picks, shovels, dishes, and other mining gear.

"Curse the dirty, yaller-hided swine!" cried Dick Scott, turning excitedly to Grainger. "What's to be done? They've come to rush the Flat again; but, by thunder! I'll be a stiff 'un afore a Chow fills another dish with wash-dirt on Connolly's Creek."

"And me, too!" "And me, too!" growled the others angrily, and Grainger, as he looked at their set, determined faces, knew they would soon be beyond control, and bloodshed would follow if the advancing Chinamen tried to come on to the field. But, nevertheless, he was thoroughly in sympathy with them. The advent of these Chinese—probably but an advance guard of many hundreds—

would simply mean ruination to himself and his mates, just as their prospects were so bright. The men looked upon him as their leader, and he must act—and act quickly.

"Let them come along, boys. Then we'll bail them up as soon as they come abreast of us, and have a little 'talkee, talkee' with them. But for heaven's sake try and keep cool, and I daresay when they see we look ugly at them, they'll trot on. How many of you have guns of any kind?"

Four rifles and two shot guns were quickly produced, and then every one waited till the first of the Chinese appeared, marching one behind the other. The foremost man was dressed in European clothes, and the moment Scott saw him, he exclaimed—

"Why, it's Jimmy Ah San! I used to know him at Gympie in the old times. He's not a bad sort of a Chow. Come on, boys!"

Grainger, who was not just then well enough to go with them, but remained in his seat with his revolver on his knee, could not help smiling at the sudden halt and terrified looks of the Chinese, when Scott and the others drew up in front of them with their weapons at the present. Half of them at once dropped their baskets and darted off into the bush, the rest crowding together like a flock of terrified sheep. The leader, however, came steadily on. Scott stepped out and met him.

"Good-morning. What do you and all your crowd want here?"

"Nothing," replied the Chinaman quietly, in excellent English, "nothing but to get down to the creek and camp for a few days. But why do you all come out with guns? We cannot do you any harm."

"Just so. But we can do you a lot if you try on any games, Mr. Jimmy Ah San."

"Ah, you know me then," said the man, looking keenly at Scott.

"Yes, I do, an' you're all right enough. But me an' my mates is going to keep this field for white men—it ain't goin' to be no Chinaman's digging'. So what's yer move?"

"Only what I said. Look at my men! We do not want to stop here; we wish to push along to the coast. Some of them are dying from exhaustion, and my pack-horses can hardly go another quarter of a mile."

Scott scratched his chin meditatively, and then consulted with his mates. He, although so rough in his speech, was not a bad-natured man, and he could see that the Chinese were thoroughly done up, and worn down to skin and bone. Then presently Grainger walked over and joined them, and heard what Ah San had to say.

"I'm sorry that you are in such a bad fix," he said, "but you know as well as I do that if any of your men put a pick into ground here, there will be serious trouble, and if they lose their lives you will be responsible—and may perhaps lose your own."

"I promise you that nothing like that will happen," replied the Chinaman. "My men are all diggers, it is true, but we will not attempt to stay on any field where we are not wanted. My name is James Ah San. I am a British subject, and have lived in Australia for twenty-five years. That man" (pointing to Scott) "knows me, and can tell you that 'Jimmy Ah San' never broke a promise to any man."

"That is right enough," said Scott promptly; "everyone in Gympie knew you when you was storekeepin' there, and said you was a good sort."

"We have come over three hundred miles from the Cloncurry," went on the Chinese leader, quickly seeing that Scott's remark had much impressed the other miners; "the diggers there gave us forty-eight hours to clear out. The blacks killed fifteen of us and speared ten of my horses, and six more men died on the way. We can do no harm here. We only want to spell a week, or two weeks."

"Poor devils!" muttered Grainger; then he said to Ah San: "Very well. Now, you see the track going through that clump of sandalwood? Well, follow it and you'll come to a little ironstone ridge, where you'll find a good camping-ground just over a big pool in the creek. There's a bit of sweet grass, too, for your horses, so they can get a good feed to-night. In the morning this black boy will, if you like, show you a place in the ranges, about four miles from here, where you can let them run for a week. There's some fine grass and plenty of water, and they ought to pick up very quickly. But you will have to keep some one to see that they don't get round the other side of the range—through one of the gaps; if they do, you'll lose them to a dead certainty, for there are two or three mobs of brumbies{*} running there. Do you want any tucker?" {**}

* Wild horses.

** Provisions.

"No, thank you," replied Ah San, with an unmistakable inflexion of gratitude in his voice; "we have plenty of rice and tea, but I should like to buy a bullock to-morrow, if I can—I saw some cattle about two miles from here. Is there a cattle station near here?"

"No. The cattle you saw belong to one of us—this man here," pointing to Jansen, "will sell you a beast to-morrow, I daresay."

Then the armed protectors of the integrity from foreign invasion of the rights of Chinkie's Flat nodded "Good evening" to Ah San, and walked back across the road to the "Digger's Best," and the Chinamen, with silent, childlike patience, resumed their loads and trotted along after their leader. They disappeared over the hill, and ere darkness descended the glare of their camp fires was casting steady gleams of light upon the dark waters of the still pool beneath the ridge. [see it here: http://www.gutenberg.org/files/24805/24805-h/24805-h.htm]

There are two things interesting about Louis Becke, author of this story, 'Chinkie's Flat': one, that he wrote autobiographical material for T. A. Browne ('Rolf Boldrewood') to use as background material for a novel Browne was writing, only to sue Browne for plagiarism; two, that he won the case with the assistance of Banjo Paterson, a poet and solicitor (!). [see it here: http://marshall.csu.edu.au/people/LouisBecke/Bio.html]

Would his ghost sue me for including part of his stuff here?

*

A letter BH wrote to bh:

Since there is no one I want to write a letter to, I think it's probably time to write one to myself. The reason is simple enough: I want to sort myself or yourself out.

[Raging about 'social mental media'. Unfair. 213 words cut—SA]

[Stacey remarks: And let me delete 67 words about racism and simply say: Racism is not what Australia is all about.]

Best regards and will talk more whenever I'm in the mood.

P.S.
Something to remind myself with, a story of a writer I know whose name I can't even reveal to myself. Let's just call him Ni Ming. A mutual friend of ours recently revealed that Ni Ming was going to write a story to enter it for the biggest literary award in China. But I scoffed at the idea saying if one had an award in mind when one wrote a story one was bound to fail and that the idea of an award should be the last thing one has in mind when engaging in literary creations. But my friend pointed out that it had always been Ni Ming's practice that he only wrote stories when there was a literary competition up or else it would be a waste of time, Ni Ming's words ringing true enough: *Literature is nothing sacred but simply another business. It's only worth pursuing if you can make it pay for you. Otherwise, one might as well spend one's days in the casino as there are always chances of winning. But for the award money in competitions, I'd have put it last on my agenda.*
When he said that, I recalled another remark he had made at the beginning of his commercial literary 'career'. In his own boastful words: *Why, I mean, do I have to write the book? I'd wait till I have bought my first property.* Now that he's bought his 20th property, he still hasn't begun on his first book.

Part III

Chapter 1

Strange Beauty

> *Love, is man unfinished.*
> Samuel Beckett[1]

> *I must be alone with life.*
> Frank O'Hara[2]

> *For there is no crime to the intellect. That…judges law*
> *as well as fact.*
> Ralph Waldo Emerson[3]

[1875 words cut as part of my on-going self-censoring process, with only the beginning part of the novel inserted here as a reminder of something posthumous written by the dead author.]

---

1 Samuel Beckett, *The Collected Poems of Samuel Beckett.* Faber & Faber, 2012, p. 73.

2 Frank O'Hara, *The Collected Poems of Frank O'Hara*, edited by Donald Allen. Berkeley: University of California Press, 1995, p. 158.

3 See the quote here: http://classiclit.about.com/library/bl-etexts/rwemerson/bl-rwemer-essays-14.htm

Chapter 2

[Stacey says: I have pondered the following for a long time and decided to leave it for the future publishers to decide whether to delete or keep.]

My report, after the assessment, runs as follows,

> Dear L,
>
> Must I be honest enough to tell the truth or simply offer platitudes as most people do? As a saying goes, that I saw on Instagram a long time ago and that can remember to this day, 'honesty is a very expensive gift. Don't expect it from cheap people.'
>
> The book manuscript, SB in short, is an unusual novel of intense qualities, so intense that it is a pity that the country it's written in is the wrong one for it. It would have found publication in France, the Netherlands or Germany. But if you talk about Australia, forget it because what this country singularly lacks is innovation, creativity and the power of imagination, qualities that this novel is full of.
>
> While I recommend it for publication without any reservations, I ask the publishers to think again what is it that they want from a book: huge sales that bring in huge profits that can feed them and their author for the rest of their lives without having to publish or write another book ever again? Or a book that brings little profit but that prompts and prods our thinking and imagination along lines hardly trodden before, offering new directions in thinking, writing and reading?
>
> Best,
> Baohui

*

My responses now to the 3 issues, raised by Stacey.

I'm sorry that I wrote the way I did but. I must confess I don't understand the bit about 'self-indulgence'. Is there a non-self-indulgence? To put it another way, is an author not allowed to take selfies because it is self-indulgent?

In regard to theory, I don't think I have found any theories adequate enough to address my kind of fiction that mixes poetry, cross-writing, cross-translation, cross-self-translation, autobiography, biography of an imaginary character, and posthumous writing, e.g. writing as if posthumously. Perhaps you could recommend a book of theory on life after death or death lived as life?

As for the bit about history, I think it all depends. History is self-made as much as it is public-made. Like breathings, like wind, much too much of history is lost or forgotten as soon as it is made. What about the six women whose names are not even traceable in any written histories of this country, officially or unofficially? If I invent a name for each of them and tell a story, would any historians, including the well-paid ones, agree? Does their agreement have anything to do with anything?

I don't have any more to say. But I think I'll work as hard as before, reading more, writing more and digging into the silence, indeed the Silence, more, myself a long and buried silence, too.

[Stacey's mini report: On the manuscript, from p. 219 to p. 228, for 9 pages, something purely external, having little relevance to the main piece of writing, the novel in question, is forcibly inserted into or grafted onto what is known as *Ah Sin, an Imaginary Biography of a Storyteller*, in violation of all the rules of storytelling, particularly that of authorship. More than once, I warned Baohui against the danger of plagiarising despite the decriminalisation of it from Kenneth Goldsmith's point of view, linking it to the obsoletion of pornography as a litigious issue. We don't really need to know whose writing this is. But an act of plagiarism will be looked upon unkindly in this country and under this climate whatever dangerous avant-gardists had to say elsewhere. My personal recommendation to the future editor of this manuscript is an expurgation in its entirety.]

Chapter 3

I spread a piece of writing paper over the makeshift table we had in the middle of the ground in our tent. There was a lingering aroma of eucalyptus in the air. Or was it of the wattle by the river? I could never tell. Then I started writing, with the pen I had bought in Robe, a bottle of ink by the side. Up to down, right to left. Up to down, right to left. Up to down, right to left. The way the writing went, it exactly matched my breathing until it caught her attention.

'Why did you write like that?' said Ciara, mildly surprised. 'why not starting from left hand and moving across the paper horizontally?'

'Good question. I have never thought of it. I just do it,' said I, my pen paused in my hand, then, 'we're all right-handed, I suppose. And rain falls, from up to down, doesn't it?'

'Yeh, but it doesn't fall from right to left, does it?'

'No, unless a wind blows it from the right.'

'But it could blow it from the left as well.'

'In my memory, all the rivers in my hometown run from right to left.'

'But, in mine, they all seem to run from left to right.'

'At least, my hometown rivers all run from East to West.'

'But mine all run from West to East.'

'Too right. Well,' I looked into her eyes, thinking, 'the heart is located in the left part of our bodies. It is not where things get started; it is where things return to, from right to left.'

'It could also be where things get started. Yes, they get started in the left, in the heart located on the left.'

'Well, I give up. You win. But since time immemorial, our writing has been like this, from right to left, like the right-handed limbs, and, from up to down, like the rain. It'll remain so perhaps until time immemorial, too.'

'I can't imagine how we can write like that in English.'

'I suppose not. It might have to be something like "ton, esoppus I", read in reverse, from right.'

'Oh, this talking makes my head ache. I'll go and have a rest.'

I held her in my arms, feeling the baby bulge, and printed a kiss on her mouth. Then I recalled we hadn't had it for quite some time now.

Her hand was touching me underneath and there was already a hard-on.

'Yes?' I said, half-audibly.

'Yes,' she said, no sound, just the moving shape of her lips. Then, 'Would it hurt the baby?'

'No,' said I. 'I'll be gentle, and considerate. I'll go from behind.'

She smiled her sweetest smile and the next moment we were at it, hard inside soft, dry mixed with wet, hot and hot, her breasts, nipples, cupped with my fingers, the pleasure of it all so intensifying that I ejaculated in six shots instead of five, my normal number of shots, while devouring the whiteness of her nape with my eyes. It was such a cleansing act of abandon. I gave my all, semen, sweat, phlegm. I always do.

She held me in her arms, murmuring, 'I love you, Sin. I love you.'

And I said back, 'I love you, Gin. I love you, too.'

'I detest the word "too".'

'I love you, Gin. I love you.'

When she fell asleep, I pulled the crumpled blanket over her and went back to my writing. It was a letter addressed to my parents. I had to write the letter on one piece of paper, both sides, minimizing the weight to reduce the cost of postage. I wrote,

> Dear Mum and Dad,
> I have not been able to write you for a long time because there are so many things that have happened since I last wrote.
>
> The main change that has happened is that I have left the goldfields for good and have started a new life in Melbourne. In fact, I share my love life with Ciara, originally from Ireland and locally from Avoca.

Soon, we are going to have a baby.

Things in the goldfields were unruly, to say the least. The white miners didn't like us. They didn't like the way we dug for gold. They didn't like anything about us, the way we smelt, the way we talked, our language, our customs, even our looks. But, most of the time, they left us alone. It's only when they thought their economic interest was threatened they'd get agitated and threaten action. And they did, so we were chased after, we were chased around, and we were dispersed.

What I found is that they really didn't like us for being good. Because they themselves found it hard to live up to the good standard expected of them they despised us for doing so.

I won't complain any more. To complain is to cost money because the page is already heavy with words.

I do have friends, most of them my old mates from the goldfields, but some of them new, an Indian, for example, and a Jew, for another. I'll tell you about them next time.

Enclosed please find a 5-pound note as part of my support to you.

How's Brother Min doing in San Francisco? Haven't heard from him for ages.

Missing you both and loving you all!

Very best,

Ah Sin, your most respectable and loving son

*

[1654 Chinese characters purged, with the BH translation that follows in the next section—SA]

They say you are an Indian. They also say you are from Punjab or even an Afghan. I don't know what's the difference. When you appeared in front of me the first day, I got a big shock: How come you are leading such a huge thing, like a moving house, yellow all over, its head taller than you, and its colour in sharp contrast with your white gown and white turban. You said your name was Khan. That sounds like the name of a king. In our language, it's called "可汗" (Ke Han). Can sweat, I thought. Because on such a hot day, you are still wearing so much clothing, unlike me, wearing only short clothing, and in straw shoes.

It was on account of my clothes and my long queue that all the locals, kids and adults alike, treated me like a monster. At first, wherever I went, they chased me off. The kids here were pretty bad. I was walking on the road, with a shoulder-pole, when they, all bad smiles, followed me on tiptoe, and gave my pigtail a yank before I realised what they were up to. In that way, I fell quite a few times, my white radish, bok choy and sweet melons rolling all over the place. There was something to be said about the kids who, after all, didn't pinch anything. They yanked my pigtail because they found it a fun thing to do. As soon as they saw me yelling, getting quite upset, they'd run away, laughing, before they threw clogs of soil at me, standing far off, on a street corner.

They weren't so aggressive when they saw you, Khan. In your hands, the camel was like a huge weapon that made everyone fearful because no one had ever seen such animals, a bit like a Guizhou donkey although much fiercer. Plus, your white clothes were whiter than their skin, which acted like a deterrent to them. When you stood there, a black face atop white clothing, with a camel the size of two horses, like a warship so submissively led away by you, even the adults were greatly afraid, let alone the kids.

When I stayed for long in this place, people gradually got used to me because I would often give kids good things to eat, such as sweet melon and sugarcane. When they ate them, the kids developed a sweet mouth and a soft hand. Some even took to call me 'Uncle'. One day, a kid by the name of Jack got a cold and was in a high fever. Helpless as they couldn't get a doctor in a hurry, his parents had to put him in a bathtub, soaked in cold water, hoping that it would reduce the temperature. When I found out about this I went directly to them as they were old acquaintances and often bought my vegetables at a cheap price. I took with me a crock, a finger of ginger and a packet of brown sugar, and cooked a pot of ginger soup. Then I got them to carry the boy out of the cold water. He was shivering all over, his lips turned purple from the cold but his head scorching to the touch. I had a warm blanket brought in, to wrap the kid tightly inside it, and fed him the soup spoon by spoon. Then I told his parents not to open up the blanket because it was meant for him to sweat it out.

You were there that night yourself. Although we both spoke poor English, but, with an exchange of glances, a headshake or nod, we could manage to somehow communicate. But, of course, your English was better than mine as you were able to explain everything clearly to Jack's mum and dad. I was so pleased to see you talk as you gestured, and to see his parents frequently nod their heads.

Our friendship began from a small thing. It was really because I was overcome with curiosity as I found your way of leading a camel so exciting. I picked up my courage, shoulder-pole on my shoulder, and went to watch while forgetting to cry my wares. I went so far as to accost you in my broken English, wondering where you had come from and where you were going, taking your camel with you.

You were friendly, unlike the white people who would either ignore or browbeat you. I learnt that you were from Afghanistan, a country I had never heard of. But I learnt from you that there were camels and men wore white gowns like you, even under a scorching sun, and that you wore white turbans as well. I asked if you were hot, you said you were not. Disbelieving it, I held my hand to touch but he stepped back at once, putting his hand out to stop me, possibly because he was afraid that my market gardener's black hands might dirty his clothes. But did he know that his face was blacker than my hands?

Just then, I heard a simmering roar, which gave me a big fright as I had never heard anything quite like it. When I turned my head around, I saw that it was the camel. As it made the noise, it spat out a long red ribbon before it swallowed it back as if swallowing the thunder back into its belly. Meanwhile, to my horror, all the vegetables in my baskets were gone. Oh, my God! There were a few chives hanging down the camel's mouth!

You burst out laughing, showing all your white teeth. I was so upset, I said, 'I've lost everything. But why are you laughing?' You threw up your hands and said, 'But there's nothing I can do about it.' I said,

'You have to pay for it!' The word 'pay' I could remember most clearly because it was identical with the Chinese character "赔" in sound and meaning. In English, all you have to do is say 'pay' if you want people to pay you, and people would understand you. But you pointed to the camel and said, 'Then get him to pay!' That reduced me to silence. Well, right, why was I so curious as to come and see the camel?

Without saying another word, you lifted the lower hem of your white gown and jumped over the camel, to sit between its two peak-like humps. And, then, when you knocked on its belly with your stick, the camel stepped forward in total submission.

I had not seen you since. I heard that you had gone to the scorching north carrying sacks of salt.

*

Golden Treasure Club invited me to go and do a story. The man from the book club spoke to me the other day as soon as I finished my storytelling in Punch Lane, off Little Bourke Street.

'You did a good job,' said a bald-headed man with a greying moustache as he held out his hand.

I held out my left hand because I was holding my opium pipe in my right and the man immediately pulled his hand back.

I realised my mistake, apologizing as I put down my pipe on the ground and held out my right hand.

The man picked it up, looking me in the eye, and said, 'I was just wondering if it is possible for you to come to our club and tell us a couple of stories.'

'Done,' I said, 'no problem.'

He pulled a black pen out of his top pocket, took up my hand which he had put down after picking it up, and wrote the address and his name on the back of it.

In one glance, I'd taken my bearings: Adrian and Dinkum Café.

*

[Stacey says: So much self-indulgence in himself, with his Chinese poems, paired with his English self-translations as well as show-offishness of the books he has read, all cut, 1202 words.]

*

So it was Sunday night that I went to Dinkum Café to meet up with the club people.

Adrian stood outside the door, smoking. When he saw me, his face broke into a smile. Without much ado, he turned his head around and pointed to the back, with an 'at the back and will join you shortly.'

I went along the narrow passageway between the counter and the tables, lit up by candles in the glass bowls, till I arrived at the back, a large space covered with a canvas, gaslit and with an overhead gas heater. Already, there was a ring of people, seated around a table with a few books on it.

Because no one said anything to me, I found a chair near a corner, pulled out my pipe, pinched, while kneading, a ball of opium from a leather pouch, put it in my pipe and lit it before I let forth a cloud of white smoke that made my head dizzy as a pleasing sense of delight came to my heart, and I peered at the faces that seemed wooden under the gaslight, hardly any of them bare-faced.

While I was stealing glances at them through the opium smoke, I heard snatches of conversation in whispered voices among them: 'A Chinese philosopher', 'Copperfield', 'Walks in beauty', and my hazy glances returned at least one result. The copy lying open on the table was by John Keats.

As soon as Adrian came back, he announced in a flat voice, saying, 'I've invited Ah Sin to come here and tell us a story or two.'

'What about our last discussion of Oliver Goldsmith's work? Are we going to continue with it tonight?' a voice queried, from a man in an overcoat.

'Yes, I mean why not,' said Adrian. 'if there are any issues you'd like to raise or discuss. Let's limit it to half an hour.'

'Since our friend what's-his-name is here, why don't we ask him a question?'

'He's Sin, Ah Sin,' said Adrian.

'While I have the greatest pleasure of meeting your honour,' said the man with a wrinkled face, as wrinkled as a crinkled parchment, 'can I ask if Lien Chi Altangi is a genuine Chinese name?'

'The simple answer is: no, never,' said I, quickly and firmly.

A chuckle was issued from a man whose face was hidden in the shadow of a book he was holding in front of him. He seemed to be hiding his face to read the book, not wanting to see me. But he said, and I could ascertain that the voice came from behind the book,

'Do you have any philosophers in China?'

'Oh, plenty,' said I, offended, and in a wounded tone, 'too many in fact, such as Lao Tzu, Chuang Tzu, Kong Fu Tzu, Meng Tzu, Mo Tzu, Hsun Tzu—'

'You can't be serious,' said the same voice. 'How can they survive? Did they eat at all? Did they only just spend their days thinking?'

'I think they did eat and they did shit, too,' said I, seriously. But my audience, not mine a short while ago, burst into a raucous laughter till I resumed, 'but it is their thinking thoughts that survived their food and shit.'

Despite more laughter from them, I kept on, 'If you look at Australia as it is right now, swept with a mad craze for gold, I'm sure nothing will be left in 10, 50 or 100 years because there's only digging, no thinking. What might survive is shit that might grow into gold in a thousand years for all I know and care. But you won't have a thinking philosopher who digs only into his own head.'

Amidst a rising murmur of confusion, puzzlement, slight disapproval and utter detestation, Adrian said, 'Now, let's give the floor to Sin and hear what he's got to tell us, Altangi or not.'

'Actually,' said I, remaining seated, as soon as I had the opportunity. 'I'll tell a story about Kong Fu Tzu, also known as Confucius. But I hope you don't mind if I use the present tense throughout as that makes you see him as if he were right here in front of your eyes. Once when someone asks Zi Lu, one of Confucius' disciples, what Confucius is like, Zi Lu says he knows nothing about Confucius even though he does. Confucius blames him for it. He says to Zi Lu thus: You ought to have told him that I am someone who reads and writes, to the extent that I often forget eating and sleeping. Sometimes, when I gain something from my reading and writing, I tend to even forget my worries. I have spent my life thus, to such a degree that I sometimes even forget how old I am.'

I paused and relit my extinguished pipe, with another ball of opium pressed into it.

'That's interesting,' said Adrian. 'In our language, your Confucius is at best a bookworm.'

'And at worst?' said I.

'Someone who's so forgetful that he probably doesn't even know what money is when placed before his nose,' the wrinkled man offered.

Ignoring that, I said, 'And there's another story related to him. As Confucius is a man 7ft tall, with a powerful book knowledge, he is asked why he is not serving the king in a royal court. The question is obviously asked to put him to shame because it suggests that he may not be as good as he sounds or else he would have been recruited by the king. But you know what he says in answer to that question? He says that if he can remain loyal to his parents and maintain a harmonious relationship with all his brothers and sisters it is equivalent to being an official in a royal court as, after all, that is what the government or the king's rule is all about: trying to maintain a harmonious relationship between, and with, all his subjects.'

'If anything,' Adrian was again the first to offer a comment. 'it reminds me of a saying, familiar to all: Charity begins at home.'

Thus ended the night, without me being able to offer them the real story that I had been turning over in my mind. It was the one about the woman, King Zhou of Shang's favoured concubine who was originally a fox spirit.

*

I lay in bed, awake, for a long time, wondering why winter nights here were so long, longer than anything I'd ever lived with, and why it was so quiet, not a single sound, except her even breathing by my side. My thoughts flowed, like a sluggish creek, each ripple the face of someone, turning up before it disappeared, with a pursuing memory that relentlessly refused to give up: Gargan who showed me his diary kept while he was a missionary in Jiangxi, Ah Liu who told me of many stories related to interpreting, Ah Mao's outburst in dressing as an emperor imitating what Charles Thatcher wrote in a poem, Ah Bo's suicide, Ah Nong's imprisonment, Ah Heng's death, Ah Ling's death, Ah Chin's death, Ah Wen's death, Ah Yin's death, death, death, death, so many deaths in this country it seemed the sky covering this land was a vast canvas of death. The eyes of the sky looked down and the hands of the eyes pointed a finger at someone walking while the tongue of the eyes said: It's you and we are going to take you back. Then you disappeared. You had nowhere to hide. You joined them in death. United in death. Re-united in death. A beautiful country of deaths. A cemetery more beautiful than life. A united state of deaths. A commonwealth of the departed. Trees feeding on death. Trees fed on death. Trees fattened on death. Cemetery trees. Cemetrees. Almost ten years now. No hope of ever getting rich. Little interest even. Just getting on. Just getting by. Death was a zero, a millionaire of zeroes. The ancients were not afraid of death. They had their eyes gouged and they were happy because they insisted on telling the truth. What was my truth? Everything was fading from memory. And the truth was told and retold in multiplied, multiple forms. And when I looked around, I couldn't find a single person I could call a friend except Ciara.

Chapter 4

I liked this line I came across and I record it here: 'It is better to die *in situ* as I shall.' (Louis MacNeice, *Collected Poems*, faber & faber, 2016 [2007], p. 3)

*

The easiest way to approach history is through figures. History in fact is an account book. What went missing from it is memory. And the other thing missing is silence, or silences. Or perhaps I need to clarify it more specifically. It's not memory that is missing. It is the mind. History has no idea what went through the mind of a fictional character in a fictional place at a fictional time. Historians, the accountants of time, want us to believe that they are the pillars of history because they have written about it, recording it, enlarging it, dignifying it or denigrating it according to their own views, based on their readings of other histories. But they never manage to record a single breath breathed by say Ah Sin, my character, or a single trace of thought that went through his mind at a particular historical moment. Do I exist to simply serve the purpose of matching my character's life in the chronology of their fictionalised histories? Or do I write from my own imagined memory, out of a silence that is as deeply buried as some gold in a pre-historic period in the mind and the heart? Are we really hollow and empty when we don't have a word in our eyes or on our hands? Don't we have things that we can pull out from the depths of the mine in us? It was only yesterday that I had this urge to interview Ah Sin to see what he thinks of this novel that I'm writing of him. Do you look at every possibility presented and say, 'No, but this is not possible,' or do you welcome it with open arms, open hands, open fingers, open eyes, open nose, open mouth, open feet and open toes? Is history what this anonymous poet says when he or she posts the lines in an online discussion group,

> History is not there until we live it
> Then it's something else, a book, a memory, a breath

[Too much about masturbation and too explicit, 496 words cut—SA]

10.22.35am. History is but a list of figures, a heap of fact sheets, that could be randomly arranged like this:

> Riots against the Chinese
>
> Bendigo, July, 1854
> Buckland River, 3 dead, more drowned, 4 July 1857
> Burrangong, incidents between November 1860 and
> September 1861
> Lambing Flat, 30 June 1861
> …
> Too countless to count
>
> And riots against the whites:
>
> 0

Conclusion: History is a tale of the strong oppressing the weak, a very, very old tale. I only love the figures. But history caught up with them, the strong, and vanquished them, time and time again.

T.B. Now, another kind of riot, in cleansing *them* from the mind, the Australianised mind, with the echoes of the old 'No more Chinese' and of the new 'Only Chinese money, no Chinese, please. We don't want them as friends.'

*

According to Andrew Marcus, only 3 Chinese women had arrived in Victoria by 1857. (See his 'Chinese in Australian history', *Meanjin*, v. 42, no. 1, 1983, p. 85.) Let me quote this from the book quoted before, *Taojin di*, by Yu:

[202 Chinese characters cut, translation below. There is an ethical issue here with Yu's work. BH should have sought his permission to include these translations. But because he died before his time I think I'd have to do that on his behalf in order that this book could see the light of the day—SA]

You have to ask the most basic question, such as this: That woman, that Chinese woman, the one from Guangdong, possibly from Kaiping or Enping or Taishan or Xinhui, did she come to Australia with bound feet? What's her first feelings when she first set her China-bound feet on the soil of Robe? Did she happen to have her period that day? If she did, what clothes did she use to stop the bleeding? And how did she hide herself from the men's eyes when she changed them? Did the blood dripping out her vagina stain the petal of a certain wild flower or the blade of a certain wild grass in a certain bush somewhere near Robe? History remains unperturbed, concerned only with numbers, dates and place names.

Oh, yes, there is something about one of the three women before she came to Australia. You want to know about her? You have it here:

[338 characters cut, translation below—SA]

From the bottom of your heart, you are someone romantic. You hanker after things faraway. Even when a young girl, you heard a story in which you learnt that as long as you rowed your boat out to sea you would one day reach the sky and you could always live in the sky, like the stars, shining. Life in the fishing village was boring. When men went out fishing in the sea, women stayed home weaving the fishing nets and kids walked around on the beach, squelching, high fiving the sands with their foot-palms. When you went asleep, you had dreams, and when you stayed awake, you also had dreams. Every time you ran across the beach, you imagined it to be a boundless gate. You made a sound by beating it, like knocking on a door. Would there be someone on the other side and when he heard the sound would he pull it squeakingly open, to invite you in to step into the other side of the earth where there were flowers and greens, no winters, no storms, always peace and quiet and satisfaction? At the time, you didn't know the word 'imagination'. All you knew was that as soon as you closed your eyes, your heart was full of things elsewhere, where you climbed down a downward-growing tree and could see only a sliver of light in the extreme distance. You kept climbing, thinking of the word 'climbing', word by word, downward, towards the depths of your heart.

And this fictional history or history of imagination wouldn't be complete without the description of a third woman who arrived on the ship called 'Young America':

[357 characters cut, translation below—SA]

You are walking on the street side by side with *Dage*, Big Brother. You freshly looked at the scenery around the street. There was a café called Shakespeare. White people were sitting inside it, drinking coffee from their china cups. When they saw you coming, they stopped, one by one. The ones talking stopped talking. The ones drinking coffee stopped drinking coffee, all raising their heads to look at thee. Thou were fretting, finding your collar a tad stiff, making it hard for you to move your neck. Fortunately, because the weather was hot, you had removed your *yunjian* (cloud shoulder, a kind of decorative shawl) and your vest. You didn't put on your skirt. Instead, you wore voluminous black trousers, atop a pair of flowery cloth shoes. In their eyes, male and female, you might look like a monster. But when thou looked at them, thou also found them strange. Yellow hair. Moustache also yellow, like Zhang Fei. If you measured a white woman's eyes, their size would be many times that of thou's eyes. And the colour of their clothes tended to be simple and elegant; they seemed to prefer the colour black, unlike thou, either loud red or loud green and unlike *Dage*, too, whose forehead was shiny and bare, half of it hairless and the back half of it all black hair, combed together and narrowed down to a huge pigtail behind his back. In certain ways, thou found, they were more men than men or more women than women. But it was scary to see them look at you from a distance, in total silence.

Chapter 5

Herbert was a client I quite liked. It was at the end of one of my story-telling sessions that he came up to me and said, 'I really enjoyed your story.' After I found out that he was a land surveyor, I told him that I had a number of friends who were interested in purchasing land and he might get business.

He raised his brow and didn't say anything, looking a little hurt. Still, when I suggested coffee, he welcomed my suggestion. Together, we went to a nearby café and sat down on either side of a table. This man, I thought, gave me an impression that there was something heavy on his mind. While waiting for the coffee to come, we exchanged a few glances. I took my time, resting up from my prolonged session of sto-rytelling, enjoying the silence afterwards, and he, possibly thinking his own thoughts or his own measurements. I had no idea what they were and I was not going to find out, not in a hurry. This was a new habit for me. Unlike most of my fellow countrymen, who were so afraid of silences that they'd never sit quiet, preferring to chat incessantly about little nothings, with their loud mouths, to the chagrin of all the non-Chinese people around them, I learnt from my observation of the daily realities with culturally different people in them. I could now, literally, regard myself in the mirror of my surroundings and other faces, mostly wooden and indifferent, in which I could see the same of myself, think-ing my own thoughts of nothing.

And I wouldn't describe it as the ice, either, the kind of situation between two strangers that would need to be broken before anything happened or could happen. It was probably just that neither of us had little to say to the other.

'But you see,' said the man with hair like a thatched roof.

'Yes?' my eyes turned from inside out and directed themselves towards his spectacled eyes.

'Can I check something with you?'

'Oh, yes, go ahead.'

'Do your people intend to stay in this country forever?'

'My people? How did you mean?'

'The Mongolians, you know,' he said, apologetically, and then, 'or the Celestials.'

'Neither, I'm afraid. These are the nicknames. In our treaties signed with the Great Britain or the United States of America, as far as I can recall, we are referred to as "the Chinese subjects". Please have a look at The Treaty of Nanking in 1842 and The Treaty of Wanghia in 1844 if you are not sure.'

'Granted you are. But my question remains a valid one: Do you people intend to live in this country indefinitely?' the man's face looked intense now, his eyes bulging behind the glasses, enlarged it seemed.

'Relax, relax,' said I. 'let me tell you a story about Confucius. You know who he is?'

'What are you talking about, man? I'm a novelist. And, as far as I know, there are two Confuciuses in the world.'

'Who's the other one?'

'Oliver Goldsmith, who referred to himself as "the Confucius of Europe".'

'That's presumptuous or is it not?'

The man raised his eyebrow again. For a Chinaman, a Celestial, a Mongolian, to attack such an illustrious figure as Goldsmith, it was more than unacceptable. But, the self-acclaimed novelist held his temper in check and simply said, in a light tone, 'Granted it is, but is it your wish, I mean the wish of your people, to stay in this country indefinitely?'

'I suppose so. Although I can't speak for others, I don't deny that everyone has his own wish and will endeavour to carry it out whichever way they can. But you don't want to hear my story?'

'Oh, yes, go ahead,' said Herbert as he took the cup, just arrived, in hand and began sipping from it.

'It won't be long, I promise. I am, after all, quite tired by now. At one stage, Confucius fell ill. This happened when he had lost his ministerial job in the royal court. His disciples treated him like a big shot assuming he'd be delighted. On the contrary, he was very much offended by what he saw as an act of deception. He said to his disciples: I'd rather die surrounded by a couple of my disciples by my side than by people who thought they were my servants and underlings. Even if I wasn't honoured with a state funeral, I would at least not die neglected on the road if I had my disciples near me.'

'What are you driving at?' said the man, 'with this story?'

'Nothing. It's just something that came to mind when you asked about "my people" going back.'

'No, I asked if they intend to stay.'

'Sorry but that sounded exactly like what it meant in reverse, in my ears.'

'Do you write?'

'No, hardly ever. I'm a storyteller. And I make a living by telling stories or I try to.'

'I like the story you told about Na Za this morning.'

'Oh, that's the name of our son, when he's born, that is.'

'Ah, congratulations, on your future son.'

'Are you married?'

'No.'

'You say you are a novelist? Are you writing a novel at the moment?'

'Thinking of doing one. But I need to sort out a few things.'

'I see,' said I, as the meaning of the remark sank in. 'Actually, most of my people, if that's the term you prefer, want to go home.'

'Why?'

'There's no future here for them.'

'But there is a great future, isn't there? They find piles of gold. They find our women and get married. They produce kids. They have their own people streaming in. They then turn this country into their own colony.'

'That's all bullshit. It's newspaper talk. You only have to look at the reality to realise that nothing of that is true, not a shred of truth in it.'

'But, surely, the written word is superior to the spoken?'

'Oh, yes. That's how my people treat it. They won't let alone a scrap piece of written paper strewn on the ground but must pick it up, put the pieces together in a heap and burn them together in a shrine, meaning them for the gods. But are you sure that the living words, right from the living mouths, are not worth anything?'

'Not till they turn into the written via the sacred hands of a writer.'

'I'm not sure. But I don't argue against it, either. In fact, all my stories come directly from written sources even though those sources may have been oral originally. Who knows what is what, and which is which, eventually? Is mouth more important than hand or the other way round?'

'Let's see what's going to happen, then,' said Herbert as he finished his cup and went to the counter to pay.

For once, I didn't fight to rush ahead of him to make the payment as it was the custom of my people to do. I thought I deserved my cup for at least I had somehow provided him with material for his novel, apart from a freely offered story which might be worth a farthing, in the scheme of things. With stuff like that, you never know.

*

In my historical mind, one that's full of historical shit as much as of good stuff, mostly racially connected, I recalled Elinor Mordaunt, that English woman writer who loved love, with her memory of the Chinese half-caste guy from Portugal in Melbourne's Little Bourke Street. Soon enough, I found the reference, on this hot day of 43 degrees Celsius, a day on which I wondered to myself why they didn't abolish living in the bush. But Mordaunt's description of the Chinese went something like this. For this guy, 'there seemed to be no historical spot in Europe which he did not know intimately, not a half-forgotten verse that he could not finish for me, not a writer whose works he had not only read, but whose place in literature and whose influence he clearly realized. And then sometimes he would quote Chinese poetry, accompanying it with a running translation which was a delight to the ear.' And his attitude towards the 'White Australia' was vividly portrayed here: 'One evening I remember some insolent, loud-voiced remarks on a "White Australia" were flipped down the table in his direction, but he only shrugged his great shoulders. "We shall see," he said; "after all it is the best who win."' (Mordaunt, *On the Wallaby*, 1911, p. 186).

She must be talking about Ah Sin, *my* Ah Sin. Was she not?

*

On the fifth day of the fifth month, on the lunar calendar, it's the Duanwu Festival again. This time, unlike before, I was prepared as I had bought a bunch of bamboo leaves, a ball of strings, some pork and a bag of glutinous rice in the market, with the intention of making Tzung Tzu for both of us. On seeing the brown-green leaves, she was perplexed and wondered what they were meant for. I didn't explain, simply said, 'When it's ready, you'll see.'

Then I started preparing the next day. It was a laborious process. I washed the leaves in the river, one after another, and straightened them, laying them in a bamboo basket. I washed the rice in a basin. Then, with a kitchen knife, I skinned the pork, taking off its skin, saved for stir-frying.

When I came back to the kitchen, I put the wok on, filled it with water, put the leaves in and lit the fire. I let them cook in the boiling water for about five minutes before I put the fire out and laid them in the cold water to keep it in their original shape. I soaked the rice in the water overnight. I then diced the pork and marinated the pieces with such ingredients as five spice and star anise seeds.

She watched me doing all this with an intensity I had never seen before. No questions asked, therefore no answers. The only thing she said and that I could remember years after was this, 'Why do you have so much tradition? And is it worth keeping it alive even when you are so far away from it?'

My answer was simple, and, in my opinion, to the point, 'Oh, yes. As long as there is love, there is tradition.'

That night, as usual, we didn't have a heavy meal, just a few baked potatoes, a number of steamed Tzung Tzu, much to her delight, and a bowl of fish soup, cooked with the freshwater catfish that I had caught in the Yarra. Tradition has it that catfish soup contains the most nutritious substance for a pregnant woman. The soup, when well cooked, turned milky and tasted like nothing else. It was pure heaven.

Over dinner, she praised my culinary skills and said how much she enjoyed everything I did, food, stories and – she paused, winking at me. I took the hint but pretended not to understand until she said, 'Tradition, you know, is something I don't have and don't want to have.'

'Well, I suppose,' said I, remembering a guy I had dealt with who was wont to make promises that he never intended to carry out, always ready with excuses. I told her who that person was.

'Oh, it's William. I don't like him,' said she.

'Well, you know, he's otherwise okay except where promises are concerned. Now,' said I, working myself up, without realising what I was doing. 'that is tradition. Where I come from, people put an enormous emphasis on the importance of keeping promises. In our language, there are many expressions that attest to that, such as yi nuo qian jin, a promise is worth thousand pieces of gold, and yan bi xin, xing bi guo, once promises are made, action must be carried out.'

'But sometimes promises are easier to make than keep, you know,' said she.

'Why make them then?' said I, recalling how William, who had borrowed five shillings from me, made constant promises to pay me back but never did.

'Perhaps because poverty made it impossible? Or people are too busy?'

'I don't know. I'll tell you one story along this line. This is about a king and how he lost his kingdom in raising false alarms. In ancient times, there were many beacon towers along the borders. If you light one up by setting fire to a pile of firewood at night, it sends out a signal that enemies are crossing the border and coming to get you. The feudal lords, princes and dukes will then come to your rescue. Now, this king, King You of Zhou, had a beautiful imperial concubine by the name of Bao Si. She was an extremely picky woman and hardly ever smiled. To make her happy with a smile, the king had in vain tried all means.

She just didn't find it amusing enough until a bad minister suggested the idea to the king about the beacon towers. Subsequently, the king ordered all the 20-odd beacon towers along the borders be lit with fires when he and Bao Si, in a pagoda on top of a hill, sat watching how thousands of troops from all around came to the rescue of the supposedly fallen capital. To the great consternation of all, this was a mere joke, but it was a joke that, for the first time, moved Bao Si the beautiful imperial concubine to a sweet precious smile. The king's pleasure did not last long for, a few years after, when his kingdom was invaded by an alien race and all the beacon towers were lit, no one came to his rescue because they all had automatically assumed that this must be another joke.'

'That's China,' said she. 'Not here, where similar things will never happen.'

Her remark threw me into silence, which I found it hard to pull myself out of. Silently, I did the dishes and, silently, I made the bed for both of us. Then, silently, I blew out the candle, when she touched me on my arm, my right arm. Her hand slid down my arm, to rest on my hip, my right half, and to move across it downwards, stopping where my crotch was, cupping my tool, already erect.

'Are you angry with me?' said she.

'Not really.'

'Yes, you are.'

'No, but there's nothing to be angry about.'

She went silent. But her hand was busy, so much so that I sat up, half reclining against the wall, and said to her, 'Please, put it in your mouth. I love it.'

She took me in her mouth, warm and wet, raising her eyes to look at me, entranced. It was not till then that I realised, in a single moment of revelation, how the word 'eyes' contained the word 'yes'. Then, hot and hard, my tool began vibrating, shooting a whole load of semen right into her throat so that she swallowed it wholly and whole-heartedly.

I kissed the semen that had smeared her lips and sucked it all clean, my own salty stuff that tasted no less beautiful than the catfish soup. And it's not till that very moment when a poem by Zhang Wei, a Tang poet, who wrote it on the wall of his friend's house, came back to me:

> Friends are made with gold
> Not much gold, no deep friends
> So whatever promises are made
> You'll eventually go in different directions, after parting company

*

Last night, I had a dream in which I saw Mum. Her hair is all silver. She is smoking a pipe, making a pattering noise in it. Then she starts talking. She says: Your Dad has been dead for many years now. That means you have also been overseas for many years. A lot of our villagers have come home. According to them, they have made plenty of money. But there are also a lot who are not back. I heard they are dead and buried in an alien land. Every time I hear someone is dead and his bones will stay behind, I burst into tears because I think of you. I can hardly hold my eyes open these days because I have wept so much, too much, my eyes bleary with tears. Men of my age are all dead. Your dad dead. Your uncles dead. Their brothers all dead. I don't know why they are all dead. Perhaps they work too hard in everything. They work hard by day. They work hard by night, too. They lose too much vital energy. I want you to keep well and come back. Even if you are back with nothing on your back, I wouldn't mind. I just want to see you whole, a live mass of living flesh. I want you to come back and marry the girl next village because I want you to keep our family name alive. The only way to achieve that is to marry the girl and have kids. It's Buddha's will. The girl, Ah Xiang, has now grown into a full woman. She is waiting. She has been waiting all these many years now. The dead spirits and I, we all want you to come back.

While listening to her, I found this urge in me to ask her questions. But everything I asked fell flat. Indeed, they fell on deaf ears. Then I found my tongue-tied questions jostling in my chest but refusing to come out. I watched her taking her time smoking the pipe and delivering her speech, sitting cross-legged, like a Buddha in her chair. When I tried my hardest to examine her sad teary eyes, I woke up with a start.

She woke up, too. And she said, 'You were making a lot of noise in your sleep. Did you know that?'

'No,' said I. 'What did I say?'

'You were talking gibberish, in your own language that I don't understand a word of.'

'Oh, I'm sorry I woke you.'

'No, you didn't. I wasn't feeling very comfortable all night and, now, I'm feeling even worse,' said Gin.

I got scared and sat up straight, from underneath the quilt, my left hand shot out in search of the matchbox in the darkness.

'I'm sorry but I don't feel well. I feel like having a crap.'

'Oh, I know what it is, I know what it is,' I said, repeatedly. 'we're going to have the baby.' By now, I was on full alert, like an arrow, drawn on a ready bow, as a rush of memory flooded across my mind, with all the details standing out vividly, the chief of which was a wooden basin of warm water, with a naked baby soaking in it.

I lit the candle, and, holding her in my arms, helped her out of the bed. Already, the sheets underneath were wet. Her water must have broken! I put her in the sofa, slid a cushion beneath her and covered her with a blanket as I went hurriedly to the kitchen where I lit the fire and sat a kettle filled with cold water. Then I heard her say, in an enfeebled voice, 'Please find the scissors and some clean warm water.' Then she added, 'A bar of soap, too.'

While I was getting ready, filling the big wooden bathtub with warm water, finding as many candles as I could and lighting them all up, my mind went through all my goldfield experiences. But I could not find a single occasion on which my gold-digging mates physically delivered a baby in my presence. There were stories galore, though, of how babies got delivered in difficult circumstances without any medical support as they were known to have come out the way ripe fruit like apples and oranges fell off the branches, simply too easy. I imagine that tonight would be the night on which I'd make an easy and pleasant job of it, too.

So, I transferred her to the tub and put her in it, half submerged in the warm water, and waited for the baby to come. Now, she had stopped crying, her eyes closed, her face a placid lake, content, and she seemed to have entered into a dream, relaxed and at ease. I waited and waited but nothing happened. All around us, there was darkness and quietness. The night felt so long as if the day would never break. I kept the water warm by replacing the cold with the warm till I felt the need to go to the dunny outside. Just as I stood there pissing, shivering, when I heard a terrifying shriek that came through the thatched roof of our hut. I went quickly back and, to my horror, mixed with delight, I saw something between her legs! A mass of wriggling flesh, crying in a voice that raised the roof.

'My baby,' I found it irresistible to cry out. 'Oh, my baby!'

I snatched a clean towel out of a small pile of them next to the tub and, with it, wrapped the crying baby up. Then I found I couldn't take it away as there was something tugging at it. Oh, it's the umbilical cord that the 'scissors' were meant for. I found the scissors, cut it then and there and went to the bed in the bedroom and put the baby half underneath the quilt. All the while I did this, I did it with complete aplomb and absolute joy, believing in my ability to do something successfully that I had never done before. But something oppressive, something ominous seemed going on as the atmosphere seemed too quiet for my liking. Then I realized that it was her.

Oh, horror of horrors! The bathtub was a pool of blood and Ciara had a face as pale as a white sheet of paper. My hand went instinctively out to her nose to feel if there was breathing. There was, but very faint, very, very slight. There was nothing I could do but seek assistance from my neighbours. I did, after I dried her and cleaned her up with a towel and dressed her up.

Lynn and her husband Dave, our neighbours, came over and gave us a hand. They helped call the ambulance which took Gin and I to the Melbourne Hospital, and they stayed behind, looking after the baby.

As soon as we arrived, a nurse examined Ciara and reported that her heart had stopped beating.

'But that's not possible,' said I as tears streamed to my eyes, blinding me. 'She's alive and well when I helped her onto the ambulance.'

'She's bleeding profusely,' said the nurse, pointing at the soaked sheets beneath her.

'Oh, oh,' I was literally choked on the word, unable to utter anything.

*

I went to Ciara's funeral. It was a fine day. The sun's light touched everything, the rooftop, the crown of a eucalyptus tree, a wavelet in the Yarra that turned and disappeared, and the face of Ava, my baby girl, held in my arms. My heart was as heavy as the gravestone, marked with these words:

> In Loving Memory of Ciaravoca Ahsin
> My Loved Wife

I had no thoughts in my mind; it was like the sky now, without a cloud in it. I had no friends to attend the funeral, either, just the funeral director Don and his assistant. And there was also the catholic priest Father Joseph. He delivered the homily, praising how chaste a woman Ciara was in all her life.

Hugging my baby close to me, I stood surrounded by the other headstones and the sunshine on them. How I wished I could stay inside that coffin with her for ever and ever! The severance was simply too much to bear. A tear broken in half, inside and outside.

Chapter 6

Dear Stacey,

One thing that may baffle you here is the seeming lack of friends on the part of Ah Sin as it conflicts with the common perception of the Chinese as a large landmass kind of people, I mean a large peoplemass, a landpeoplemass or peoplelandmass, that went everywhere en masse in those days, a people that seem always on the move in twos and threes if not in twenties and thirties or two hundreds and three hundreds.

Nothing is further from the truth. As far as I know, and from my own experience, they were the loneliest people in the world. They lived apart from the whites and other people of colour, both as a result of the government's separatist policy and of their own reluctance to mix indiscriminately. They even lived apart from themselves, the way they did back in their own country, each clinging to their own clan or village, like a large plate of loose sands, not my words, but the words of Sun Yat-sen. Because emperors throughout the centuries were mostly oppressors and exploiters, people were quintessentially survivors doing their best to protect themselves by making the best of a bad situation and moving on.

And the other common perception of the Chinese is that they were steeped in tradition. The second they open their mouths, they quote Confucius or Lao Tzu. They won't begin a ritual without setting off firecrackers. They'll burn incenses at the funeral and have a great meal to celebrate the event in what they call a white happiness, as contrasted with a red happiness meant for weddings. But Ah Sin was not like that. He spoke English. He mixed with people of all nationalities. He lived with an Irish woman. He did have a few friends, like Ah Fong and Ah Mao but they were either busy or living in a mental home. He had acquaintances, too, such as Get Sling and Ah Liu. But they were also busy. Besides, Ah Sin was not someone who would readily seek help or sympathy from the others. He was self-reliant enough to do things his own way: do them himself or pay for them to be done. Neither was he a man given to emotional display, whether for show or for real. He was as committed to love as he was to the bringing up and education of the fruit of his love: his baby girl, which is why he did what he did, as I described previously.

One must also understand, and remember, that Chinese people as a race were the most denigrated, the most despised and the most belittled then, and it's almost as if this race should be totally erased from the face of the earth. Ace, race, erase, see the connection? How about create a new word 'erace'? How could they be allowed to continue their existence for so many millennia? Didn't Mark Twain once refer to a New York Chinaman as 'the friendless Mongol'?

Henry David Thoreau, that philosopher whose thoughts and practice influenced so many followers who didn't dare follow him in practice, just taking pleasure in the thought, once said this below,

"Nations! What are nations? Tartars! and Huns! and Chinamen! Like insects they swarm. The historian strives in vain to make them memorable. It is for want of a man that there are so many men. It is individuals that populate the world."[1]

I always maintain that Chinese civilisation is one on its own, a mixture of everything, like the face of a Chinese that looks Caucasian with an 'asian' in it, albeit lower-cased, perhaps deliberately, mixed or fucked – forgive the expression – to an inseparable degree. You think they think and behave like you until it is too late when you realise that they neither think nor behave like you, which explains the profound sense of loneliness within them.

Best,

BH

---

1 See here: https://www.azquotes.com/quote/942377

P.S.

[Anti-theory, no good, 615 words cut – SA]

*

Dad sent me a WeChat message last night after I had switched off my phone and gone to sleep. I'll skip the trivia and keep the essentials. I'll even ditch my original thought of including the entire message or parts of it in Chinese by providing a parallel text in English.

The key message is this that if there is any moral support these days it has to do with 'Like'. He said he wouldn't mind being unhappy about my behaviour lately which he thought was very ungrateful. As a supporting father, he said, he didn't expect any financial returns from me. Nor did he expect me to be always respectful in a boring way, beginning every message with a 'Dear Dad' and closing it with things like 'Very best' or 'Many thanks and much appreciated'. He wouldn't mind being called 'Mate' as long as the contents of the letter or message were dutiful and respectful. But he was sorely disappointed that there were no such things anymore. Fact is, whenever he sent me shared postings, about anything and everything, in Chinese, I never bothered replying, with a 'received with thanks'. Worse. He said that whenever I put stuff in Moments on WeChat, he would click 'Like'. However, there was never a return of kindness on my part because I never clicked a single 'Like' for anything he'd posted or shared in Moments. He wondered why I did that and if I as his son had ever thought how important it was to 'Like' someone, even if it was his father. These things were trivial, he admitted. But didn't we all live in an age of self-media, self-trivia, in which one's self is self-exposed on a moment to moment basis, for all to see, particularly for the loved ones to see? Wasn't anything even worth a 'Like' by one of one's loved ones? Where does one show one's love, or even like? Does one have to wait till one dies to hear or see a 'Like'? Is that possible? Does that make sense? Why do we so hate to Like? Why are we so stingy with Likes? If honesty means not to Like, are we honest enough to admit that we do like to be Liked but we just don't like to

Like? After all, you were brought up by Mum and Dad with love and like, why can't you return that with the same? Do we have to invite you to like us as some do on Facebook? How awful is that, inviting our son to like his parents?

It is for this reason that he revealed that he'd partially blocked me by not allowing my Moments pictures or captions to be viewable by him and not allowing his to be reviewable by me, thus, at one remove, getting rid of the anxieties caused by the lack of Likes or unreciprocated Likes.

*

[Stacey says: Throwaway remarks on literature, irrelevant to this creative thesis. 1115 words cut.]

*

Chapter 7

Before I left for home, with my baby girl, renamed Na Za, I had one more commitment. I had been invited once again by the book club in the Dinkum Café, to run another story session. For that, I had got myself prepared, this time in Chinese, with Ah Liu as my interpreter, on a Sunday when he was not working.

I caught up with Ah Liu, in my humble hut, before we went together to the Café. When he saw me, the first thing he said to me was, 'I'm sorry that your wife—'. I cut him short by saying, 'No, please', then I thanked him for agreeing to interpret for me as I poured him a hot cup of Iron Goddess of Mercy.

'How did you go?' he started, looking at the baby sitting on my left lap, 'she's lovely, isn't she?'

'Oh, yes, my best and only companion now,' said I.

'Oh, no, don't say that. You've got plenty of friends. We all are, you know.'

'Thank you for that.' I knew what it was like. But I couldn't say more than that. 'And your work busy?'

'You bet! I'm dragged from court to court, interpreting for all sorts of people in all sorts of cases.' Once he got started, Ah Liu found it hard to stop. 'But I can't give you any details because by law I'm not allowed to divulge any information except to say that it's all about shit stuff, involving murders, manslaughters, robberies, thefts, suicides, arson attacks, mental patients, prisoners, and what not.'

'You know what? You can write a book of stories based on these cases.'

'Oh, there are heaps of stories for sure. It's one thing to interpret for people who tell you stories and quite another to put them down in a book. You might be found doing this against the law, you know.'

Up to that very minute, my baby had been fast asleep. But the word 'law' sounded like a clap of thunder that sent her into a loud, shrill cry. With one accord, both of us burst out laughing, our laughter mixed with her cries till she came to an abrupt stop, her eyes, wide open, staring at me in amazement before moving on to stare at Ah Liu. Then she burst into tears again when I said, 'Please don't, Na Za. Ah Liu is a friend, not a devil. And he is not the law, only that the law makes him busy.'

'Oh, yes,' said Ah Liu. 'the law makes me work like a devil.'

I wiped the tears from Na Za's face, with my sleeve, and said to her, 'Be brave for you are Na Za who dares the devil.'

'Is that her name? I must say it's a great name even though it's originally meant for a boy.'

'But it's better for a girl, for my girl,' I said as I lowered my head and printed a huge kiss on her white face.

'She is both Mandarin and English,' said Ah Liu.

'No. She is both Mandarin and Irish,' said I.

'What are you going to talk about tonight?' Ah Liu changed the topic, not forgetting to add, 'but it's very hard to tell her apart from either.'

'I'll keep that a secret. You'll know as soon as I start talking. The only thing that worries me is this baby. What if she wakes up in the middle of it? What if she bursts out crying, like just now? And what if she is kept awake all night by the noise of storytelling and people talking?'

'You really should have told me earlier. Else, I'd have got my girlfriend Fran to come along and she might act like a temporary nanny, you know.'

'Don't worry. We'll see how it all goes. And we shall limit the whole thing to under one hour.'

'Done,' said Ah Liu as he rose to go.

*

This time round, when I arrived, there was a changed atmosphere, quite unlike the charged one last time. Piercing glances were now replaced with kindly looks. Friendly hands were extended to shake mine. Greetings were exchanged. Remarks were made, mostly on my baby, in praise of how long her lashes were, how big she was, and how white. Again, like last time, there was no woman in the audience.

Quickly, I compared notes with Adrian, letting him know that I'd prefer to sit and do my story while holding my baby in my arms, wrapped up in warm clothes, because it was less tiring that way. He was obliging enough, saying that I could go for as long as I felt comfortable and that I could be the first to go. I thanked him for his kindness and plunged into my story straightaway while, of course, introducing Ah Liu as my interpreter.

The first one was a short Buddhist tale of a five-coloured deer. It saved a drowning man at its own peril and told him not to betray its whereabouts. The man promised that he'd never betray him. But, when the king's wife fell ill and was told that only a five-coloured deer could save her life, the king offered a huge sum to get the deer caught. It was not till then that the man, saved by the deer, came forward and claimed that he would reveal where the deer was if he was awarded with the money. The instant in which he said that, his face was covered in impetigo. Soon enough, the king's army located the deer and surrounded it. The deer emerged from its hiding and begged the king not to order his soldier to shoot it. It told the king how the drowning man had begged the heavens, the gods and all the deities to save his life when it was the deer itself that had jumped into the water and carried him to safety. The king, deeply moved, gave the order not to kill the deer. Afterwards, thousands of five-coloured deer came flocking into the country, and brought with them everlasting prosperity and peace.

I finished the whole thing in one go, in Mandarin. While Ah Liu was interpreting it, I took the time to feed Na Za with a bottle of milk, kept warm in a leather bag. She was very good, her dark eyes shiny with a light that reminded me of her mother. My heart ached at the thought. Then I heard my name called as they were asking me to move on to the next story if there was one.

'Yes,' said I. 'Let me begin by asking you a question, all of you: Have you heard of a Chinese poet by the name of Li Po?'

An utter silence. I heard the pattering of a beginning rain outside. And I was startled: How can I carry my baby home in the rain?

'Don't worry,' said Andrew. 'if no one knows, you do and you can tell us, correct? Isn't that the very reason why we had Sin here again tonight?' he turned and asked the audience.

'Oh, yes,' a chorus of voices rose and I had my moment of vindication.

'He's one of our greatest poets,' I began. 'born about 1100 years ago, he died at the age of 61. He is not only known as a poet but also as a drunkard, or drinker-poet. One short poem he wrote was known to nearly all the Chinese people. Entitled, "Thoughts on a Quiet Night", it goes thus: "Bright moonlight in my bed / like frost on the floor / I raise my head to look at the moon / and, lowering my head, I miss my home."' I said all this in English and as soon as I finished I could hear a couple of appreciative oomphs and ohs in the audience. Nodding my head, I went on, 'But little is known of him as an interpreter.'

As I said that in Mandarin, my audience was left confused, but only momentarily as Ah Liu quickly took over and started interpreting. He was fluent and expressive as he accompanied his words with gestures, adding a couple of things I didn't even know, as if he was translating my story, as he said, 'Just as Captain Cook had an interpreter by the name of Tupaia, history was full of interpreters forgotten by people, such as Zhao Xian, one of the last emperors of the southern Song dynasty, who became emperor at the age of four and was dethroned two years after when he was taken prisoner by the invading Mongols. At the age of 19, he was sent by Kublai Khan into exile in Tibet where he became a Buddhist monk and spent the rest of his life translating Buddhist texts between the Chinese and Tibetan languages until he was cisi (blessed with death) by Emperor Yingzong of Yuan because of a poem he wrote in which he missed his lost paradise when he was the emperor himself.'

'To make a very long story short,' said I, eyeing my baby, who was breathing evenly in the crook of my left arm. 'there was a reception in the royal court in which the emperor was presented with a letter by a foreign emissary from Balhae, a small kingdom in Manchuria,

Korea and the Russian Far East. But neither the emperor nor any of his ministers or their assistants could understand a word of it. At the time, Li Po was taking the civil service examination. Because he was such a genius, it took him little time to answer all the questions and he was the first to come out of the exam room. As soon as Yang Guozhong and Gao Lishi, two of the emperor's most favoured ministers, took a look at his examination papers and recognized his name, Yang commented that it was no good and such a writer was only good enough to grind the ink for him while Gao echoed by saying that he was fit for pulling on his boots for him.

'When no one could understand the letter from the emissary, He Zhizhang, Li Po's poet friend, recommended Li whose name was quite familiar to the emperor. Despite Yang and Gao's protests, the emperor decided to get Li Po to read it. I will only give you a synopsis as the letter is quite long. But the gist of it, as Li Po revealed, is that Gadokbu（可毒夫）, the king of Balhae, demanded that the Tang emperor grant him an annexation of 13 states from Goryeo or else he would order his troops to invade Tang.

'Emperor Xuanzong of Tang was both pleased and concerned, wondering if Li Po could write a letter back in the language of Balhae, to which Li readily agreed but on one condition only that Yang must grind the ink for him while Gao must pull on his boots for him. The two men, deeply resentful, had to do it for fear of incurring the ire of the emperor.

'Then, in the presence of the emissary, Li Po wrote the letter in one go, right in front of a watching emperor, in a tone that was neither humble nor arrogant, reminding the Gadokbu that Tang was a great country to which all the surrounding countries paid their tributes, that a small country like Balhae, a mere attachment to Goryeo, was not even worth reckoning with if it came to war and that, should a war break out, Tang would smash it to smithereens, and soak it in blood'

Just then, a shrill cry from my baby broke my talk and silence befell an enthralled audience. Lowering my head, I had a look and 'oh'ed as I saw a pool of water coming out of her nappy, my forearm getting instantly warmed. I let Ah Liu do the talking and interpreting while quickly disappearing in the nearby toilet. There, I changed the nappy, using a few freshly cut pieces of my old bedsheets, making her comfortable, before I came back.

By the time I tiptoed back to the entrance, my baby in my left arm and a bottle of milk in my right hand, I could see in one glance that the whole thing was over as some had already stood up, making their way out to the toilet, and Ah Liu was talking with someone about something. By the intense look on his face, I could see that he was trying to explain something. But the man who was listening didn't seem quite happy. I went over and asked what they were talking about when the man, wearing a top hat, turned on me and said, 'But that sounded very much like what you people have been doing all these many centuries, even millennia, haven't you?'

I, blinking my eyes, was totally lost and said, 'I'm sorry but what do you mean?'

The man, George I think his name was, had very small eyes and a spade face. He went on to say, 'You have invaded Mongolia, Korea and Tibet, and, now, you are invading this colony. Did you realise that?'

'Actually,' said I, as I pulled out the nipple from Na Za's mouth, causing her to start crying, when I put it back in again. 'if you have the slightest knowledge of Chinese history, you wouldn't have said that. I mean, you ought to have known that China's is a history or has been a history of repeated invasions by the foreigners. The Southern Song fell when the Mongols invaded China in the year of 1276. The Ming fell in 1616 when the Manchus invaded China. But, as a matter of fact, each time China was invaded, it grew stronger as it had the ability to absorb all the foreign elements into the Han and turn them into one.'

The man seemed to have grown less aggressive, albeit still not quite convinced. Ah Liu, the constant peacemaker, cut in, with a remark that went, 'I don't think it really matters who invades whom. Ultimately, I think, the strong will swallow the weak up even if they seem vanquished by the weak in the beginning. Savages and barbarians always win at first but at last they are the ones defeated because it is civilisation that will triumph over savagery.'

A few other club members, standing in a circle and remaining quiet for the length of the talk, either agreed by nodding their heads or disagreeing by raising their brows, without saying anything, except William, who said, 'The Mongolians are always a problem and they can't be civilised.'

I was about to say something when Ah Liu held out his hand, like a stop sign, and said, to William and Adrian, 'Can we say thank-you to Ah Sin for his wonderful stories and let him go as he's got his baby to look after?'

Prompted, Adrian said the same and I took up the opportunity to thank Ah Liu for doing a fantastic job interpreting my stories.

*

I, B.H., found myself scheming again. And I don't think it's George; it's actually William, the one who wrote *White or Yellow?* I should have added that William showed Ah Sin a sample of his writing, part of a novel in progress, actually, two, one of which goes,

> I would not do a black man harm or a yellow man or a green man for that matter but I'd sooner see a daughter of mine dead in her coffin than kissing one of them on the mouth or nursing a little coffee-coloured brat that she was mother to... (Lane, *White or Yellow?*, p. 9)

And the other one goes,

> Perhaps under all their meekness these Chinese were braver, more stubborn, more vigorous, and it was doomed that they should conquer at last and rule in the land where they had been treated as outcasts and intruders. (Lane, *The Workingman's Paradise*, p. 10)

Ah Sin never heard back from William again. Nor did he contact him because William didn't leave him a contact address. It was not till that trip back to his home village with Na Za that he read the pieces. Without a word and nodding his head towards the second piece, he wiped his arse in the ship's toilet with them and flushed them.

I did two things today. First, I Googled sex change. And the first piece of info came from a very unlikely source, at DFAT: https://www.dfat.gov.au/about-us/publications/corporate/passports/online-pass-port-information/Policy/Identity/Sex/Changeofsexsexandgenderdi-verse/index.htm , with the very first passage that goes,

> The Australian Human Rights Commission (*Addressing sexual orientation and sex and/or gender identity discrimination 2011*) defines the phrase 'sex and gender diverse' (SGD) as referring to the whole spectrum of sex and/or gender identity. For the purposes of issuing passports, this includes 'trans' and 'intersex' persons. 'Trans' is a general term for a person whose preferred gender is different to their sex at birth. The term 'intersex' refers to a person who has genetic, hormonal or physical characteristics that are not exclusively male or female. A person who is intersex may identify as male, female or as being of indeterminate sex.

I found this less enlightening than I wished for. I then went in search of information written in Chinese about sex change and if sex-change would make it easier for one to secure a permanent resident status even though it's not really what I was after. My search quickly ended up in tapping into sex with sex-changed people, with websites I had watched and self-censored. The truth is my dic—my preferred way to refer to the word 'dick'—remained tragically unerected the whole time. If I did go through the process I wonder how much sexual drive I would lose and have to enhance with medications or hormone. The idea appalled me.

The other thing I did was sex-change my name, secretly, to my-self. Instead of Baohui（宝辉，Treasured Brilliance）, I now turned it into a woman's name: Baohui（苞蕙，Budding Orchid）. Well, I liked it so much that I now officially called me that, in private. Like the one stone that killed the two birds, this self-initiated stunt made me like myself no end.

*

Because of the baby, Ah Liu and I took a cab and went back to my den. He didn't say anything about my stories except that he found the Li Po story quite amazing as he had never known that Li knew a foreign language. I said — by now, both of us were in bed, side by side, after a simple meal consisting of two bowls of hot noodles and after I fed my baby and put her to sleep in the cradle next to me — that Li was in fact not a real Han-Chinese. He was born in Suyab, or Broken Leaf, a city in Kyrgyzstan. His father's name was Li Ke, a rich merchant there, Ke an important indication that they may have migrated there from China because the word meant 'guest'.

'Just like you and me,' said I.

'Are you also of Hakka origin?' said Liu.

'Oh, yes. Didn't I tell you? My people have originally migrated from Henan, you know.'

'My people have migrated from even further away.'

'From where?'

'Hubei.'

'Yes, people from everywhere in the north migrated to the south for centuries.'

'Five exoduses as far as I know,' said Ah Liu as he recounted how the Hakka people started their first exodus from as early as 300 AD at the end of the Upheaval of the Eight Kings, then another one in the Tang dynasty, a third one at the end of the Northern Song dynasty, the fourth one at the beginning of the Qing dynasty and the fifth, at the time of the Taiping Heavenly Kingdom Movement, and that's when the largest exodus began in history, one that moved overseas and spread all over the world. 'you know, I have cousins who are in Cuba, Peru and Brazil.'

'You sounded like a scholar, you know.'

'I'm interested in history and if I get enough money from interpreting I may one day go to study history at the University of Melbourne.'

'Oh, that's a nice idea.'

'It's not just an idea. I'm going to put it into practice one day.'

'You know what?'

'What?'

'When one is in power, one should keep an air of the mountain and the forest and when one is in the political wilderness one should keep one's ambition alive to run the country again.'

'That sounds familiar. Are you quoting someone?'

'It's from The Cabbage Talk: 居官应有山林气，在野须怀治国才.'

'I think I know that one from memory.'

'You are like that, in the wilderness now. But.'

'You, too. Who knows what one is capable of doing one day? One's potential lies too deep for one's discovery, like a volcano, like an earthquake, like a tsunami.'

'Well, I admire you for that.'

'You are doing well, too.' It's not till then that he said something that faintly sounded like praise. Unlike the Australians, who were overflowing with words like 'thank you', 'good on you' and 'well done', my people hardly ever said these things. It's all expressed in expletives such as 'ha', 'ow', 'hao', 'umph' and etc. It would sound insincere to praise someone too much and it would also hurt oneself if one did that too much. Most of the time, remaining silent would be the best choice. Still, I learnt the white ways. I learnt to praise. I learnt to at least sound kind. And I did all that feeling guilty inside. And I told him that.

'You know why?' said Ah Liu.

'No. Why?'

'Because we are too honest for that. If we don't feel admiration for someone, we don't express admiration that we don't feel in the first place. And we don't pretend that we know something that we don't.'

'Not like the fellow what's his name who challenged me with all sorts of questions that essentially laid himself bare as an ignoramus.'

'Worse. I may be accused of being someone who never apologises. But I don't like the way they apologise, then act as if nothing had happened. I won't name names or give more details than necessary. But when properties were destroyed and people got bashed up, they appeared in court and always managed to get away from it with an apology or two. It's slightly better than America where Chinese are not allowed to be witnesses.'

'No? Not even when they see a murder happening under their noses

242

and with their own eyes?'

'Sadly, no.'

'Why?'

'Because they consider the Chinese as habitual liars who have no knowledge of perjury as a crime.'

'Ha, ha, ha. That's just so ridiculous.'

'No. It hurts. I've seen so many of them telling lies. They say they'll turn up at one o'clock. But they either turn up at 3pm or never turn up. They say they'll pay you promptly. But they never do after you write to them asking for it again and again and only pay you months after. They make a promise to do something, then they forget it, and apologise.'

'Oh, yes, that's so true of them and perhaps because it's so ingrained in them they have the expression, "white lies", right?'

'Right. There are no known yellow lies or black lies or brown lies. There are only white lies. And how can you get these compulsive tellers of white lies to act as witnesses? How can they be trusted?'

'Tell me a tale or two,' said I, prompting him.

'Promise that you won't tell anyone and promise that you'll keep that promise.'

'I promise.'

'Again, I won't name names, just A and B. A is running a shop. Each commodity comes with a tag of price stuck on it, some 1 shilling, some 6 pence and some 1 pound and so on. B comes into the shop and selects an item, but not before he changes the price tag from 1 pound to 1 shilling. I know this sounds unbelievable. But it's what happened. Then A and B have an argument, A accusing B of tampering with the price tags. B, denying it, flies into a rage and hits A in the face. Even when the case proceeds to the court where I interpret for A, B denies that he has ever done the tag-swapping. In the end, A loses the case and ends up paying more than 1 pound as court costs.'

'That's awful. But why?'

'I said I can't tell you more. Well, we are losers everywhere, aren't we?' said Ah Liu.

'Right,' said I, recalling my experiences in the goldfields.

'Most of the indentured labourers in Cuba died as a result of the extremely harsh circumstances there. Few survived. I have no idea if my cousin there is still alive or dead.'

'I'll make enquiries when I go home.'

'When will you go?'

'Maybe when winter ends in August and spring begins in September?'

'Good time. I'll spread the news.'

'No, don't. I don't want anyone to know.'

'But surely they'll have letters home that they want you to take with you, don't you want to do that?'

'Oh, yes, I forgot. Well then, I can't act as a free courier but I'll do that for friends or acquaintances. I don't have many friends, you know.'

'Neither do I.'

'Well, at least, I've done a few letters for some of my friends who are illiterate. It's all in the style of "The Pearl Tower", a song that sings of letters home from afar as "good doctors" because they cure the heart diseases by telling lies.'

'Hearts like lies better than the truth, sometimes.'

*

As an afterthought, I intended this section to be a moonlit night on which Ah Sin started having ideas about his daughter's future education. He had no idea what he wanted Na Za to be in the future. But the first thought, or one of the first thoughts, that came to him was that he wanted her to be a poet like Li Po. To do this, he had a simple method, in the steps of his own father and the village teacher, Master Wang Long, or Ah Long. That is, to recite all the poems available in memory, passed on from generation to generation.

While he blew off the candlelight and lay down by Na Za's side, Ah Sin was wide awake. By the way, this was the night following the story night. The beam of moonlight that came through the cracks of the wattle walls, walls woven with wattle branches, kept him awake and was reminiscent of one particular poem by Li Po. It is one in which the poet gets so drunk that he mistakes his own shadow for his companion and begins a threesome dance that includes himself, his shadow and the moon, a surreal companion. He started going through the poem from the first character to the last and, without realizing what he was doing, he found the poem melting with the moonbeams in an automatic flow from his heart via his tongue, low enough for himself to hear and not to wake up the baby,

Drinking Alone with the Moon

A pot of liquor among flowers
I drink alone without friends
Lifting my cup, I invite the bright moon
With my shadow, we become three persons
The moon does not understand drinking
And the shadow merely follows me about
In temporary company with the moon and shadow
One should seek pleasure when it is spring
I sing as the moon saunters along
And I dance but the shadow messes around
We share the joy when awake
And we scatter when drunk
We roam forever, letting ourselves go
And will meet one day, high on the Milky Way

Amazingly, the baby didn't wake up as he thought she might. But a serene smile crept up a corner of her mouth and spread across her face, lighting it up like a moonbeam shot with poetry, absorbed by her brain lying dormant.

Ah Sin heard a voice saying within him, 'We, two, are three, including the moon.'

Chapter 8

[Stacey says: I am afraid that I have to shed this section even though I like it, simply because it's irrelevant, getting distracted into other areas such as his meeting with Chinese-Australian artists and their perennial complaints about being denied chances of winning the Archibald Prize however good they are. I think they are being precious. And I think they don't have to attach *that* much importance to the prize if they are independent enough. Artists have to stop worrying about not winning prizes. 1478 words shed.]

*

[Stacey says: I'm not sure if I should remove the following passage. I'd hate to see it go, though. When honesty is white hot and truth is so scary one dares not look it in the eye, that's how it feels when I came across this. I think I'll just hand this over to the editor of the manuscript to decide. They can always remove it if they deem it detrimental to the reception of the book if and when it comes out.]

The remark BUP said that I forgot to put in the segment above kept me awake half the night, ringing persistently in my ears, like a refrain. 'We are Chinese. But we are the Indian variety, Brahmins turned upside down, literally turned into the Untouchables, living in a country with an invisible caste system. We remain at the lowest rung of the social ladder. Who would give you the highest award in the country for anything related to the artistic and intellectual achievements if you haven't suffered the worst, like the indigenous people of this country, if you are survivors doing relatively well and if you keep being wealthy enough to want to be comfortable, and not involved with the politics? If you haven't been vanquished financially, physically and spiritually, and remain a threat to them in all those regards, who would acknowledge that you are the best by giving you the best? If they acknowledge that you are the best, it is an automatic admission that they are not as good as you. They have beaten a huge retreat from the past by allowing you into all walks of life in this country. But God knows how long it is going to take to vote one of you in as the next PM? And, more importantly, God knows how long it is going to take to award one of you this good. Just you wait. But I wouldn't give a fuck because, you know, I am the best and I am the Untouchable.'

*

Finally, I've managed to catch up with Stacey. Does it sound real? Is it part of an imaginary scene? Does it matter if it's real or imaginary? But I sit across the table from her. I'm sitting across it, I mean. I can see there's a streak of white hair. I don't comment on that. I keep my line of vision away from it. I look at her. I look into her eyes. Chestnut? No. Hazelnut? Sort of. Olive-shaped, quite. Nice looks? Not really. Determined? Yes. Resolute? Yes. Manly? A bit. Relaxed? Sure. She returns my gaze. What does she think of me? Too inexperienced? Still groping in the dark? Writing all this rubbish without realising it? Thinking of replacing herself with someone else because too hard to handle? Her shoes, I'm thinking. No socks. Just a pair of runners. More man than man. I still remember the only classes I went to in which she taught poetry to the beginning students, in their late teens or early 20s. Her hoarse voice ringed with smoke. Did she smoke? Not that I can recall. She drinks, that's for sure. Chardonnay or a bottle of Billy Button.

With a start, I woke up from my memory-revelry. 'Sorry,' said I, 'what did you say?'

'I was saying,' Stacey said, with a smile, 'here's your coffee.'

'Oh, thank you,' said I, glancing with admiration at her white even teeth revealed by her smile.

'How did you go with your writing?'

'Hard-going, soft-going, medium-going, all-going,' said I.

'How do you mean?'

'Sorry about playing with words. It goes okay.'

'Now, seriously, are you going to turn this into something unreadable?'

'Readability is marketability is likability. I'm not into any of that.'

'What are you into then?'

'No idea.' I said, then, 'maybe into Beckett.'

'You mean Samuel?'

'Why not? Anything wrong with that?'

'No. Depends how you want to proceed.'

'I just like going against the grain.'

'You do? Show me an example or two.'

I produced a crumpled piece of paper, bearing a found poem I arranged based on what Samuel Beckett said and showed it to her.

She read it and returned it to me, without a comment. Then she said,

'You sound exactly like a few years ago when we first met.'

'If everything can be instantly turned into money, how boring would life be?'

'But if you don't have money, you don't even have this coffee to drink.'

'Australians are a people fixated on money, from birth to death. There's no escaping it.'

'You are so unkind. It's not just the Australians. People all over the world love money.'

'I'll only show my kindness when I get further away from humoney-ty.'

'Did I detect something new or funny from the word you used?'

'Yes, you are so asute. It is h-u-m-o-n-e-y-t-y.'

'You've got so little respect. Hope you are not suffering from depression or some such things.' And she paused, as something seemed to have sunken in. 'Did you say ascute instead of astute?'

I ignored that and said, 'Well, if I did the way Nietzsche, Dostoevsky and Hesse did, I would be overjoyed. Treat me as an absolute social misfit.'

'I think you need go and see a doctor, a psychologist or psychiatrist even.'

'You've got to be kidding.'

'I'm serious. We've got a staff member who recently killed himself, without any reasons, or any apparent reasons. On the surface, everything seemed okay. He never argued with anyone. He always came and went with a big smile on his face, or at least when he ran into people. He's divorced, yes. But that's probably not the cause of his suicide. I don't know. I can't work these things out.'

'Neither can I,' said I, without knowing why I said so.

'Let me tell you something. I won't make any suggestions, let alone corrections, except that you follow your own instincts and take it right to the end. Then, there is always time for you to go back and revise it, multiple times if necessary. If you really are suffering from depression, it's even better because you can take it as a source of inspiration. Nothing works better than a worst-case scenario.'

'This sounds like a Chinese proverb.'

'Which one?'

'Sheng yu youhuan, si yu anle.'

'Meaning?'

'One survives disasters but not pleasures.'

'There seems more to it than just that, is there?'

'You are right. If you do a literal translation, it would be something like this: One dies in pleasure but is born out of hardship.'

'I couldn't agree more.'

'Heteroglossia,' said I. Then as if tasting the word on my tongue, I said it again, 'heteroglossia.'

'You are getting there,' said Stacey as she finished her coffee and rose to go.

*

[Stacey says: Uncomfortable with the two found poems BH created for his own amusement with material from Beckett's 'Worstward Ho' and *Watt*, I decided to remove them. Literary experimentation will have to submit itself to the market demands or die its own quiet death. Who wants to read experi/mental stuff anyway? Not even the experi/mental people themselves.]

And, curious enough, I bumped into this website (https://lostallhope.com/suicide-methods/firearms) where I found my fingers quick to copy some of the words and paste them here:

1. Using a shotgun rather than a gun or rifle.
2. Firing into the head rather than the body.
3. Using a gun that works properly and ammunition that is not old.

Then these three points:

-For those attempting a suicide aiming at the chest, the heart is target.
-Using a shotgun if aiming at the chest will also increase the chances of a fatal outcome due to the fact shot spreads out and can cause extensive damage even if not aimed quite correctly.
-For those aiming at the head, the most popular site is the right temple.

The internet is such a wonderful place, I thought to myself, that one could wipe out the world if one could find the right website with the right information.

*

Talking about something fading from memory, I recall how forgetful I am these days, particularly when it comes to writing fiction. Wouldn't it be wonderful if everything's as easy as eating? But when I wrote about the night on which Ah Sin and Ah Liu slept together, I forgot to put in a lot of things and, in an act of honesty, I refuse to revise it by inserting the bits I thought I should have included. If I have a reader, a reader outside Stacey, I must tell him or her that this is my way of being honest, not revising anything done. How can we revise – I mean – how can I revise my life lived the day before yesterday or yesterday or even a minute ago? Don't people cheat themselves by thinking that they can somehow make things perfect by resorting to constant revision? Don't they ever manage to maintain a surface reality by not allowing others to peep into what lies hidden underneath? Don't they find revision synonymous with making up, like the kind of new-age stop-hole stickers that can cover up everything shoddy and make things look anew? I might have to adopt a third-person narrative here if I am allowed, or if I allow myself to, when it comes to that story.

Every once in a while, Ah Sin sighed. When Ah Liu asked why, he remained silent. Then Ah Liu said, 'Are you sighing for home?'

'No,' said Ah Sin.

'Oh, I see. I'm sorry,' said Ah Liu. 'I'm so forgetful. You must have been feeling sad about Ciara's passing away.'

'That goes without saying,' said Ah Sin.

'You know what?'

'What?'

'I've been attending a course at the university in my spare time.'

'Attending a course? Where?'

'At the Melbourne U, in the department of history.'

'What for?'

'Just for self-enrichment, you know.'

'Good on you. At least you are not like them, enriching themselves with the only thing they know: gold.'

'Right. Gold is their God and has replaced God as their only god.'

'I recall that story again about Chuang Tzu.'

'What story?'

'The gist of it is that his third wife is not happy with his non-interest in the pursuit of a materialistic life. She wants a life full of money, lived with a beautiful man. When she poisons him to death and puts him in a coffin in the backyard, she meets with her handsome man at night and is about to go to bed with him when he falls to the ground. The man's father, half-drunk, tells her that he is suffering from an old condition. Whenever he gets overexcited he falls down to the floor. The only cure is to feed him with the brains of a dead man. The woman, remembering her dead husband in the backyard coffin, picks up an axe and hacks open the coffin and is about to hack open her dead husband's brain when he sits up, giving her the shock of her life.'

'Is that real?'

'Well, sort of. No stories are real as long as they sound real.'

'But this one doesn't even sound real because how can a dead man sit up in his coffin when it's re-opened?'

'Such things do happen. Our warehouse of ancient stories is full of tales in which women wake up from death after their men make love to them. And vice versa.'

'Love is the most difficult thing, you know.'

'How did you mean?'

'I mean it's hard with a woman, particularly from a totally different culture.'

'Like what?'

'Uriella, you know, is a nice girl.'

'Yes?'

'But she's demanding.'

'In what ways?'

'She wants me to be more than myself.'

'Which is what?'

'Simply put, she wants me to be knowledgeable, to be learned, to be not as vulgar as a Chinese person.'

'What did she mean by that?'

'Not to wear a queue, not to wear our traditional attire, definitely not to smoke opium, not to care about money as the only thing that matters in life, and not to—'

'Not to what?'

'Not to have anything to do with the Chinese as a race any longer.'

'Because?'

'Because they've been so denigrated that to be with them means to be with sinners and devils.'

'What if you do prefer to be with them?'

'Then there's no relationship.'

'Come on, that's no deal. There are no such things between Ciara and I. We came together on one thing only: love.'

'Yes, you are right. But not everyone is like you and Ciara. There are so many varieties of love nothing guarantees anything.'

'I'd say drop her and go for someone else then.'

'More easily said than done.'

'Meaning you've gone over the top, the love top?'

'Oh, we've done all that is supposed to be done in love. But when it comes to marriage, there are strings attached. You can't get around that.'

'How about go back to See Yup and marry one there and bring her back?'

'Out of the question.'

'Why?'

'Because I've gone beyond that. They cease to interest me after a while. Once I've slept with a white woman, I don't think I can sleep with women of my own race anymore.'

'Is that so?'

'You'll know that when you go back to your country.'

'Not your country anymore?'

'Not really.'

'How can you talk like that? That's shocking.'

'Nothing shocking. It's a reality. Quite a few of us have decided to stay, without ever wanting to return.'

'Let's see how things pan out then.'

*

One correction in regard to the place name of See Yup. I know that the normal spelling of it is Sze Yap, meaning four counties. But because they in the old days loved making fun of the Chinese in general and the Chinese gold-diggers in particular, the Australian writers twisted the name into 'See Yup', meaning they had eyes that see up, with the corners of their eyes tilting upwards. Once they got that as a stereotype, white actors and actresses across the film world would have their eyes taped to see up, in the See Yup way, without knowing a thing why it was the Sze Yap or See Yup people who had more people outside them than inside them, for all sorts of reasons, such as tradition (they started migrating as early as the Tang dynasty), poverty (for them it was always richer and better overseas), and family (members of the same family would involve more going out in their wake). Still, if I made a mistake putting it down as 'See Yup', the reason to keep it in without correcting is as strong as to remove it in order to be correct.

And, Stacey, I'm sorry that I have only realized that I should have followed your advice right from the start by casting a female character in my fiction or focussing the story entirely on one or more female characters in order to tie in with the current literary climate or, better still, the current literary climate change. Perhaps I have only my dick to blame, my Chinese dick that refuses to be Westernized by either having it castrated or going completely limp or simply casting its amorous glances West-wise. I am hopeless, Stacey, did you realize? And isn't it too late for me to change the whole story women-wise just so that I may somehow get published eventually? Shouldn't I die, really, as one of my male writer friends put it: If you are a male writer these days, the best thing for you to do is write a book and kill yourself. After all, I have mentally and psychologically made myself asexual so that I won't be falling in love with anyone anymore because to love is to be prone to make mistakes.

*

[Irrelevant dribble, 1520 words cut—SA]

There was something else that I must remind myself to do in this novel that keeps me forgetful about things. The haircut, for example. One of the things Ah Sin kept doing throughout his stay in Australia was he practised haircutting not only for his fellow countrymen but also for himself. If Australia was full of people like him, barbers would permanently go out of work. Fortunately, he didn't do too many heads and he didn't have time to do that, either. Besides, he cut hair for his friends and himself for free. That was really nice, in a way. In my imagination, I saw him squatting by the side of the Avoca River, looking at the flowing water, in fact his own image in the water, as he raised his right hand with the scissors, chopping, chipping and cutting away at his hair, first at the right temple, then at the left temple, dexterously, skilfully, and a little reversely, while looking askance at his own image in the water. This would have happened before he moved on to other sites in the goldfields, the way Ah Kut the philosopher did, on his regular walkabouts. It was a most enjoyable moment to watch his chopped hair drop strand by strand into the water and flow away with the ripples, with occasional fish coming to the surface, mistaking the hair for some new food. Before he went to China, he had planned to visit Ah Mao and give him a haircut. But this plan was thwarted by the guard at the entrance to the mental home because they didn't allow anyone to go in with tools that enabled the inmates to harm themselves. As a result, Ah Sin left, feeling despondent, without even seeing Ah Mao, but promising in a note that he'd come back to see him again.

To prevent me from forgetting this, I've recorded this one above and will find time to insert it wherever it belongs in this text. But I can't promise. If I forget, I hope Stacey, as my editor, might either do the inserting or remove it as something irrelevant. As for my non-existent readers, I don't give a damn what they think.

Part IV

Chapter 1

In my memory, Four-Family Village when I left it was a small village of a few households. All the males, except the aged and the very young, had gone overseas, leaving their women behind. Some had gone to Panama, others had gone to Peru or Cuba or America. A few of us had come to Australia. In my mind's eye, my house was perched on the side of Dragon Creek. It was such a clean creek that in summer when I was a little kid I would jump in from the balcony and swim. Old villagers said that if you swam with the stream further south you'd arrive in the sea and then the world was yours to be had. You could go anywhere and reach the end of the earth. And that was one of my earliest dreams.

As the creek wandered away from my village it became a river, filled with seawater when the tide was in, and the banks were dense with a red forest, hong shulin, our term for their mangrove, neither making sense, as the 'red forest' was not red and the 'mangrove' had nothing manly about it. The absurdity of the words was reflected in the absurdity of the lives we lived back then: people seemed to have been born for elsewhere. They grew up with a face turned seaward and a heart for transplantation; anywhere was better than home. Unlike Ciara who didn't want to return to Ireland, her homeland, where she had no one waiting for her, no family roots to dive into, I had always wanted to return to my home village, particularly with Na Za, my 7-year-old daughter. I had a pet name for her: 'Daa Seinn'. I wanted her to learn not only English, her mother tongue, but also Mandarin, her father tongue, her father's tongue. After weeks of travelling by sea, weeks of seasick days, sunshine and rainstorms, waves and wind, thoughts of death and dreams of home, and after weeks of distances gained wave after wave, breath after breath, moment after moment, cloud after cloud, seabird after seabird, we arrived, in a small boat along the familiar river sandwiched between green rice-paddies, freshly planted with rice-seedlings and occasional willow trees. It was the flight of a spring swallow that flew low across the rice-paddies that set my heart pit-a-pat with excited longing and trepidation. I had not seen the bird for nearly two decades now.

'Did you see that?' I said to Daa Seinn, pointing at the swift swallow, gone in a second.

'What?' she raised her head and looked. 'I didn't see anything.'

'A swallow,' said I.

'A swallow? Something to swallow?'

'Clever girl,' said I, remembering the character 嚥 I had explained to Ciara on the night when we made love to each other. 'the same words in both Mandarin and English.'

'What is that?' she uttered a little cry as she pointed.

Following the direction of her finger-pointing, I saw an old man behind a dark-grey water buffalo, his hand on the plough. Before I had time to tell her what it was she had blurted out, 'Is that a Chinese tiger?'

All on board burst out laughing, making her very shy and ashamed.

'No, it's a water buffalo,' said I, explaining that it was a beast of burden that did all the fieldwork for a peasant, from ploughing the rice paddies to pulling a stone roller to thresh the grain.

'Can I ride on it?' Daa Seinn said.

'Can you ride it? Oh, yes,' said I, recalling how I did that as a young child and how I fell off it onto the rice paddy, my whole person blurry with mud. It was Dad who pulled me out of the rice mud and let me swim myself clean in the nearby creek, years before he died in a war, fighting as a Taiping army soldier.

'I want to ride it, I want to ride it now,' said Daa Seinn, jumping up and down for joy, impatiently.

I did my best to quell her newly born appetite for riding a water buffalo, promising that we would do that first thing as soon as we arrived home.

*

The road that led to my village, my former village, remained the same except that it was now wider, not the little path that was full of mud when it rained or raised dust when the sun shone. And the village, in the distance, was nothing like what I had imagined it to be in my memory, a row of low-roofed houses, consisting of whitewashed mud-bricks and black tiles. There was a number of what was known as *diaolou*, a building that looked like a fort, in a combination of styles, ancient Greek, Roman, Byzantine and baroque. Though there was no one meeting us at the mouth of the village, with gongs and cymbals and drums and flags, a troop of kids had heard the sound and soon emerged from nowhere, converging on us with delighted cries. They gazed at us curiously as if we were foreigners. They were particularly interested in Na Za's looks: a pale face underneath a headful of black curly hair, atop a brownish dress, half concealing a pair of black boots. Then they cheered up when they saw Na Za produce something that they had never seen before: a life-sized kangaroo that I had handmade, its belly full of gum leaves and its skin patched up with the rags that had served as nappies in her babyhood.

All became quiet when they accompanied me to the door of my former home. A greying wooden door with a rusty lock. The kids — little boys and girls — disappeared as suddenly as they had turned up. I paid the porter off and slumped down on the steps. For the first time, I heard the roosters, sounding so sonorous and solitary. Na Za sat down next to me and said, 'Dad, I'm so tired.'

'Tired.' What a word! An exact description of my current situation, and, indeed, of my entire life. Why do I come back? To see whom? Where is home? Just this wooden structure under lock and key? And kids running around curious to see strangers like ourselves? I raised my head to look at the sky as tears ran down my cheeks. There were no tears; I just imagined them. Then, I thought I heard someone coughing. I looked up again and saw an old man coming, his wooden stick knocking the bluestone road with a clicking sound. As he got closer, I could see that he had a white beard, white brows and white hair, with a long pigtail behind his back, his black gown so long it covered part of his black thick-soled shoes. He came to a stop right in front of me, the clicking sound also coming to a stop I rose and made a bow, with both my hands folded in front of me. He returned my bow with the same courteous gesture but somehow dropped his stick, which crashed onto the road with a loud clink.

'Let me pick it up for you,' said Na Za as she rose to her feet and was about to take the stick in hand when the old man held out his hand and said, 'Please don't.' And as he said so he bent and picked it up himself.

'I'm sorry,' said I, introducing myself as Ah Sin.

'I know, I know,' the old man said. 'I'm your Grandfather III. But you don't remember me because I've aged beyond recognition.'

Grandfather III? As far as I could remember, there were a number of uncles and aunties on my father's and mother's side. By the time I was born, my paternal grandfather was dead. Even though my maternal grandfather was alive when I went overseas I had no idea that there was another grandfather. But I was dutiful enough to oblige and said, 'Grandfather III, how are you?'

He said nothing in reply. Instead, he brought out a key from underneath his black gown and gave it to me, saying, 'They are all gone now.'

'Give the key to me, give it to me,' said Na Za as she held out her tiny hand.

I let her have it. She tried it this way and that. But the ancient lock wouldn't work. I took it over and put it in the middle of the butterfly-shaped bronze lock. With a cranky click, the lock opened. Impatiently, Na Za pushed the door open when her face turned pale, amazed by things she had never seen: a dark cave-like space, with a square of sky shown overhead and a large square sunken in the middle, right below the square sky, strewn with brown fallen leaves and wet with rain water.

The old man stood by the door, looking in, refusing to come in. But he said he'd organize something tonight by letting the other villagers know.

I opened the door to my parents' room. There was a table against the wall, with a half-burnt candle on it. A mosquito-net hung over the bed in a corner, with a thin quilt, neatly folded, placed in the middle of a bamboo sleeping mat. On the facing wall hung a painted portrait of each of my parents when they were relatively young. The table was covered in a veil of dust and so were the portraits.

As Na Za was getting hungry, I fed her a piece of bread wrapped around some brown sugar, and let her drink tea from a bamboo container I carried myself. Then I let her out, to mix with the other kids, advising her not to go near the creek as it was dangerous for her to go and play with the water for she might drown in it. Then, with the main doors ajar, I sat down, on the edge of the tianjing, the skywell, and started smoking. I smoked and thought. I smoked and thought. But my mind remained blank. If there was any thought, it was this: I have managed to return from death to death, from one death to another death. When I left, everyone was alive, my parents, my grandmas, both paternal and maternal, my grandfather, and my siblings. Like a flood that had receded overnight, they were all gone in the couple of decades I had spent in Australia. I knew my younger brother had gone to America because he had believed that it was a better country than Australia. But we had never written each other. I knew my two sisters had married people outside the village. But that was that.

But how was it possible that five people I held dearest to my heart died one after another in such a short time? Am I dreaming? Is this a nightmare? I pinched myself hard on my leg and it hurt. Sitting here and smoking, I became aware of their ghosts everywhere.

*

Dear Baohui,

To be honest with you, I grow increasingly concerned with the way the story goes. I have problems with three things:

    1. Too much author intervention

    2. Too little circumstantial information on Ah Sin's life with his young daughter for 7 years

    3. Too little circumstantial information on Ah Sin on his return to his ancestral village

Do you want your readers to believe that this is a believable story or do you want them to know that you have deliberately written an unconvincing story to thwart their expectations?

Let me know what you think.

Stacey

*

Following is my reply in a diary entry I never sent.

[I literally hate the following, so I decide to shed it all, 960 words in total—SA]

I have a story here to tell myself, that is, my readers, about a conversation I had with Dad.

'Why Greece, of all the places?' said I.

'"Poverty and Greece are sisters," ' said Dad.

'How do you mean? I don't understand,' said I.

'It's not my words; it's the words I quoted from a book I read years ago.'

'What's the book?'

'Something called, Map of Love.'

'Who by?'

'Don't remember it any longer. But Greece is a case in point. Right now, Greece is still one of the poorest countries in Europe, an underdeveloped country, exactly why we need to go there and support them and include them in the Belt and Road Initiative.'

That fragment of the conversation about Greece interested me enough to find the book, completely forgotten in the library, and I quickly located the page, p. 59, where the quoted words are actually the title of a subsection. Then, a page after that, I found something that lit my eyes that says, 'Man is here isolated and rejoices in this isolation', followed by a poem that I love,

> I love no one and feel tenderness for none;
> My friends betrayed me and my foes detest me,
> My kin insult me and the strangers wrong me

Even in hell I wish to be alone
I want not love nor to be loved...(pp. 61-2)

To be honest, I remember saying to Dad over the WeChat voice call, that I wasn't interested in making money. Afterwards, I wondered if my lack of interest in money would make my characters less passionate about it than otherwise. And I also wondered if my unprofessional interest in poetry, that is, my unambitious interest in poetry without wanting to be a published poet and an award-winning poet for that matter, would also colour the way in which I represent my characters. Stacey is probably right when she says that all fiction is about money, about people loving money because money is life, about people falling out with people because of money, and about people happy with it and unhappy without it. What she didn't know was that she sounded like she was preaching about the merits of good bowel movements to me: If you have good shit, you feel happy. If your bowel doesn't move like Alexander Portnoy's father for two weeks in a row, you don't feel happy.

*

Talking about the ghosts, I, Ah Sin, felt like one myself. When I went in search of gold in the Victorian goldfields, I left my shadow in my village. The shadow must have been cast by the sky across the ocean, a shell vacated of its substance that remained a living shadow with my family members and the villagers until it became fainter and fainter as I entered deeper and deeper into my Australian existence. Now that I was back, my shadow disappeared, gone back to Australia. But why did I come back? Did I have anything to do with this, this village, this country? And why did I bring Na Za back? To show whom?

The thought of Na Za gave me a start. I looked wildly around me and, looking down at the five or six cigarette-butts lying on the blue-stone skywell, I realised that she had probably gone out far too long. I went out. I looked in vain for the crowd of the kids on the street. Quickly, I went around my house to the back, to the edge of the creek, half concealed by the tree branches and leaves. There, I was moved to see her squat by a cluster of bauhinia flowers, intent on something in front of her.

I stole over, wanting to see what was going on, when I grew tense with fright: there was an earthen-coloured snake, half-raising its head at her, its forked tongue flickering, and she was gazing at it with a fixed stare, seemingly fascinated.

I didn't know how long this had been going on. But I quickly went over and took her up in my arms from behind and snatched her off the scene. Quickly turning its head, the snake slid into the grass and disappeared in an instant.

*

Dinner that night was a great fanfare. The whole village turned out, it seemed. Kids. Old men. Old ladies. Middle-aged aunts. A few young girls. Cousins, nephews, nieces. People I didn't know. Among them a white man and his Chinese wife. My ancestral house was lit from inside out. Tables were brought out, laden with food and drink. Candles and kerosene lamps everywhere. No more ghosts. Smiles on every face. Loud chatting. All eyes examining stuff I'd brought back: sheets of sheep skins with white wool, short boots made of kangaroo skin, bars of butter soap, ties of all colour, including the green and the kangaroo colour, and bars of chocolate. When we sat down around the table and began eating, Na Za next to me, holding a pair of chopsticks in her left hand, all eyes were directed at her and casual comments were made.

'She's left-handed!' a woman's voice.

'Shush! Don't say that,' another woman said.

'Isn't she good-looking?' a third voice.

'She's very Chinese,' then the voice tapered to a whisper, 'but also very foreign.'

I heard that but pretended I didn't. Instead, I offered a smile towards where the voice was issued and saw the woman across the table, sitting by the side of her white husband. I nodded my head to her and to her husband and each of them nodded back to me. Then I started looking for the old man who had handed me the key in the morning. But he was nowhere to be found. As I did so, I kept busy picking pieces of food with my chopsticks and putting them in the bowl in front of Na Za: a piece of duck, a piece of chicken, a piece of roast pork, and a piece of steamed carp after I made sure it contained no bones. But she did not touch the food. She just sat there, looking at people all around her. When I asked why, she said that she just wanted to have bread, so I left and came back with two pieces of bread that I had bought in Hong Kong during our stopover there, not the kind of daily bread we had in Melbourne that you could spread butter and jam over but the flowery, sweet kind that contained raisins or nuts. Just then, I heard a remark, in an unmistakable Australian accent, that came across the table.

'Where did you guys come from?' the white man across the table said.

'Can you tell him?' said I, to Na Za.

'Oh, we come from Richmond,' said Na Za. 'Have you been there before?'

'Oh, no, but is that Richmond, London?' the man pursued.

Baffled, Na Za looked up at me, imploringly.

'Nah, it's Richmond, Melbourne,' said I. Then, 'what about you? Where did you come from?'

'We came from Sydney,' the man said as he turned his head aside to look at the woman sitting beside him. 'Rushcutters Bay, actually.'

'Oh, that,' said I. 'isn't that a place where Chinese market gardeners concentrated?'

'Oh, yes,' said the man whose name by then wasn't known to me, nor mine to him. 'In fact, that's where the Irish convicts had coined the saying much earlier.'

'The saying?' I was bewildered.

'Beyond the hills lies China,' quoted the man without the spectacles.

As people began dispersing, I found the man and I had somehow got closer, sitting side by side on the same bench, his woman on her own, sitting from us across the table.

'Way Woo Wo,' said he as he thrust his hand towards me.

'Ah Sin,' said I, as I did the same.

Woo Wo laughed soundlessly.

'Oh,' I uttered a little cry of surprise as I recalled something. I found a tin of coffee and a tin of brown sugar, brought them out and put them on the table. I was about to go to the kitchen when the man stopped me by placing a hand gently on my wrist and said, across the table, to his woman, 'Sarah, can you go and make some hot water for us please?'

'Yes, yes, yes, yes, yes, yes, yes,' the woman said as she rose to her feet and went to the kitchen. I noticed the dark flowery dress she had on. It was something I hadn't seen before, quite appealing.

'I hardly say "yeh" more than once,' said I, without meaning to criticise, simply saying.

'You know why?' said Woo Wo.

'Not really. Why?'

'You don't read classical Chinese poetry, I gather?'

'Oh, yeh, I do.'

'Like what?'

'Plenty, things like wulü and wujue or qilü and qijue.'

'Then you must understand that in a qilü or qijue poem, each and every line consists of seven characters.'

'That's exactly right,' said I.

'There you have it,' Woo Wo said.

It took a while to sink in, the while in which Sarah, the man's woman, came out with teacups filled with freshly brewed coffee. The second my lips touched the edge of my cup, I 'ah'ed.

'What?' the man asked with concern. 'Did you get scorched by the coffee?'

'No,' said I. 'rather, I got scorched by the thought of that yeh and the number of times it was uttered: exactly seven times, not six, not eight, just seven!'

'You got it,' the man was delighted and took his coffee in one gulp, finishing it to the dregs, holding his hand out with the empty cup, straight to Sarah. 'Do me a favour, will you?'

As Sarah went back to the kitchen, Woo Wo said, 'It is no longer possible to know which comes first, poetry or the poetic way people say things. My wife learned English after we met. Even though she is still struggling with it, she can manage on most social occasions. As she grows more and more English-oriented, she retains the poetry of her own native tongue, which is what you see in the pattern of rhythms when she uttered something like "yeh".'

'Are you a professor of language?'

'No. I am the local priest.'

'What church?'

'The Anglican Church.'

*

[BH: a self-musing below.] [Musing? Not even amusing, 559 words deleted—SA]

*

That night, after all the guests had left and I put Na Za to bed, I told her a story of the two-headed bird, one head called Ja Lo Cha and the other, Yo Bo. When Ja Lo Cha is asleep, Yo Bo must be awake. One day, when Ja Lo Cha is asleep and Yo Bo is awake, the wind blows a flower from a sugar-apple tree to Yo Bo's side. Yo Bo thinks to himself: 'If I eat it both of us will be happy and energetic.' So, without waking up Ja Lo Cha and telling him, he eats it. When Ja Lo Cha wakes up, he feels wonderful and says to Yo Bo: 'What happened? Why do I feel so good? Why does even my voice sound so beautiful?' But when Yo Bo tells him of what has happened, Ja Lo Cha feels quite upset, wondering how he could have eaten it himself without sharing it with him and deciding that he'll do the same in future. One day, when both of them see a poisonous flower somewhere, Ja Lo Cha thinks to himself, 'When he goes to sleep, I shall eat this flower so we both can die together.' Which is exactly what he does. When Yo Bo wakes up, he feels awful and learns, to his great chagrin, what has happened. He starts singing a poem:

When you go to sleep, a flower drops by my side
I eat the beautiful flower, to your dislike
I wish to never live with a fool again
No point hurting others while hurting oneself

By the time I finished singing the poem myself, Na Za had fallen asleep. By the candlelight, her face was serene, white and angelic, a miniature of her mother and I myself. I love you so much, my daughter, I said to myself as I lowered my head to kiss her on the cheek, hearing her heartbeats and her even breathing.

*

As I, Baohui, walked towards the local post office, I thought of Woo Wo, the local priest and his story of movement from England to New England then to Four-Family Village where he met his Chinese wife, recently pregnant. I overheard him talking to Ah Sin that he felt happiest when he was in China. Surely, most people were poor. But that was exactly the point: there is hope only among the poor. The rich had only one way to go: not the richer but the poorer. Moreover, to be rich or poor was beside the point. In their desultory talk, they wandered further and further away till all they talked about was whether they could fit in anywhere. For Woo Wo, he never felt comfortable either in England or in Australia. In the former, a highly class-based country, someone like him from a lower-class background would have no hope of ever getting beyond his current status. In Australia, a former British colony, the culture was heavily stained with its convict past. The English language, for example, was full of expletives. If he had kids, he would not have them educated in Australia. Moreover, racial tensions were rampant. And there were issues in the Church, too. At that point, he decided not to say any more. But when it comes to China, particularly the Canton part of it, he couldn't help heaping praises. People were friendly. Food was great. The culture was family-based, self-reliant and full of poetry. He had long felt an outsider, either in England or in Australia. But, in China, it seemed home. He had all the respect in the world. People were kind and helpful. And he was kind and helpful in return. Gradually, with the acquiring of the language, he was able to read Chinese poetry in the original and enjoyed it immensely.

In a dream I had last night, Woo Wo, this character of mine, comes to visit me. Without prompting, he says to me: *That's what I like about the Chinese. They don't want to conquer the world. They are happy to be conquered by the world so they can enjoy the pleasure of being conquered and in turn conquering the conquerors, without lifting a finger, just waiting and drinking their tea. They did that to all the barbarian rulers in the past, including the Jins and the Mongolians. They will do that to all the rest of them and each time they are conquered they become stronger and better enriched.*

When I woke up, I wondered if I had got him mixed up with Albert Gervais, the French doctor who spent time in China and wrote about China so interestingly, quoting Hollington at length that I quote here at a shortened length:

> A Chinese who becomes too European will regularly lose the qualities of his own race without acquiring those of the people among whom he is a guest. What is good for some peoples may not be good for others; and the conventional, rather puerile moral system of Confucius can never be compared to Western idealism, at least as certain spirits like Goethe, or Dante, or Saint Francis, have understood it. China follows a different road from ours. The dead are the true masters of this civilisation. Behind a front that changes like the chameleon's colours, the nation is profoundly conservative, stubbornly refuses any real alteration in its age-old traditions...They have copied the worst tendencies of the West, its pitiless materialism, its vulgarity, its taste for money, its need for useless and indifferent diversions. (pp. 302-3)

Although my naming of Woo Wo (no me or I-less) had preceded my reading of a poem by Heine in Chinese translation, I thought it had gone further than Heine's recommendation about "完全成为他自己本人" (to become completely himself) (p. 273). The Western notion of individuality, of being completely oneself, is boring to a murderous degree whereby all one individual ever achieves is to kill scores of people, or, if it was a Hitler, millions of people, and, on the other hand, all he ever achieves is to keep adding zeroes to the 1 he has established himself to be. But if you start off as a 0, there's no point adding more 0s, because all will be 0s anyway. And that is the state of being me-less or I-less and that is the state of complete happiness. And then when everyone is an individual and thinks he or she or they thinks differently, aren't their thoughts the same again even when individual?

When I realised that it was not by Heine but by Shelley and the poem was 'Political Greatness', I decided to let the mistake stay because it helped with the process. I liked the mistake so much that I found the poem and the ending words, 'being himself alone', which, in a way, was wrongly rendered in Chinese after all. The double mistake pleased me no end because of my created connection between the individuals and the I-less.

Ah Sin, for his part, expressed his honest opinion about China, too. While agreeing with everything Woo Wo had said about it, he admitted that he would perhaps agree to disagree. China, he said, had such a chequered past that people had to be selfish, self-protective and do their best to eke out an existence, preparing for the worst because the unexpected was always around the corner. By comparison, Australia was good where people could manage a life very much the way Lao Tzu had prescribed and believed in: jiquan zhi sheng xiangwen, laosi buxiang wanglai. As he said so, Ah Sin spelt it out for Woo Wo: People don't make contact with one another although they can hear the dogs and roosters around them. An ideal society, Ah Sin said, in which there was no need for any wars as everything was resolved on a business level. You pay, you buy; you get paid, you sell. Then you lead your life the way you prefer. It's that easy.

When I arrived at the post office, it was empty. Dimitry stood behind the counter and said 'Nihao'. In return, I said, 'Ya su.' 'This parcel to China?' he said. 'Yes, please,' I said. As he got busy weighing it and putting the address on the envelope, I started enthusing about the Greek Festival held in Lonsdale Street the other day when he cut me short, saying, 'I'm not interested in all that.'

'Oh, really?' said I. 'Why not? I mean, aren't you a Greek yourself?'

'Yes, but that doesn't mean I have to be part of it. In fact, I never am.'

'Do you know that Oakleigh is now the largest Greek-concentrated area?'

'Of course, I do. I've been there a few times. Everyone I see on the street turns out to be a Greek. No, I don't want to see that. I'd run miles away from it all.'

'Like me. I hardly ever go to the Chinese New Year's festivities on Little Bourke Street.'

'Oh, really?'

'Yes, really. What's the point seeing something that celebrates the shadow of something real, year in and year out? Boring, mate!'

'Right,' said Dimitry as he announced the price, '58 dollars or 58.50 if you want the tracking information provided.'

'Yes, please,' said I as I tapped my credit card on the machine, instantly charged, when a thought came to me: Ah Sin's story had to be told from multiple points of view, not just 'I, I, I'.

And I thought of Chen Tianhua, a poet who died at 30 and whose poetry, almost forgotten in China and certainly unheard of overseas, provides an insight into the time when Ah Sin, my imaginary character was alive, in a writing, titled, 'A Sudden Head Turn', that mixes poetry and prose, in a seamless eruption of emotion. Here we go,

[320 characters cut, translation below—SA]

And my translation below:

> The land has sunken for hundred autumns, with rolling smoke and running blood.
>
> When you, heart-broken, enumerate the things of the past, who, of your race, will revenge?
>
> After being destroyed for two hundred years, China, my family, is but a vanquished nation.

In my early teens, I got acquainted with a slave's knowledge and I wanted to become a slave official. Quite unexpectedly, the ban was lifted on maritime trade and, with it, like the rushing-in of clouds and wind, came the English, the French, the Russians and the Germans, to do business in China. In less than 50 years, they reduced the Chinese people to poverty and they exhausted their resources. Not only that. They would frequently raise armies to invade our nation. As they fought and won, we fought and lost. Japan took Taiwan, Russia took Lüshun, Britain took Weihaiwei, France took Guangzhou Bay and Germany took Jiaozhou Bay, allowing us no freedom in our eighteen provinces in their spheres of influence. The Chinese government acted like their slave and the Chinese people were treated like their cows and horses. And, in addition, there were clusters of Christian missionaries that were like wolves and tigers. If you didn't treat them well, they'd do whatever they wanted to do to you. Although China has never been carved up before, now it looks like carved up already, like a melon.

Even though Bertrand Russell was quoted as saying, 'Every nation would be richer if every nation abandoned nationalism,' (qtd in Pickering, p. 79), it was easier said than done, particularly for someone from an invading country, not the invaded one. For the sake of exegesis, here's what I thought and did. Instead of providing a historical background to the story by writing about it from the perspective of an authority or a number of authorities, I'd simply do so by interlacing it with forgotten poetry, such as quoted above, because it is my view that poetry is better history whatever else it is. And, after that, when I checked online, I found this by Aristotle: 'History describes what has happened, poetry what might. Hence poetry is something more philosophic and serious than history; for poetry speaks of what is universal, history of what is particular.'

Or perhaps Aristotle is wrong because he doesn't know how to use a mobile phone, let alone a computer?

*

It took me a long time to fall asleep and even when I did it felt as if I wasn't asleep for, with my eyes open, I saw Mother come in. She stopped by my bedside, picked up a loose corner of the quilt and pulled it up to cover me right below the chin. Then she went on to tuck all the loose corners around my feet and my sides. All the while, I had wanted to say something but words refused to come out of my mouth, a moment described by Woo Wo as 'tongue-held' or 'tongue-tied' when he decided not to say anything about the Church vices because he quoted the Bible as saying that the tongue was one of the most poisonous organs on a person, in fact the most poisonous. Then I saw Mother sit down on the edge of the bed, saying to me in a gentle and low voice: 'Son, I'm so pleased to see you back after so many years. I had always thought you are dead until the last letter you wrote me, us. Then I kept praying to Buddha that you are safe and sound and soon back. I am sorry I can't take that long to wait. While I was working in the rice paddies planting the rice seedlings, I got bitten by a snake and died as a result. But I have never forgotten you. If you come back with a child, be it a son or a daughter, please go to this spot underneath the bed. There, I've kept something for you. It's a golden lock. Please dig it out and get your son or daughter to wear it around the neck for it has the power of protection.'

As soon as she said those words, she disappeared. It was not till then that I burst out with my first flow of words, 'Mother, where are you going? Come back!'

In the listening darkness of the room, my senses were restored to their wakeful state. A dream as real as the reality.

*

[BH's self-musing in response to an accusation arising in his own heart.]
[Stacey: If disliking is reason enough, let it be, 1032 words cut]

More of this. But I'll put Ah Sin first. Ah, Sin always to always put first.

And with what Stacey said constantly in mind, too, as I put that in a reminding list:

> Keep it to a minimum, said she.
> Do the right thing, said she.
> Be serious, said she.
> Be market-oriented, said she, and corrected she, be success-focussed and conscious.
> You have to be the best and I won't settle for less, said she.

By 'it', did she mean poetry and the other language that they called LOTE? I have often wandered to myself without daring raise the issue with Stacey, the word 'dare' Ibsen, such an idealistic writer, used so many times in his An Enemy of the People.

Chapter 2

Sure enough, I found the golden lock in a hole in a corner underneath my parents' bed that I now lay on, side by side with Na Za. When I wiped it clean, it shone and felt heavy in my hand. She had a look, delighted, and said, 'What's this, Dad?'

'A long-life lock,' said I, handing it over to her.

She stared at it, touching it, touching it again. When her stare changed into a gaze, her face softened into a question, 'What do I do with it?'

'You put it around your neck and it'll serve to protect you, to keep you whole,' said I. I picked it up from her open palm and was about to put it around her neck when she wriggled, her neck moving this way and that, saying, 'but it smells,' and refused to wear it.

'Oh, I'm sorry,' said I as I took it down and went to give it a wash, with soap. Then I remembered something. I went back to the bed, removed the bedrolls and the bedsheets. Right where my feet were when I lay down to sleep at night, there was a baina yi, a garment of a hundred patched-up pieces.

This one, unlike the golden lock, attracted Na Za's attention at once, with an immediate question, 'Is that meant for me?' Her left hand already shot out to grab hold of the garment.

'No,' I held her hand and, gingerly, pulled her hand off it. 'You've got to be careful with this one.'

'Why? Why? Why?' she raised her sunflower face and spat out the rapid-fire question.

'Listen,' said I. 'I'll tell you a story. Then we'll go to ride a buffalo. Okay?'

'Yes, yes, yes!' she held my hand in both of hers and looked into my eyes. Instantly, her mother came back and my heart was warmed up.

'My grandma, your great grandma, came to visit me last night while you were asleep. She said to me that over the years she had collected clothes from all the households in our village and the surrounding villages in order to make a garment of hundred patched-up pieces in preparation for my child. Before she left, she had put it away in a safe place and asked me to retrieve it so you can put it on. Like the golden lock, it is meant to protect you, particularly in illness.'

'Does it mean I shall never fall ill again when I put it on?' she looked up at me as she twisted my index-finger around her thumb.

'Most likely you won't,' said I.

'But where is my great grandma?'

'She's dead.'

'If she's dead, how did she come?'

'She came in a dream.'

'Then she must be still alive.'

'Oh, nothing dies. No one really dies. Just now, I saw Mum in your eyes.'

'I dreamt of Mum a few times already.'

'What happened in your dreams?'

'I can't remember anything, just a faint figure of someone calling me by my name.'

'I'll get this little garment washed, too, so you can feel comfortable wearing it. Then we'll go and ride the buffalo.'

*

[BH's diary, one entry.]

> 10.53.16am. I overslept again because the alarm set for 7 a.m. did not go off. Which means I have slept another 9 hours. 9 hours! If I sleep 9 hours a day, I must have slept 3285 hours in my last posthumous year. I was about to put 'financial year' when the word 'posthumous' cut in and I quite like the hang of it, so I include it here. And it seems to make a lot of sense, too. I have lived and I don't seem to have lived. Everything is posthumous. Now, if a

posthumous year costs 3285 hours to sleep, I shall have slept at least 114,975 hours. That's 4790 24-hour days, and 13.125 365-day years. I have slept at least 13 entire years out of a mere 35! That's more than one third of my life. I'm such a waster of time! But isn't living a life also a wasting of it? I've worked out something about Rui's suicide — Rui, an old friend of mine in China – 'ui': Sruicide! – it must have been because death was so fantastically alluring to him that he found it impossible to resist its temptation, forgetting that he was standing on top of a five-floor building, the edge of it, and intent on throwing himself into the enticing arms of the stunning woman waiting for him down there on the construction site. And he did, consummating with her in the instant impact that achieved his long-wanted success: union and reunion of permanence. There are failures and there are successes. And this is the kind of success that he pursues, not the more vulgar kind of money-measured boredoms awardable only to the mediocrities. He jumps to his death, his most faithful woman who never says no to the likes of him and who, indeed, always welcomes the boldest. And the other possible explanation I've worked out for the ruicide is that deep in his heart he knew that if he died at 41 he will remain 41-year-young, not even 42-year-old.

A fragment I wrote the other day, on a scrap piece of paper that lay next to a 10-dollar banknote, said something to this effect: 'Is there an easier way to get to the top rather than spend one's life getting stuck in this shit, day in and day out, without ever seeing the light, let alone the high light, of the tunnel at the other end?' I picked up the note and binned the scrap.

Meanwhile, I keep reading poetry, realising that it is an increasingly obsolete activity. I guess I do this as an act of rebellion against all the odds geared up for one purpose only: adding endless numbers of zeroes to that first figure 1. And I can't believe that someone like Heamus Henea, oops, I meant Seamus Heaney, sometimes falls short because he has to resort to using such hideosity as 'through thick and thin' (*Human Chain*, Faber & Faber, 2010, p. 74). I immediately decided to apply this to Na Za. When Ah Sin told her that he had always loved her Mum through thick and thin, she said, 'I'm sorry? What did you mean by "through think and thin"?' And Ah Sin said, 'Actually, I like what you have just done, changing the whole wordscape.' 'In fact,' said Na Za, now a pupil studying English in a missionary school run by Woo Wo. 'I prefer "through thin and thin", "through thin-thin" and even "through thick and Ah Sin.'

To fill you in, whoever you are, my dad has just divorced my mum and has married someone younger than him by thirty years, about my age.

*

I went to Grandfather III's house, this time without Na Za. She would be bored, so I let her out to play on her own. The first thing that caught my eye when I arrived at the door was a huge black lacquer coffin that occupied a large part of the hall. The old man I called 'San Ye' (Third Grandpa) was sitting on a stool by the side of the door, smoking. After an exchange of greetings with me, he pulled another stool out for me to sit on, next to the coffin, and offered his opium box, made of silver, with a dragon carved on the cover. I declined, indicating my own pack of tobacco, and offering it, too, with both of my hands. He did not even glance at it. Instead, he put a pinch in his pipe, lit it and took a deep draw on it before he puffed it out, in a white plume of smoke. Without any preamble, he said, 'Your dad was killed in a fight.'

I looked at him, looked at the deep troughs, three of them, on his forehead, looked at his heavy, thick, black brows, like two horizontal wooden clubs, looked at his slit-eyes from which one could see nothing, like the eyes of a dead fish. He went on,

'The locals and the Hakkas had had a series of fights from the Xin-hai year onwards. It was like seesawing. You won, I lost. I won, you lost. The locals blamed the Hakkas for taking up their land by building their houses on their land and speaking a different dialect from the local speech. The difference was like that between fire and water. No mutual tolerance. Most of the Hakkas took their residence in the hills where they built fortified houses of multiple storeys, strongholds against the local invaders. A few, like your family, had arrived earlier, in a more peaceful and peaceable time, so they were able to mix with the locals amicably until bad feelings became the order of the day. Since the Fifth Year of Xianfeng, fights between the locals and Hakkas have been going on for more than a decade in Xinning and its surrounding areas. In Chixi alone, more than 20,000 people got killed. This village used to be Ocean-Watching Village and because the number of families was reduced from dozens to four families, it has got its current name. All the young and strong males have gone overseas, looking for gold, looking for work, looking for any opportunities that might exist elsewhere. Any countries would do. You name it. America, Australia, New Zealand, Cuba, Panama, Peru, Singapore, South-east Asia, India, and a whole lot more. I am the only one who has chosen to come back, from California, because I want to die here, in my ancestral land, to be buried with my parents, my grandparents and my great grandparents. If I die in America, they can't even get my name right on my gravestone. And I die absolutely alone, buried alongside the animals, those who have killed us, bullied us, cheated us, trod us underfoot, treated us like animals, dismissed us as lesser human beings, ignored us as non-existent, obliterated us as non-beings. Now, look at me. I am an achiever. I achieved my goal of making my coffin for life, for the rest of my life, for my death. The Changshou (Long Life, a euphemism for coffins) coffin you are sitting next to is my dream, realised once for all. When I die, I shall be comfortable in the thought that I have a tiny house with a tiny bed to sleep on, just my full length, with a bit of footroom and headroom. And when I die, I shall live, forever. I know, I know. Everything, including myself, will rot to dust. But that's why the soil in this village and elsewhere is so rich, because it is filled with dead bodies, their blood and their flesh. That's the best nutrition for the earth, essential ingredients for crop-growing.'

All the while I listened to him I thought of my own thoughts. The blue ocean at Guichen Bay. The kangaroo-coloured paddocks all the way to the goldfields. The riots. The roarings of the whites. The pulled pigtails by the root. The tears. The suicide of Ah Bo. The mental hospital of Ah Mao. Ah Fong's restaurant. My wife, my dear wife. And my dream of visiting Ireland with her one day.

'Grandpa,' a gentle voice came from inside the house behind the hall. 'Here's your tea and the tea for our guest.'

*

Dear Baohui,

I haven't heard from you for a long time. What's going on? Why don't you ever say anything about anything I posted on WeChat Moments, or sent to you directly for sharing? Why are you always so short of words whenever you reply, just a 'yes' or 'no' or 'received', not even with a 'thanks'? What's going on? Don't you ever miss me, your Mum? I miss you. I sometimes miss you terribly, particularly after your dad has recently divorced me. He's gone with someone so young that she could be your sister. Shame on him! Shame on her! Shame on both of them! But a good riddance, too, because I don't have to cook for him, to wash his dirty, shit-stained pants, and to pretend on public occasions that I am overjoyed with his achievements. Nothing of that anymore.

Have you found a girlfriend, someone after your own heart? Can I recommend a few? I know someone from a very good background. She is not only pretty but also smart. Her parents, both highly educated, work in important positions. She is finishing her MA in financial management and she has a good command of English. I know because I have taught her. Her name is Zenzen. I attach a photo of her for you. Please let me know as soon as possible what you think. I want you to get married and lead a comfortable life.

This PhD thesis you are working on. How is it coming along? Is it interesting at all? I always stress this: You don't have to if you don't want to, and that applies to PhD theses, too. As far as your dad is concerned, you can join him in his Greek project. I think you'll have a wonderful time there even though I've divorced him. A man should not engage in literary pursuits anymore. This is not the right age for it. It's a woman's business. Even if you really want to pursue it, you might go for something else, something like filmmaking. That's how you can earn an instant fame, worldwide.

In my opinion, there is no future for literature by men. Don't I know? I've got my MA in Sydney. I've mixed with men and women of letters there. What a pathetic mob! When a book is launched, few go to the launch and fewer buy a copy. Absolutely appalling! It's like the dead spirits moving. I married your dad because he was rich or had the potential of becoming rich. Now that he's rich, what has he done?

[No, I'm sorry; I can't allow anything anti-Australian here,163 words cut—SA]

You have to come back to China as she is now one of the most powerful countries in the world, and I'd say the most after the U.S.a. Yes, a small 'a', like this: 'U.S.a.' because it is no longer a world leader in everything that can be categorised as 'A'. Once you come back to Shanghai, we — your dad, my divorced ex-husband — will find you a job and a girlfriend.

Do you miss me? Say you do, say you do. And be a good boy.

Your long-suffering Mum

*

I raised my head in surprise. I had thought Grandpa III was living alone. But here was someone so young, barely out of her teens. She didn't greet me but her face registered the faintest smile. She put the tea set on the table, rinsed two cups with hot water, put one pinch of tea leaves in either, poured water in and waited a couple of seconds. Then she used a wire strainer to let the water out, keeping the leaves in. She did all this with skill. I couldn't resist looking at her black pigtail hanging down over her shoulder on her back. I found her flowery blouse so appealing to the eye. And below her wide and loose pants, reaching only to the shins, were a pair of black cloth shoes that indicated that her feet were not bound.

Meanwhile, San Ye went on with his talk, to no one apparently, after a fresh replacement of the opium. The topic had slightly changed its direction, now more to do with the origin of the Hakkas. He said, 'Why are we called Hakka? Because we are kejia. Ke: guests. Jia: family. We are from all over China. We spread all over the world. We have a long history, so long no one can remember it. Wherever we go, we are guests. Even when we strike long roots, we are not locals. Can never be locals. Not regarded as locals. We are guests. We settle as guests, from generation to generation, century after century. That's why no one takes us seriously. They treat us like guests. They bully us. They chase us off their land, thinking we have no titles, no rights. But our people always fight even as they retreat and go away, continuing to be guests. No one in our families talks about this because it's a shameful history. You don't know because no one told you about it. But it's in your blood that the minute you were born you started dreaming away. You never think happiness can be found in a fixed and settled place because that is too easy. Happiness can never be found anywhere; it's an illusion. You can only find it in a dream or in a dreamless sleep. Or you can only find it when you are constantly on the move. Once you stop, it's gone. That's us. That's us guest family people. You don't take roots. You are indeed ashamed of taking roots. We are as mobile as money itself. We are money, in a curious sort of way. The only thing that moves in this world is money. If you move, you have money. If you know how to move, you have money. If you know how to move with money, you have more money. That's why they hate us because we have money. We go everywhere and money goes with us because money doesn't strike roots. Only trees do but trees are not money. We move money everywhere and when we go money comes with us; it follows us. There are two things you can't miss with the guest family people. They kick up revolutions and they go with the foreign. Remember Hong Xiuquan? He's the leader of the Taiping Rebellion against the Qing Dynasty and he started a Christian movement in China, believing he himself to be the younger brother of Jesus Christ and that it was his mission to spread Christianity across China. See? He is a revolutionary leader and he sided with a foreign religion. Only someone from a Hakka background can manage to do that. And, you know, many of you originally came from Henan, all parts of

Henan. But that, more than a thousand years ago, was a place where many Jews went and settled. These are a people like the guest family people. They wandered and roamed around the earth. I haven't seen them here in my place. But seeing you and seeing other guest family people is seeing them because your blood is visible through your thin skin as everyone can see your wandering gene, with your wandering heart, in it. I have wandered enough to not want to wander any more. See my coffin that I've made for myself? It's made of the best wood ever, the Phoebe nanmu. This is a real slow growing tree. Although the old saying goes that it takes 10 years to grow a tree but it takes 100 years to grow a person, the situation is reversed when it comes to this tree as it takes at least 100 years to grow into usable material. The beauty of it is that, in its full prime, when the sun strikes on the trunk, you can see streaks of gold in it. This is why it is called the golden-thread nanmu. Because it is highly resistant to decay, it was used by a Ming emperor to construct the Forbidden City. I want to sleep in it forever and I want it to serve as an example of someone who comes to his final rest after wandering all his life.'

By now, San Ye had downed no fewer than 12 cups of tea that I refilled and served. He had even smoked the tobacco I had offered and nodded his approval. He liked the leaf from Brazil because it had a smell he had never smelt before. I smoked and listened. But my mind was entirely taken up by the girl who had taken the tea set out and put it on the table in front of the shrine. Who was she? Was she really his granddaughter? Or was she just a servant? But if she was the servant, she wouldn't have called him 'Granddad'. Or – I held my thought when it came to an abrupt stop because I didn't want to go further by thinking more about her.

*

My WeChat response to Mum was simple enough, in typical punctuation-less WeChat lingo style:

Got it with thanks Mum I do miss you in fact all the time but I am so busy I haven't got the time to miss people all the time have a wonderful time in your post-marriage life

Just then, I had a thought, actually, two, that offered themselves to me. In one of them, I heard San Ye tell Ah Sin that he had in fact been sleeping in his coffin for years, in all seasons of the year. Even though this sounded like pure boasting, Ah Sin said nothing to dispute it. He was willing to believe anything that came out of a toothless mouth. The other thought was related to something I saw in the sky as I was taking a walk outside in the park. I saw, with my own eyes, that I had been turned into Ah Sin himself, a shoulder-pole on my shoulder, switching from one to the other, with my own belongings in the two large bamboo-baskets, walking alone across Australia, from goldfield to goldfield, walking in fact from China all the way to Australia across the seas, seeing the gold all the times, like some distant lights at night that defied approaching. I could weave these into the fabric of the story. But it's too hard for me to find the right spots to squeeze them in. Why bother? I thought to myself.

*

[Meandering thoughts about poetry, irrelevant and uninteresting, 1008 words cut—SA]

*

I was sleepless that night, thinking, thinking of, thinking of her, thinking of the black meandering pigtail on her back.

I looked at her, my little Daa Seinn, lying in her own quilt beside me, her placid face, like her mother's. The girl was totally exhausted after a long day playing in the fields, riding a buffalo, falling down off it, and riding it again till she could sit on it and sing. Then she went swimming! How dare she! But I was told she had no problem at all. Without anyone teaching her, she could paddle in the water like a puppy dog, her clothes all wet. When a local boy by the name of Ah Tien saved her and got her to change into his clothes, she didn't object to it; instead, she put on the long and loose garment like her own, forgetting her own multiple-patched clothes. But the golden lock she never took off her neck. Then she had lunch at Ah Tien's house where his mum cooked for them while they played hide and seek. Obviously, she had the time of her life.

But what about me? Why am I back? Now that they are all gone, I live my life without a purpose. I have been a drifter ever since I set foot on Australian soil, from Bendigo to Castlemaine then to Melbourne, a guest everywhere, now, more guest than guest, back on home soil. At least I have to do these things: finding Na Za a teacher, visiting Woo Wo in his home church and doing the tomb-sweeping. As for myself, what is left there for me to do? Oh, yes, Aunty Chai next door wanted me to read a letter for her and write a reply for her son in Cuba, too. My thoughts got entangled as the night deepened. The cock crowed. The first cock crow. Then another cock, another cock, till all the cocks in the surrounding villages started crowing. And, afterwards, I fell asleep, dropping into a bottomless hole, a goldmine of dreams that ghosts kept drilling till they could never hope to get out of it ever again, buried alive with gold.

The next morning, after I got up, washed myself and prepared the breakfast, congee with sliced salted turnip and salted fish, and steamed bread, I woke Na Za. The first thing she said when she opened her eyes was, 'Dad, I had a dream. I dreamt of you with a woman.' I asked who it was. She said that it was a stranger that she had never seen before. 'Was it maybe your Mum?' I said. 'No, it's not Mum. It's someone else,' she said, frowning. I ignored the remark, letting it sink in. Afterwards, when we finished eating, Na Za and I went to Aunty Chai, our next-door neighbour.

Aunty Chai's husband had died in a fight between the guest family people and the locals. She was living with her mother-in-law, on the ir-regular remittances sent from her son in Cuba, on the rice she planted with her own hands in her own rice paddies and on the vegetables she grew in her backyard.

When we appeared at the door, she was sweeping the floor, her 80-year-old mother-in-law Mrs Chan was sitting by the door, sewing the sole of a shoe. Aunty Chai greeted me and waved us in. But Na Za was hesitant because these were two strangers to her. Aunty pulled out two bamboo chairs and put them by the low table, one on either side. Then she served me hot tea, with a hand extended to Na Za, holding a handful of candies. Na Za looked at her, at her hand, at me, then at Mrs Chan, sitting there and sewing. She was hesitant. Then she said, 'Dad, can we go?'

'Hang on a tick,' said I to her. 'I've got work to do.'

Just then, a pig came wandering to a shallow pit, not far from the door, and lay down in it. That caught Na Za's attention as she went over and squatted, looking at it, ignoring my warning, 'Don't get close; it's dirty.'

Aunty Chai took out a letter from a flowery oblong lacquer box and, with both of her hands, handed it over to me as she said, 'I've got this recently from Cuba. Please read it for me.'

Carefully, I took the contents out of the envelope with what looked like a Spanish stamp and a Chinese seal on it, and unfolded the one-page letter, quickly scanning it from top to bottom and from right to left before I started, with a whimper,

> This is not from your son but a friend of your son. He says that they have recently been involved in a war of independence led by a man whose name is Carlos Manuel de Céspedes. Many fellow Chinese who have gone to Cuba as indentured coolies have joined the army fighting for independence from the Spanish. However, recently, something has happened. In one of the fiercest battles fought in Bayamo, the city was reduced to burnt ashes, many died and a few went missing, your son among them. Please rest assured that your son may come back alive one day and please also find a one pound-note enclosed he asked me to forward you.

When I finished reading the letter, I could see that Aunty Chai's head got lower and lower until it reached her lap, buried in her cupped hands, her whole person trembling, like a leaf in the wind.

Her mother-in-law, who had been sewing the sole thus far, stopped her needlework in the middle of it, her eyes staring outside at nothing, tears running down her wrinkled face.

Na Za, unaware of what had been going on, was still squatting in front of the pig. In fact, she was scratching the pig's back, playing with its hair, stroking it. The pig was feeling so comfortable that it rolled onto its back and spread its four legs as it oinked.

Just then, a white duck waddled in and stopped before Na Za, raising her head to look at her, first with one eye, then the other eye. Na Za was so amused by the pantomime that she held out her hand to touch the bill. But the duck, quickly to its own defence, winced and waddled back, with a series of fierce quacks. Just at that moment, Aunty Chai came over and said, 'Don't be afraid, she's a gentle duck. You two could become good friends.'

Sure enough, Na Za came back and the duck also came back, to her. After their first encounter, stranger to stranger, both became more relaxed and Na Za was more prepared because she got a handful of sunny grains of rice and scattered them before the duck. As she watched her pecking at the grains, a smile spread itself over Na Za's face and a thought suggested itself to her: What if I leave? Would she follow me? No sooner had she thought of it than Na Za stood up and made as if she was about to leave. The duck raised her head and stoppied pecking, quacked and started waddling towards her. Afterwards, Zuoshou, Na Za's pet name for the duck, and Na Za became close friends when Aunty Chai gave the duck to Na Za as a gift.

*

[Too angry and self-indulgent for my liking, 1274 words cut—SA]

*

Back in the village I was born in, we – Na Za and I – lived an idyllic life of indolence, accidental visits and expanses of unoccupied time bar one thing: love. There was a lot of love between Na Za and I, her love for her dad and my love for my daughter. And her love for her Left Hand (that's what 'Zuoshou' means), a duck who would follow her everywhere, rising early to wake her up, pecking at the hems of her skirt to ask her out for a walk and follow her everywhere in the village, not just to the waterside but also to every family Na Za happened to stop by, on top of giving Na Za or us one egg every day, now all the eggs filling a big bamboo basket that neither I nor Na Za wanted to ruin by eating. But that was far from enough. I was hankering after physical love with a woman. I wanted to love a woman, from eye to body, from clothes to stripped clothes. But.

The other day, Na Za and I went to pay respects to my family members buried in the nearby Green Hill. We brought with us a lot of things: paper money, firecrackers, bunches of incense, milky-coloured candles, a bottle of rice wine, a plate of fruit, two bunches of white chrysanthemums, a small broom, scissors, and a red lacquer box, with carved flowers, of a prepared meal, with braised pork, braised fish and steamed phoenix claws (chicken feet).

There were two graves, side by side, one for my parents and the other for my grandparents. I laid one bunch of the chrysanthemums before either gravestone. I swept the gravesites clean. I then laid out a long string of firecrackers but did not light it before I sprinkled their gravesides with the rice wine, in an act of libation. Awed by the solemnity of it all, Na Za watched me do these without a word. It was such a fine day. The sun touched both of our faces warmly. The creek ran away, twinkling in places where the sun struck. Here and there, there was an occasional buffalo ploughing in the rice paddies. When I set off the firecrackers, the staccato explosive noise startled Na Za so she ran away to stop at a distance, where she covered her ears, watching.

'Is death the shadow of life?'

'I'm sorry?' I said, turning around to see her intense eyes.

Daa Seinn repeated what she said, 'Is shadow the death of life?'

'What did you mean?'

'Nothing,' said Daa Seinn. She bent to wipe a muddy spot from the face of the gravestone.

When this was finished, I started burning the paper money, to Na Za's bewilderment. I explained that people were not really dead. They were still alive in another world, an underworld, where they needed to use the money and they also needed to eat and drink. She said: But you are burning it. You've burnt the money. I explained that only by burning it could the dead start using it because fire was the medium by which money could turn into a usable form when it reached the hands of the dead. She stood, her mouth shut tight, her head moving from side to side, in a defiant way of saying no, of disbelief, refusing to understand the logic.

When the meal was offered, in three large bowls, as the final ritualistic presentation, Na Za could no longer contain herself. She yelled at me, saying, 'But why? Why do you do this to them? How are you ever going to make them eat these?'

Without a word, I pulled her into my arms and I said, in a tearful whisper, 'I'm sure they won't be able to eat these as they are dead. Ours is a culture – culture, you know, a sky under which things are different from elsewhere – in which people who are dead are never dead, particularly those closest to you, your family members, your parents and grandparents. We do seem to cheat ourselves by doing these things but only because we have love and our love is undying. I love you, Na Za.'

'I love you, too, Dad,' said Na Za. 'But I don't want to eat them when I am dead. I want to eat them when I am still alive.'

'You can eat them now, if you like,' I said.

'Are you sure?'

'When did I lie to you?' As I said so, I picked up a chicken foot with a pair of chopsticks and put it in her opened mouth.

*

I admit to myself that my writing about Ah Sin came very slowly, almost word by word, moment by moment and breath by breath. But, hey, something happened. Nothing these days allowed me to stop to think, never allowing me to say things like 'I'm bored. Let's have fun', in one of those tons of trash emails I receive daily from women I do not know. Each and every morning, it's as much my sacred duty to clean myself up as to clean up my email inbox. One said, *I want to have sex. I can't wait.* Another said, *Come between my breasts and my thights.* I deleted them but I liked 'thights'; it's almost like thoughts turned thights, a transformation. But it's bad timing as my own thighs no longer generated any thoughts. They were like two surfboards sandwiching a rock.

Charlie, a friend of my age, called via WeChat just now. When I asked how he went in search of a girlfriend, he started,

> Not easy Mate. Asian girls do not go for Asian guys like me. They flock to the whites. They find them fun, infinitely more interesting than us. Who are we but just the last resort, the backups to rely on when everything else fails? Even a black man is more enticing in his I don't care about nuffin ways. Only last night, in a joint, we saw this Asian girl hooked up with a black guy. The guy was absolutely relaxed and everything. He made the girl laugh her head off like she had never lived before. She would never be that happy with an Asian guy because the guy might remind her of her own strict taunting dad.

'Why don't you try a white girl then?' prompted I, thinking of a white girl I studied with whose name was Rosie.

'No way, Mate', said Charlie. 'Let me put it this way. I don't really care about the woman's racial or ethnic background as long as she is my type. But there simply are no matches on the apps I'm using, things like Tinder and Bumble. These days, it's not your call but theirs. If they choose you, set their sights on you, then there is some chance, some small chance. I got a few coming my way, all gone now. But so far, I haven't got a single white girl coming after me. You know G? I mean he's Asian and he's got a white girl but only because he plays sports, has tattoos, smokes, and bluffs his way into all sorts of situation, like a white guy. You have to be like that to win the heart of a white girl. Problem is: how long is that going to last?

'Ho, ho, ho,' said I. 'you want it to last? You might as well ask a hero's statue to last, covered in white bird shit.'

'No, I mean, it's better long-term than short-term, no? Still, I wouldn't mind having a few one-night stands to ease into it or them and see what happens.'

'Listen,' I said as I couldn't help tittering to myself that he had remained a virgin after all these many years. 'You might consider going to Ukraine.'

'Why on earth would I consider going there, as if MH17 was not bad enough?'

'Well, I haven't got all day to fill you in on that, nor am I running a dating agency. But if you check into SN, Saturday Night, there's a program they did on how Aussie men found their partners in Kiev, I think, or Odessa, I'm not sure. But with a population of more women than men, twice as many, I think, a man can find any women there.'

'But I don't want to find any women; I only need one.'

'Fair enough. Just go and check it out on YouTube. I'd love to go there one day or perhaps we could both go together, not till you make up your mind whether you like them enough to go.'

*

[293 words cut—SA]

Chapter 3

We were walking towards Zhaoge, the nearest town. As we walked, I explained, pointing things out for her to know. This was rice. That was wheat. That was an ox, pulling a cart, piled with chairs. This was a shoulder-pole, with a basket on either end. Na Za got impatient, waving her hand, for me to stop. 'Dad,' she said. 'Tell me a story. I don't want to know about these.' So I told her a story of King Nan Tuo, who was such a huge lover of money that he ordered that all the treasures be sent to him for storage to be spent in his after-life. As he had a daughter at a marriageable age, he stipulated that all who were interested in proposing marriage to her must bring treasures, pearls and money. There was a young man who had fallen in love with the king's daughter. But he had no money. His mother, a widow, grew worried watching him becoming gaunt and thin, pining for the king's daughter, till one day she pulled her son to her side and told him to go to his father's graveside. She told him that if he reopened it he would find money. Sure enough, when he did so, he found that there was a piece of gold in his father's mouth. When he went to seek the king's daughter's hand, with the piece of gold, the king was enraged because after his order no one was supposed to be so rich. He must have stolen it from the king's hoard. The king ordered to have him tortured. But however hard and harshly they treated him, the son would not admit to the crime. Eventually, he told them that this was the gold he had found in his dead father's mouth after he received his mother's instructions. The king's men followed him to the grave and found it to be true. It was not till then that the king felt greatly ashamed of what he had done in comparison with what the son's father had done: he had saved nothing for the after-life except one piece of gold in case of need. After this, the king decided to scatter all his treasures across the country among the poor.

Na Za fell into silence after that, not like her usual self, full of questions, except for a short remark, like an after-thought: 'Why is love so closely related to gold? Is gold worth it?'

Then, it was my turn to fall silent.

We arrived at a teashop, called, First Tea. The shopkeeper, a man wearing a black silk melon hat and a long sleek pigtail, rose to greet us, with a 'hello'. Na Za was quick with a 'hello' in reply, as her hand shot up in a friendly gesture. But I was surprised. Why didn't he address me in Mandarin? Did I look like a complete foreigner? A few words with him confirmed my suspicion. Mr Weng, on seeing me wearing a Western suit, with a Western-featured girl alongside me, thought that it would be most polite if he addressed me in English. He asked us to sit down while he prepared tea for us, sitting in front of his tea set. Na Za sat down on a high stool. But I didn't. As Mr Weng went the rounds introducing his varieties of teas to Na Za, his only audience, I walked around the shop while lending him a casual ear, looking at the scrolls of calligraphy hanging on the wall. One scroll, written in a wild-weed style, featured The Classic of Tea by Lu Yu. Although I had difficulty recognizing much of the contents, I could make out a few things that made sense. In my interpretation by guesswork, the writer was saying that, of all the waters for stewing tea, the mountain water was the best, the river water was second best and the well water was third best. The best mountain water was the one that slowly ran over the milk stone. The best river water was the one that was far away from humanity whereas the best well water must be from a well most often used by people. Then, my eye caught these two lines that went:

寒夜客来茶当酒
竹炉汤沸火初红

I turned them into English, uttering the words, in spite of myself:

When the guest came on a cold night, we drank tea, like wine
The tea was boiling inside the bamboo stove while the fire was burning red-bright

Mr Weng's ramblings about his tea products came to an abrupt stop as he rose and came to my side with a cup of tea in hand, saying, 'You like these poems?'

'I do, actually,' said I, taking a sip from the cup he offered. 'What's this?' I nodded towards the tea and said again, 'but what is this?'

'Oh, you mean this tea?' said Mr Weng. 'it's Ti Kuan Yin, from Anhsi in Fukien.'

'Yes.'

'You've got such a fine taste. It's simply the best.' Mr Weng showed me around, taking samples of tea in a wooden tea chest, running through their names, such as the Golden Osmanthus, Buddha's Hands, Hairy Crabs and Big-leaved Oolong Tea, with Ti Kuan Yin being one of the Oolong teas that's between green tea and red tea amongst six major teas in China, the green, the red, the dark-green, the white, the yellow and the black.

'Do you happen to have White Cloud Tea?' I cut him short.

'Oh, yes, it's the best tea in Taishan that comes in three varieties, the red, the yellow and the green.'

I said, 'I'd like to buy five kilos of it please.' As I said so, I had a look around, searching for Na Za. But she was nowhere to be found.

'Where is my little girl?' said I, concerned.

'Oh, mister,' said Mr Weng. 'she's in the backyard, playing with my daughter.'

*

That night, when I came back, I found I was writing something down. I wouldn't call it a 'diary'. I just called it 'a piece':

> Mr Weng and I became instant friends, not just because he had also come back from Australia but also because his two wives and Na Za got on well. May, the younger one, in her early 20s, taught Na Za how to jump rope. She wasn't quite as pretty as the older wife, Pandi, but certainly was livelier. The second wife, about Mr Weng's age, was knitting a pair of woollen socks for May as she was in the

family way, so from time to time she cautioned May to tone down, to be less active playing with the kid.

I was slightly jealous, in my heart of hearts. But I made sure no one detected anything on my face. As I sat drinking tea with Mr Weng, he filled me in on his years spent in Ararat digging for gold. He was one of the few who had struck it rich in the Canton Lead and had decided to return to China without wanting more. This was because he had a dream in which a fortune-teller, after examining his facial features and his palm lines, warns him against staying for too long. When he, or his dream self, asks how long is too long, the fortune-teller simply says: as soon as possible. As he was deeply superstitious, Mr Weng decided to pack up then and there. And he now congratulated himself on the timely decision and was forever grateful to the fortune-teller for his fortuitous warning. From what he had learnt afterward from people who came back much later or from the letters from those who stayed put, theirs was not a life worth living, one full of violence meted out by the white claim jumpers, lost properties, robberies and utter solitude without the company of a woman. He certainly was happier now, with his two wives and a number of other shops he was running, one a cloth shop and the other, a bookshop.

In our conversation that lasted throughout lunch and into the late afternoon, we basically covered everything we knew or had read about. When he wondered if I had any future plans, I said I had none. He then suggested that I ought to find a woman to form a family. When I said I was thinking, I saw May glance at me. Our eyes met and her face instantly flushed red. Then, he talked about something that I had never heard of before. He mentioned a name, Low Fan Pak, as someone who had established a republic in Borneo. He said he was very interested in going to have a look-see at least.

My curiosity aroused, I wanted to find more about that.

*

[Stacey remarks: One problem with creative writing students in relation to fiction they are creating is that they tend to confuse nonfictional realities with fictional ones, putting them in, not leaving them out, thinking self-lovingly that they might somehow work, without trying to create an organic link between the separate stories in the totality of the novel. I'll keep the first sentence and cut the rest of the following Hong Kong story, 384 words cut.]

I had yum cha with Yang Jin and his wife as well as his son and his son's wife.

[Stacey remarks: I don't like any incorrectness in a work of fiction, particularly when it comes to climate change. The following anti-climate change remarks are offensive and unhelpful. I hereby exercise my discretion as the supervisor to shed 190 words]

We listened in open-eyed silence and when he finished, I applauded and said, 'This is resistance literature at its best.'

'Literature?' he was shocked. 'it has nothing to do with literature.'

'Sorry,' I said. 'I was thinking of something else.'

'You are obsessed with the literature that you are writing. That's why.'

[Stacey remarks: Part of the continued Hong Kong story, 172 words cut.]

After I finished the words above, I went out for a walk in Pangu Park. Don't wonder if you haven't heard the name. It's a park I invented myself, both the name and the surroundings. Although it was only around 10 a.m., the dew was still heavy. The grass in the distance was white-green. That's dew's work. Here in Pangu Park, everything was ugly, the tree stumps, the chopped-up, peeled wood blocks, the broken branches, the pale-stemmed grass that I later found to be achnatherum splendens, all over the place, never with any hope of being anything else or anything better, unharvestable, its fate to be burnt to ashes, or mowed down before being burnt to ashes. Indeed, at certain places, a fire must have raged through the gum trees. A tree stood in black, bare of leaves. A cluster of trees stood together, but there was no solidarity, as each stood apart in their togetherness. That's what I liked about the place, more and more, because it was a total rejection of the romantic and the snobbish. Nothing ever invited the camera to take photographs. Nothing ever induced one to express oneself in wonderful terms as when one stood on top of Mount Everest or over the Niagara Falls or Uluru. But its ugliness was its very beauty. All was low-key, unpretentious, honest to the degree of unworthy. But I never tire of being here as I come daily to breathe in the air carrying the smell of gum leaves and dewed-grass stems. Occasionally, you see a dog-walker or two. But they are whites and they seem harmless, occupied with themselves and their dogs. Between us there will be no exchange of anything beyond a faint smile for the rest of our lives. In Australia, eternity is synonymous with death.

On my way back, though, I saw the usually empty park encircled by vans. As I approached, I realised I had come to a farmers' market, vans with stands in front of them selling stuff from gnocchi, fruit and veggies, dumplings, pizzas, dips and spreads, pies and samosas, as well as raw honey, selling at 30 bucks per 3 kilos. I wasn't particularly interested in any of those. But I stood before a man playing guitar and singing along, with his mate in accompaniment. A white boy, aged about 12, stood in front of them, too, holding a wooden stick in his arms. Basically, we two were the only audience. When the man finished singing, he talked to the boy, commenting on his stick, saying how great it was and it might be worth twelve hundred dollars one day as it roughly resembled a digeridoo and part of a cello. The boy turned his back towards them, but his face was only half turned. Although he didn't say a word in return, he had a half smile on it that suggested he was listening, not missing a single word. After the man mentioned cello, I noticed that the way the boy was holding the stick did resemble the way Yoyo Ma held his. The boy and I exchanged a glance. But our glances at once wandered away. Still, I wouldn't say I didn't like him. It's just that we were of two entirely different species on this planet that there was no way we could ever become united. Ever.

On my aimless wanderings in Pangu Park, I thought of how Ah Sin had eventually reached his destination, at least spiritually, if not physically. I'm not sure if I should close the book by sending him to his destination and getting onto the sequel to this book, in an intended trilogy. A trilogy of what? Perhaps a trilogy of the republic, called The Lanfang Republic?

On the other hand, he was a man full of jouissance. He loved women, his thoughts never far away from them. His eyes never wandered away from them without wandering back. The more pretty a face was, the more attention it commanded, from him, that is. But this is common sense. No men in his times don't like a pretty woman. She who is physically beautiful remains a stirrer of the heart. I know I'm only speaking the platitudes and I need to stop. But Ah Sin was living in a time of a different paradigm. The righteous accusers of other people as wrong-doers did not as yet exist. He could love whoever he wanted to love as long as it fell within the limits of social acceptance and official sanctions. He wanted to marry someone young and pretty and Chinese. And then, when he returned to Australia, he wanted to marry again, to someone Australian and white and pretty, too. Living with two women, of two different cultures and languages, would be the pinnacle of his ideal, like living with two countries, at the same time.

Talking about the 'official sanctions', I was reminded of a practice in the Qing dynasty. The government officials, banned by the government rules from visiting the brothels, were free to visit the 'xianggong', a corrupted version of 'xianggu', like-girls, male prostitutes. In those days of sexual laissez-faire, Ah Sin must have had his fill of pleasure from the 'xianggong'.

'Why don't you write about it?' I said to myself. Then, once again, I thought of the project I have so far neglected to do for Stacey, the work involved in gathering material about gay and lesbian literature in ancient China. Gosh, I must say, they had a great time as neither gays nor lesbians were discriminated against in those days, at least not in fiction, and, cut that short, will you, Baohui? Just tell us a story, not to illustrate a point but to tell a story. Simple as that.

The town is Mitsein, Rice Fortress, if you like. There is a fad for the gays, known as Xiaoguan, Little Officials. they take hold of the area known as Li Yao, vacated by the local prostitutes because all the males in town have stopped visiting them, instead going to enjoy the male flesh. The prostitutes protest to the local court, arguing that the gay prostitutes have ruined their business. The nutshell of the story is that they have won the sympathy of the judge and the injunction from him that prostitution by gays is forbidden. As a result, the area is again taken up by the prostitutes and business is revived. Interested readers with a knowledge of Chinese are referred to the novel, titled 《龙阳逸史》 （1632）.

On the other hand, what is neglected is the story of how a Westerner seeks sexual comfort in China, by their own account. These days, if you do that, you either end up in prison and killing yourself like Jeffery Epstein, or you pretend that nothing has happened. Unlike Doctor Gervais who was so honest that he gives a detailed description of how he found a local young prostitute in his book, A Surgeon's China (1934). Because I don't want to give my readers, and most important of all, my supervisor, the wrong idea that I am approving his behaviour, I won't quote you the salacious passages in their entirety. I'll just whisper in your interested ears that it's in pp. 111-114 and say: Go and enjoy yourself. If you happen to be PC and SC (sexually correct), forget it. Just act as if I had not said anything.

*

I, not Ah Sin, am feeling more and more disgusted with myself. I can never aspire to a life playing golf in Windsor Castle, like Prince Andrew. Nor can I ever hope to marry a woman like Imelda Marcos when she was young, or any woman of her status, like Ivanka Trump. Even if I become general manager of the port in Greece my father is intending to buy, my nationality remains a stigma that I can't wash off my back. Writing a novel dressed as a PhD, or the other way round, writing a PhD dressed as a novel, I don't seem to have much of a future. Oh, yes, I saw a posted picture on Instagram this morning and I liked what I saw.

It's a remark by Jim Carrey that goes: 'I'm starting to realize that relationships are for beginners. Experienced people stay single.' Exactly! You have to be honest enough to face the world or else you just pretend, and pretend real hard.

Ah Sin, though, knew nothing about what was or is happening with me. He definitely didn't know that he even existed. Nor did I know what he meant to do or what was happening with him. Despite the advancement of telecommunications technology today, we still can't telephone, email, WeChat, Snapchat, Whatsapp, Facebook, Twitter, Instagram or Pinterest anyone alive in his time. Are we too stupid for the past? At least this much I can do, for him, because he started talking in my mind this morning without being invited. He said,

> I always talk to Ciaravoca before I go to sleep, to her ghost, I mean. Usually, this happens after I talk Na Za to sleep, with a story or two. Then I talk to Ciara's ghost. I tell her how Na Za is. She is growing fast, tall and thin now, with a pigtail. Her hair is blonde, with streaks of black hair. She has black eyes, not quite Chinese, not quite Irish. Just both. With a private tutor, Mr Ma, she is learning Chinese and can recite the beginning of 'San Zi Jing', *The Three Character Classic*. The first two lines have struck roots in her: 人之初，性本善. (In the beginning, human nature was good.) I know the Bible says it differently. Psalm says, 'Behold, I was brought forth in iniquity, and in sin my mother conceived me.' But I want her to remember the Chinese lines because if we are born sinners we may remain sinners and there is no hope whatsoever for us because money cannot save us, progress cannot save us and the only people who can save us are ourselves. What's more, if love is sin, what is not sin? In my one-sided talk, she never takes part. I never receive a comment. But the very act of talking eases me and lulls me to a comfortable sleep. Or else I'll have to rely on opium-smoking to numb my nerves. One thing I never tell her is in regard to women. A man never tells his woman about another woman or the other women, particularly when the woman comes from another cultural background. Back in Taishan, relationships

are fluid. Men and women come together and leave. I have had my fair share of it. But that's as far as I can go. At this point, I happen to recall a story written as far back as 795, the story of a prostitute falling in love with a student. Even though Gin's ghost has disappeared and the night has deepened, I want to renew my memory of what happens. In a nutshell, Zheng Yuanhe, a student with a big ambition, goes to Chang'an the capital to attend the civil service examination. There, he visits a brothel and meets Li Wa. He is handsome and she is beautiful, so they fall in love and live together for two years. At the end of the two-year period, when he runs out of money, he is chased outdoors and she disappears. The penniless Zheng falls sick on a street. But an assistant in a funeral parlour saves his life. In return for his kindness, Zheng starts working as a funeral singer for the dead and the mourners. Zheng's father happens to spot that when he goes to the capital on business. He is so furious that he gives him a sound beating. Thereafter, Zheng becomes a beggar. On a snowy day, he happens to arrive at the door of Li Wa.

Deeply moved by Zheng's misery, Li decides to quit her brothel life by paying her madam a large sum of money. Then she looks after him and buys books for him till he is fully recovered. A year later, when he passes the examination with flying colours, they get married, with Zheng's father's blessing and approval. Ever afterwards they live a happy life, the man working as a high official and the woman assisting her husband and their kids.

Sometimes, I stop to wonder to myself if a similar life is possible. Ah Xiang, for example, is someone I've met recently. Right now, though, I'd like to sleep.

Now, that's what Ah Sin spoke to me about in my head this morning.

Chapter 4

Ah Fa, whose nickname was Ah Fat when he was a little playmate of mine when young, was a salt merchant in Canton and he invited me to stay with him for a few nights. Because of the secret business he wanted to show me, I had to leave Na Za to the care of San Ye and his servant girl, Ah Mei.

The first night I spent in Canton was an eye-opener. This was a city with a history more than 2000 years old, longer than its Italian counterpart Venice, criss-crossed with rivers and creeks, where the three major rivers, the West River, the North River and the East River, joined. Variously called City of Five Sheep, City of Sheep or City of Ears of Rice, the city had a legendary story of its origin that goes that, in the beginning, five deities in garments of five different colours came riding five 5-coloured sheep, an ear of rice with six stems in their hands. When they arrived and gave the ears of rice to the people there they flew away, leaving their sheep that turned into stones. Because the city was rich in waters, it was also rich in women and sex, and the men seeking them. As far as I knew, love and sex abounded where there were plenty of waters. In Hangzhou, for example, there were what were known as huafang, the painted boats, and, around the Qinhuai River in Nanjing, the sex scene was active, too, captured in two lines from a play, The Peach Blossom Fan, by the early Qing playwright Kong Shangren, that go, 'the sound of oars and the shadows of the lanterns are miles long / while the singsong girls and their flower boats play the muddy wavelets.'

We rode in a horse-carriage till we arrived in Xiaodongmen. When I disembarked, my eyes were dazzled by what I saw: boat after brilliantly-lit boat lined the dock, all of them painted red and carved in loud images of dragon and phoenix, as well as lotus flowers and peony flowers.

There were small boats alongside the big boats, ones that looked like floating pavilions, with painted beams and carved pillars, and colour lanterns hanging in front. This, Ah Fat told me, was what was known as Zidongting, or, literally, Purple Hole Boat. When I couldn't help laughing out loud at the name, Ah Fat was puzzled and wondered why. I told him. He 'oh'ed and said that it wasn't that for Zidong was the name of a village Mai Yaoqian came from when he was an official in the early Qing dynasty. He had a boat made and named after his village to ply between Zidong and Canton.

Then, he lowered his voice, and said, 'Follow me and don't do anything till told.'

Along a wobbly springboard, we stepped on board a floating pavilion, when a servant-like boy, lantern in hand, appeared from nowhere and bowed deeply before us and said, 'Please', with a hand extended, indicating inside.

The interior of the boat was so huge it was like a hotel lobby. The only difference was that there were chairs sandwiching tables around the side beneath the windows. And there were tables and chairs around them in the middle. This was because, according to Ah Fat, that place was meant for both diners and accompanied entertainment. By 'accompanied entertainment', he meant that he and I wouldn't be sitting there alone. But we would have company of our own choice. In fact, several girls were standing about, in an eye-glanced blur of colours, chiefly scarlet. My nostrils were met with a sharp aroma that recalled the time immemorial in classic Chinese poetry. For some reason, the girls didn't stay long, but left one after another, leaving only one whose name was Qing Ye, green leaf. I stole glances, not daring to look at her directly. One glance told me she was in blue. Another glance said she had a melon-seed face. A third glance revealed that she had tiny feet. That induced a half erection. But as soon as we sat down and Ah Fat invited her to sit by my side, she refused, leaving me bewildered. She then went around to sit down by Ah Fat's side. While waiting for our food to come, I felt bored and went to one of the opium-smoking chairs by the window where I started smoking my opium while watching Ah Fat and Green Leaf talking in small voices. I couldn't hear what it was about but I looked at her feet again.

Moments after, while I was entering into a semi-delirium, induced by the opium, relaxed in every bone of mine, and every nerve, Ah Fat came back and sat down in the chair next to me, separated by the table with the opium set on it. In one half-opened glance, I convinced myself that the girl was gone. 'But why?' said I to Ah Fat.

'Don't you worry,' said he. 'it's because of your dress.'

'My dress?' said I. 'what's wrong with it?'

'Nothing wrong,' said he. 'it's just that it's too western for her.'

'What?' I was taken aback. 'Did you mean she didn't like me because I was western?'

'No, not that. It's because she had thought you were a savage man from the west by the way you dressed yourself in suit and tie, and didn't wear a pigtail.'

'Come on. That can't be true. I've never heard of such stupidities in my life.'

'It's not stupidity; it's probably wise of her not to want to have anything to do with westerners. For one thing, they are rude; and, for another, they always act in an overbearing manner. They stink, too. And they are hairy, like monkeys.'

'Yes and no. Some are good, some are not so good, and others are downright bad.'

'When I told her that you were a true-blue Chinese, she expressed her disbelief, wondering why you wore Western clothes. To prove my point, I actually took her to your side to have a closer look.'

'And?'

'She seemed convinced by the skin of your face. But she detested your clothes so much that she decided to leave then and there.'

'Well, bad luck then.'

'Don't worry. I'll make sure we'll have company tonight in a little while when everything gets ready.'

*

Baohui, to himself, in an email, 'I am troubled by something I can't adequately weave into the Ah Sin story. I could have easily stolen the piece and smuggled the detail in, e.g. the one related to kids where Ah Sin and Ah Fat visit this flower boat. I can describe them as sitting dexterously, trying to avoid sitting on rolling babies or stepping on their heads. I can also have Ah Sin curiously going to the captain's cabin to observe how the woman captain is adroitly manoeuvring her way out of the piled-up boats. I can also have Ah Sin and Ah Fat making love with their chosen women the whole night on the boat while the woman captain is smoking her pipe, with one baby each, soundly asleep in her arms. But the point? I am no longer into that game of cheating that is called fiction. If there is some good stuff there, why can't I simply copy and paste it here? Or type it up if it's not electronically available? Well, that's what I'll do.'

And following is what I've just typed up,

> Babies, and again babies! They teem everywhere. The East fairly creeps with them. They are China's main product; and are all of them the dearest, smilingest, chubbiest little beggars in the world. If you take a sampan, the captain of the boat, who is always a lady, will be carrying one on her back. There are probably half-a-dozen more under the hatchway; and it is ten chances to one that you are unconsciously sitting on another. The only really safe thing to do to avoid this brand of mischance is to shin up the mast. But that has its drawbacks. It is a very unpleasant sensation for a sensitive person to find himself sitting on a new baby; and this Eastern habit, of leaving them littered casually about, develops in the visitor a cautious expression of countenance before sitting down. For my part, I haven't outgrown that yet. I find myself suddenly starting up from my seat in a tram, dreaming that I have been sitting on a mislaid infant. Imagine the humiliation of returning it to its parent, with excusesthe flattened remains of her offspring! One could hardly say, 'Pardon me, madam! I'm afraid I've spoilt your babybut I will get you another! And yet some sort of apology would be deemed essential. [Alf Vincent, p. 76]

Is fiction truer than nonfiction or, the other way round, nonfiction truer? What if I decide to suppress this by using the detail and imagining it back? I was reminded of an argument I had had with a historian with a limited understanding of the Chinese language. I was telling him that fiction doesn't make sense in Chinese because it is *xugou xiaoshuo*, literally, virtually constructed small says. I was saying *xiaoshuo* (small says) began as a discourse in spoken words about things that are small and that are spoken about. I was saying that discourse translates into Chinese as *huayu*, *hua* meaning speech and *yu* meaning language, the former spoken and the latter, written. I was saying that all *xiaoshuo* (small say) has this distinction of being small about the small issued from the small, e.g. a tongue, a head with the imagining brains, and a mouth containing the talking tongue, the very way Ah Sin practices telling his stories, based on what he has heard about, observed or read about, in real life or imaginary. I was saying that in ancient China *xiaoshuo* (small say or fiction) was actually *fei xiaoshuo* (non small say or non-fiction). I cited him an example from *yuewei caotang biji* (Pen-notes from the Yuewei Thatched Hall), informing him that this is a book of what is known as *biji xiaoshuo* (pen-notes fiction), in fact a misnomer because the notes Ji Yun took and included in the book were all from his real life experience, nothing fictitious. I ended the talk by telling him about Yu who had invented his own genre called *biji feixiaoshuo* (pen-notes non-small-say or pen-notes non-fiction), an attempt to restore the genre to its actuality, all, it seems, to no purpose, as the historian turned a deaf ear to all that before he went back to Europe.

My own theory towards the quotation above is that if there is something readily available to be found, let's just find it and use it, creating a new genre, to be called 'found literature' on top of 'found poetry', or, at least, 'found fiction'.

The day I wrote that, I was reading *Practicalities* by Marguerite Duras, a thin book that I loved. Good books have to be thin, that's my view. Fat PhD theses can go to the dogs. The second the term 'found poetry' came into my head, I stopped at a spot and said to myself: Go and find it, and turn it into a poem, exactly as what I did below [from her book, pp. 12-3],

Funeral

The funeral was to take place late the next afternoon.
We made love in the hotel in Aurillac, then made love again.
And again the next morning.
I think it was then, on that journey, that that particular desire
emerged clearly in my mind.
Because of him, I think.
But I'm not quite sure.
But yes, it probably was because of him, because he had it too,
the same desire.
But it could have been anyone.
At random, like the last customer at night.
We'd had hardly any sleep, but we set out again very early.
It was a lovely drive, but terribly long, with bends every hundred
yards.
Yes, it was on that journey.
It's never happened to me again.
The place was ready.
On the body.
In the hotel rooms.
On the sandy banks of the river.
At night.
It was in the château, too, in their walls.
In the cruelty of the chase.
And of men.
In fear.
In the forest.
In the wilderness of the rides through the forest, the lakes, the sky.
We took a room by the river.
We made love again.
We couldn't speak to one another anymore.
We drank.

He struck me, in cold blood.

In the face.

And parts of the body.

We couldn't be near one another now without fear and trembling.

He drove me through the grounds and left me at the entrance to the château.

The people from the undertaker's were there, and the wardens of the château, and my mother's housekeeper and my elder brother.

My mother hadn't been put in her coffin yet.

*

[Stacey says: I have recorded all the cuts in a separate document for future literary historians as well as interested lawyers in case BH raises an issue with this in hell through its legal institution because, as far as I understood from him, that's where injustice in the human world is fixed in traditional Chinese literature where when real people can't have their grievances resolved in a real world they often have them resolved in hell by its judge after they become fictional.]

*

After we did that — in classic poetry, it's always referred to as *yunyu*, cloud and rain, but in everyday speech one just says do it, did it or let's do it — Bi Xiao and I didn't immediately go to sleep. Instead, I tried my best to bring the poems about *that* to mind and tell her. There was a poet by the name of Niu Qiao who wrote much about men and women in love, doing it in love. One line goes, "须作一生拚，尽君今日欢": 'the imperial concubine tries her hardest to please the emperor at night.' Another line goes, "一倒一颠眠不得，鸡声唱破五更秋": 'the man and the woman are tossing and turning, sleeplessly, till the cock crows at about 5 a.m. in autumn.' A third one goes, "对垒牙床起战戈，两身合一暗推磨。菜花戏蝶呒花髓，恋蜜狂蜂隐蜜窠": 'Like the two armies pitted against one another, in the ivory-carved bed

310

/ their two bodies in one, pushing the millstone; / the playful butterfly, among the flowers, is sucking the marrow of the flower / while the wild bee, for love of honey, goes into hiding in the hive.'

'You are so good with poetry,' said Bi Xiao, in a tired voice.

'I just got a good memory,' said I, remembering how my dad asked me to memorize ancient Chinese poetry and how I strayed into the wilderness, learning stuff by heart that he would have frowned upon.

'Are you coming back tomorrow?' she said in a whisper.

'Oh, yes, definitely.'

'That is so kind of you,' said Bi Xiao.

'Not at all.' Then, I remembered something at the dinner table and said, 'did you say you are good at telling stories?'

'I said that just for fun, to amuse the strangers.'

'But you must tell me one at least.'

She squeezed my hand beneath the quilt and said, 'No.'

'Yes,' I insisted.

As I felt her hand release its tight hold, I sensed that she was about to give way.

Sure enough, she said, 'But I'll tell you a very short Buddhist story, shall I?'

'By all means.' I kissed her on the mouth, a mouth that might have been kissed by many but more exciting because of that, and smelled the scent that never failed to induce a hard-on.

'After, okay?' she said, and then, 'A kitten, when born, asks his mother what is there to eat. His mother says: People will teach you. One night, the kitten goes inside a house and hides himself in a stack of kitchen utensils. When someone spots him, he advises the others to cover up cheese, milk and meat and put the chicks on a higher place to avoid the cats eating them. The kitten therefore knows exactly what is there for him to eat.'

'This is so lovely!' The kitten now seemed to be me, knowing exactly what he wanted to eat now that he was acquainted with the knowledge of the eatables.

We began mouthing each other, breathing in each other's breaths, our private parts engaging and enmeshing, my presence filling her absence, her presences delighting my absences. We were one, our bed our only intimate watcher and listener, and the walls of the room, also a constant watcher and listener, more faithful than others, and seeing more clearly than the muffled and tumbling bed.

And what was most thrilling was her feet, so tiny, and, according to her, so painful. But when cradled, first in my arms, then in my cupped hands, and finally in my mouth, I felt as if my whole person was set on fire. Holding up her three-inch lotuses in my hands, one on either side, as if on wings, I pushed and pushed, feeling bigger each push, till it became disproportionate in size, growing a-wing, taking flight into the air, seeing blue, seeing golden, seeing a blur of colours and feeling as if my whole person was melting inside her, to the accompaniment of her small cries of pleasure, uttered in an accent I had never heard before, the more enticing.

Afterwards, when I asked her what accent it was that she spoke, she said she's from Hunan.

*

The other day, when I masturbated myself, while watching porn online – it's so easy these days that the multitude of porn sites seem like my private harem, in which I am a king, playing my own part apart – I realised for the first time in my life that I was in fact homosexual, literally a gay. I comforted myself, a self-comforter, with my own hand, my right hand, a right-handed self-comforter that I am, relying not on someone else's hand, which didn't exist, not even on an imaginary hand, which wouldn't work, unless assisted with my own hand. My hand was a male hand, which goes without saying, and it is this male hand that, one morning, when held up to brush my teeth, made me realise I had been gay all along. I love my own love. I watch others to make myself cum. I have little time for my mother. I have little time for other women, either. I like men. But I don't love them. I don't think I can allow anyone to thrust themselves into my anus. I have a terrible phobia about not being able to download stuff from my bowels if something like that happens. Even if it may make it easier for the bowel movements, I am still scared of the consequences of anal penetration: pain, bleeding, mixed with shit, and what not. In a way, now I think about it, I stand between a fucker and a fuckee. Or, put another way, I am both a fucker and a fuckee. I, the fucker, and me, the fuckee. Absolutely no physical involvement with anyone other than me, or Mee. I might call myself Steve Mee, a role model for anyone who doesn't want to follow in the footsteps of people, no names named, felled by MeToo. Why do you want to fuck anyone when you have got yourself, your self, to fuck? (One correction I'm thinking to make if this word 'fuck' tends to offend is I'll replace it with 'fark', so people will see 'farker' and 'farkee'. If they don't see the word truth but a half-concealed word-truth, they have themselves to blame.) I'm both heterosexual and homosexual, deep into self-sex and self-love until they are no longer hyphenated but become merged words: selfsex and selflove.

[Stacey remarks: I find BH's attitude towards LGBT offensive albeit funny, 239 words cut]

And, now, Stacey, do you have any idea that this may have anything to do with the past? It's time you were educated. I'll tell you but I won't tell you, not with this text, or with that bit about you removed after applying self-censorship, that it is my conjecture, my supposition, my guesswork and my all these three rolled into one that my fellow gold-diggers in the past (I'll come to that if I find time) who appeared in that video clip in Gum San Museum in Ararat: a cluster of faces, wrinkled, creased, furrowed, crumpled, puckered, shrivelled, wizened, weather-beaten, time-worn, leathery, and, curiously, feathery, too, that were thronging to the foreground of the screen to impinge on my eyes. Tears came, without warning, taking themselves by surprise. All male, male eyes, male noses, male brows, male hair, male mouths, male teeth, male lips, male ears, male wrinkles crinkles shrivels furrows: all male Chineseness that goes nowhere, that is recorded as history but not History, the custodians of which have no idea which hands they masturbated themselves with to spend their sexual lives, without impinging on any members of the other genders. They were clean and pure because they got their own hands to help themselves. If history or History is above all that, it is no better than a eunuch.

I wonder why I can't write poetry and if I ever do I don't seem able to produce anything longer than two lines. Curiously, Na Za or Daa Seinn seems to take after me in that.

*

Stacey Ahsin's editorial remark: Baohui's description of his masturbatory activities, cut, remind me of a line, written by Danish poet Inger Christensen, that goes, 'They masturbate their skeletons'. (*it*, tr. Susanna Nied, New Directions, 2006 [1969], p. 166]

*

I liked the word 'Xiao' – firmament or small – and told her, as honestly as I could that the country I came from didn't give me a job. There, I wasn't qualified for anything. I was a mere storyteller, scraping a living, on a day to day basis. She immediately wanted me to tell her a story, which I did. Following was what I told her, a few nights after, also a Buddhist story:

> There is a merchant by the name of Chengjia Baza, from a rich family background. But the family has suffered a decline. As a result, people in his village regard him as someone of no worth and pay little attention to him. He leaves, an unhappy man, for Rome. Years after, he has made a fortune. When they learn of his homecoming, the villagers line the road in a welcoming ceremony. Deliberately, Baza wears plainclothes and walks in the front of the procession, all his goods carried on a donkey's back. Because he is aged and his facial features have since changed, no one recognizes him. When they ask where Baza is, he says he is at the end of the procession. When they ask the person at the end of the procession where Baza is, they are told that he is at the head of the procession.

Then they blame Baza for not telling the truth, when Baza says: This Chengjia Baza is not myself. He is carried on the back of a donkey. Because when my person is there people ignore me. When they hear of wealth they come and welcome, which is why it's on the donkey's back. The villagers are all confused and say: But we don't understand what you mean.

Then Baza says: When I was poor, all of you avoided me. When I am rich, all of you welcome me. You come here not for me; you come here for the money!

Xiao listened in total silence. Then she heaved a deep sigh.

'Why?' said I. 'Did something bother you?'

'Yes,' she said. 'your story reminds me of my own story.' She then told me of how her family used to be very rich in Yuanling, her birth-place, dealing in Jietan tea and silk, until they were rich enough to decide to move further south to Canton, acting on the advice of a blind fortune-teller who had predicted that movement south would bring in more fortune and security. What with the constant fighting between the Qing army and the Taiping rebels, and the lootings by the local bandits, the family businesses were subject to constant change, ups and downs, then downs and downs and downs, all the way down, till she was the only one who was able to move south with my sisters. And she survived, because of her good looks.

While I lent half an ear to her story, I was thinking of my own thoughts: I must marry her and take her and Na Za with me and go back to Australia. Even if we didn't have a place there, we could man-age on our own as long as no one bothered us. I'd go on telling stories and perhaps become an interpreter as I had good enough English to cope. Another alternative was the Lanfang Republic, the ideal society in the Pacific, a physical utopia for overseas Chinese.

'You were not listening,' she said, turning her face up to look at me before she turned her back towards me, her naked back.

'Yes, I was,' said I. 'you said you had a sister who also went with you.'

'How did you know?' she said as she turned herself half back. 'But I didn't say that. I said "sisters"'.

'I know, I just know,' said I. 'I have a fortune-teller's eleventh sense of telling.'

'What is the other 10 senses then?'

'Senses of smell, sight, touch, taste, time, hearing, direction, pain, balance and country.'

'Then what is this eleventh sense?'

'It's a sense of love.'

'Is there such a sense?'

'Oh, yes. There is even a twelfth sense.'

'What's that?'

'A twelfth sense of story.'

'Yes, yes, yes. I've got that.'

'So, what happened?'

'Well, my sister, she's two years younger than me, and I were sold to a flower boat brothel. That's how.'

'Have you heard of Australia?'

'No. Where is that?'

'It's a country. No, more like a colony, a colony kind of a country.'

'I don't even know the difference.'

'Don't you worry. But I'm thinking.'

'What are you thinking? Tell me. Tell me.'

'I'm thinking of—', I stopped short of saying what was on my mind.

'Of what?'

'Of taking you there.'

'But I can't leave without my sister and she dislikes foreigners.'

'We'll have to talk about that.'

I didn't know why. But when I thought of her sister, I felt slightly warm around my crotch.

[Stacey says: I can't stand Zi Ya; he's too critical for my liking. This is not an academic treatise, least of all a polemic, but a fiction. 1265 words shed although I'll keep an explanation by BH below.]

I'm so forgetful that I have not provided something necessary about who exactly Zi Ya was. He's lived in Australia for so long that he's forgotten how old he was. A joke or reticence, I guess. But he's also a total failure, according to himself. Whatever effort he made arrived only at failure because he was a Chinese who refused to surrender to white values. There was in ancient China someone by the same name, born in about 1036 BC. This was an old man famous for fishing with a hookless line. He went fishing daily with that hookless line for many decades, becoming a laughingstock of the local people, until he was in his early 80s when King Wu of Zhou found him and promoted him to the level of generalship. It was not till then that under his military leadership the Zhou army defeated King Zhou of Shang, thus founding the Zhou Dynasty. Now, this latter-day Australian Zi Ya was my literary advisor in order that I could successfully complete my PhD novel.

*

One thing Zi Ya didn't know and I didn't tell him, and didn't intend to tell him about is my fear of bad influences. As a result, I had to censor myself in relation to the ancient Chinese emperors or kings. I could have put all the bad stories in Ah Sin's mouth for fun and have done with it. But because of my strategy in making him a good guy, thus a good buy, I'd rather bear the responsibility—accountability or fictional accountability is it?—for telling a bad story or two that, hopefully, won't incur a bad influence. Gao Yang, for example, Emperor Wenxuan of Northern Qi (526-559), was a jealous and angry man who had the habit of wearing heavy makeup and women's clothes and recruiting beautiful women he spotted out on the street for his own sexual pleasure in the palace. Out of these he fell in love with a stunningly beautiful woman by the name of Xue Pin, literally loving her to pieces. Because he was given to fits of temper and changing moods, Gao Yang could be one moment loving and the next moment murderous. In love with Xue Pin, he was also sleeping with her sister. When Xue Pin thought it an opportunity to advance her father's career in the royal court, she was rebuked by an enraged Gao Yang suddenly turned nasty, so much so he had her physically sawn in half and beheaded before going to a dinner party with her head held in his arms, throwing the party into consternation. Then he ordered that her thighbone be made into a pipa, a musical instrument, with which to play funeral music at her funeral.

Gao Yanzong (544-577), Gaoyang's nephew, was the 6th emperor of Northern Qi, only for a single day. But he was notorious for his wayward ways when he was Prince of Ande. For example, he would shit from the rooftop for his underlings to receive it in their open mouths. Or he would mix his own excrement with food for officials under him to eat.

I often wonder if this is appropriate for me to do, telling the wicked stories to innocent minds made sublime by the sublime. But if I can manage to set Ah Sin free from this I can at least gain some peace of mind knowing that I have done a good thing for the past.

*

[Stacey says: Another Zi Ya related story, with 2 poems, one by Thomas Hardy and the other, by Yu, in Chinese, removed, with 1625 words. I mean, who wants to hear a migrant intellectual's bitter story? If he doesn't sing praises, he'd better shut up.]

*

I'm scared. Lying sleepless between my two women, I thought to myself: What am I going to do to keep them, my daughter and myself alive? In some way, I am approaching the state of He Daqing when he is kept in the nunnery by Kong Zhao (Empty Shine) and Jing Zhen (Quiet Truth) for their daily and nightly pleasures, in that story from *Stories to Awaken the World*. Bi Xiao and Yun Xiao are nothing like either of them. They always are careful not to go too far to exhaust me. They are good sisters to each other and are like good sisters to me, and they treat Na Za like their daughter because they take pity on the motherless child and like her for what she is, a girl who speaks English and is now quite fluent in Mandarin and Cantonese, too. I can stay here for the rest of my life, have kids, and watch them grow into adulthood as I grow old myself.

They always say that one day I'll go back to Australia. Now that I have the two women, originally from the flower boat, living with me under the same roof, the rumour spread far and wide that I will definitely leave, never to come back again. It's almost as if my life were transparent, like a mirror in which everyone can see their own wishes pampered and realised. But no one knows about my worries and concerns. If I go back to Australia, there is no place for me. 'It's a white man's country,' Harry once said to me and I still remember the remark. My brothers, from the surrounding villages or counties, didn't give a damn and they went despite all the difficulties. And they persisted in their ways regardless. They made money, they bought the properties and they settled down. No ambitions higher than a mere desire to eke out an ordinary existence. [Probably a good spot to insert that remark that goes, 'Dreamers don't go to Australia; dreamers would not have the time to dream there'? (from The French Consult's Wife: Memoirs of Céleste de Chabrillan in Gold-Rush Australia, translated by Patricia Clancy and Jeanne Allen, and published by The Miegunyah Press, 1998, p. 255)—B.H. noted]

But if I return, what is there for me to do? I can't continue to do the story-telling from street to street. Working as a court interpreter is a possible choice. But is there enough to support this family of four? Oh, yes, Bi Xiao did say that she's good at knitting and that she could sell her knitwork. And Yun Xiao said that she was a good cook and that we could open a restaurant there. As for myself, I am not a bad cook, either.

What bothered me most was Daa Seinn, the love child of ours, Ciara and I. She was all agog with excitement on first arrival, finding everything fresh and new and making friends with everyone, animals included, such as the big white water buffalo that she called 'Cheese'. After a while, she went quiet, then quieter, cutting herself off from the rest of the village world. She hardly had anything to say to me; she had even less to say to either Aunty, refusing to call them as I directed her to: Da Ma (Big Mum) and Xiao Ma (Small Mum). It was either with her nose in a book, sitting next to the skywell, or simply shutting herself up in her own room, allowing no ears to hear anything; no one knew what she was doing there. Although on more than one occasion, the issue of her future marriage when she reached 16 was brought up between her Big Mum and Small Mum, I was the one to quell their voices by saying that she might eventually go back to Australia as that really was her home. At this stage, though, I had no idea what she really wanted. I must have a chat with her one of these days.

*

Daa Seinn's poetry:

> The eye of the sky is blue
> Like mine. But why are their eyes as black as the night?

*

And, once again, Na Za or Daa Seinn picked up the heavy tome of *The Doctrine of the Mean*, written in Chinese by Zi Si, also known as Kong Ji, grandson of Confucius, and went straight to the page bearing the remark about the big and the small. Subsequent to their visit to the graveyard, she was given a copy of the tome because Ah Sin thought it most important to give her a goldfield to dig for gold. If he had to raise her in China, in its long cultural tradition and language, she must be somehow fed with the best food for thinking that went right back to the beginnings. Would she understand a word of it? Ah Sin was not concerned with that as he was convinced that, given time, she would grow big to know the meanings by speaking the language, reading it and understanding it. There were altogether 29 characters. At first, she didn't understand a single word. By and by, she recognized a sky, an earth, a big and a small. Then, there were people, a gentleman, and a break. Today, as if blessed with something from the heavens, she instinctively 'ah'ed to herself and said, 'Oh, I see. Is that what it means?'

She immediately went back from the shade of the riverside tree and found Ah Sin. 'Dad,' she held the book out, with her left index-finger pointing at the remark. 'I know what it means now.'

Delighted, Ah Sin said, 'Tell me what it means then.'

'However big the sky and the earth are, people are not totally satisfied. That is why when one talks about bigness, it is so big that not even the whole sky can cover up and when one talks about smallness, it is so small that no one can break it up.'

Ah Sin stepped back, took a careful look at Daa Seinn as he shook his head, his lips trembling, finding it hard to express himself. Then he blurted out, 'My girl, you must be a genius! How did you find out? And how well you put it!'

But before he had time to drink it all in on top of asking her to put it all down in English, with a thud, the book was dropped onto the floor as Daa Seinn ran out of the house, in the direction of the river again.

Part V.

Chapter 1

All good things come in pairs. The day both Bi Xiao and Yun Xiao vomited and felt sick, the granny next door came and had a look.

'Have happiness le,' she said, laughing her toothless laugh, indicating that they were both pregnant.

I was immensely pleased and proud. My daily workload was doubled with helping out about the house until Bi Xiao suggested that I could hire a maid or two. But Yun Xiao objected to it as soon as she heard the idea. According to her, they could help each other out themselves, with Na Za in her early teens providing help from time to time. I, as a big man, should not concern myself with too much domestic stuff. I should focus on my studies in preparation for the civil service examination as that would lead to a future career as a government official. I said I had no interest in pursuing anything like that. Yun Xiao lost her temper, accusing me of being a good-for-nothing. I kept silent; I didn't talk back. I actually liked women when they lost their temper. It's in their nature to lose their temper. If they had periods, they were restless, prone to temper tantrums, like an active volcano. I had my ways of appeasing them. When they erupted, I'd fall silent, say nothing, take out my cigarette and sit down on a stool by the side of the door, smoking past the storm, cigarette after cigarette. It wouldn't do the way I used to do to Gin. When she got upset, I would go up to her, hold her in my arms and gently kiss her on the cheek while saying a few kind words. She would then say, 'Can't believe you Chinese people are so sweet-tempered!' when I would say to her, 'Oh, no, that's because you haven't met the ferocious ones, the bastards who lose their temper and beat their wives like hell.' Even when I said that I was aware that there was a note of sarcasm and exaggeration because most of them I knew were quite good-natured and good-tempered men, which is one of the reasons why Thai women liked to marry a Chinese man. Ciara, bless her, never used the derogatory term 'Chinaman' to refer to either me or my friends, not even when she got upset. Our arguments were so few it seemed we were then living in a paradise. She was as unambitious as me, content with the kind of life we were living or trying to survive. That's the best part of it. One wasn't stressed for anything. You made money, you spent it, you made money again and spent it until you reached the end of your life.

Bi Xiao was, in a way, like my mother. Kind-hearted, caring, and generous, she was protective like a hen, treating everyone around her like little chicks, including me, putting them under her wing. My life with her was satisfying in every way. But this very satisfaction was dissatisfying because it lacked a drive. Yun Xiao, perversely, or naturally, provided that drive. She egged me on. She threw tantrums. She was fiery-tempered enough to push me around, stumbling forward. After spending a few years of do-nothingnism, dabbling in all sorts of books that I had not read before, in both English and Chinese, going to drink parties with friends and, on extremely rare occasions, visiting brothels, when on business away from home, I had something resembling hope that shaped itself in a question: What are you going to do, Sin? What prospects do you have in the future? And what plans? You know you are a talented person but you don't feel you belong anywhere and there doesn't seem anyone worth your serving. Do you want to follow the example of Jiang Shang whose talent remained undiscovered until he is 80?

As my mind went along this line of thinking, blind to all the things happening around me and deaf to Yun Xiao's squabbling, smoking till my throat got hoarse, I saw the mailman appear at the end of the village road. His appearance was always a good sign for me because he would bring me tidings of another world. Sure enough, there was mail from Australia and something that bore a stamp that I had not seen before.

I opened a parcel containing many newspaper cuttings, and found the letter, written on a piece of white paper that went,

Dear Ah Sin,

You've probably forgotten me by now. I'm the guy who you invited to the opium den in Little Bourke Street that night, the writer who subsequently collaborated with you by getting you to tell me the stories and writing them down before submitting them to various newspapers and magazines, remember? And we had agreed that when there was payment we would go half and half, right?

In any case, I have since managed to put most of your stories down and got some of them published. Enclosed please find them.

I hope you like them.

Yours most sincerely,

Harry Alan Taker

16 July 1865

My stories published? That was amazing! My hands, visibly shaking, went for the pile of newspaper cuttings and took the first one, spreading it open. One could immediately see that it was a newspaper called *The Tribune.* The very first story, a very short one, that caught my eye, went as follows,

The Carriage

By Harry Alan

When Kao Chu Mee, a minister from the State of Cheng, paid a visit to Duke Hsiang of Chee, the latter had him arrested on charges of conspiracy and plotting against the State of Chee. The punishment he decided was known as 'cart-splitting', or 'splitting of the carts', quite similar to our 'splitting the bills' or 'splitting the payments', if only semantically.

When this punishment was carried out, it involved five carts on two wheels, drawn or pulled by five buffaloes, in five directions. The condemned, facing upwards, was spread out, with each of his limbs tied to the last horizontal bar of the cart, and his head, tied up in a rope, also to a cart.

When the order was given, the five buffaloes went in five

directions, all at the same time, pulling the body, still alive but not kicking, apart. And, instantly, with a noise resembling a thunder that split open the sky, the limbs and the head were carried away by the carts, leaving his body, limbless and headless, on the ground, in a pool of blood, still steaming and hot.

Ah Sin, when he told me the story, actually suggested that this punishment be applied to the criminals, such as the bushrangers, in Australia. If no buffaloes were findable, one could find five kangaroos to do the job, perhaps more effectively.

Did I tell him that? I started wondering before I burst out laughing. The guy must have played a trick on me by sending me up.

*

Another story I read that he had got published in *Argus* went as follows,

The Head

By Harry Alan

My friend Ah Sin was a good guy. He came from China, in a place called Hsing Ning. When we fossicked for gold in Castlemaine, he was one of the very few Chinamen who would wander across the line from time to time to our part of the camp and share a tea or coffee with us while smoking his incessant opium. Unlike any other Chinamen I had ever set eyes on, he seemed a totally different kind of fellow, full of stories. Following is one that he had told me.

Chia Shi-tao was a good-for-nothing when he was young. But, as luck would have it, he grew up into a government official and flattered his way right to the top. In China, if you flatter, you'll have your way because emperors like praise; they don't like criticism. This is what Ah Sin said.

One day, Chia Shi-tao went with his entourage, his concubines and servants and maids, on a tour. In a lakeside pagoda where they stopped for a rest to watch the scenery, one of his concubines was heard admiring the two handsome young scholars who were just disembarking from a boat.

Chia Shi-tao immediately said to the concubine, 'Fair enough. I grant that you will be married to the two of them, this minute.'

When the other concubines heard this, they were quite amazed. The concubine in question, of course, was immensely delighted.

Not long after, a maid came up, holding a box in her hands. Chia said, 'I have organized all the paperwork for her engagement to these two men.'

As he said so, he got the two young scholars to open the box.

It was opened to reveal the severed head of the concubine. The two scholars, so shocked, fell swooning into the water, while the rest of Chia's concubines, flabbergasted, covered their eyes or faces in utter dismay.

The moral of this, if any, according to Ah Sin, was not really a moral but his own discovery that women, like men, also have an appreciative power. They observe men and enjoy the sight of them from a distance the same way men observe them and enjoy their good looks.

But the extent to which this royal minister went is a bit too far. He should have himself beheaded in actual fact.

*

The next one also appeared in Argus, a newspaper I didn't remember reading as I only read *The Age* when I was there.

The Iron Mouth

By Harry Alan

Again, this is a story Ah Sin, before his departure for China, had shared with me.

Chang had a nickname, 'Iron Mouth', because, as a fortune-teller, he was known for the accuracy of his predictions.

The other day, he was sitting in front of a shop in Little Bourke Street, an opium shop, actually, when people came from all directions and asked him to tell their fortune.

He made an announcement, saying: If I tell you the truth, you won't like it.

But everyone present ignored the remark, pressing him for his predictions.

He pointed to a man with a long and fat pigtail and said, 'You are going to head back to China soon, in silk robes, and shine an illustrious light on your ancestors.'

The man, very pleased with that, dropped a few coins in Chang's clinking bowl.

He then said to another man, with very narrow eyes, 'And you, this much I can tell you, will get married with a gweilo girl pretty soon and have lots of kids, nearly all baby girls, only one boy.'

Amidst a raucous laughter, the narrow-eyed guy, red in the face, went past Chang as he dropped one single coin into the bowl, without even saying a 'thank you'.

Then Chang said, 'But I have got nothing more to say now.'

'More. More,' the crowd chanted in unison.

Chang said nothing. He took out his pouch, dug out a pinch of shredded tobacco, put it in his pipe and lit it, before he spewed out a plume of white smoke. He puffed and puffed till he seemed content with all the smoking spirits dancing around him.

Then, without raising his eyes, he said, as if to the piece of muddy ground in front of him, 'I've said enough good things. But if you want me to tell more, it may not be fortune alone.'

'More. More,' the crowd chanted again, in unison.

'Well,' Chang said, taking his time, allowing a few forceful drags on his pipe till he inhaled all the smoke deep into his lungs before releasing it in ball after ball of deity-like smoke, 'I won't say who but there is one among you whose size of face, length of hair, length of the brows, the shape of ears and the size of nostrils are all signs that point to an unmistakable destiny in which', he stopped, breathlessly.

'Did you mean me?' in a sudden hush that descended, a man whose shape seemed all out of shape, not before the description, but after the description, said.

'I don't mean you or anyone,' said Chang, not looking at anyone, as he rose and said, 'I'm getting 颈渴（giang hod）, thirsty, and must go and get something to drink. Can someone watch my money bowl for me please?'

He had hardly taken three steps than he heard a swooping noise coming from behind. Before he realised what it was, he was covered in a rain of flying coins from the bowl that was hurtled at the back of his head, by the shapeless man who thought he had been humiliated by the unvoiced suggestion that he might have some terrible misfortune befalling him shortly.

And the moral of the story? As his friend Mr Ma said, 'Everyone loves flattery. But no one likes the truth that hurts, not even false truth.'

A postscript: I have adapted this ancient story from the horse-mouth of Ah Sin by setting it in contemporary Melbourne. I'm sorry if I have taken too much liberty by even changing the course of the narrative. But I guess that if a poet has what is called a poetic license, I, as a storyteller, or joint storyteller, must at least qualify for a fictional license if ever there is one.

One thing about Cantonese. May I reveal a secret embarrassment that I do not speak Cantonese? To admit this deficiency for a Mandarin-speaking Chinese is like to admit that one could not speak Irish for an English-speaking person. To cope with my Cantonese-speaking characters, I have to decide early on to bypass all the linguistic subtleties the way I had read in a novel about Chinese people by a white person, in which the Chinese language matters little. Although I forgot the novelist's name, it being a very bad book he had written, I thought his was a good example to follow, not the way to write a bad book but the way to dodge the inessential issue that potentially could become essential, though not without a lingering sense of guilt. To make up for this deficiency, I dipped into Cantonese, watching episodes on YouTube from time to time, until I was convinced that I would never be able to acquire the language or the dialect unless I went to live in Guangdong and got married to a Cantonese woman. The best I could manage is that I noticed that Cantonese had much borrowing from English, its 爹 哋 （de di） deprived from 'daddy', its 阿 Sir （Ah Sir）, a merging of Chinese 'Ah' with English 'Sir' to mean the police, and its K 士 （kei xi）, another merging of both languages to denote the word 'case'. In a way, Cantonese heralded the marriage of the English and Chinese languages that French did to English in the Norman conquest of England in 1066 because Canton was one of the first ports of call where English entered China, also one of the first ports of recall where things happened in the nation's memory.

*

I looked in vain for anything to do with cloud and rain [a euphemistic ancient Chinese expression that refers to having sex—BH]. I recalled I had told him quite a few stories on one occasion in a bar while we were having a drink. He'd always have a pen and his notebook ready. I told him of how a young man of 18 was seduced by a middle-aged abbess in a nunnery. Located on a hill, the nunnery had a winding path that led downhill to the side of a lake. One day a pale-faced young man came by a boat and disembarked. He then climbed the winding path that led to the nunnery to have a look around. It was an old one hidden among the dense foliage and tall trees. The abbess, as soon as she set eyes on the boy, felt as if her desire was set on fire. She closed the door behind them and pulled him into her arms. Then she took his yang ['yang', as in yin and yang, is a word that refers to male—BH] thing in hand and rubbed it. The instant erection of his own yang thing took the young man by surprise. She then kissed him till he opened his mouth when she stuck her tongue into it for the young man to suck on it like a lollipop. Then they had cloud and rain. Afterwards, the abbess kept him in the nunnery, got him shorn of his head, and took possession of his person for a few nights on end before she allowed another nun to share him, alone or together, three of them in one bed. The man died two years into this life of debauchery and iniquity. Shortly after she buried him, the other nun also died, of a broken heart.

Why he didn't put the story down in words and have it published was beyond me. But I suspected it had a lot to do with our talk about the Victorian values, an expression that he had taught me, and an expression that, to me, was quite laughable. When he wondered why, I said to him that it sounded hypocritical. A man loved a woman and wanted to sleep with her, that seemed to me the most natural thing in the world. The same thing happened to a woman. But the thing is, you just couldn't write about it or you were not allowed to write about it, let alone see it in print. What hypocrisy! I, for one, would, if I could, write about my love life — loved life, loving life — for all and sundry to read. What was shameful about it when you were not ashamed of doing it physically? 'Values, values, values,' I could still hear his voice booming in my head. 'these are the chains that bind the society as they bind the minds. If you speak or write against it, whatever you produce will be deemed valueless and will inevitably be bowdlerized. In our age at least, or in any other future age, I gather, to live is to pretend and pretend hard. You have to be what you are not or what you seem. It's not exactly deception. But it helps. And it helps things happen.'

Ignoring what sounded like philosophy in what he said, I counteracted by saying, as I recalled it, 'which is exactly why you need to come to my native land, the Celestial Empire. We both have monarchs, oh, no, you don't. Oh, yes, you do, a colony with a queen! What a shame! A like-country with a fake parent. When I say a "like-country", you know what I mean? In my native land, rich men have multiple wives, the big wife, Wife No. 1, followed by a number of small wives, known as concubines or, even better, as ru furen, "like-wives". In that sense, this country, known as "Australia", is in fact a like-country, like a like-wife, run by a non-blood-parent from thousands of miles away across the ocean, probably the second largest concubine in land area apart from Canada. Yes, a concubine-colony of Father England. But us celestials certainly led a much better life than you poor white guys, bound in the chains of so-called values that rendered everything else valueless and made people ashamed of themselves on all Sundays and the rest of the days throughout their lives. Why do we need to live if we don't enjoy ourselves? You tell me. Where I came from, men enjoyed themselves smoking opium, without anyone telling them that it was a sin to smoke and knowing that it was the British who had introduced that from India in the first place. Then they would go and visit the yaozi (brothels) and have fun. Love between men and men was more common. Stop shrieking! It's not a crime, I'm telling you. No one goes to jail for that. You can find men in brothels and enjoy yourself playing with them with no problems. This is true of the government officials. There are rules against them visiting brothel women. But no rules exist against them having fun with men. It's a much freer country than here if you know what I mean.'

That conversation, I now recalled, seemed to have left him visibly disturbed and quite grumpy. He didn't like any innuendoes suggesting that his 'country' was not as good as someone else's country, particularly the celestial empire. His sense of hierarchy would never allow the celestial empire to sit on top, regardless of its history of thousands of years. If all that long time, in his opinion, contained only accumulated excrement, one might as well go without. Despite his convict roots, originally from England, Harry was a proud man who believed in progress and improvement in anything and everything, and, at the same time, he was fascinated with mysterious things that were older and that came from afar, the further away the better. I was his source, his informant and assistant. And I was happy to play the role.

But I didn't have a problem with his declining to write these obscene stories down. It's up to him and to the society that restrained him. I'm happy as long as I lived, with the knowledge of things that had happened in that regard. A superior mind was an inferior one if it held itself superior in wilfully going blind. I don't have time for that.

*

Over dinner, I showed Bi Xiao, Yun Xiao and Na Za a 10-pound note

I had received from Harry as part of the royalties he had received for the publication of our joint stories. I explained the way I collaborated with Harry. Yun Xiao, sitting opposite me across the table, wondered how the readers responded to our stories. I said that, as far as I knew, I had no idea because Harry never made a single mention.

Bi Xiao turned the note back and forth a few times, examining it, uttering small cries of exclamation. 'It's so green and so light! Doesn't feel like money,' she said as she fingered the texture of the note and passed it on to Yun Xiao, who took it in her hand, with long painted finger-nails. 'But who is this woman?' she said.

'Let me have a look, let me look,' said Na Za, as she reached out for the note.

Without a word, Yun Xiao thrust it into her hand, picking her own chopsticks as she began eating.

'Why did she do that to me?' Na Za turned to me and said, in English.

'Don't you worry about that,' said I. 'Aunty was hungry. She wanted to eat. Her baby—' before I could finish my words, I heard a 'bang' on the table and saw a flash of the chopsticks that flew, right in my face. I ducked my head and the chopstick landed on the floor behind me. The other one flew nowhere and I didn't even hear the sound of its fall.

Yun Xiao stood up and went back to her own room. I immediately followed her. But she banged the door closed. I tried to push it open, but she resisted, holding the door down with the weight of her whole person. Afraid that I might apply too much force to cause a fall, I gave up and went back to my seat at the table.

'What's going on?' said Na Za, visibly upset. 'Why did she do that? Such a termagant!'

'Don't use words like that. She's your second mum.'

'No, she isn't.'

'And I'm your first mum,' said Bi Xiao, breaking her silence with a big smile. 'no?'

'Yes, you are,' said Na Za. 'and you have the most wonderful feet I've ever seen.'

With that description, Na Za was very pleased with herself and was about to pick up a red-cooked pork belly when Bi picked up one for her and put it in her bowl. Then she picked up a choice piece of fish-belly from the red-roast carp and put that also in Na Za's bowl, much to her delight, as she said, 'Thank you so much, Big Momma!'

'What did the girl say?' Bi turned to me.

'She said,' I replied in Chinese. 'that she wanted to thank you for all your kindness.'

'I know that,' said B. 'but what did she say after that thank-you?'

'Oh, that,' said I. 'She's calling you Big Mother.'

'Good girl!'

As this went on, the 10-pound note lay ignored, on a corner of the table, along with the story that I had meant to tell them that it really was a hell of a lot of money. In the old days, when they first arrived in Melbourne, that was the worth of the head tax slammed on their heads, the amount that would cover the whole passageway from China to Australia. One'd have to toil and moil for 10 years to save that much money to be able to go to Australia. But, then, we had better ways because we had successfully dodged them by landing in Robe and travelling overland. Oh, those days, those days, all enshrined in this simple note that didn't have a tongue to tell its own story, a story lost to them all except me.

Without waiting for either B or Na to finish eating, I quickly finished and went to Yun's door and pushed it. Surprisingly, I met no resistance as the door opened by itself without a sound. The room was dark. By a shaft of candlelight that came from outside, I could tell that she was sitting on the edge of the bed. I closed the door behind me and went to her, asking if she was alright.

She didn't reply.

I encircled her head, covered in her hair, with my right arm and sensed a relaxing of her nerves.

I sat down, next to her, and held her in my arms as I put my lips to the side of her face.

She began sobbing.

'What's going on?' said I. 'What happened?'

She refused to say a word.

'I hate that girl. I simply hate her!' I thought I heard these words muttered under her breath. But they might as well have been uttered in my own mind by an imaginary voice.

'Are you hungry? I'll bring your meal in.'

As I said so, I rose to go. But I felt my sleeve being tugged. My heart softened in that instant. I sat down again and we began kissing. The kisses felt like food, filling. I was filling. I went to the door, stood and listened. There was no sound from outside. I listened again. Then I could hear giggling arising in another room, Bi's room, where she and my girl were chatting and laughing, as happy as ever.

I pulled the low table over against the door in case it was pushed open from the outside, then went to Yun.

We had the best of clouds and rain afterwards. It was so satisfying and filling that I forgot to tell her of the important matter that I had wanted to announce at the dinner table.

*

Something I kept in store at the back of my mind but subsequently lost track of, something that I meant to include as part of the story, indeed as part of Daa Seinn's education by Ah Sin. It's just that the book, titled, *Zengguang xianwen* (A Supplementary Collection of Adages), published in the Ming dynasty, containing the ancient wisdoms, was somehow lost, nowhere to be found. When I found it a couple of days ago, it was not the book but a printout copy of a version published on the internet, bearing traces of reading, with the liked ones ticked from time to time. As I read them, a picture appeared in my mind. After darkness fell, Ah Sin would light a kerosene lamp and ask Daa Seinn to sit next to him. He would begin with these words, "人不通今古，马牛如襟裾". Daa Seinn—I must say I have to drop Na Za in preference for Daa Seinn as I like it more and more—rolled her eyes and said, 'Oh, Dad, why did you have to torture me with all that crab?'

'It's not "crab",' Ah Sin corrected her. 'It's crap. But, no, it is not crap. It's essence. But tell me what it means?'

'It means: Go and eat the shit,' Daa Seinn said.

'No. Be serious. It means: When a person is not knowledgeable about today and the past, it's like a cow and a horse wearing human clothes,' said Ah Sin.

'Sorry but I don't think I need to know all that. I'm fed up with this place. I just want to go away.'

'Soon enough, soon enough,' said Ah Sin. 'But I like this. Listen to what it has got to say. 逢人且说三分话，未可全抛一片心。'

'Xin? I know. That is heart,' said Daa Seinn.

'You are good, aren't you, good girl!' said Ah Sin and, seeing that she became more lively after being praised, he said, 'You only tell people one third of what you really want to say as you can't chuck out all your heart.' See what I mean?'

'I don't "see". I heard,' said Daa Seinn.

'It reminds me of an English poet who wrote a poem, exactly along the same line, that I can recite to you. Here we go,' as he said so, he delivered the poem off the top of his head:

> When I was one-and-twenty
>   I heard a wise man say,
> "Give crowns and pounds and guineas
>   But not your heart away;
> Give pearls away and rubies
>   But keep your fancy free."
> But I was one-and-twenty,
>   No use to talk to me.
>
> When I was one-and-twenty
>   I heard him say again,
> "The heart out of the bosom
>   Was never given in vain;
> 'Tis paid with sighs a plenty
>   And sold for endless rue."
> And I am two-and-twenty,
>   And oh, 'tis true, 'tis true.

'He's too old for me as I'm only 13,' said Daa Seinn.

'I'll give you one more adage before I allow you to play on your own,' said Ah Sin.

'Adage?'

'A wise saying, such as this, Shui zhiqing ze wuyu, ren zhicha ze wutu.'

'Meaning?'

'If the water is too clear, there will be no fish in it. If a person is too strict with others, he will end up with no friends.'

'That's you. You are too strict with me, so you'll end up not being friends with me.'

'Oh, no. That's too hard on me,' Ah Sin groaned as he pulled Daa Seinn to him, intending to hug her, when she ducked and ran away. As she did so, she chanted, 'Ching Chong Chinaman gave me know-how, Ching Chong Chinaman went so loud, Ching Chong Chinaman had no idea, and Ching Chong Chinaman had a lot of fear.'

A newly-arisen thought interrupted the flow of this story in my sub-conscious, suggesting I go and check about A. E. Housman. When I did, I shook my head and said, 'Forget it, an anachronism, as he was not born until 1859.' Then, to myself, there being only myself to talk to these days, I said, 'What does it matter if I put it there? What would they know? How would they know? What would they bother even if they do know? Who's so perfect as to have an exemption from any errors, historical, mnemonic or anachronistic? And, ultimately, who cares?'

It so happened that not long after I bumped into this 'Gold Rush Game' on the website of National Museum of Australia: https://www.nma.gov.au/av/goldrush/ , which was so boring and time-consuming that I had to give up a few split-minutes [Stacey, if they can say split-seconds, can I not say split-minutes, my minutes all split up anyway?] into it. Then a wandering thought offered itself to me: The past is not recoverable in its physical forms except by technology and that in itself is a crast—I meant a crass—and inevitable anachronism, an anachronism only the ones alive now are capable of.

*

Dear Stacey,

As requested, I attach a copy of my translation from that book, afore-mentioned, that's *Zengguang xianwen*, translated as *The Wisdom of Ancient Aphorisms*, or, in my rendering, *A Collection of Good Broadening Sayings*. They may sound trite today but had influence for centuries since the Ming dynasty. See a few examples below:

'There are direct trees in the mountains but no direct people in the world.'

'It's easier to get close to a strange tiger than a familiar person.'

'The human relationship is as thin as a piece of paper the same way each chess game is new when played.'

'If you raise a boy and don't educate him, it's like raising a donkey, and if you raise a daughter and don't educate her, it's like raising a pig.'

'You want to sharpen a knife / But a sharpened knife hurts'

'When you are poor, you are at least at ease and at self. But when you are rich, you have so much to worry about.'

'When you are poor, you talk little, the same way when water remains level with the ground it doesn't flow.'

'Enjoying favours one needs to recall one's humiliation in the past and living in peace one must worry about the incoming danger.'

'It is easier to run people down than praise them.'

'It's no good if you keep praising me. But if you criticise me, you deserve praise.'

'The net of skies never leaks.'

'It takes a century to meet in the same boat the same way it takes a millennium to sleep on the same pillow.'

I might have to stop here as it is a fitting adage for the joining of Ah Sin with his two wives later on.

Best,

B.H.

BTW: A couple of days ago I came across a book that I have not decided to read. It's *Ways that Are Dark* by Ralph Townsend. Judging by its reception as a bestseller in the States and the controversy it kicked up, I felt reluctant although Zi Ya wanted me to at least read it because, according to him, the 'more poison they contain, the more salutary their effect,' quoting E. M. Cioran (*The Trouble with Being Born*, p. 80), which, believe it or not, reminded me of an age-old wisdom in Chinese: "良药苦口利于病，忠言逆耳利于行" (Good medicine, bitter, is salutary to your condition the same way kind advice, against the ears, is beneficial to action.)

Chapter 2

Dear Mr Ahsin,

I, Wong Ah Long, have the pleasure of introducing myself to you as the secretary-general for the current and eleventh president of the Lanfang Republic. Ours is a thriving republic that you may not have heard of but that has been in existence since 1777, in fact only one year after the United States of America declared its independence in 1776. Founded by Luo Fangbo, our beloved and respected first president, this republic had its origins in Kongsi, managed by the Hakka people, that moved to Western Borneo by invitation of the local sultans to work in gold and tin mining. As the republic grew, we have set our capital in East Wanjin, a prosperous town of tens of thousands of people.

As we grow and expand, there is an increasing need for education and culture, education because our kids are having difficulties living in an environment of mixed languages and cultures, Indonesian, Dutch and Chinese, and culture because both the mining communities in the Republic and their children need to have something uniquely from them and about them that can hold them together. For this reason, we need to build schools. We need libraries. We need writers and historians. We need poets especially because they are the spirits of a culture without whom the culture would be bottomless, like a building without a foundation.

Right now, the Lanfang Republic has entered into a critical stage for development and we have cast about for talented people, capable of speaking both the Mandarin and English languages, throughout the world, particularly in the Asia-Pacific Region, including, of course, Australia.

Mainly by word of mouth, we have learnt about you as an illustrious storyteller of great Chinese classics in the past as well as a gold-mining specialist who has first-hand experience in gold-mining in Australia, apart from a wealth of knowledge about Australia and China. To make our republic go from strength to strength, you are exactly one of the people we are looking for.

In fact, we would like to offer you the position of Cultural Minister of this burgeoning republic as you are qualified in three regards: that you have a high command of the two afore-mentioned languages, that you are well-experienced in both Chinese and Australian affairs and that you have well served the communities in the countries where you were a citizen or temporary resident, of which many an individual we have approached has spoken highly.

Please can you reply to this letter at your earliest convenience and let us know if you decide to accept this offer? Hereby can I quote you a well-known remark by Mencius when he said, in Chinese:

舜發於畎畝之中，傅說舉於版築之間，膠鬲舉於魚鹽之中，管夷吾舉於士，孫叔敖舉於海，百里奚舉於市。故天將降大任於是人也，必先苦其心志，勞其筋骨，餓其體膚，空乏其身，行拂亂其所為，所以動心忍性，曾益其所不能。
人恆過，然後能改。困於心，衡於慮，而後作。徵於色，發於聲，而後喻。入則無法家拂士，出則無敵國外患者，國恆亡，然後知生於憂患而死於安樂也。

Which, in my translation, is as follows:

Shun was used in the middle of farming his land. Fu Yue was used while he was working on the construction of a wall. Jiao Ge was used while he was making a living as a seller of fish and salt. Guan Yiwu was used when he was in prison. Sunshu Ao was used while he was living as a hermit by the sea. Baili Xi was used after he was brought from a slave market. All this goes to prove that when heavens want to entrust someone with a great task, it will work him hard, mentally and physically; it will starve him till he grows weak so that nothing he does pleases it. As a result, he grows so strong in character that he is equipped with abilities that he didn't used to have.

Only when one constantly makes mistakes can he correct them. If one is troubled at heart but seeks a balance in his mind, he will then be motivated, the same way that he will be understood if he allows an expression of his inner thought and feelings to appear on his face or in his sighs or his chantings.

Likewise, a country will come to nothing if its ruler is not assisted with talented people, if the country is not run with a good law and if there is no constant awareness of possible invasion from the surrounding countries. Then, only then, will one know what it means when one says that one dies in pleasure but is reborn with worries.

In awaiting your favourable reply, I remain your obedient servant.

Yours most faithfully,

Ah Long Wong

*

I was reading Confucius. When a student asked if it was good to befriend everyone in his village, Confucius said no. When the student further asked whether it was appropriate to keep a distance between him and the rest of the village if he disliked them, Confucius said no. What should he do then, the student wondered. Confucius' advice was: Befriend only the good ones and distance yourself from the bad ones.

I put down the book and thought of my own past. There were times, particularly after I arrived in Australia, I felt like a criminal. When I found a nugget of gold, for example, it felt like a stolen piece of property. When I lived with a large group of my fellow Chinamen, it felt like living with a group of sinners who had nothing sublime in mind except dig for more gold before they went home. I often had a desire to distance myself from them all but found it impossible as I had to sleep, night after night, between my fellow diggers in cramped space. Likewise, I had also the desire to be close to the white people who I had always thought to be fair-minded, full of justice, sublime and spiritual.

When they went to church and pray, it was not about money but about a true belief in God, someone who they never saw but believed existed regardless. When we went to our joss house, it was always about practical matters: to expel the evil spirits so we could make a quick recovery from our varied conditions, to keep our fortune safe and sound and growing, and to ensure a future of constant income. But the distance from the whites was enormous because they had a way of keeping it that way. It's not as if they were all sweet-tempered and mild-natured. They could erupt like a volcano, an earthquake or a tsunami, like when they jumped our claims or rounded us up in a wholesale attempt to drive us off the diggings. And their action was warranted by their seemingly impeachable sense of justice. Even when law intervened, the violent people were often found innocent and acquitted. If they believed in God, if they acted justly and if they had the power of violence and innocence, who wouldn't want to be associated with them? Even God seemed to be on their side. But it is they who kept distance as if we were the bad ones. The report about us was always bad. Nothing we did was good. We smoked opium, bad. We worked too hard, bad. We didn't bring our own women, bad. We needed love and women, bad. We found our own women and lived together with them, bad, both bad. We believed in our gods, bad, not gods, but idols. We had our own religious beliefs, bad, pagan beliefs, not real, not authentic, not good. Nothing about us, nothing we did, was good. So the distance deserved to be placed between us. Confucius never talks about these things. He only talked about villagers in answer to his student's questions about human relationships. That relationship was limited to people of the same skin colour. He had never gone overseas in his lifetime. He had never actually met a completely foreign person. He could not possibly address the issues that faced me. If I asked him a similar question, I wondered how he would answer. If, for example, I asked him: Are whites inherently superior to people of other skin colour the same way a white tiger, a white lion, a white piece of paper, a white swan, a white fly, a white kangaroo, a white fish, a white bird, a white tree, a white cloud, a white snail, a white worm, a white-eyed wolf, white eyes, white days, white hair, white waters, white wine, are superior to their respective counterparts of opposite colour or colours? I had no idea what he might say and I couldn't imagine what his answer would be. But I could never forget a casual remark made by a white man who commented on my fellow Chinese in a sweeping gesture that included them, the diggings in which they were busy working and the dry hills behind them: Look at them! These are the working ants and working bees and working horses that the world has never known. You may expect money to grow out of them. But you may never see these people produce a single book, a single poem, a single Shakespeare, a single anything in the way of spiritual wealth that will impact the rest of humanity. They are the lowest of the low and you can't go any lower. If they have history, that history can't be any better than what they themselves have shown to the rest of this world. I recalled how much I disliked what he said and how helpless I felt in trying to defend my own people. I was driven beside myself, inside myself. I could have told him a story to counteract his blasphemy. I could have even challenged him to a duel. But I lacked the courage. And I didn't have enough of the language to cope. The newspapers were overwhelmingly against us, so much so that I was gradually taking their view that we were born bad, innately, inherently, and instantaneously. The very fact that we were associated with the native people, the blacks, the Irish and our own fellow countrymen was just the proof that we were so. Someone suggested that when we had children of mixed blood, they would be even worse because they inherited the bad qualities of both races without retaining anything good of either.

I resisted. I always resisted, with my stories because I knew that there were good ones and bad ones among these people, as Confucius said, and that I, instead of following his advice, which I had never learnt of till now, had always kept with both the best and the worst. But even what was the worst might not be strictly speaking the worst. Ah Mao, for example, couldn't be described as the worst simply because he was suffering the worst condition and was detained in a lifetime institution, and even then he was to me a thinking man, with an entanglement of emotions. I liked them all for whoever they were and whatever they had done.

And my enlightenment came when I started living with Ciara. She told me that her people had suffered a similar fate to ours. They couldn't find a job because they were Irish, their image tarnished with famine, suppression and rebellion. They were unwanted because they were thought of as dirty and cunning, their men habitually bashing up their women when they got drunk and they had such a temper! It was comforting to know this but, at the same time, I wondered if anyone was perfect and if everyone was always subject to judgement and criticism by someone else. And, moreover, if the strong always tended to judge the weaker harder and unkinder.

Shun was one of the five ancient emperors. Fu Yue was a minister of King Wu Ding in the Shang dynasty. Jiao Ge was the grand councillor, also in the Shang dynasty. Guan Yiwu was a reformer in the State of Qi, in the Spring and Autumn Period. Sunshu Ao was a court minister serving King Zhuang of Chu in the Eastern Zhou dynasty. And Baili Xi was the prime minister in the State of Qin, also in the Spring and Autumn Period. I wasn't their match although I was also a nobody, like them when they lived in anonymity, at the lowest level of the low, before they were discovered and 'used'. Surely, if human beings were not equipped with decent eyes to discern, the eye of the sky would come in to help?

My heart was filled with gratitude for the opportunity that offered itself. If I could go and serve the new republic and do my bit, I'd give up on everything else and give it my all.

Two lines came to mind from Zengguang xianwen, that I had taught Daa Seinn, which go,

蒿草之下，或有兰香
茅茨之屋，或有侯王

'What did it mean?' came the constant question from Daa Seinn and my answer, from a century or more ago, came, 'It means: Beneath the wild wormwood, there may be fragrance of an orchid /And inside a thatched roof hut, there may possibly be a king.'

*

Dear Mother,

I miss you so much ever since I came to China with Dad. I can still remember seeing you when I came out of you, from a place so low I could hardly see any light till blood smeared my budding eyes. When I opened my eyes wide, I could see through the curtain of blood your face as white as an unwritten piece of paper. When I woke up again you were gone, my ears filled with dad's sobbing. How much I slept, in the first few days of my birth! And the next thing I remember of you is a box they lowered down in a hole in the ground. I didn't know why. But I cried, in dad's arms, till I went back to sleep again.

China is a good place. But people are so different. They don't accept me as one of them. Even if they do, I refuse to be one of them because I don't think I belong. Nobody really cares either way. And I miss so much about Australia, everything that is bright and sunny, the clean air and the fragrance of the tree leaves, with my memory of you saturating just about everything that I think in association with Australia.

With Dad having two wives now, I feel like an orphan, like you, the three of them total strangers. How can I ever get along with them? Enlighten me please!

Daa Seinn
Your dearest daughter

*

'But why do we have to go to a place where the weather is as hot as hell and the people are as savage as the primitives?' said Bi Xiao in my arms when we lay together.

'But it's a new country, a new republic,' said I.

'But what is a republic, a country without people?'

'A republic is a country without a king. You can tell by what it is not. It is not a colony, like Australia. It is not a kingdom, like Great

348

Britain or China proper. It's not anarchy or confederation.'

'There are too many strange words that I don't understand.'

'Don't worry. Just bear this in mind: when we go there things will be even better than either here in China or over there in Australia.'

'Why but we are already quite well-off here, aren't we?'

'Yes, we are. But things are in flux. One moment you are here and the next moment you are there, never fixed and stationary. But if you are fixed and stationary, you feel restless, like I am now. In this country, I don't have confidence and I don't have much of a future.'

'I don't know what you are talking about,' said Bi Xiao. 'We are having a good life here. If you try hard, you may be able to pass the civil service examination and become a government official, in the provincial government, or at least as head of a county.'

'No. I'm not cut out for that. None of the good ones are cut out for that. Pu Songling never passed the civil service examination and he wrote *Strange Stories from a Chinese Studio*, published after his death. Li Ju-chen never passed the civil service examination and he wrote *The Marriage of Flowers in the Mirror*, published shortly before his death. Zhang Nanzhuang wrote many books and was virtually unknown but his book, *Ho Tien*, is a great work published after his death.'

'These are all losers. Their work can't be any good.'

'But they are appreciated, I can tell you. If you ask Woo Wo, he'll tell you how much he likes them.'

'Who's Woo Wo?'

'The English priest of the Methodist Church.'

'But we don't believe in their religion.'

'I'm not asking you to. But if he is the priest, his words must carry weight.'

'I don't know about that. What I do know is that the other day when you took us three with you to the church the man was devouring us, particularly Yun Xiao, with his eyes, as if he had never seen a woman in his life. I don't like that.'

'That doesn't sound like him.'

'But it's him. If you don't believe me, you can go and ask Na Za because she said something.'

'What did she say?'

'She said the man had a hungry look in his eyes.'

'Is that what she said? I thought she was too young for that.'

'Come on. She's already had her first period!'

'Oh, my God. I didn't know about that.'

'Why would you men want to know? It's our women's business.'

'No, the thing is — where was I?'

'You were talking about books by those losers.'

'Oh, yes. I was going to say that there are a lot of people who quite like their books.'

'They must then also be the losers as losers always like losers. It's like what they say, hsinhsin hsi hsinhsin.'

'Yes and no. But I'm not going to argue with you about this. You may be right, after all, for women are always right, aren't they?'

'That's not true. It all depends.'

'But I want to go to this new place where, in my new position, I may find my total freedom.'

'Why do you talk like a baby?'

'Baby?'

'Yes. You said, "total freedom".'

'I was just putting it a bit too strongly as I know there is no such thing. But that's exactly what I had thought of before we went to Australia.'

'And?'

'Free for some, not free for others. And it all comes down to this: If you don't have money, you aren't free.'

'That's probably true here, too.'

'Everywhere. But you know what? Money is not guarantee for anything as so many of my fellow countrymen had got money but lost their lives.'

'Let's not talk about this, shall we? I am so tired. My baby, our baby, is also tired. Can you hear?' she pulled my head towards her and hold it down on her full belly.

'Ba-dum, ba-dum, ba-dum,' I heard a faint heartbeat, accompanied by a bigger sound of 'boom, boom, boom'.

'I love it so much,' I said to her, then, 'can we have it tonight?'

'No, no, no,' said she. 'if you want, you can always do it on her, the bitch.'

'You are still upset.'

'I'm not. I just want to sleep,' she said, turning her back on me.

For a long time afterwards, neither of us spoke. When I thought she had gone to sleep, I went to the loo. It took me quite a while there. When I went back to bed again, she said, 'what did you do?'

'Nothing. But I thought you had gone asleep.'

'I was listening and I heard the noise.'

'What noise?'

'You know what it is, don't you?' as she said so, she held her hand out from her back and took hold of my thing, limp and shrunken.

'You shouldn't have done that,' said she.

'But I can't force it on you or her.'

'Why did you mention her again? I was—'

'You were what?'

'I was going to – call you back.'

'Really?'

'But you can't do it anymore.'

'Yes, I can.'

'Are you sure?'

Chapter 3

A BH authorial intrusion:

I can't believe I have allowed myself to fall into silence for so long, only because of a simple remark by a friend. When we met the other day, in his new restaurant in Bulleen, he said, 'The way you write, it seems it has nothing to do with the present world around us.' When I asked him to say more along that line, looking into his beady eyes and orange-peel face, he said, 'I haven't read it, your work I mean. But you have to write in a way that makes money, big money, like a lot of the *wangluo xieshou* (net writers) who gross millions of dollars with the kind of stuff they write, chapter after short chapter that hooks you and makes it impossible for you to stop because the story keeps going. I haven't read Australian fiction for a long time now; I ceased doing so a long time ago. There isn't much, to say the least. These days, though, there isn't much in anything because words are not friendly to the eye or eyes are not friendly to the words. Anything that is not image-related is bound to suffer. Apart from those I mentioned, a writer can only write about himself; he can't write about anyone else because he doesn't have the connections. Nothing is real anymore, only money is. You see, another deliverer guy, this time an Indian, who delivers food for us with Uber Eats. This is one third of our business. You need stop thinking about theories and innovation because these things are limiting. They can't reach out. There's nothing wrong with sensational stories. They catch eyes. They have readers.'

I listened and looked at the blank walls of his restaurant. There was not a single decent painting hanging on the wall, only two fake oil paintings that he said he had bought for 20 bucks apiece.

The artist, sitting at the head of the table, said nothing so far. He was staring at me, from under his face-covering mop of white hair, and thinking. From time to time, he nodded . But it's obvious he's not nodding in agreement with whatever my restaurateur friend said. It was more like he was nodding to flashes of thought across his mind. Then, when the money issue was brought up again, he said, as if at the drop of a hat, 'It's no longer viable to engage in the business of painting. Galleries collapsed one after another in recent years. Nathan, the gallery owner, has run his gallery for 16 years but he has recently decided to close it down. For six months, he told me, he did not sell a single painting. I myself have a garage full of my own unsold paintings and I'm thinking: when I die, who's going to buy them? If I can't commit suicide like Mark Rothko or Arshile Gorky, I may one day go down the path of John Baldessari by burning all my paintings and turning them into a giant gallery of ashes. Oh, God, what's the point of painting? Why can't I live a life constantly bathed in the admiration of people and gross, keep grossing, big dollars from my sales?'

Meanwhile, the restauranteur had moved on to some other topics, including a very brief one about the controversy between Sun Yang and Mack Horton. He told me that the attack in Chinese social media on Horton was massive and intense. Fortunately, few in this country read Chinese, probably only 130, as reported. He suggested that I check that out on sina.com.cn and moved on to gambling.

I did check and found it here:

http://comment5.news.sina.com.cn/comment/skin/default. html?channel=gn&newsid=comos-hytcitm3608466&group=0 , all in Chinese, with 1113 comments, most of them very negative about Horton and Australia. I'll quote only one that goes, in Chinese, "澳大利亚的欧洲裔人口，原是英国留放过来的犯人，霍顿，一个犯人的后代，就这点德性了", and provide my English translation here, 'The European population of Australia is originally the convicts from the U.K., and Horton is just the offspring of the convicts. That's how much morality he's got.'

Then I realised that the artist wasn't there at all. It was only an illusion. In a state where two people kill themselves on a daily basis, anything may happen suicide-wise. The only one who wouldn't have any qualms about such matters would surely be the restaurateur, all his life a continuous process of money making, so much like the Chinese gold-diggers alive in my imagination.

Outside, as I walked in the cold winter night towards my car, I raised my eyes to see the stars. They were not there. In their place were the undying city lights. Even if they were, they were too far to reach anyway. I recall my friend Hui's laughing remark from a past occasion, 'Go there. Fly. Without a destination until you are totally gone.'

The amount he quoted for a flight into total disappearance in the unknown was around 1 million US dollars. It was fast and might take a few dozen hours before it all came to an end. But, otherwise, everything else sounded like a slow death. I was so disappointed with myself and in myself that I thought of it again.

Indeed, this was not the first time I felt like a dead man talking or walking. I wouldn't mind telling Stacey about it although she wouldn't want to hear it. Instead, she would suggest that I go to see a psychiatrist, or, at the very least, a psychologist. I didn't want to be bothered with either her or the 'ists'. All I ever want is to continue my existence as a ghost, trawling through my life as a shadow of the past, alive with people I have never seen but have always seemed to live together with. My life seems to have been split apart in the middle, one part gone to the past and the other, to the future, one of a possible life in which I spend my days with my numerous dolls, updateable ad infinitum, or I have my brains uploaded to a terminal in a virtual country and live there forever despite the complete destruction of my physical body.

With my self split into two parts, I retain nothing in the middle, it all being hollow and empty as it is and has been, in parallel with an all-shrouding simulacrum, no, more accurately simulascam, a reality that is truly false until one dies, when one truly lives.

I know I don't make sense. I don't care.

*

Woo Wo's abode was also his church, family church, where he lived with his wife Sarah. One wondered why they never had kids. But they just didn't and they didn't seem to worry, either. Inside the hall, it didn't look like a church, though. There were scrolls of calligraphy featuring classic Chinese poetry hanging on the sidewalls. A bare table in the middle of the hall served as the altar, facing east. Behind the table was a miniature statue of Jesus on the cross, hanging on the facing wall. Over the week, the table would be put back against the wall. It's only on Sundays that it was pulled out so that Woo Wo could deliver his sermons behind it underneath the Cross. Villagers would come and sit around the house, listening to him preaching, in the local dialect, which he had learnt from his wife and from his daily discourse with the villagers.

A non-believer, Ah Sin never paid visits to this part of the village. But he chose Monday as his first visit, carefully avoiding the preceding Sunday. He was an atheist out and out even though he liked to mix with people from all religious backgrounds, always with an intention to learn. Secretly, he had an opinion of his own. But he never voiced it.

When he arrived, with a small basket of eggs, as a gift on his first visit, he could see that Woo Wo was pacing in the hall, holding a book in his hand, eyes half closed. It looked as if he wasn't reading, but reciting, checking against the words from time to time. He stopped in his tracks, watching.

Woo Wo, as part of his daily practice, was reading the Bible, standing or slowly walking around the house, reciting or checking when he wasn't particularly sure about a word or expression. When he came to a stop, he opened his eyes from the weighty words, shot through with story, and was delighted. There he was, Ah Sin, from Melbourne, standing outside the door, with a big smile on his face, watching.

He put his Bible on the table and went over with extended hands. They shook hands and sat down on either side of the table. As he did so, Woo Wo kept saying, to Ah Sin about the eggs, 'You shouldn't have. You shouldn't have.'

After an exchange of greetings, Ah Sin produced the letter from his pocket and wondered if Woo Wo would like to have a read.

Woo Wo took the letter in hand, carefully took the contents out, unfolded the paper, read it, folded it, put it back inside the envelope and handed it back to Ah Sin.

'What do you think?' said Ah Sin.

'Well,' Woo Wo paused, then said. 'What do you think? Are you going?'

'Perhaps.'

'___'

'What's your opinion?'

'I don't have an opinion.'

'Well,' Ah Sin felt uncomfortable on a sudden. He had never felt so awful before; it almost seemed as if he had come here to beg for food but received a slap on his face by way of rejection.

'Not a problem,' said Ah Sin as he rose from his seat. 'thank you so much for your help.'

Woo Wo watched him leave, not saying a word, not rising, until he reached the threshold, when he said, to his back, 'I think you ought to go, to give it a go.'

'You think? Why?' Ah Sin, one foot outside the threshold and the other inside it, said, his back half turned towards Woo Wo.

'My opinion, if you ask for it, is simple enough: Try your luck there. It's like digging for gold, but a different kind of gold-digging than Australia. I would welcome the opportunity with open arms. A republic is a country of freedom, with no ties to the past, a country of the future, a country looking forward to the future. There's no king or queen sitting on top of people, kept alive by the people, fed by the people, raised by the people. If it is a republic, it must be one based on the idea that it is of the people, by the people and for the people. I hope you have a great future there.'

With that, he lowered his eyes, took up the Bible, opened it where a bookmark was inserted and resumed reading.

Ah Sin took his inside foot out and, when both of his feet were outside the threshold, he strode away, like a happy horse, having accomplished a major task.

*

It's not till after I finished writing this and re-reading it that I found I had made a fatal mistake. Instead of writing in the first-person narrative, I wrote in the third, addressing Ah Sin as 'Ah Sin', not as 'I'. This means I haven't pretended hard enough. And I have lapses of memory in my pretensions. One voice says: But there always is a scope for revision. True. Nothing dies. Everything is subject to revision, either by the person who did the writing or by those who publish it post-him. That's the reason for the raison d'être of the future, or it seems. When I first heard of Maurice Blanchot, as I recently did, I was amazed by the similarity between us even though he did what he did decades ago. I found his book and this in it by accident, as if said for me alone,

> 'I feel myself deadno; I feel myself, living, infinitely more dead than dead. I discover my being in the vertiginous abyss where it is not, an absence, an absence where it sets itself like a god. I am not and I endure. An inexorable future stretches forth infinitely for this suppressed being. Hope turns in fear against time which drags it forward. All feelings gush out of themselves and come together, destroyed, abolished, in this feeling which moulds me, makes me and unmakes me, causes me to feel, hideously, in a total absence of feeling, my reality in the shape of nothingness.' (*Thomas the Obscure*, Station Hill Press, 1988, p. 104)

It prompted me to wonder if human thoughts are not the same across the ages, races, cultures and countries except for one essential difference: language. Ignorance will remain as long as languages exist, not possible to be merged into one that is intelligible to all. Even if it is the same language, like Mandarin, it is not the same after decades of evolution into the traditional and simplified scripts as texts from millenniums ago would have to be translated in order to be rendered understandable. But what is literature? The very question bothers me. I try to forget it. I try to tell a story when it doesn't exist in the first place. I write from the void of my mind. By the sheer mystery of words, the story takes shape, looks like a story, then comes into being, a bad being, nevertheless, and possibly even into bin.

Sometimes, to be honest, I really love banality. To be as banal as someone suffering from a condition for life, without ever having to work, without ever having to have an ideal is the very ideal itself. In fact, as I found out lately, the word 'ideal' is banal in the extreme, just an 'i' and a 'deal'. But it has got to be combined with a 'with' to make sense or else who do you want to 'I deal with'? And it all comes down to deal and dealings. Striving for perfection or near perfection, and the constant pressure for it, is the real cause of death. Go and get someone to love and fall in love with him or her or even they, Baohui, instead of getting stuck in this unholy shit of fiction.

When I look back at what I've done before, I realise that I have been telling lies, one after another, and never stop doing it, never even feeling ashamed of myself. But if one is 100% honest with oneself and the rest of the world, one might as well commit suicide and burn all his stuff, leaving nothing to anyone, not even to one's closest friends or relatives or family members.

This is hard. We live in a physical world of lies and when we enter into fiction we live in a parallel fictional world of lies. But it seems people prefer that as if it were a much better world.

In any case, I'll write something that deeply interests him. I'll probably revert back to 'I' again or I'll even try a second person narrative before I tell you, the only reader in the world, my supervisor-reader, how I spent a day on duty in a gallery a friend of mine is running.

*

You set your sights on her mainly because of her feet. You looked at them and you were turned on. Then you looked at her face before you moved your eyes down to her feet again. You liked her feet much more than her face, which was round and full. Her feet were so tiny it's about the length between your thumb and your index-finger when you spread them out, in the shape of an inverted 'L'. You actually bent yourself double and measured her foot, encased in a red silken shoe, embroidered with peony flowers. The silk was soft and noisy to the touch. The shape of the foot was like a tender bamboo shoot, so sharp that, with a mere glance, your yang tool raised its head straight away.

She was shy, so shy she withdrew her foot and hid it behind another foot. But in so doing she revealed the other foot, which you took in your hand and put your nose to it. Later, when you were sleeping together, you told her how wonderful the smell was, to her huge amusement. She told you that it was actually quite smelly, a bit like, a bit like. She cut herself short. You didn't mince your words when you responded with a 'like your yin thing.' She, ashamed, hit you, like a drum, with her soft, fleshy fists, which only made you hold her tighter. And when you entered inside her, she was so wet underneath it felt like a pool, a pool of poetry that merged all things beautiful, including the pain. She had been in pain since a child, she told you, but it was pain for a practical purpose. Mum kept telling her that a woman without her feet bound would be a woman good for nothing and that she would remain a spinster for the rest of her life as no man would ever want her. She cited many examples in her village as failures for life. So and so refused to have her feet bound and was rejected time and time again until she was picked up by the poorest guy in the village. There was no one like you who raised pain to an aesthetic level even though, like the rest of the male humanity, you worshipped the feet more than the face. In your eyes, beauty is born the second something is transformed into something hardly like itself. A cloud that turns into the peak of a mountain. A river that spreads like a vast fan of tree branches. A sky that resembles a library with hanging books. A pair of feet that are as pointed as unopened lotus-flowers, as pink, and as deformed in its deformation as anything transformed, and as stinking as the durian, but more tasty. When you told her this, she didn't say a word, a smile perched on her face like the mysterious smile on the Buddha's face. She was as intoxicated as a drunken cat, twisting and turning in your arms, uttering small cries of pleasure that made you madder in your reckless thrusts till both of you melted in the water of love, in the waste of love. In one night, you had cloud and rain with her six or seven times. You held her deformed, transformed, not-yet-reformed, feet of the tiniest size in your hands, putting your nose to their deep cracks, and entered into her on the strength of the smell coming from her toes, her soles and her heels, all knocked out of shape and the more beautiful because of it. When you, in one of your storytelling sessions in Melbourne, revealed what you had seen of women's bound feet in China, in your village, you found people growing curious and asking you questions about the pain and the deformation. You couldn't tell them much except the poems you had read by the poets about them because you hadn't had any physical experience although you grew up with a keen sense of them walking around you, all those tiny feet tip-toeing about, it seemed. The direction a man's eyes traversed would always be downwards, upwards, then downwards again as if the feet were the key to everything, the centre of attention, of interest, of sexual appeal, and, indeed, of everything a man was hoping for and living for. Beauty, you said, to yourself, to others and to her, at various times and places, came at a price and was priceless. Only a woman knew to turn herself into such a beauty and only a man could appreciate it. When you had your first cloud and rain with her, you felt the tightness of her yin tunnel and its powerful sucking ability. Ah Fat was right when he said that the weakening of the functions of the feet actually increased the power of the crotch, its clamping force so softly, suckly that nothing would remain intact in it for long. It is only afterwards that you began appreciating her face, such a round moon of happiness, that you lay, with your own face, cheek to cheek, by its side and fell asleep as you never had. The next morning, when she woke up, washed up and made up, you noticed that she had changed into another pair of lotus shoes, a white pair with black rolling edges, so lovely you had an instant hard-on again.

On the other hand, Yun had big feet. She told you that she had a bad temper, couldn't stand the pain and took off all the wrapping cloth when her Mum put it on her feet. Time and time again, she fought with her Mum, with one wrapping her feet up with the 'stinking' cloth, in Yun's own words, and the other, constantly unwrapping it, with the result that her feet were only slightly deformed. She grew into what her Mum called her a woman of dislikes. She disliked foot-binding. She disliked cooking. She disliked needlework. She disliked embroidery. She disliked anything that was traditionally associated with women. She even disliked the idea of having a baby because she disliked the pain and blood. Why didn't a man have babies, she asked. What did she want? She had no idea. She didn't want to know. But she didn't want other people to know for her. She was in fact prettier than Bi. But few men took notice of her because of her big feet. After making careful comparisons, you decided to take her on, too. You liked an honest character. And you liked her face, too. From time to time, you recalled what Ah Fat had said about women's feet. He said that they were like their external sex organs. If they were well deformed they would resemble flowers of all kinds, images of all beauties, and they invited the instant entry of men's eyes without themselves lifting a finger. But the big feet turned men off. It served as the sign of a closed door.

Your woman is now by my side, and is stepping down the stairs in a gingerly, provocative manner, from more than a 150 years ago.

*

I was helping someone out on duty that afternoon, in Gallery ZerO ZerO ZerO. There was a coffin of poems in a corner, in which the poet of the poems lay face down in it on the opening night. Despite the sign that said: 'No Photographing', people formed a circle around it and took mobile phone photographs unhindered and uninhibited. He lay there face down and didn't get up until the opening speech was finished, after 3 minutes. When he got up and stepped outside the coffin, or the shape of it, built with white bricks, I could see this was a deeply ashamed man, who seemed guilty of what he had done, so offensively to his audience. Even the smile he offered seemed bitter. Instantly, he turned into an object for photographing. He had hated its guts. But, on this occasion, he was prepared to let them do whatever they liked, allowing whoever wanted to be photographed with him, like a living moveable prop, taken hither and thither, before this painting or that.

People only took pictures. No one, though, wanted to be photographed sandwiching him or alongside him.

In the middle of the gallery was a row of transparent wings, with images painted on both sides, that turned on themselves, operated by the hanging batteries. This created a perpetual motion, in which the

pictures seemed to be a-wing, and one could see the coffin and the poems filling it on the other side of the wings that, like moving cutters,
chopped them into floating fragments.

On the facing wall across the floor, was a huge scroll of painting,
done on white French rice paper. I didn't quite understand what it was
all about. But it seemed like an echo of the Mountain and Ocean Classic, with ancient characters all over the breast and face of the painting. In the middle of it all was a figure of undying spirit. All black
and white, the figure alone was blue. Someone in the audience said:
This could indicate the water. I turned around and saw that this was no
other than the poet himself. Before I could pick up enough courage to
introduce myself to him, his attention had already been caught by two
young women from a book club. They were enthusiastic about his coffin and wondered if they could get him involved in one of their book-
related activities when the man cut them short, with a curt remark,
'Why bother with those activities? What's the point of doing that if
you don't even buy a copy of the poet's book when he is still alive? You
either buy his book or you don't. Simple as that. Who wants to do all
those activities? It's a pure waste of time and energy!'

With that remark, the poet went around the crowd and got to the
backyard where he started smoking with the artist, as I could see
through the open backdoor.

But, today, as I sat in front of the heater, listening to the traffic outside the main door, not far from Victoria Market, and thinking those
past memories, I saw no one coming. There were constant passers-by
going in two directions but not one of them stopped and looked in
through the door for a single second. The big flag-like sign bearing
the words 'Gallery Open' stood on a pole, right in front of the gallery. I
thought of poetry and I thought of painting. I had thought that poetry
was the hardest thing to sell in the world. Now, it looked as though
painting was in an even worse position. No wonder the artist and his
partner were so intense in the hours before the gallery was opened.
They were so prone to temper tantrums that one cross word might
cause tempers to be lost on both sides.

I thought of what Father had told me of his experience in Frankfurt years ago when he went to the annual bookfair. He said that in one of their visits to the city centre, they stopped near a market, not far from a street lined with galleries. He went in one of them and had a look. The girl behind the counter was well-spoken and very good-mannered. She rose from behind the counter, greeted him and started introducing the gallery in German. Embarrassed, my father had to speak to her in poor English, explaining that he wasn't good in either language. He quickly came out of the otherwise empty gallery and, deciding not to be embarrassed again, he went down the street, past one gallery after another, peeking in from the outside. All he could see was that not a single gallery had more than two people. They were like glass coffins, filled with the bones of paintings, however good they were and by whoever.

The more I dwelled on the impossibility of art — who would want to buy a coffin of poetry and take it home no matter how sublime the idea was? — the more frustrated I felt. If I were to be the owner of a gallery like this and an artist myself, I'd kill myself before the year ran out or give it all up in no time. It is nice to talk about art, to pretend that you love art, but it is a totally different matter to live with art, to marry art and to survive with art.

I smiled at a comparison that came to mind when I thought: What if the gallery was as busy as the Queen Victoria Market and the Market as empty as the gallery? Then I defeated myself with the thought: Provided the earth and the sky had swapped places, each becoming the other.

The curse, I thought, was the prevalence of photography and the shrunken size of it. When everything comes in a size that fits the mobile phone screen, the urge to see the real thing disappears. When distance disappears, enabling the eyes in Melbourne to see something instantly in New York or London or Paris, indeed anything anywhere, there is no point going any further than the mobile phone held in one's own hand. Except for the investors who purchase art, no one will bother with it, let alone buy it. Sharing is good but its cost is the death of art. Banksy's destruction of his own art heralds a future of self-destruction, soon to come.

'So what was the title of the coffin again please?' I heard myself address the question to BUF again after he came back from the two young women.

'Tingshijian,' said he, nonchalantly.

'Can you write that down for me please?' I said as I handed him a piece of paper.

'停诗间,'with a flourish of his hand, he put the characters down.

I laughed, realizing what the joke was of his play on characters as it literally meant 'a morgue of poetry'. But English wasn't good enough to convey the sound of the morgue of corpses and the morgue of poetry as both sounded exactly the same in Chinese.

I told him what I thought.

The man seemed pleased, with his invention, and with himself, until he blurted out, 'But I think they should have called their gallery a different name.'

'Like what?' I pursued.

'fART Gall/ery, or even f阿t Gall lery,' said he as he left, without saying anything.

*

Dear Stacey,

As part of my research as required by your honour, I supply you with a partial translation I did of a novel, titled, *Ku shehui* (苦社会), literally, *Bitter Society*, written by an anonymous person and published in 1905, telling the story of how three Chinese intellectuals go to Peru and greatly suffer on board the ship and how they later find their way to America where they likewise suffer discrimination and expulsion meted out to them by the American government. All the sufferings and misery in the latter half of the 19th century can be summarised in one word, 'ku' (bitter), as attested to by the title of this book and of another, *Ku xuesheng* (苦学生), or, literally, *Bitter Students*, of which I shall also provide you with my translation of a randomly selected piece or two.

The following is a description of what happens on board a ship carrying hundreds of Chinese coolies on route to Peru and the *yangren* (ocean man) referred to is a Peruvian:

There was a group of people, lying in a mess, one on top of the other. When a sailor saw it, he cried out, 'How can you be doing this? Get out of here!' The crowd uttered an 'oh' in a low voice but remained unmoving. The sailors found it strange as a foul smell rose right from the bottom, making their stomachs turn. They then went to report it to the yangren...As a matter of fact, about seventy to eighty people lay about, their faces smeared with blood, their bodies a mass of indistinguishable flesh and clothes. All one could see was that, amidst the blood and the pus, the locked chains on their hands and feet had come loose. It was not till the yangren bent down to look that he realised that they had all died, their hands and feet losing skin, and their bones broken. Without realising what he was doing, he began vomiting. Immediately, he directed the other sailors to go up to the deck and bring down seven to eight huge bamboo baskets before getting them to shovel the rotting corpses off the floor and to throw them in the baskets overboard.

In the course of writing this novel, I shall provide you with my translation of the choicest pieces from the old writings that I'm sure no one reads except the most stubbornly persistent.

I'm sorry if my long delay in doing this has caused you any inconvenience in frustrated expectation.

Have a very good one over the weekend despite the rain.

B.H.

*

Of the two sisters, Yun was the younger and the prettier one. In the past, despite her big feet, she had clients of her own. When Ah Sin bought them both, she and her sister, by paying their debts, she was happy for a while. Then, she was unhappy again, periodically, pestered, it seemed, by a past that refused to leave, with its landscape littered with personalities like a lantern of revolving horses, its days of sleep and nights of revelry. These were rich merchants, big Yamen officials, or officers from the army. Occasionally, there were scholars. For them, it was mostly a one-off. They couldn't afford to keep the relationship going as it was time-consuming and, more importantly, money-consuming. She hankered after a day when she could be bought out of the brothel by someone rich and live with him happily for the rest of their joint lives. She was pleased that Ah Sin offered to buy her out of her bondage. But, at the same time, she was displeased that he wanted to also buy Bi. They were known as 'sisters' but actually were not the real ones. They were from the same village, spoke the same dialect, but came from two very different backgrounds. Bi's was a big family of many kids. But they died one after another when young, as a result of famine and floods. In the end, the family could not survive without selling her to the brothel. Yun herself, as described before, came from that family of merchants. But because they were robbed and the shop was burnt down to the ground, the family was reduced to paupers and had to sell her, too, to a brothel, the same one in which they met and became sisters. As far as she knew, though, she was different from anyone she had ever met before, either in her village, or in her brothel, because her family was different, their backgrounds different. According to Father, their family had descended from a people known as believers in a religion that advocated the removal of animal tendons when cattle and sheep were killed. Hence 挑筋教 (tiao jin jiao), a religion of removed tendons. Father had little memory of what the religion was like because the family, after generations, had been absorbed and assimilated into the local Han culture to the degree that they had stopped going to the Synagogue a long time before. By Father's generation, they had long lost their language. The only one word they could remember was 雅威 (yawei) or Yahweh, a word that was mighty by the look and sound of it. Literally, it was elegant power. As he explained, Father wrote something down that Yun had never seen before: יהוה and said that that was what 'elegant power' looked like in the original language. Yun was impressed with the way it looked because the first letter and the third letter looked very much like the Chinese character for 'door': 门, whereas the second letter looked like '7' and the last one, like the tip of a brow. In fact, Father said and Yun remembered, they looked like twigs fallen from a tree that got scattered over the ground. Afterwards, Yun would find her eyes involuntarily looking at the twigs or branches lying on the ground in patterns of all sorts except that they didn't make any sense to her; they were just resembling radicals in Mandarin Chinese, such as these: 丶, 一, 丿, 丶, and etc.

She had a temper when she was little. The temper grew with her, into adulthood. A glance from her client that went downwards to her feet would decide her then and there whether to accord him the reception he would have if he had not sized her up with her feet as the ultimate measurement. Ah Sin came at a right time when the number of her clients had dwindled to a trickle. Her eyes, deep and dark, would often find themselves looking out the window at the trees. Like a woman of rancour and resentment, who had lived a long life languishing in the prison of a harem after being abandoned by the emperor, she was getting more and more used to the indifference gathering around her like accumulated dust, consoling herself with the thought that her life would one day be like the little bird outside, hopping from one tree branch to another, picking at something she found eatable, before she moved away, tirelessly in search of food, not freedom, as keeping alive was her sole condition for survival, with an unshakable inner sense of freedom.

Father's teachings, as she could remember from time to time, were always this: We are a wandering people and we go places. If we like the place and the place likes us, we stay. Otherwise, we move on. We have been on the move for thousands of years. Our freedom is our movement. If life is purposeless, we take purposelessness as our purpose. We believe in 雅威, and we believe in money, too, which is why we are good at it. But there are those who want none of that, believing in neither. Instead, they believe in the language of twigs that I have drawn and showed you. These are the people with more Yahweh than 雅威, their power so elegant that it stays the course, word-wise. The spirit, though, never dies.

Ah Sin, to Yun, was someone unlike anyone. She hated him because he loved the bound feet. She hated him because he had a daughter born from foreign wedlock. She hated him because he was sometimes not quite resolute. He wanted to appeal to all but he didn't know how to tell the good ones from the bad so he could decide to go only with the good ones. He was easily tempted and would easily go astray.

But even when there were so many things she disliked, she had to admit to herself that Ah Sin was the best when it comes to clouding and raining.

On one occasion, Ah Sin recalled, they were about to cloud and rain when Yun stopped to ask, 'How many times did you have it with her?'

'That's a very awkward question to answer,' Ah Sin heard himself say to himself in silence. 'No woman would ask a man such things.'

'How many?' Yun poked him in the ribs.

'Oomph, not many. Just once or twice,' Ah Sin heard himself say.

'You are lying. You spent a few nights there already last week when I complained about my condition.'

'Yeh, we just slept but didn't do it.'

'You want me to believe that?' Ah Sin had his ear pinched and blurted out in pain, 'Maybe three times? I forgot.'

'You forgot? You forgot? I'll teach you to forget,' As she said so, Yun took out Ah Sin's dick, holding it swollen already in her hand and slapped it across its head three times, very gently, as a punishment for his waywardness.

*

Sometimes when I'm tired of writing and of reading, I amuse myself with copying. You won't know who I read and what I'll copy until I show you or share with you. My nature being such, I never share it through social media towards which I remain cold and hostile for a simple reason: It's disrespect to dead authors to share the best of their writings without their permission; one ought to buy their books and consume them in private. In the last remaining days of a book world, a booked world, I recall, in pain, how Father has grown his library to a bursting degree, without ever finding time to read a single page while at the same time exceedingly proud of his achievement which puts all the colleagues or relatives of his to shame because, as far as he knows and

I do, most Chinese families don't have a private library. From a recent photo of my father's private library, shared on the WeChat Moments, I can see three titles, *Fifth Chinese Daughter* by Jade Snow Wong, *A Biography of Friedrich Nietzsche* in Chinese translation and a copy of 《同性恋在中国》 (*Homosexuality in China*) by Fang Gang. As far as I know, he hasn't read any of those nor have I. Chinese people hardly read any more. To read the shared news or knowledge on your mobile phone, that is the order of the day, the cheapest way to get by on a day to day basis, and all shit. That is what Mother prefers to do, not because of the money factor but because of the need for gossip. You need to keep in the loop of your one thousand and one connections. You need to be aware of who's marrying whom, who's divorcing whom, who's having affairs with whom, who dies where and how, who's eating what, who's bought what handbag at a more expensive price than whom, assisted and proven with constant pictures. And, occasionally, you need to show to the rest of the WeChat world that you are such a knowledgeable person that you can actually quote a few quotable quotes, solid evidence that you have philosophy, you have art, and you have everything others may not have, all shared, transferred from one site to another, nothing innovative or creative by oneself, all a gigantic piece of eternal banality.

I never click 'Like' on anything Mum has posted.

And, talking about 'affairs', I must confess that I know something about Dad. He has someone in love with him somewhere in a country, someone about my age. But I kind of admire Dad for that. No, I mean, I have mixed feelings. I do know of this tycoon in Malaysia, with a big family of nine, who has a beautiful young woman, about 30 years his junior, as his on-call escort. If he goes to London on business for a week, he'll book her in, fly her over and stay with her for a week before they fly back, each to his or her home. I forget to say she's based in Hong Kong. I wonder if that is what Father has been doing and where his girlfriend is based.

I talk too much and give too much away. I need to stop for quotes.

Giorgio Agamben quotes Heidegger [I misspelled him as 'Highdagger' and quite like my mistake] as saying,

Mortals are they who can experience death as death. Animals cannot do so. But animals cannot speak either. The essential relation between death and language flashes up before us, but remains still unthought. It can, however, beckon us toward the way in which the nature of language draws us into its concern, and so relates us to itself, in case death belongs together with what reaches out for us, touches us. [*Language and Death: the Place of Negativity*, 1991, p. xi]

Agamben then asks the question, 'And what if humankind were neither speaking nor mortal, yet continued to die and to speak?' [p. xii]

I don't know why but I think I quite like the fact that I am what I am not and I am not what I am, and, in essence, I am a holder of nothingness. No, a placeholder. A platzhalter.

[Stacey remarks: And after BH's departure, I decide to remove the lot, from here onwards, too long, too repetitive, and so irrelevant albeit some good stuff, all attesting to BH's wide-range of reading. 456 words cut.]

Chapter 4

Why 'Chapter 4'? You ask. Because the sections separated by the '*' tend to be too numerous and something like a 'chapter' needs to come in and provide a break. So much for the explanation.

Is there a conflict between the past and the present? There is. Right now, instead of writing about Ah Sin – I was thinking of writing about Na Za or Daa Seinn even before I got out of bed this morning – I am thinking of writing about someone else. Her name is Anon. Yvette Palazzo told me so. She's an artist.

[Stacey says: 1013 words shed because it's another irrelevant story to do with an artist and her hatred of anything literary. The novel is about Ah Sin, not an artist or artists. Not even about BH. He's already too much for us, our imaginary readers.]

Oh, yes, but before I do that I must remind myself that I have quite liked what I read, in a biographical dictionary published in Chinese, about Artaud as someone who is into experimentation in all aspects, turning the metaphysical into physical realities, with no considerations for his audience, and that he is fed up with Western drama for its too much concern with logic, correct wording and grammar. This is Dictionary of Modern Culture, published in 1988 in China, and the source of this can be found on p. 21.

*

Qu Fei, a name that literally means Go Not, is a coolie who is tricked onto a big ocean-going ship by being shown around it when the person who does the tricking disappears all of a sudden and he is left alone with hundreds of coolies, total strangers. Before he realises what is happening, the ship weighs anchor and sets sail on its way to Brazil. After weeks of suffering on board at sea, they arrive, only to face even worse suffering, living in pig-sty-like huts, getting up before dark and resting after dark, each eating three boxes of black beans a day, like horses, and getting whipped 6 times every 3 days. In a short time, out of a total of over 10,000 arrivals, only 300-odd people survive, the rest dead from illness or cruel treatment As luck would have it, Qu Fei manages to save himself from the adverse circumstances as he is a traditional Chinese doctor and gathers herbal medicine wherever he goes in Brazil. Fortunately enough, he escapes from the camp and finds his way out of Brazil until he arrives in New York where he bumps into his own father by pure accident after twenty-odd-years of separation!

Stacey, that's a summary of what I have got out of the novel, The World of Gold (pp. 127-129), as my daily routine to provide you with historical material that can also be regarded as part of the background material for this novel. [A note to remind myself—B.H.]

*

'Na Za,' I said to her as I sat down at the edge of her bed, lit by an oil lamp, her face in an aura of the lamplight. 'do you know why I gave you the name?'

'No. I don't want to hear. I don't want to know!' she moved and kicked, like an agitated fish, just out of the water.

I said nothing. I lit a cigarette by the lamp fire and waited. Then I said, 'You said you had a dream. Tell me about it.' As I said so, I lifted a corner of her quilt, a silken one with red flowers, and pulled it across her, cautioning her not to catch cold.

'Oh, yes.' The word 'dream' seemed to quiet her down. 'I dreamt of Ireland.'

'Ireland, of all places?'

'Yes. I go there with Mum. You are not coming with us. Perhaps you are dead.'

'I'm dead? Ha, ha, ha. What a joke!'

'Yes, you are. You are definitely not there. Just the two of us.'

'And?'

'There are so many potatoes. The black ocean filled with potatoes. And we are standing on the edge of it, watching. There's no one with us. We stand watching, on a cliff. In the rain. Which then turns into a fog. You watch but you can't see anything. Then Mum points and says: Look. I see a church loom large in the distance. A very grey one, as solid as the sky around it, solider. We enter the church and see dead bodies everywhere, in the shape of potatoes. Headless and footless. I grow fearful and turn to Mum for help. In that instant, she is shrunken to half her formal size, her head level with my chest. She seems to have aged years, like someone in her eighties. Her hair all grey, her eyes so terribly wrinkled, I find tears streaming out of my eyes. But I can't hear my crying voice. The more I want to make a sound the less I can make it until Mum holds me to her heart and says: Aurora, I love you! It was at that moment I woke up from the dream, not understanding what the word meant.'

'It means dawn and it's the dawn that woke you up, I guess?'

'Yes, and I think I like that name more than Na Za.'

'But I could call you "Aurora Na Za" if you don't mind.'

'No. I prefer Aurora.'

'Let me tell you something,' I repeated the story I had told Ciara before Na Za was born.

'But it's a boy's name. People laugh at me all the time because it doesn't fit me.'

I decided to tell her the whole story, nothing but the story, that I had read and grown up with as a child. After his birth, Na Za, the third son, was playing with water in the East Ocean when he came into conflict with Ao Bing, the third son of the East Ocean Dragon King, and killed him as a result. He had also burned Goddess Shiji to death along the way. Then, he pulled out the tendons from Ao Bing's body and made a belt of them as a gift for his father Li Jing.

When the Dragon King pursued Na Za in a punitive expedition, Li Jing was so scared that he threatened to kill Na Za. This sent Na Za into a great rage that he killed himself by removing all the flesh from his own body, returning it to his mother, and scraping all his bones clean, returning them to his father.

Thanks to Taiyi Zhenren, Lord Taiyi of Salvation, Na Za was revived with a new body made of lotus-flowers and a lotus-root. Na Za wanted to revenge himself on his father Li Jing. But he was vanquished by a deity known as the Lamp-burning Taoist who put him under with the Exquisite Seven-pearled Pagoda for thirty-three days until he agreed to make peace with his father.

Afterwards, Na Za helped Jiang Taigong win over the King Zhou of Shang for the King Wu of Zhou. His weapons were well-known as he went about on his fire-and-wind wheels, his universe ring and his sky-covered red ribbon, invincible because he was unkillable, in a body made of lotus-flowers and lotus-roots.

'Unkillable?' Na Za mumbled, in an almost inaudible voice, as she was drifting into sleep.

I looked at her face, placid now, like the surface of a windless lake, and heard her even breathing. I felt, in that moment, her face was like a living monument of her mother and I, supposing I was dead, as she described in her dream. A smile stole to my lips as I sighed and blew the light out.

*

In the morning, I wrote a note to remind myself to this effect: B.H., don't forget to include the violent scene here from the novel, Huangjin shijie, and forward it to Stacey when the translation is done.

What happens is that, following that fracas, Bleg, the ship supervisor, came below deck to count the number of people, and he used his whip to organise the coolies into easily countable groups but his whip accidentally hits Ms Chen who was crying against the iron wall, her face buried in the crook of her elbow. This is what follows, in my translation,

> She bursts into tears, to the chagrin of Bleg who is about to give
> her another whip when he changes his mind and says, 'If you

don't find it comfortable here, would you like to move to a cabin above?' Ms Chen stops crying but does not say anything. Bleg says, grinning, 'Let me help you.' As he says so, he drops his whip and holds out his hands, which Ms Chen takes with her own hands. Ah Jin, her husband, stands watching, enraged, but he can't do a thing. Just then, he sees his wife lower her head and open her mouth, to take a bite from each of Bleg's hands. on top of slapping his face on both sides.

What follows is another bigger fracas that almost grows into a mutiny. But I don't have time to dwell on that. Let someone in the future dig it all out or turn it into academic deadwood for all I care.

Oh, I almost forgot something. Stacey said she wanted me to include a section on my visit to Ireland. At first, I was reluctant. Then I changed my mind. But I was faced with the difficulty of choice. There was poetry I wrote. This I did in both English and Chinese. There was a diary I kept. This I did daily. There were also impressions I wrote everywhere I went. This I did either in my computer or in my mobile phone. When I did it on my phone, I used the speech recognition device. It was not till I started searching for stuff includable here that I realised why I was initially reluctant: The diary I kept was entirely in Chinese! While most poems I wrote were in Chinese, I could let them go. But I would be reluctant to translate my own diary entries into English just because Stacey wanted to see what I wrote in Ireland. The alternative would be to simply create two pieces as part of a student assignment and have done with it. Well, here they are below.

Room 14, Saturday, The Leeson Lodge, Rathmines, Dublin

The city, by the look of it, is not vastly different from either Melbourne or Sydney except in one thing: its bilinguality. I have always thought that Ireland is nothing but another England, speaking English in an Irish accent, often in a way full of ire, like a couple of Irish people I had come into contact with in Melbourne. I wonder if the country's name was not based on the word 'ire' because it's a land of ire, with people of ire, although I must admit that people I met here, including hotel staff, were quite friendly.

What caught my eye when I first arrived at Dublin Airport was signs in two languages, with something sitting on top of English that I had never seen anywhere in my life. Checking through the photographs I took, I found this one: 'Fáilte go hAerfort Bhaile Átha Cliath/Welcome To Dublin Airport' and this 'Naisc Eitilte/ Flight Connections.' It reminded me of what I used to see in Hong Kong where all the signs were bilingual, still are, with English words sitting on top of Chinese characters. If you compare both cities, you realise how Irish people are much more attuned to the politics of languages. By allowing Irish to sit on top of English, they achieve the powerful status of linguistic sovereignty very much in the position of powerful buttocks sitting on top of a toilet.

Room 14, Sunday, the Leeson Lodge

I was kept awake nearly all night by the people talking in the café downstairs. It was not as if I had not stayed in a hotel, in China, in Hong Kong or in Australia. But nowhere had I experienced anything quite like this, people laughing and talking boisterously all night, particularly women whose shrill and excited voices stand out as something I had neither physically heard nor read about. I wondered who these women were and why they didn't go home for the night and if they were together with their own men or not their own men. Their noisy night formed a sharp contrast with the total graveyard quietness in the hotel where, for the first time, I came across the name of a writer that I said I must read: Léon Bloy. I lay in bed, lights off, and listened to them, the women and the men, laughing, talking, doing nothing but laughing and talking. What a great community there must be in this country? Why did I never encounter anything remotely like it in Australia?

*

'It's about time I killed myself.' This is a recorded message I sent to myself over WeChat. I don't want to give the time and date when this was recorded. No one has any right to demand that of me nor am I interested in sharing that with anyone. I'd rather talk to the changing clouds about it. Sharing things with the clouds is the best option one has these days, or with the sky, without a single trace of clouds. No one, in this world or next, not even in the underworld, is fit for me to share anything with. That's how firm I am in my position. If I do not fear death, I do not fear anything.

Now, her ways are not my ways. She, Yvette Palazzo, in Sydney, her exact address, even if fictional, suppressed the same way mine is, produces paintings without ever wanting to show in any exhibitions, not even in a private exhibition. She has pre-booked her death. Having nothing to do with the rest of the world. Having nothing to do. Having nothing. Having. That's Dasein, Da: there, Sein: being. Being there. Being-there. Being-there with her own paintings that she lives to produce and she lives to see the death of. Which is probably why the few people who happened to see her paintings burst into tears when seeing them, for the first time in their lives, when they realised that she was a painter, an artist, very much the way people wept at the sight of paintings by Mark Rothko.

I haven't produced much except this non-book kind of a book. There's no comparison between her and I. But we both have something in common: we are good and do not have a name. She is committing suicide artistically, creating without exhibiting, creating without entertaining any ideas of generating a sale. She is, in my opinion, the quintessential new-age artist living entirely for herself, a living challenge to the art world overrun by capitalism. I – what is there to talk about 'I'? A mere idea. See that 'i' in the word 'idea'? If you add 'th', it is perfect.

The letter I wrote the whole night last night I now am reading again.

Dear Zi Ya,

Hope this email finds you well.

I now treat you the way I used to accord to Stacey my supervisor. I no longer do that. I have a problem, as deep-seated as the rest of the world. You said you had stopped bothering about making friends. I found that awfully true, in this country in particular. In a separate manuscript I have not included in this, I have Ah Mao talking to me about his case in detail. He says that it is so hard to die. Ever since he checked into the psychiatric institution he has wanted to die. But the doctors have always managed to kill off his desire for death by medication. To silence himself, he has bitten off the tip of his tongue. But the doctors have cured it with more medications. Eventually, he commits himself to pen and paper; he commits himself to words, the only source of his comfort. After a decade or so getting stuck in the institution, when all his efforts at taking his own life have come to nothing, he stops blaming himself for his own stupidities. He stops blaming the celestial empire for its weaknesses and he stops blaming England's colony for shutting him in a mental institution for life. Instead, he writes a series of suicide notes about his failed attempts to take his own life. What is the colony good for but suicides? The guilt is so heavy and profound and piercing it's almost as if the sky were an unbroken piece of steel hanging over everyone, including us newcomers.

I know I am a loser. The very act of writing this note is an admission of defeat. I have in fact written a couple of other novels that I have not shown anyone. Yes, they have been rejected again and again until I realised I am a no hoper, good for nothing, not even good for money when I have it. I don't want to fight on, as someone, a friend, suggested. I simply want to let go. If I want to get rid of the manuscripts all I have to do is click on 'Delete' to disappear everything without a trace.

The pressure is so much on you from everywhere and everyone. They want you to be good. If you write, they want you to produce something that either sells millions of copies or wins the top award for best writing. If you fail at both, you are a loser. Your choice is to either stay the course with a career that sees no end of failure in itself or opt out for something easier.

While saying all that, I do admire you for your tenacity and adherence to a belief that goes beyond belief. No one believes in failures or losses anymore. The only thing we ever want to achieve in life is achievement. But there is never enough to go around. The world is simply inhabited by too many people. It won't complain if it is minus one or two. On the contrary, it will feel relieved, with one more burden gone.

To be honest — I have to be very honest, with myself and with you, before I take my own life — persistence in literature is persistence in death, an ever increasingly profitless persistence. You spend years living a death-like life writing a book, getting multiple rejections till it's accepted, see the publication receive lukewarm reception in the media, hear all the good words about it without seeing many sales, go to this literary festival or that and get a few copies sold here and there, see your book long-listed, short-listed and stop short of getting something worth a mention. You repeat the process by spending more years in hard work, producing one book after another, one death after another, blind to the fact that the world has long stopped reading. You see authors pop up newly published books with their smiling faces atop them in Twitter or Instagram. And you see readers turn away with the click of a 'Like', as if they had bought a copy.

I don't like what I see. But I don't want to persist in what is not even a dream. I have laid out a bright future for Ah Sin, though. Yes, I must not forget this. In a nutshell, the family of three women and one man, Ah Sin with Bi Xiao, Yun Xiao and Naza Dasein, are on their way to the Lanfang Republic, and his two wives give birth to two sons on board the ship. When they reach Borneo, they are given a big reception by the officials and locals from the republic. Thereafter, Ah Sin becomes the Minister of Culture.

I can't give you any more details than this, the desire to take my own life becoming overwhelming. The Lanfang Republic story may well become another novel. But it's not for me to write. Or, put another way, it's for me to write in my death or after my death.

There's one story, a Buddhist one, that Ah Sin shares with his women on board the ship bound for the Lanfang Republic, which I must share with you before I disappear:

[400 words shed, too long and irrelevant——SA]

*

A continuation of the BH email to Zi Ya:

Have I changed my mind about taking my life after a night's sleep? Sort of. But not even when I decided to move to the Lanfang Republic, defunct about 100 years ago, would I change my mind. I'm no good at human relationships. My face is a sunshine I offer to the world. My heart is a 24/7 night, all darkness and negativity. There are very few people I admire in this world. I have very little respect for any presidents or prime ministers of any countries, of any description. The admiration and respect I have I reserve solely for dead writers and dead poets, sometimes very well-unknown ones, such as Svevo and Huysmans, no hopers till dead, and dead kings and emperors, such as Liu Bei. I don't want to list them because you already know who they are. It's not for me to share with anyone else after you. I have little interest in interacting with my neighbours. In fact, I don't have neighbours. They, like me, live their secret and secretive lives, with no desire for communication or interaction. If one wants that one can easily have it in a market or supermarket by talking to the shoppers and shop-assistants. I have no interest in finding a woman for partnership. If I need sex, my right hand is always there to help me meet my needs. And it is the cleanest way to prevent me from having anything to do with MeeToo, or HimToo, if ever there is one. Or even ItToo, when the world is filled with sex dolls and sex robots. Every morning when I wake up, I do so with the thought that I'm alive for another day and what a waste! I thought of Yvette's mother before her death. Every day she cried for death upstairs, saying in a loud voice, 'I want to die! I want to die!' Her daughter cried from downstairs, saying, 'Stop crying! Stop crying!' She was reduced to silence, but only for a short while, before she was heard crying for death again, day after day, and month after month. Then she couldn't cry anymore and died. In the process, she said, 'It is easy to live but hard to die.' When I heard that, I said to myself, offering a smiling face to Yvette, 'That's because you are chicken. If you have the guts, you can easily take your own life, as easily as you snub out a cigarette.' Talking about Yvette, I thought of the list I have done for you, the list of Australian-Chinese artists, which I have compiled and will send you in a separate file. I won't mention them because they are familiar enough to you except to say that I have included Yvette Palazzo, an artist that no one has heard of. Talk to her about the Archibald Prize and she'll say, 'Never heard of it and can't be bothered.' Compared with those eternal failures who enter into the prize draw year in and year out, she is a refreshing cooling agent as no successes are more successful than her failure, her refusal to participate in a community of created failures and successes.

I now remember what Ah Sin said, on the threshold of his departure for the Lanfang Republic, to himself as well as to his bewildered wives, 'I have a new future awaiting me in the new republic. The colony is a dark place to which I shall never return. There, anything to do with Chinese or China is deemed bad and remains bad indefinitely. My fellow countrymen over there will never get anywhere except in their own comfort zone of moneymaking. Nothing superior will be accorded them or awarded them. Staying stuck in the lower orders, they will serve the money and the people as no one else can and they shall never rise above the multitudes, not because they don't have the abilities but because they do and because they do better, exactly the reason why an invisible hand, the victor's hand in the beginning, that of the ruling class, will keep them falling low and forever outside the pantheon of the best. I won't stay in my own country, either. Its history is simply too long to move out of its stupor and slumber. Addicted to opium and run by a foreign race, people of the Han race have become total slaves, without hope of salvation and liberation. The foreign powers of high noses and sunken eyes are up to no good, either, as they come to China for the sole purpose of profit-making, their ideals of freedom and universal brotherhood never extended to the people they had vanquished with their guns, gunboats, gunpowder and cannons. I'm leaving my former colony and my present country behind for a republic where everyone is equal to everyone else and universal brotherhood is the order of the day. In my former colony, people are stuck with their skin colour and they will not transcend it for a long time to come. That's their limit and their limitation. I shall devote myself entirely to the construction and development of this new republic for the rest of my life and I shall see my children born in the republic, free from the colonial ills and the celestial corruption. And I shall see the republic rise in the world amidst a forest of nations. We shall have our own artists, our own philosophers, our own poets, our own musicians, our own novelists, our own playwrights — we shall have every variety of art flourishing and thriving in this new republic free from discrimination based on gender, class, race and skin colour. Bi Xiao, Yun Xiao and Naza Dasein, I love you all.'

I remember that from a dream. But I think I'll stop here. I'm tired of everything, of people who post stuff on Twitter to attract one like or five likes, just keep adding zeros, of the same on Facebook, of developments that only mean the added numbers of zeroes, and of the world increasingly turning into one of AIs, rendering billions of 'I's powerlessly invalid.

The other day, when I wandered as usual in the Pangu Wilderness, of my own naming, I thought I saw my own body, lying among the river red gums, like a section of a felled and skinned tree. It was in fact the dead tree. But I liked to think it was my discarded body and that I was its departed soul and shadow, or the shadow-soul, regarding it in my composure. How nice it must be to lie like that day after day, night after night, week or month after week and month, and year after year, presenting to the eye no prospect for regeneration and renewal, just evidence of something that has lived and is no longer liveable.

*

'I want to offer myself a challenge,' I said to the book lying a few meters away from me, sharing the same room with me. 'by getting myself to re-tell part of the story in *The World of Gold*, without checking and re-checking the historical facts, no, the fictive facts for accuracy, fictional accuracy. What an irony! But when the woman is thrown overboard, presumed dead, her body is set adrift till it reaches a desert island where she is found breathing and her life is saved. There, in a Chinese village, where, for two generations, Chinese migrants have been living, she is given a second life and is asked to teach English in a local school. She declines, citing her lost husband and her strong desire to find him. The head of the village organises a trip to Cuba, with a 20-person crew. But when they arrive, they are denied landing because they do not have necessary documentation. They then go on to England where they stay for a few months to study before they set sail to Singapore where, when they arrive, the woman bumps into her husband and is overjoyed. Then the husband tells of his own miserable experience sustained in Cuba, his escape from the labour camp and the help he received from a Cuba-based Chinese elder who bought him a ticket so that he can reach Singapore, safe and sound.

In challenging my memory, I can see that it hardly holds water because I can't remember the village head's name nor the name of the woman. All I can ever remember is the man's name: Ah Jin, or Ah Gold, as well as a lingering taste of bitterness throughout the novel.

You are right, Stacey, that this novel has got to be translated into English in its entirety. My only concern is who is going to pay for it to be translated and who is willing to put in money and effort to publish it and then who will be interested enough to buy a copy or two. There doesn't seem to be any guarantee in anything, not even the one that I can fully remember every little detail of, although I can lay my hands on the book and open it to the page where the story happens. [A journal entry, 3rd June.]

*

P.S.

Those who really want to die will die no matter what. Because death is their destiny. Because. Words are deaths, too. Eyes are now skipping them to look at pictures. Picture is future. Both share the word 'ture'. Picture is future is failure. The three share the word 'ure'. Picture is future is failure is endure. The four share the word 'ure'. I don't think anyone really cares whether one dies or not. Life goes on, death goes on. The two in parallel as night and day, woman and man, sky and earth, water and desert, past and future, hand and foot. Why are there no three eyes, no three nostrils, no three ears? Don't people want more? Hasn't this wanting created enough dearth in the world? Desolation, devastation? Isn't there enough of that? Too much is too much is too much.

These were the thoughts that came to me as I took my daily stroll along the Criminal Creek in the Pangu Park. For a long time, I didn't know what the creek was called. Even though I found out its name, I can never remember it. I called it the Criminal Creek because it was deliciously alliterative and because it was quintessentially Australian. A hundred and fifty years or so years ago, many Aboriginal people must have been murdered and their bodies must have been thrown into this creek. At the thought, my nostrils were filled with the smells of rotting corpses. This country will forever live, I thought, with the smells lingering in its nostrils, or tens of millions of nostrils.

I have also called this creek 'the Critical Creek', when I am in a right mood or good mood. [Stacey says: I read the 'critical' bits and am critical of them myself, enough to cause myself to say, repeatedly, 'No, no, no,' even when he tempered them by calling them 'Self-critical Creek'. That he has the cheek to include me in his attack on the comfortable academics is beyond my comprehension and endurance. 772 words shed.]

I have thought of writing a few separate letters to my parents and to my supervisor. But I don't think I have time for that. I'll write them below.

When I read Sartre I became instantly united with Ah Mao in

that remark Jean Paul made, 'I live alone, entirely alone. I never speak to anyone, never; I receive nothing. I give nothing.' (*Nausea*, p. 6), to which I might add, 'But I do speak to my shadows in the past, long dead and alive.'

*

A pre-death meditation by B.H., based on a self-quoted passage from his writing journal:

11.01am: A search throughout the MS just now returns about 16 Chinese passages. I did so because I was beginning to wonder if I should delete all of them, leaving only the translations. But it's a painful thought because I love the way the Chinese texts intersperse with the English ones, the same way a Chinese man intersperses with an Irish woman or any other women of European extraction. They look so good by their mere appearance. Perhaps, to be able to survive in another country, another language and another culture, the first things to be deleted or destroyed or sacrificed are these things that speak to our hearts or heart-minds. If one allows one's sense of numbness to grow and overwhelm one, one may succeed in another form or format, but one experiences a death, too, willingly or unwillingly. Perhaps I have to pay the price of death by allowing these things to exist textually? [68 words cut, partly on racism, a bit too much—Stacey]

Do I sound like I am speaking to you, Stacey, even if I didn't intend to email this to you? I can make this part of my will, though, that you have my permission to delete all the Chinese passages, including a few of my poems written in Chinese, from the manuscript in their entirety, if their existence means the demise of the text in English. But what about the fact that this unpublishable book is written by a Chinese suicide about the Chinese gold-diggers and particularly about a Chinese gold-digger who is, or used to be, a storyteller? Does that alone mean that the whole book is evil and should never be allowed to exist? Would the world be a better place when Chineseness is totally terminated without a trace, as Henry Lawson once remarked, 'The Chinaman had to be either killed or cured', now to be definitely killed because incurable?

*

Baohui's letter to his mother.

> Dear Mother,
> This is the source of my imagination.
> Imagined remembrances.
> Remembered imagination.
> Memories of a past I have never lived.
> In this country, there are many who pretend to be dead
> N, for example, is one who pretends to be dead
> I've learnt a lot from him, the most important of it all being
> The ability to pretend to be dead
> If you send emails to him, he ignores them
> If you use any other media to get in touch, he ignores them
> Even if you call, he uses the answering machine and never returns the call
> When he is really dead, his photo will appear in the media
> It is not till then that you will realise that he really is dead
> But there is no difference between his real death and his fake death

I'm sorry, Mum, that I've written the above. It's not meant to be part of my letter. It's just the fragments I recorded on WeChat as I walked along the Self-critical Creek not far from where I live. When I turned the sound pieces into words, I forgot to create a separate word document, instead putting them in this one. I had thought of copying them and pasting them into another document when I changed my mind. It would be good if you are puzzled when you first read this because it would feel like you've just chanced upon my mind sliced open, like a watermelon, right in front of you, and see everything there, as fresh as when they were first recorded, carrying the sound of my breathing with them and the occasional call of a bird.

You know I am the selfish one. That is because I have chosen to be selfish. Ours is a world geared towards making everyone selfish and self-protective. And ours is the Gen-Self, generation of the selfish, one living for oneself and no-one else, one loving oneself and no-one else, and one remaining with oneself and no-one else till the end of the day.

But what's the point of talking about this movement or that if I have already decided to take my own life because my movement is a movement that removes itself from the face of the earth?

To be or not to be is simply not the question for me. To be is more than enough. Not to be feels quite right, quite alright, and quite marvellous.

See you in another century and have a very good one.

Amidst a rising chorus of voices, 'Kill him! Kill him! We're sick of such a sickness,' I'm quitting.

Baohui

*

Dear Dad,

How you going, Old Mate? Still making loads of money are you? Why, I mean, I don't seem to have much to talk to you about anymore, to be very honest, even though you, Dad, are my boss. I have also completely lost interest in going to work in your company in Greece. Next life, maybe. I think I'm going to join Ah Sin in his career and enterprise in the Lanfang Republic. Never heard of that? Then read my book or my book manuscript. I am a more idealistic person than you, Dad, if you know what I mean except not in the sense you promote that someone like me should learn to sing people's praises, always speaking highly of everyone around him no matter what. I'm not cut out for that. If I can't even sing praises of this person that is I, how can I sing anyone's praises? Are they worth it? I'm not the kind you thought I was, into a future of more money, more women, more pleasure-seeking. But I really am not suited for anything that's mapped out for me. I need the intensity of quietness, so intense that the world has ceased to exist for me. They say I'm suffering from what is known as Asperger's Syndrome. Nonsense. It's more like Asparagus Syndrome, whatever it is. Yes, that's what I am: to be eaten by the earth as an asparagus. I'm not suffering from any condition or conditions. The only condition I'm suffering from is one in which I am a being never entirely Dasein, never entirely at self or let self. Even in my dream, I am not there, not Da. I'm elsewhere, always far away from myself, in a place I can't find back, in a place I can't go back to, in a place I can't dream back of again. Life is a place on cruise control, on its willing mission of self-missing and I'm on board it.

A novelist's life is not for me. I'm not cut out for it. To secure a title of Dr Zhang Baohui, with a doctorate in creative writing? What good does it serve when I go back to China? Have you heard this remark that goes, 'If you are smart enough to earn a PhD, you are smart enough not to pursue one.' (See it here: https://www.cbsnews.com/news/12-reasons-not-to-get-a-phd/ for all the 12 reasons). Already, people there are wondering why they have to learn English and whether the language is relevant anymore in this day and age of rising nationalism in a country that has suffered bashing for nearly two hundred years until it finally raises its head, straightens its back and squares its shoulders. Who wants to be constantly reminded that one is never good enough, can never master the Language, can never write it properly, can never produce anything acceptable without multiple revisions and editings? Why don't we let them learn our language to experience the same frustrations, the same criticisms, the same pickings, the same corrections, the same revisions and the same editings? It's super-high time they did.

But I'm not blaming either Mum or you for getting me to choose to do this PhD in creative writing. It's all my fault. There is hope, though, because I won't pursue it now. In fact, I have stopped doing it altogether because I have finished it and I refuse to go back and revisit my past, of doings, rightdoings or wrongdoings. The past is something that has happened and that refuses to be revised. You either live with it or ignore it. You can change it if you wish, like you change yourself, from a gendered person, to an ungendered person, even to a disgendered person or multi-gendered person, and from anything to anything. I'd rather not change it but go back to live with Ah Sin in the Lanfang Republic.

I'll talk to you more about that.

There is one book that I'd like you to read. It's *Beyond Human: How Cutting-Edge Science is Extending Our Lives* by Eve Herold, already published in Chinese translation. All those future possibilities she talks about in the book are meant for the rich, the one-way journey to a self-selected planet, the transmigration to settle on Mars or the Moon, the option for freezing at ultra-cold temperature for say 500 years before waking up again at your current age of 64, the replacement of all your body organs with fantastically new electronic organs that last you centuries or the uploading of your brain onto a terminal where, saved onto a mega-byte USB, you will be able to live for eternity, and, when installed on a robot, you'll be alive, and go live, again.

All these can be realised as long as you've got money, heaps of it.

But none of these are for me. I'm going, going, and will be gone pretty soon.

Cheers,

B.H.

Chapter 5

Hi, Stacey,

I'm a very ugly person. Look at my teeth. They are horribly crooked. Which is why I hardly smile because I have a fear of revealing my ugliness even though I'm short in the tooth. English is such an ugly language it has long in the tooth but not short in the tooth, only shortcomings, no longcomings, only no way, not yes way, only for good, not for bad, such a one-sided language I often think of killing it or reinventing it.

It's funny that I recall some of the trailers I saw, all featuring actors throwing tantrums or bursting into tears as if that was the true status of a character. One could be living with someone else or with oneself for ages without any emotional disturbance, do they know that? What remains below and unseen is perhaps the truest state of mind that needs to be covered, uncovered, discovered or re-discovered. This forms part of an interview I did with myself and, if you are interested, please let me know instead of laughing it off as an absurd idea. There are times when only a self-interview is the best way of discovering oneself, like a selfie, a psychological and psychiatric selfie. You probably already know it without me telling you although you haven't had the guts to try it because you are so high in your position of power that you consider it beneath your dignity to conduct a proper interview with yourself and that only someone condemned would be willing to do so. Well, I am that someone if you know what I means – don't correct it as 'mean' for that 'I' is already an object, a living corpse.

[Stacey says: I don't like his comparison of himself to being an Aboriginal person. Quite impropriate and preposterous. 375 words cut]

Sorry about my rambling on, my ramblings, ram/blings, ram/blingblings. No more, Stacey, I promise. Your criticisms and advice have greatly helped and I really appreciate it, and because of that, I was able to think more widely and more freely, read more laterally and write more erratically. I do not think that writing needs to be an ordered thing, arranged and re-arranged with the ancient rules of a game, set by the ancient, intolerable, unwieldy whites. Just now, I googled 'literary canon' and found one article, titled, 'Revision of the Literary Canon', its bibliography containing names like Paul Lauter and Leslie Fielder, but not the top name on the tip of my tongue, who seems an everlasting decider of the good over the bad, the beautiful over the ugly, in terms of literary cannoning. Curiously, I just can't recall his name.

Let's move on and don't worry about my 'novel'. It's dung when it's done or dunged.

Au revoir! Auf wiedersehen! Zaijian!

Your most humble servant-student,

Zhang Baohui

*

P. S.

[Stacey comments: This section, of 322 words, is removed even though it's struck through with a straight line throughout.]

[BH to himself: I'm not sure about this. I'll have another look before I decide to keep it or remove it.]

*

Part of a self-interview with BH by BH, self-suppressed by BH till he decided to 'leave', as the title of a found poem suggests before, as follows,

Q: How did you imagine the feelings about bound feet?

A: I didn't imagine. I experienced them.

Q: How?

A: I ejaculated my semen onto a woman's pair of bound feet.

Q: Did you really? How?

A: Hear me out. I ejaculated onto the pair of feet in a photograph, taken I don't know when but I have a vague memory that it was taken around the turn of the century, in or around 1900.

Q: Why did you do that?

A: Because the very look of them gave me such a thrill that I couldn't help doing it and it felt better than anything that's easily available now.

Q: Don't you think it's a disgrace on their society that they demanded their women to go through such pain in order to create aesthetics, a paramount sense of sexual beauty?

A: I have no interest in talking to people who judge the past with the standards of the present. Regarded that way, people born 5000 years ago might as well have not been born at all because they were downright wrong, mistakes that ought to have all been corrected now, or, better still, erased.

. . .

*

Note: It's Daa Seinn, formerly Da Sein, speaking. They look at the bump. The interested eyes, particularly of the women, and the bumped heads, whispering, mouths to ears. The bump, on the bumpy road, to where, no idea. A road of bumps, then babies. Bumpy babies. A smile that steals onto a corner of my mouth has caused a female tongue to comment in Cantonese. I know what it says. I don't want to translate it, not even for myself. I touch the bump. It feels good. Neither Big Mum nor Second Mum will force anything out of me even though they don't. Dad wouldn't care less. Would he? He's too busy to notice anything. It's the ghost I've fallen in love with. And it's written on the wall that I shall make the delivery in Australia, nowhere else but Australia. So I arrive on a day like this, a whole plum tree bursting into bloom in the sky, in a place they call Suspence. I hope I won't be written into death when my new baby is born. I lie in bed, watching the branches starting to turn into snow of flowers. I am happy with no company except strangers that are nurses and doctors. I am relieved that I have returned to the new world, with another world in me, within me, throughout me, in my blood, me a body of running creeks, all interconnected.

Please give me another life in another life. When the baby is born, if it's a male, I'll call him Mitsein. If it is a female, I'll call her Fitsein.

*

P.S.

This is not the end of the story. This is actually the beginning. In my death, I shall write my next novel, to be titled, *Memoir of a Republic: A Sequel to Ah Sin*.

*

There was a lapse of memory on my part. In preparing to tell Ah Sin's story, I wrote an imaginary piece about his love affair with an Irish woman and a daughter subsequently born to them, in Chinese. I found the piece and put it below:

[452 characters, translation below—SA]

Let me attempt a self-translation to see if it works:

All right. Forgive me for my constant diversion. What I was meaning to say was that after I had that illicit relationship with the Irish woman she disappeared and gave birth to a baby girl. A few years after, she came back and handed her to me, saying: I can't afford to raise her. You take her away! As she said so, she thrust her into my hands and left without even turning her head back. I asked our daughter what her name was. She shook her head. I asked her the question in English, she still shook her head. I tried many ways but she refused to open her mouth. I found out soon enough that she was a mute person.

I took a look at her. She had golden hair. But her eyes were black. There was a sense of something combined, both Oriental and Occidental, around the way she looked. I began writing characters for her, with a gum tree branch. I wrote down two characters, "爸爸", as I pronounced them for her. She stared at me, nodding her head as if she understood. A feeling of love rushed to my heart. When I thought how hard it was to disembark at Robe and to overcome all sorts of difficulties to reach Beechworth in those days, I thought I must somehow find a way to commemorate it, so I named her 'Robe', after the place.

Oh, yes, after Ah Xiang died, we buried him in the Beechworth Cemetery where dozens of Chinese miners had gone to sleep earlier than him. After the burial, we found a stone to carve his name, the name of his village, Beiliu Village, and a line of poetry that I thought of for him: A life of peace, flowing with wind （祥和一生，风流一世）. In a few decades, I thought, the characters would become unrecognizable. Well, for a man, his whole life can be summarized in two characters: 金 （jin） and 精 （jing），gold and semen.

*

Why must it happen at the same time that I came across this on the day I wrote that? It goes, '…and the woman I loved is dead, like broken jade and buried incense.' (Lin Yutang, p. 108)

*

These mistakes or lapses are part of an organic growth of a personal history, or, to be more exact, a fictional personal history that refuses to be revised. How can one go back and tell one's former self in one's teens that one ought not to have dreamt of stealing? How can one take it into

394

one's head that one can revise history and set it right with mere apologies? How can one hope to rewrite history when one remains a member of the master race? Dreams are being dreamed precisely because of these impossibilities and more.

*

And when it comes to gay and lesbian love, let me provide you with something I may have neglected in telling you because my familiarity with the matter blinds me to the fact that people living outside the language and the culture may have no idea what's going on. Take gay love. While officials in the Qing dynasty were banned from visiting brothels, the government turned a blind eye to them if they sought sexual comfort in boys, known as *xianggong*. No possible translation, sorry. Or, if they were rich enough, they could keep a *shutong* (book boy) or two in their own houses for their own pleasure.

Women, too, had their freedom, a word not the exclusive property of the West. In the old Canton, women formed what was known as Jin-lan hui, Golden Orchid Society, in which they were united as sisters in their refusal to be married with men. There were stories of girls, forced into marriage with men, who killed their male partners. And there were also stories of sisters marrying one man in order to have their own pleasure right under the nose of their man. I think this is part of the story I meant to tell about the two women Ah Sin was married to, who were actually lesbians, pleasing Ah Sin at the same time when they were pleasing themselves, without Ah Sin's knowledge or, perhaps, with his encouragement, given that he was a very open-minded man.

But, I've lost the energy. And I have lost track. If Stacey is interested, she can pick up the thread wherever I leave it and carry on with the story by removing something here, dropping it or taking it somewhere else. It's all for the taking. Or another book for me to write in my death if you believe that death isn't a place where nothing happens. I've got heaps of material, historical, poetic and literary that I can send to her by email. Standing in a vacuum-like space where I can't place myself, not knowing whether I am gay or lesbian, or questioning, or asexual, or even A (for Australian), B (for British because I write its language), or C (for Chinese), or anything of anything except a breathing thing, or simply a breaTHING.

*

My third lapse of memory is my haphazard dealings in writing with the Aboriginal people. I knew it was a sensitive subject, one that makes one edgy and fearful because of the constant accusation that one doesn't get it right or one is into tokenism. I didn't have a problem with that. My problem is I couldn't find an Aboriginal person to befriend. I had to imagine a friendship in words while there is no physical reality. In my preparatory writing in Chinese, there is one chapter written without any punctuation where a reference is made to the whites, comparing them with their Chinese counterparts:

[127 characters cut, translation below—SA]

I now render a self-translation below:

> All of you in our eyes are the most abject people in the world except the Aborigines but even more abject than them because they at least do not worry about money do not worry about property they eat wherever they go they drink wherever they go they shit wherever they go they live wherever they go the skies are their eyes the land is their skin the fauna and flora are their flesh but what about you all your eyes have grown into the money

Just then, I recalled an incorrect remark made by Septimus Burt in 1892 to this effect that 'I have come to the conclusion myself, and have done so for years, that the only way of effectually dealing with all these coloured races, whether blackfellows, or Indians, or Chinamen, is to treat them like children.' (Qtd in Henry Reynolds, *Aborigines and Settlers: The Australian Experience 1788-1939*. Cassell Australia, 1972, p. 26.) My immediate reaction to this is: If this was correct then, it must be wrong. Can we draw a conclusion from that that anything said now will prove to be wrong in a hundred years? I had no one to answer that question, so my musing went on:

> If we can be friends with them, if we can throw tantrums with them, if we can criticise them and be criticised by them, if we can treat them like real human beings, not ritual performers, if we can visit them and they can visit us back, if we can engage in all sorts of real human relationship and interaction with them, life would be more tolerable instead of a constant demand for PC until the real stuff is all but gone. That's not what I said but what I thought. I didn't write about it because I was full of PC-related concerns; I wrote something else, again in Chinese. Please Stacey, forgive me if you think this is too hard on you. When I die and you take it over from me, you are welcome to edit the whole thing whichever way you like:

[445 characters cut, translation below—SA]

I'm now translating it myself, in an act resembling that of self-pleasuring or self-comforting, safe in the knowledge that the only person who would read this manuscript would be my supervisor. If so, why not? I don't care; I don't care anymore. I'm a dying person. Literally, I'm a dead person. I'll disappear myself in a country known for the number of its people gone missing. One never knows when the country itself will go missing one day, very possibly on the day when I do:

> You were gone earlier than I. Before you died, you asked me to turn your bones into an erhu. You said that when one played on the bones it would sound better than on any other wood instruments. I thought you were joking, so I said: Let me wait till you rot, with only bones left. But the waiting may take years and I may have already gone back to my home country before you are completely rotten. You said: No use waiting. In time, my leg will

397

break off by itself ahead of time. You can then keep the thighbone to turn it into an instrument because my spine can't be turned into a *qin* (instrument), it being shaped of breakages, no good as a *qin*.

Surprised, I took a look at you. Your leg was safe and sound. How come it will break off? And ahead of time? You couldn't explain. You said it was a feeling. But the feeling was most odd. If you felt something might happen, it would happen. For example, the other night when I saw the Irish drunkard, I felt that something might happen. Sure enough, something did happen afterwards.

Now that you were gone, I got an Aborigine to remove your thighbone, making an *erhu* based on the drawing I did for him, fitting the strings onto it that you pulled off the other night. The result was not hard to imagine: the sound was hoarse. But the actual result was that it was an exquisite work of art. The cleaned white bone looked like a piece of jade. That night, I ripped a tattered jacket apart, and pulled out a large bunch of horsehair. With the best bit of it, I made a bow. No ears needed, just eyes, to look at you as a work of art.

End of the Story:

To end the story is to end my life. To end my life is to end the story. I might have never even lived if you know what I mean. All I am is that voice you have heard from the cemetery at the start of the novel. In the beginning, there is the grave.

Rather than find a spot where I can fit in this story by making up a story in which a Chinese miner saves an Australian boy from a rushing river and refuses to accept a fat gift from his gold-mining dad, say, a tiny piece of gold, I'll tell a story off the top of my head after reading *Lü's Commentaries of History* (in Chinese 《吕氏春秋》). It is beyond me why they didn't translate it as *Lü's Spring and Autumn* and why they rendered it as 'commentaries of', not 'commentaries on'. English as a language, I must say, is as flexible, creative and poetic as its

Mandarin counterpart. But there are bad translators galore that have done sorry jobs. Do let me, though, have a quick job with it to get the story out of the way and my life as well.

In ancient times, in the State of Lu, there was a law that stipulated that the government would pay anyone for helping a Lu person working as a servant in another state outside the State of Lu and back to it. When Zi Gong, one of Confucius' disciples, did so but refused to be paid by the government, Confucius said, 'It's no good. Once you start this practice, no one will ever help anyone out of their slavery.' Then, when Zi Lu, another disciple of Confucius' saved someone from drowning and was offered a cow, he took it. For this, Confucius highly praised him, saying, 'I'm sure the Lu people will never ignore the drowning people again.' (《吕氏春秋》, 2007, p. 151)

Do you, readers and Stacey, want me to go back and find a spot to slip this in so that it becomes an organic part of the story without breaking the organic streak and strain of it all already there?

Part VI

I, Stacey, have to start off by apologizing that it's not Zhang Baohui but me who has to write this part, in a post-him and post-pandemic period and I am poignantly reminded of a remark he had made before the virus arose in Wuhan and spread to the rest of the world: *I'd better finish myself off before the world goes nuts when something unprecedented happens.* In a way, I think he is a genius. He made a great decision to take his own life before he succumbed to Covid-19 or might have succumbed to it.

One more thing. What I need to add is that I have, in my final edit, cut another 4000 words or so from the manuscript in its entirety, feeling simultaneously sorry and pleased on behalf of BH or for the sake of him, and also that translated sections of fiction without the accompanying characters in Chinese are all from a Chinese novel by Yvonne, now deceased, about the Chinese gold-diggers' journey from Robe, SA, to the Victorian goldfields.

But I shall cut the crap by getting right to the point with an interview I've done with him, my former PhD creative writing student, in his death, and, instead of presenting it in its entirety, I shall quote parts in accordance with the themes we talked about, as follows,

On love
SA: I remember you were saying, in a conversation we had over coffee, that you didn't suit love or love didn't suit you.

BH: Love is winter, which is why it is November. I mean Nlovember.

SA: What about self-love?

BH: Self is the most detectable thing. It shits every morning.

SA: You wrote a poem and showed it to me, partly about love. Do you still remember?

BH: Show me. I don't remember.

SA: It's here.

Thus spake bh

I procrastinate
For months I don't put in a word
I masturbate
Often there's nothing that comes out
I don't love anyone
I don't even love myself
I don't know who I ought to blame for this
Most of the times I sleep with myself
When I wake up
I'm disappointed to find myself alone as ever
Occasionally I sleep with a woman, a being as casual
as myself
But no copulation leads to any fruition
I am still myself
I am always myself
Half man, half woman
Half animal, half human
How can I be whole?
Why would I have to be whole?
Who should I please?
Why would I have to?

BH: Oh, that one, just a throwaway. And I am reminded of something.
You said to me that you were impressed with how I called myself in my
self-introduction: Not an SOB, but an SOP (son of a poem) and decided
on accepting me as your student just on that.

On Regrets
SA: Would you have any regrets now that you are no more?
BH: Yes, lots. My biggest regret is this that I wish I had cast a woman
as the main protagonist.
SA: Why?
BH: I have learnt here in hell that to have any success in this country,

I mean, in that country, with fiction, a woman protagonist, well cast and positively portrayed, would do one loads of good whereas an Asian male protagonist has to be avoided at any cost.

SA: Why?

BH: I'm not interested in answering that question. I'm so tired. I need a holiday in hell.

On His Supervisor

SA: Would you mind me, your supervisor or ex-supervisor, being a self-appointed editor, cutter, remover, reviser and censor, of your manuscript please?

BH: Why do you want to do that?

SA: I'd like to help it see the light of day.

BH: Well, it's up to you now that it's in your hands. Keep what you'd like to keep and cut what you'd like to cut. Do anything you like. It's not my book anyway.

SA: How do you mean?

BH: You know what I mean, don't you?

SA: In the main, I think I'll probably purge all the poetry from the book.

BH: But that's not fair.

SA: It's your original idea as evidenced by a poem you sent to me while you were still alive.

BH: I don't know what you are talking about.

SA: It's here below. Read it for yourself:

Advice to him who listens

Remove all the negativity
It's not the business of a novel to criticise
But to tell a story
A story of love to its full capacity
However unhappy the author is
He should not allow his unhappiness to interfere with his
    fictional progress
He should always bear in mind that he should do his best to endear

his characters to his readers instead of otherwise
Failing that, he is advised to pursue poetry
Along the lines of psychological violence and vitriol
By engaging in constant criticism
By way of relentless satire/irony/malice/attack, or simply,
   meaninglessness

Make your mind up whether you want to be loved or hated, or
   both

SA: Is that what you wrote that you emailed me months ago before you took your life?

BH: I don't remember ever doing that. Is this some sort of a joke or what?

SA: In any case, I don't think it's a good idea to put too much poetry in a work of fiction. It stops the market going.

BH: You mean it stops the bowels moving?

SH: Oh, Baohui, when did you become so disgusting?

BH: In regard to ascription, please call the novel written by Baohui-Zhang-Stacey-Ahsin.

SH: Will definitely do.

One Final Thing
SA: Is there anything you'd like to add please?

BH: There's one regret I neglected to mention. I wish I had gone through sex reassignment surgery to become a fully-fleshed female.

SA: Why?

BH: In this hell here no one asks why. They know what is what and they say no more.

SA: Okay, that's fine. Now, can I quote a poem you wrote about experimental fiction please?

BH: Don't you think putting too much poetry in this already disgusting novel will put more readers off?

SA: But because of the nature of your writing, I think including that poem might help make things clearer to them.

BH: Well, it's up to you.

406

SA: Readers, please find the poem below,

《阿门》

'Experimental fiction is fiction
that refuses to stay
within the boundaries laid out

either by traditional realistic
literary fiction or by
the standard genres of thriller

, mystery, sci-fi, romance
and so forth. We
might say that experimental fiction

is non-escapist literature in
that it does not
seek to seduce its readers

into a dreamy forgetfulness
. It is fiction
, instead, that often unsettles

, that makes one
feel uncomfortable or liberated
, because it breaks rules

and invents new ones
. Ideologically, it
undermines the common conceptual categories

by which we understand
and navigate the world
; it rejects the normal

rhetoric of how we
describe things. If realistic
literature is a series of

check-boxes on a preprinted
form—a checkbox
for character, a checkbox for

exposition, boxes for theme
and pathos and storyline
—experimental fiction is the

guy who can't fill
out the form, who
has to create his own

checkboxes or add footnotes
or perhaps just puts
a match to the form

and burns it up
. Experimental fiction is
like a foreigner in a

new land—a
stranger who doesn't know
the social etiquette.' 阿门

(a found poem based on the re-arrangement of a passage from an article here: http://www.mapliterary.org/on-experimental-fiction.html , in stanzas of first two 4-word lines and third 5-word lines, including stand-alone punctuation counted as a word)

BH: And I wrote a novel, titled, *Australia White*, in Chinese. If you like, can I get you to read only one short chapter in it please?

SA: Yes, just send it.

BH: See it here. [The following is that chapter in Chinese that I don't know a single word or character of but decide not to censor—SA]

声音

妈妈，不要生我了。这个国家不适合我，不适合你，不适合爸爸。不适合你们那个国家的人。我们肤色不够白。要是有可能，妈妈，你就趁我还没有出生之前，就把我的一身黄皮剥了，换一身雪白的肌肤，让我白得能看见充血的青筋毕露，全身遍布河流，就像你们来自的那个国家。你吃的米很白，妈妈，比你们从前那个国家的米还要白，一进你的肚皮，这白米就化成鲜红的血水浇灌着我的肢体。我好happy。妈妈，你对我真好。总是躺在那张沙发上不动，怕动了我的胎气。其实动一动也没关系，因为这样我就能跟着你动。我的周围好黑呀，从来都没有白天，每时每刻都把我在血水里泡着，热得人难受。我还能听见有人在跟我用一种将来时讲话，......无论你怎么写，写多少，都只能是用文字填充一个个呼吸的空间，而当文字被一种不属于你颜色的颜色框定之后，文字就被带上了脚镣手铐，沉重地行走着不再进入未来，而是向着过去迈进，你成了罪人，不被发表，不被重视，不被写进历史，不被授奖，而在故意的记忆中被遗忘。你向一百年前的那个时刻弯下腰，低头看着晚霞和朝霞结合，像迟暮的婚姻，流着血，喊叫着，一只手长长地伸过空间，捏着粉碎的心，用英文的语法压迫着时间，你的鸡塞打着霜，前倾了，颠覆了，鼓舞着，放肆地再生，令规矩颤抖，那些惧怕寂寞的人又用时间把自己的弱脑灌醉，笑得苍白一片，如一个名叫威尔德布拉德的人，小胡子翘了起来，眼睛瞪着，牙齿细得像米。你要写得永远都无法让任何人重复，难以进入并难以就范。你写的时候，你就死了，现在不复存在，像那片天空永动永不动，永远不存在地存在于不存在的存在之中。你早已不能忍受身边的一切，包括人特别包括人，所以于是然而本来但是即便终于这才你从现在淡出，与过去交友，……这次不行，我们就回去，再也不来了。我想念家乡的肉。透明虾子的虾须在舌尖上扎痛的感觉。早早黑下来后点亮油灯时那冒出黑烟的刺鼻一瞬。丝绸在皮肤上刮擦的细腻感，女人感。睡在上风头，让细软的风从大脚趾甲上拂过，香云纱飘飘的。怀着自己的肉，给肉唱歌：肉宝宝，宝宝肉，你胖胖，妈瘦瘦，妈想你把梦做错，你想妈做梦出来。嗨呀嗨，嗨呀嗨，妈妈是你小白菜。你别跟我捉迷藏，别想像水一样地躲开火，冬天一样地躲开太阳，我不会像第一次那样生不下来。爸爸在河边滩地上种的菜都一垄垄地出溜得肥壮阔大，长势喜人，我就不信不能把你这个小杂种生出来！你知道我是属猪的属狗的属鼠的，一起都属，属得种什么生什么，不怕你跟我耍赖。我就差不是属鱼的，否则，我会亮晶晶地一生一大串，就是家乡鱼塘的鲫鱼，一次也能产10万到30万个鱼卵。别笑妈妈不会生，上次流产，是因为在海上颠簸太久，结果把肚子里的一团血肉都从口里吐了出来。当然，这是妈妈跟你开玩笑，妈哪有那个本事，等你爸爸申请到许可证，我们就可以留下来，我呢，就把你生下来，你呢，就把我生下来。我能生下来，也就等于你能生下我。这是我们女人的逻辑，你长大就会明白的。

SA: Maybe nothing of this is real. I'm only imagining things. But I feel much better after this interview as if a huge burden had been lifted off my heart. I'm freer than ever before. Oh, there's something else I forgot. There is an entire section on me in which BH presents me as a divorced woman with a lesbian orientation. I didn't say anything but simply cut it without further ado.

References

"200年前，第一个中国人踏上澳洲这片土地": https://www.sydneytoday.com/content-101822369269070

Anon., 'Xing xiang zi', http://www.shicimingju.com/chaxun/list/915077.html

Artaud, Antonin, *Antonin Artaud Anthology*, ed. Jack Hirschman. San Francisco, City Lights Books, 1965 [1956].

Biheguan zhuren, *Huangjin shijie* (The World of Gold), included in Ah Ying (ed), *Fanmei huagong jinyue wenxue ji* (A Collection of Literary Writings Against American Restrictions of the Chinese Labourers). Zhonghua Book Company: 1960.

Buchanan, Keith, *Map of Love*. Pergamon Press, 1970.

Che, Jixin (ed), *Zhongguo huangdi quanzhuan* (A Comprehensive Biography of Chinese Emperors). Shandong Education Press, 1991.

Chekhov, Anton, *Sakhalin Island*. Alma Books Ltd, 2015 [1895].

Collins, Tom, *Such is Life*. Halstead Press, 1962 [1903].

Cronin, Leonard (ed.), *A Fantasy of Man, Henry Lawson Complete Works 1901–1922*. Sydney: Lansdowne, 1984.

Dictionary of Modern Culture (《现代世界文化词典》). Jiangsu People's PublishingHouse, 1988.

Eco, Umberto, 《误读》 (*Diario Minimo*), published by China CITIC Press in 2015.

Chen, Tianhua, 《猛回头》 ('A Sudden Head Turn'): https://baike.baidu.com/item/猛回头/8077025

Chin, Frank, Jeffery Paul Chan, Lawson Fusao Inada and Shawn Hsu Wong, *Aiiieeeee! An Anthology of Asian American Writers*. Penguin Books USA, 1991 [1974].

Donne, John, *Complete Verse and Selected Prose*, edited by John Hayward. Nonesuch Press, 1962 [1929].

Feng, Menglong, *Yushi mingyan* (Stories Old and New: A Ming Dynasty Collection):http://www.dushu369.com/gudianmingzhu/ysmy/

Fitzgerald, J. D., *The Ring Valley: A Novel of Australian Pioneering*. London: Hodder, 1922.

Gervais, Albert, *A Surgeon's China*. London: Hamish Hamilton, 1936

[1934].

Gong, Shuduo (chief editor), *Zhongguo jindai shi: 1919-1949* (A History of Modern China). Beijing: Zhonghua Book Company, 2018 [2010].

Guo, Shuyun, *Yuanshi huotai wenhua: samanjiao toushi* (Living

Primitive Cultures: Perspectives on Shamanism). Shanghai People's Publishing House, 2001.

Lane, William, *White or Yellow? A Story of the Race War of A. D. 1908*, in Boomerang, 18 February–5 May 1888.

Lane, William, *The Workingman's Paradise*. Sydney: Cosme Publishing Company, 1948 [1892].

Lin, Yutang, *Six Chapters of a Floating Life*, a translation in English of 《浮生六记》. Beijing: Foreign Language Teaching and Research Press, 1999.

Ling, Mengchu, *Erke pai'an jingqi* (Slapping the Table in Amazement [Part II]). Beijing: Zhonghua shuju, 2014.

Ouyang, Yu, *Representing the Other: Chinese in Australian Fiction: 1888-1988*. Cambria Press, 2008.

Owen, June Duncan, *Mixed Matches: Interracial Marriage in Australia*. UNSW Press, 2002.

Pascal, Blaise, *Pensées*. Penguin Books, 1995 [1966].

Pessoa, Fernando, *The Book of Disquiet*. Penguin Books, 2002 [1998].

Pickering, Michael, *Stereotyping: The Politics of Representation*. New York: Palgrave, 2001.

Qian, Chunqi, *A Select Collection of Poetry by Heine* (《海涅名诗精选》), translated in Chinese. Taibai Literature and Arts Publishing House, 1997, p. 142.

Richardson, Henry Handel, *The Fortunes of Richard Mahony*. William Heinemann Ltd, 1954 [1930].

Roth, Philip, *Portnoy's Complaint*. Penguin Books Australia, 1971 [1967].

Shelley, Percy Bysshe, *Select Lyrical Poems by Shelley* (雪莱抒情诗精选), tr. Jiang Feng. Taibai Arts and Literature Publishing House, 1997.

'The First Landing, The Chinese Invasion, Shipwrecks in Guichen Bay':https://www.robe.sa.gov.au/webdata/resources/files/The_

First_Landing.pdf

'The Growing of Big Smoke', *Zhongguo yinyue shilue* (A Brief History of Chinese Music), written and edited by Wu Zhao and Liu Dongsheng. Beijing: People's Music Publishing House, 1993, p. 313.

Twain, Mark, *Mark Twain in Australia and New Zealand*. Penguin Books, 1973 [1897].

Wang, Zichen (annotated), *A Four Books Reader* (《四书读本》). Beijing: Beijing Bookshop, 1986 [1936].

Vincent, Alf, 'Vagabonding in Asia', *Lone Hand*, 1907, included in *The Oxford Book of Australian Travel Writing*, eds by Ros Pesman, David Walker and Richard White. Melbourne: OUP, 1996.

Ying, Wu, *A Beginner's Buddhist Scriptures* (《佛典入门》). Bashu Press: 1998.

Yu, *Taojin di* (A Land of Gold-diggers), a novel in Chinese. Nanjing: Jiangsu Literature and Arts Publishing House, 2014.

Acknowledgements

First, I'd like to thank the Australia Council for giving me a grant for two years to write this novel to make it financially possible for me to drive all the way to Robe, SA, in early 2019, and back through Ararat, Ballarat and Bendigo; to go to Taishan, Guangdong, China, in February, and to fly to Ireland in March of the same year.

I'd also like to thank Alex Miller for introducing me to David Bannear, an archaeologist, and to both Alex and David for showing me around in the ancient site of gold-diggings and the graveyards around Castlemaine.

My thanks go to Feng Zhenjiong, a poet originally from Enping, Guangdong, and now based in New York, who showed me around in Taishan and introduced me to many local poets, such as Tan Xiao and Yang Fan.

My thanks also go to Evelyn Conlon, an Irish novelist based in Dublin, who, along with her partner Fintan, a musician, treated me with warm hospitality while I did my research there.

I'm most grateful to Bruce for providing valuable comments and to Sandy for her useful feedback.

I'm full of gratitude to David for publishing this book and doing all the editing work, making it possible for the book to see the world.

My thanks go to Alex and Declan for providing the blurbs for the book.

And, as always, I am indebted to my wife Lu for her continuing support in making my life as comfortable as ever, as an insightful and appreciative companion.